POSITIVELY HEROIC!

"This way!" Indrajit whispered, and dragged Ilsa with him.

"Beneath the stage," she said again. "There's an exit that only *I* know."

Indrajit had already picked his way out, and didn't want to risk getting lost. He dragged the singer along by main force. "There's an exit this way!"

"To my dressing room, then!" She pointed.

"No time!" he panted.

"If you want to hide me," she rasped, "I can't go outside looking like this."

Good point.

Indrajit stood in the door of her dressing room for just ten seconds while she tore off her stage helmet and glittering train and threw on a black hooded robe. He noted a pair of windows, open and facing out onto the street. Cool night air, painted yellow by torches and oil lanterns, drifted in from the Crown.

"I hope you're good with that sword," she croaked. "I'm unarmed."

"I'm excellent," he lied. "Positively heroic."

He also had no idea where to go. The shared garret where he'd been sleeping on a pile of rags in the corner? Though he was in arrears there, and the landlady, a three-legged woman with a bloblike, trembling knob of flesh on a long stalk that hung before her like an esca, might not let him in. The Blind Surgeon, where apparently his credit had been restored? Holy-Pot's office?

The last idea seemed to be the most commonsensical—Holy-Pot had resources and knowledge—but he wouldn't be in his office at night, would he? And Indrajit had no idea where the risk-merchant lived.

"This way!"

BAEN BOOKS by D.J. BUTLER

The Cunning Man Series
(with Aaron Michael Ritchey)
The Cunning Man
The Jupiter Knife

The Witchy War Series
Witchy Eye
Witchy Winter
Witchy Kingdom
Serpent Daughter

Tales of Indrajit and Fix
In the Palace of Shadow and Joy

To purchase any of these titles in e-book form,
please go to www.baen.com.

In the Palace of Shadow and Joy

A Tale of Indrajit & Fix

D.J. BUTLER

IN THE PALACE OF SHADOW AND JOY

Copyright © 2020 by D.J. Butler

A Baen Books Original

Baen Publishing Enterprises
P.O. Box 1403
Riverdale, NY 10471
www.baen.com

ISBN: 978-1-9821-2553-0

Cover art by Don Maitz
Maps by Bryan G. McWhirter

First printing, July 2020
First mass market printing, August 2021

Distributed by Simon & Schuster
1230 Avenue of the Americas
New York, NY 10020

Library of Congress Control Number: 2020015802

Pages by Joy Freeman (www.pagesbyjoy.com)
Printed in the United States of America
10 9 8 7 6 5 4 3 2 1

*This book is for my friend Steven L. Peck,
whose lectures on evolution in
science fiction and fantasy
directly inspired this story.*

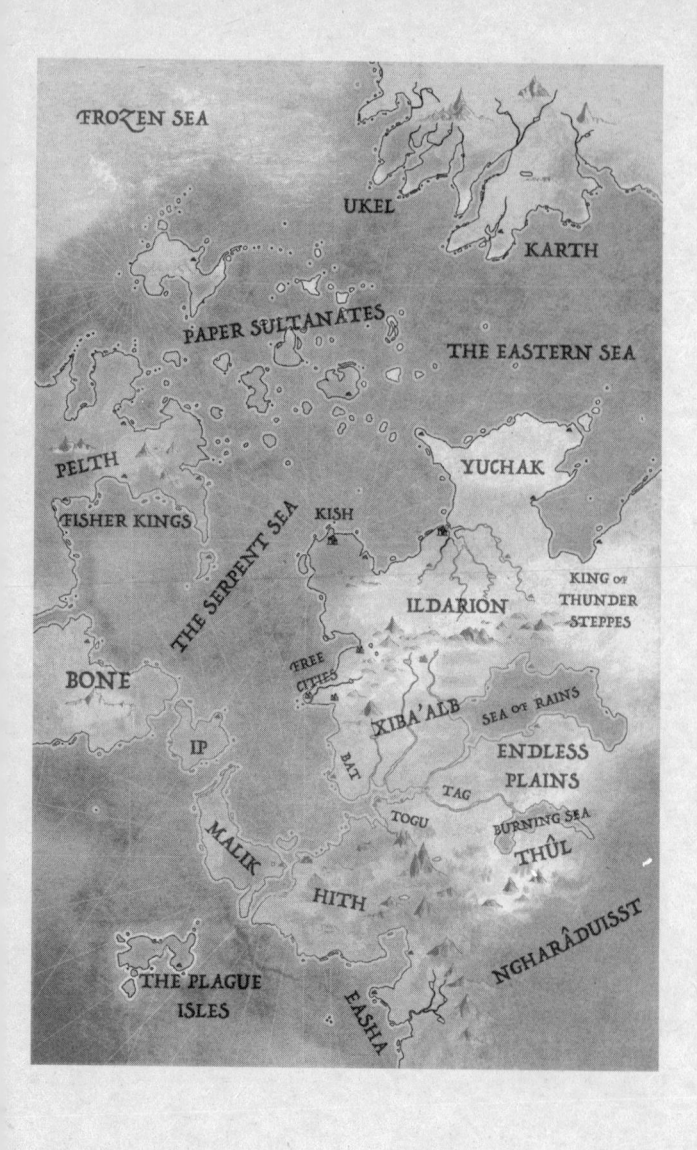

The Shelf

The Spill

West Flats

East Flats

The Dregs

The Crown

The Lee

Caravanserai

Necropolis
↓

The ANCIENT & FREE
CITY of KISH

Chapter One

〰〰〰

"DON'T THROW ME THROUGH THE GLASS," INDRAJIT Twang advised his captors. "You'll like the big crash it makes; it'll be very dramatic, but your boss won't thank you. Glass is expensive."

The thugs hesitated. There were two of them, one a hard-muscled wall with a flat face and an ashen-brown complexion, and the other a blubbery, fishlike pile that seemed to have three mouths, and definitely had four tentacles. The second ruffian had no legs, moving across the floor with a snail-like lower half that contracted and expanded in a continual arching and stretching motion. Whichever of the thousand races of man tough number two belonged to, Indrajit had never seen another member.

Indrajit pushed into the hesitation, trying to lengthen it into a reprieve. "Look, I can't pay right now, but I can pay . . . soon. Or with work. How much do I owe?"

Ash-Brown looked over his shoulder at Anaximander Skink, the owner of the Blind Surgeon and also its bartender. Skink was a Wixit, furred except for the pads of his hands and feet, nimble, and about two cubits tall. Skink stood atop the bowed wood of the bar and growled.

"You owe a full Imperial, you sack of Smork droppings."

Indrajit didn't know what a Smork was, but the other patrons of the Blind Surgeon, who smelled like fish and oil and sweat, appeared to. They bared teeth and tusks and laughed at Indrajit.

"Come on," Indrajit pleaded, "you can't charge me interest on a bar tab."

"I'm not charging interest." Skink rolled back black lips to reveal jagged yellow teeth, like a dog's. Skink's people ate carrion, and Indrajit suspected that the location of the Blind Surgeon on the West Flats had been chosen so that the smell of fish intestines and brine and fishermen would cloak the stink of flesh Skink left hanging in the back room to rot until it reached the perfect tenderness for his liking. "And I'm rounding down."

Indrajit hadn't really kept track. "That seems excessive."

"Yes. *Excessive* is a very good word for your tab. That's why I'm throwing you out." Skink nodded to Ash-Brown. "He's right about the window. Just drag him out and beat him up."

"What if I became your bar's resident poet?" Indrajit hooked a toe into a protruding board at the base of the bar to stop the thugs from carrying him out. Their strength, and the fact that he was wearing sandals, resulted in immediate sharp pain to his foot. "I could recite every night. Stand in the corner and declaim. All the best drinking establishments have resident poets."

A stage to work from might even help Indrajit find what he was looking for.

The Wixit snorted. "No, they don't."

"You could start a trend, then. Attract a new class of clientele, instead of these uncultured swine."

The uncultured swine jeered.

Skink waved a crooked digit at his thugs and they stopped pulling. "New poems?"

Indrajit took a deep breath. "I don't really *write* new poems. Not like you're thinking, anyway."

Skink snorted. "No one wants to hear the Blotch-iad, Twang."

Indrajit wanted to straighten himself up into a dignified stance, but the thugs prevented him. Writhing, he managed to push his chest out a few inches. "The Blaatshi Epic is the great song of my people. My parents were deeply honored when I, as a young boy, was selected to learn to perform it in its entirety, in thirty thousand lines. They sacrificed two goats in celebration."

"First of all," Skink said, holding up long-nailed digits to count off his objections, "it isn't a song. There's no music; it's just like the parts where the actors talk in high opera."

"Recitative." Indrajit sniffed.

"Secondly, nobody speaks Blaatshi, so it just sounds like you're a Spirit Talker, standing in the corner babbling in a trance."

"I could translate," Indrajit offered.

"Thirdly, I've heard your translations of sections of the Blotchiad, and it doesn't sound like poetry. It sounds like people making grand vows and prophecies and threats, in the most long-winded fashion imaginable. It's boring!"

Indrajit gasped.

"Boring!" one of the Blind Surgeon's fisherman patrons roared, raising his wooden mug.

"Boring!" the others shouted, raising their own drinks in response.

"Fourthly, you then try to make listeners stand up and act out the scenes."

"That's the art," Indrajit said. "You don't understand the glory of what I do. This is the entire history of my people, from the Darkness that Ate the World to my great-grandfather's time. The deeds and words are too important to be smothered with music, and the act of emulating the historical figures imprints key passages on the minds of listeners. It is participatory drama, and I am four hundred twenty-seventh in the line of artists who have devoted their lives to performing it. I'm a storyteller, an actor, and a historian. The performance of the Blaatshi Epic is the greatest spiritual, artistic, and cultural experience a person can have."

"You know what I think a great performance is?" Skink asked.

Indrajit shook his head. "Tell me."

"Anything that makes people buy more drink. The Blotchiad makes people want to kill themselves." Skink nodded to his bruisers. "Make sure he remembers this. Break, say, two bones."

"Do you have a preference for which ones?" Ash-Brown asked. "Maybe that bony nose-ridge he's got?"

Skink turned the question to Indrajit with a polite raising of the dark hairs at the base of his forehead.

"How about a metaphorical bone?" Indrajit suggested. "What if you just deeply wound my pride? As indeed, you already have, with your callous and uncultured disdain for the pinnacle of my people's learning."

"How many of your people are there?" Skink asked. "In that valley over there on the other side of Ildarion, or wherever it is you said you come from?"

"Three hundred," Indrajit said. "When I left."

"So, what? Maybe two hundred now, given how bad recent harvests have been?"

Indrajit ground his teeth. "My people *fish*. You would know that if you paid attention to the Epic."

Skink shrugged, a gesture that folded his little body nearly in two. "Three hundred green fishermen no one's ever heard of, lords of nothing, living nowhere special. Nobody wants to hear your epic. Nobody ever will. Of all the epics of all the thousand races of man, if I had to rank them in order of which I'd most like to hear next, the Blotchiad would come in dead last, after Smork farts."

The furry innkeeper's words stung. Skink was right, no one wanted to hear the Epic. No one wanted to learn to recite it anymore, either; this was Indrajit's great challenge in life. "We're not green. Our skin has a pleasing mahogany tint with just the faintest hint of green to it."

"There's lots of brown people," Skink said. "Forgive me for noticing the green, but it stands out more. Are you going to pick two bones to get broken, or am I going to raise the number to four?"

"How badly will you break them?" Indrajit wasn't sure whether he was asking Skink or the thugs.

"Does it really matter?" Skink growled.

Indrajit Twang wished he hadn't sold his sword. He sighed. "The left arm. Upper and lower."

"You know what? I'm feeling generous. Just break the forearm, boys. Mind you, I want him bruised, too, and leave a little blood on the stones. It'll let other customers know I'm serious."

The two thugs dragged Indrajit toward the door. His sandal heels scraped across the baked clay floor.

"I could make up new poems!" Indrajit wasn't sure he could, actually. He knew the rhythms and rules of the Epic deep in his bones, and could spin out new verses to it as easily as he could breathe—indeed, one of his duties was to add a new generation to the Epic, the generation of his grandmother—but that wouldn't satisfy Skink. Skink would want low bawdy, or love poems, or popular songs, the kind that got printed on large sheets of paper and sold in the street for two bits each.

"Too late!" Skink snapped.

"But this squares us up, right?" Indrajit called. "We're even?"

"No." Skink dropped down behind the bar, where a series of planks nailed together to form a walkway let him stand eye to eye with customers. "No, you still owe me an Imperial, and your tab is closed until you pay in full."

Ash-Brown and Blubber dragged Indrajit outside.

The knotted, salt-encrusted strips of leather that hung in the doorway and served the inn for a door scratched Indrajit's face. Outside, despite the proximity of the water—only thirty paces away or so down a tangled alleyway, Indrajit could hear the slap of waves on slimy rocks—the air smelled marginally better. Cleaner. More salt and bird and fish, less sweat and tooth decay.

"Can I pay you guys _not_ to beat me up?" he offered.

Ash-Brown and Blubber hurled him to the rocks.

These were wide, flat paving stones of old Kish, laid in Imperial times. This close to the water, they might even be older: Druvash work, most of which was buried under the thousands of years of detritus and construction that created the sagging heap over which Kish lay slung.

"You can't pay Skink. How could you pay *us*?" These were the first words Blubber had spoken. They sounded soft around the edges and slow, as if he were speaking through a mouthful of water, and a thin stream of mucus fell from his lips.

A trickle of sewage flowed past Indrajit's head across the stones. It must flow down from the heights of Kish above him, but the watery stools of the wealthy denizens of the Crown smelled no better than those turned loose natively upon the West Flats.

From his position lying on the ground, the two ruffians looked enormous. "I could owe you."

Ash-Brown laughed, and then punched Indrajit in the stomach.

All his breath rushed from Indrajit's lungs. By instinct more than by skill, he kicked at Ash-Brown's knees with both feet. Scoring a hit, he knocked the thug over backward and into the stream of filth.

Blubber made a bass squeaking sound.

Indrajit rolled away from Blubber to climb to his feet, but found a hostile wall of hands, claws, and tentacles to meet him. The other patrons of the Blind Surgeon, the paying ones, stood in a beer-soused and laughing row. They grabbed Indrajit Twang and threw him back at the two thugs.

"Boring!" the patrons yelled.

Ash-Brown was standing, his hand grabbing the

wire-wrapped hilt of a big chopping knife at his belt. Indrajit danced to the right, wound up, and threw a punch.

He hit Ash-Brown in the face and dropped him to the stones.

Blubber grabbed Indrajit Twang from behind with all four of his tentacles. He raised the poet into the air with sudden and surprising force, turning him upside down. As his feet left the ground, Indrajit's thoughts were ripped from the scene, and he found himself wondering three things.

First, how dense must Blubber's muscles be? He was as strong as a horse, but no bigger than Indrajit himself. And if his muscles were that powerful, were his bones made of iron?

And also, by what right did Indrajit think of Blubber as male? For all he knew, the thug might be a female, or intersex, or some kind of other option.

And finally, was he, Indrajit Twang, four hundred twenty-seventh Recital Thane of the Blaatshi Epic, about to die of a broken back?

"Stop."

This was a new voice, a man's, baritone. It spoke with the gravel of authority, and Blubber froze.

Looking down on the scene from his vantage point eight feet off the ground, Indrajit saw that the new arrival had a retinue. Four lavender-skinned men with tails—Zalaptings, one of Kish's most ubiquitous races of man, and he knew they were men because they had ragged blue beards under their long, lavender snouts—held the tips of their spears poked gently into Blubber's skin. Zalaptings were notoriously difficult to tell apart, if you weren't a Zalapting yourself. These

Zalaptings wore linothorax like professionals, but no visible insignia. Jobbers, maybe?

Behind the spearmen stood the speaker with the gravel voice. He had no arms, and legs with knees that bent backward and ended in claws, like a bird's, and a solemn face nesting inside a collar of wiggling antennae. The speaker was black as jet, but for his bright orange legs.

Blubber bent as if he might set Indrajit down, and Bird Legs shook his head. "Hold still."

The thug froze.

Indrajit's kilt fell down around his belly. "Hello," he said, as politely as he could. "Do I know you?"

Bird Legs ignored him, and instead faced Skink. The Wixit bounced on his hind legs, shaking his fist at the new arrival, apparently unconcerned about the presence of the four spearmen.

The tavern's patrons booed. "Break his arms!" Several took a step forward, as if intent on intervening in the face-off, but Bird Legs glared lightning at them and they stepped back into place. "Show us some blood!"

"This man owes me!" Skink squealed. "My employees are administering a legitimate beating!"

"I'd be interested in hearing more about your ideas of legitimacy." Bird Legs's voice dropped into a deep purr. "But he owes my master a prior debt. And unless your prices are *surprisingly* high, a larger one."

Skink hesitated. "You have . . . court papers?"

Bird Legs looked thoughtfully at the innkeeper. "What does Indrajit Twang owe you?"

Indrajit cleared his throat. "I'm happy to be on a first-name basis, but, ah, you have me at an advantage." Two of Blubber's tentacles gripped him around the hips, and they were cutting off the flow of blood. His feet were beginning to tingle.

"Two Imperials," Skink said.

Bird Legs stared deeply into Skink's eyes, and the Wixit took a step back. Then the obsidian-skinned, two-limbed man laughed. "Meaning that he owes you half, and you told him he owed one."

"Hey!" Indrajit said.

Skink flared his nostrils and crossed his arms over his chest.

"Very well." Bird Legs coughed several times, a deep, phlegmy, grating sound, and then spat on the stone. The blob of phlegm struck with a soft metallic clink. "You will find *three* Imperials in there. My master now owns your debt."

The Blind Surgeon's patrons, disappointed that no blood was to be shed, were shuffling back into the inn. Skink rushed to the blob of mucus and quickly extracted three coins, running a digit around the rim of each to check that they hadn't been clipped. "Fresh from the Mint," he commented.

"My employer is one of the lords of the Paper Sook," Bird Legs rumbled. "He wouldn't pass light coins."

The Paper Sook. Indrajit's heart fell. "Ah . . . so, your master is—"

"Holy-Pot Diaphernes, of course."

Anaximander Skink's spine went straight as an arrow and he bounced back into his doorway.

Diaphernes was a risk-merchant. This was a business Indrajit understood only poorly, and his one foray into the field, a brief recent stint working as a collector for Holy-Pot Diaphernes himself, had ended badly. He'd only managed to collect part of the debt owed to Holy-Pot by an Ildarian baron's son, and hadn't been able to bring himself to break the man's legs to encourage him to come up with the rest. Worse, though Indrajit had intended to hand what he *had* collected over to Holy-Pot, he had . . . failed.

He hadn't *intended* to spend the money, but somehow the money had been spent.

That was a week earlier. He'd been avoiding Holy-Pot since.

"I see we have a friend in common." Indrajit smiled. The blood pooling in his head was making him feel dizzy.

"Holy-Pot Diaphernes is no one's friend. Not mine, and certainly not yours." Bird Legs frowned. "You are summoned. If I order this man to let you down, will you go to Diaphernes's office?"

"Yes. Holy-Pot and I are . . . overdue for a meeting."

"You acknowledge your debt."

Indrajit nodded. "I pay late sometimes, but I pay."

Bird Legs nodded at Blubber, who dropped Indrajit to the ground. Shaken and aching, Indrajit stood. Looking up and down the street, he saw a steady flow of traffic—fishers and merchants—but no uniforms, no one who looked like law enforcement. He stooped and took the chopping knife, sheath and all, from Ash-Brown, shoving it under the rope belt that held up his kilt.

Blubber murmured in protest but did nothing.

"Who shall I say sent me?" Indrajit asked Bird Legs.

"My name is Yashta Hossarian," Bird Legs said.

On wobbling legs, Indrajit walked up toward the higher neighborhoods of Kish.

"Your tab is open again!" Anaximander Skink hollered after him.

Chapter Two

~~~~~~~~~

THE COOL, WET BREEZES OF LATE SPRING BLEW
up Indrajit's kilt and across his bare arms as he
climbed the ramp from the West Flats up into the
Spill. Higher on the knob of ruins, sewers, caves,
and natural stone on which Kish perched, the Spill
was bounded by the East Flats on the far side, and
below it and to the north, the Shelf. Like the West
Flats, the East Flats and the Shelf were all strewn
with wharves, the shacks of fishermen, and the cheap
dives the fishermen frequented. South and above the
Spill rose the Crown, home to the temples of the
city's five major gods, clinging like barnacles to the
city's highest knuckle of stone, the Spike.

The Spill itself was full of warehouses and shops, of
all kinds imaginable, or at least all imaginable goods
that came to Kish by sea. The goods generally became
more luxurious the closer one climbed to the Crown.
The Spill's buildings did not have the elegance and
wealth of those of the Crown; nor yet did the Spill

reek of fish and dung-smoke like the neighborhoods clinging to its sides. In the Spill, business got done.

At the top of the ramp, Indrajit turned into the gate leading into the Spill. Like all his people, his peripheral vision was good. That came of having eyes set far apart in their faces, almost, some would say, on the sides of their heads; with his excellent peripheral vision, he could now see he was being followed. The man was a Yifft; they looked like any ordinary, unremarkable man, caramel-brown in color and of middling height like the race of man commonly called *Kishi*, but a Yifft could be spotted by the lashless line across his forehead that was all one could see of his third eye when it was closed. When the eye was opened, the Yifft were said to possess uncanny powers of vision through it, though the tales also said that every minute they held that eye open was a minute less that the Yifft lived. They were often employed as spies and seers by the great families, and one could find them in less exalted quarters as gamblers, hucksters, and fortune-tellers.

This Yifft wore a dirty yellow tunic and a loincloth, a faded purple turban with a loose length of cloth hanging down over his left shoulder, and rope sandals. Indrajit had seen the man in the Blind Surgeon and thought nothing of him, but now the Yifft was following him.

Indrajit stepped through the Spill and breathed better. This was not the rarefied air of Bank Street or the Avenue of Heroes, but it was the air of merchants and burghers, rather than the oozy smoke of vice dens salted with the oily stink of fish.

Indrajit had been summoned to the Paper Sook, in the northeast corner of the Spill; the most direct route would follow most of the first leg of the Crooked Mile, the long street that zigged and zagged up the Spill's slope to the Crown. Good. This was an innocuous highway that might be taken by any traveler.

Indrajit looked for an opportunity to turn the tables on his tail. His long, quick stride carried him past a cobbled square where the players of a game of Street Rûphat threw elbows into each other's throats, kicked at each other's ankles, and pushed each other to the wall as they jostled to throw the ball through the octagonal stone goal. This was a public court, and the goal protruded from the wall of an adjacent dry goods merchant, who had probably built the court to drive traffic, or perhaps to appease some god.

A thousand races of man and ten thousand gods, though, depending on whom you asked, both those numbers could be larger. Kish itself honored five gods above all others, five gods borrowed from unrelated pantheons rather than a pantheon native to the city. Five gods, and, some said, a sixth.

None of them was Blaat, the Sea Mother.

Indrajit cut across the Rûphat court, earning shouts from two players. He smelled roasting tamarind seed pods, without seeing the vendor. Ducking through an alley at the back and following it through two quick turns, he put himself again on the Crooked Mile, heading for the Paper Sook. He chuckled—let the Yifft try to follow him, and catch a beating from irate players.

He stopped chuckling when he turned his head to look into the stall of a merchant selling polished copper idols and saw the Yifft emerge from the same alley Indrajit had used.

Indrajit passed a line of robed and barefooted women, chanting a song he didn't know. Some kind of doom cult, probably; Kish was full of them. He bent at the knees and walked like a bird, trying to stay out of sight. A small troop of thin, short men with ragged cloths about their hips and feathers at their knees and elbows saw Indrajit and began to follow him. Their skin was a mottled gray and they sniffed the ground as they scooted along. Just a pack of scavengers looking for a meal; Indrajit ignored them.

He passed a wealthy Bonean man, surrounded by a troop of scimitar-wielding soldiers. The Bonean was likely noble, judging by the profusion of astral tattoos that covered his body, and by the fact that he sat in a sedan chair carried by four tall, pink-skinned slaves. Indrajit paced the sedan, matching his steps to those of the largest bearer, until the Boneans turned aside.

Still the Yifft followed.

More direct action would be required.

The scavenger pack hooted, sensing some kind of game and maybe an opportunity for a meal. They flashed sharp teeth and scratched at the skin of their own throats.

Indrajit saw his chance, in the form of a bawdy show. The actors stood on a low platform made of planks, just tall enough to raise their heads above the crowd. They projected their voices admirably, but this was no Epic recitation: the actors hit each other, danced, mimed gigantic farts, and pretended to rut like beasts. One of them wore a papier-mâché mask in the shape of a horned skull, suggesting that he was supposed to be Orem Thrush—more properly,

Orem Thrush the seventh, head of House Thrush, said to be the richest of the seven great families of Kish, and the current Lord Chamberlain. Thrush was by far the most flatulent of the characters, and also tried to hump the young female characters any time the older characters turned their backs.

So the bawdy was political.

Indrajit didn't care. What he liked was the crowd, which was thick and noisy with jeers, laughter, and catcalls. The audience was getting thicker by the moment, too, growing like a Zalapting warren.

He turned his shoulders to slide as neatly as he could into a wall of spectators without breaking their ranks, then crossed a thin row of young pipal trees, their drooping leaves a rich, dark green. On the far side he ducked and stepped sideways, creeping out of sight until he could shelter behind the band.

The musicians consisted of a girl playing a forked shepherd's flute and two men playing bang harps. The harpists seemed much more comfortable with their drone strings and the percussive butts of their instruments than with the fretted melody strings; Indrajit cringed at the roughness of the music.

The Yifft struggled to get through the crowd and passed right by the musicians. Indrajit orbited sunwise around the band to stay out of sight, and almost laughed when the Yifft began looking left and right frantically, and picked up his pace.

Moving catlike on the balls of his feet, Indrajit rushed to catch up to the man following him. The Yifft was muttering under his breath; Indrajit tapped him on his shoulder.

The Yifft turned.

His face was angry and his third eye was beginning to open. Having lost Indrajit, then, he was turning to his magical gift to find the poet again. Indrajit chuckled as the anger turned to surprise. He saw just enough of the Yifft's eye to notice that the white of the eye was a deep yellow, thick with mucus.

Then he punched the Yifft, right in his sorcerous orb.

Indrajit Twang was a tall member of a tall race of mankind, and the Yifft was off-balance and surprised. With a shrill yelp, the snoop dropped to the paving stones and lay still.

Passersby looked, but no one looked twice.

This was Kish, after all.

The Yifft's third eye opened fully. Indrajit now saw that it had a horizontal iris, like a goat's eye. Looking at that eye, he felt a trickle of sweat run down his back, and an unsettled feeling in his stomach.

Grabbing the Yifft's turban in both hands, he yanked it down to cover the eye.

"No fair watching me while you're unconscious," he said.

With yelps of delight, the gray scavengers swooped down upon the Yifft. Indrajit kicked two of them, and then drew his knife to chase away the others.

"Not for you!" he called to them.

The Yifft had followed Indrajit, but he hadn't done anything worse than that. Indrajit dragged the unconscious man to the cluster of musicians, tossing him into their midst to keep him safe from the scavengers. The bang-harp players glared and hissed, but kept playing.

Indrajit resumed his walk. He picked up his pace, stepped off the Crooked Mile, and deliberately took alleys and byways, cutting away from the Paper Sook before angling back to reach it. He stopped twice at shops to pretend to examine first a saddle and then a glazed clay jar while checking for another tail.

He seemed clear.

Surely the Yifft was Holy-Pot's man, sent to make certain Indrajit complied with the summons. But Indrajit needed no urging; he owed Holy-Pot Diaphernes and he knew it, and if Holy-Pot had wanted to make an example of him, he'd have had him killed in the street, rather than summoned to a meeting.

Unless, of course, he had a more excruciating fate than mere death in mind. What if he intended to torture Indrajit, then hang his corpse up over the Paper Sook as a warning to future employees?

But no, surely Holy-Pot had some job that needed to be done, something distasteful or dangerous enough that he preferred to call in his debt with Indrajit rather than send an employee, or a more ordinary jobber.

Or maybe he needed someone with good peripheral vision. Or an epic poet.

The Paper Sook was the least comprehensible of the markets in Kish, and, if tales could be believed, the one through which flowed the most money. Everything traded by the merchants here sounded to Indrajit like gambling: bets on foreign currency, bets on ownership in companies, bets on next year's prices of grain, lumber, and bronze, and counter-bets to cover all the other bets. He couldn't understand for the life of him why anyone would want to trade in the Paper Sook, unless they simply had a taste for taking blind risks.

The sook itself was square, and from dawn to sunset, every day of the week, was full of shouting, spitting men who handed each other chits and scratched notes onto paper with stubby bits of charcoal. The merchants who traded in the Paper Sook had offices in the narrow alleys around the sook, and so did the professionals who helped them: guards, lawyers, assessors, surveyors, scribes, porters, and risk-merchants.

Holy-Pot Diaphernes was one of the latter. Holy-Pot's office was in the back room of a blacksmith's shop, allegedly so that the noise of the smith's hammer on his anvil would prevent eavesdropping on Holy-Pot's work...or, according to other versions of the story, so that anyone trying to negotiate with Holy-Pot would be distracted by the loud banging.

A stone bench across the alley faced the door that opened into Holy-Pot's office, and served as a waiting room. A person who came to see Holy-Pot didn't knock or announce himself. He sat on the bench and waited for the door to open. Holy-Pot apparently had a spell that told him when anyone was sitting there.

When Indrajit arrived, a man sat on the bench. He was of average height but of solid and muscular build. His complexion was dark brown, and he had large eyes set close on either side of a beaklike nose. His hair fell in a simple black bowl around his skull.

He looked Xiba'albi, but they were copper-skinned, and this man had a Kishi complexion. Maybe from Bat, or the Free Cities, or some cheerful mixture of all of them?

Like Indrajit, the man wore a kilt and sandals. Unlike Indrajit, he was bare-chested and heavily armed. He held a long falchion lying across his lap, a spear leaned against the wall of the building beside him, and two knives and a hatchet hung from his wide leather belt. After looking at Indrajit, the man turned his gaze down, at a sheaf of paper in his hands.

"Buying risk, or selling it?" Indrajit asked.

He wasn't entirely sure *how* one bought risk, really, but he'd heard Holy-Pot use the phrase. Also, staring intently at his papers made the man seem studious. Like someone who might be in the trade.

The man looked up, squinted, then returned to his reading. "I'm here to see Holy-Pot." His voice was gentle and high-pitched.

"So am I. You won't mind if I sit, then."

"This is Kish," the man said. "Make your own way."

A few minutes passed. Cries of dismay in the Paper Sook turned to hoots of joy and then back to sorrow. Runners rushed to the sook with news, and rushed away with different tidings again.

Indrajit fidgeted. "What are you doing there?"

The other man didn't budge. "Just reading this fascicle."

Indrajit nodded. "I'm Indrajit Twang."

The other man didn't look up. "I'm Fix."

"Are you a builder of some kind?"

"Are *you* a *minstrel*?"

Indrajit furrowed his brow. "What? No, why would you guess that?"

"Your name is *Twang*."

"But I'm not carrying a harp or anything."

"And I'm not carrying a level or a hammer or an awl, so the fact that my name is *Fix* shouldn't make you guess that I'm a builder."

Indrajit grinned. "To be fair, you *are* carrying a hatchet."

Fix looked up, his expression mild. "That's for chopping *people*."

Indrajit nodded, then cleared his throat. "Did I hear you say you're reading a *fascicle*?"

Holy-Pot Diaphernes's door opened.

The Doorman emerged. Indrajit didn't know another name for him. He could call the man the Usher, only that would risk confusing him with Sigil Hoazza the third, who was the Lord Usher in the same way that Orem Thrush was the Lord Chamberlain. They were the heads of two of the great families of Kish, whose ancestors, key servants of Kish's last emperor, had stepped in to impose order when the empire fell.

The Doorman was the most nondescript person Indrajit knew. He was brown, like most men, but of a middling hue, with bland facial features, and average height and build, a true Kishi. His hair, if he had any, was concealed beneath a faded red turban that matched the faded red robe, the sort whose upper half was arranged to resemble an aristocrat's toga. A brooch on the Doorman's shoulder was a disk of baked red clay incised with a cuneiform character. Indrajit had seen documents and other objects marked with that same sign, and they'd always been associated with Holy-Pot Diaphernes.

"Indrajit Twang," the Doorman intoned in his sex-less, flat voice. "Fix."

Indrajit raised his eyebrows at Fix. "If you have the same appointment I do, you must be a real piece of work."

Fix laughed, a girlish sound deeply incongruous with the wall-like man from which it emerged.

They followed the Doorman into the building.

"Also," Indrajit said, "just *Fix*? One name?"

Fix said nothing.

The Doorman gestured at a bead-filled doorway and stepped aside. Indrajit found that his heart was beating fast; despite his assurances to himself to the contrary, there was no guarantee that Holy-Pot hadn't brought him here to kill him.

"Fix," he whispered. "Does Holy-Pot Diaphernes want you dead?"

"Probably not." Fix walked through the bead curtain.

Taking a deep breath, Indrajit followed.

The room behind the beads was dark, lit by a pair of candles—genuine wax, not cheap tallow—standing on a single sconce beside the doorway. The atmosphere was further darkened by a thick smoke. Indrajit sniffed—not yip or tobacco, but also nothing else he recognized, either. Maybe just incense.

Behind a table against the far wall, in front of another beaded doorway, sat Holy-Pot Diaphernes. He looked tall, but that was probably just the result of his being thin. His skin was the gray of a porpoise's hide, and his long arms ended in thin fingers that drummed a complex pattern on the red-stained tamarind wood of the table. Holy-Pot's visible face looked directly at Indrajit and Fix, golden, catlike eyes unblinking and thin lips pressed together. His long forehead, pointy chin, and pale complexion made his face resemble the crescent moon.

On the left side of Diaphernes's head was a second face. Indrajit had never seen it, and didn't know anyone who had, but that side of Holy-Pot's head was covered with a veil. Exhalations where a mouth should be lifted the bottom half of the veil rhythmically, and when it rested, Indrajit could make out the profile of a long nose and chin.

Indrajit had no idea what the *pot* was. Vaguely, he thought it meant that Diaphernes was some kind of priest, though not of one of the city's five favorite gods.

"Indrajit," Holy-Pot Diaphernes purred. "Fix."

"I'm here because I owe you," Indrajit said. "The amount I . . . failed to return."

Holy-Pot nodded. "And the amount you failed to collect. And your fee."

"Fine."

"What's the job?" Fix asked.

Did Fix also owe Holy-Pot money? Or was he just a regular hireling, a solo jobber?

"What do you know apout risk-reselling?" Holy-Pot's voice sounded like that of a cat about to pounce on its prey, though his expression was mild. He had trouble pronouncing the sound *B*.

"Nothing," Indrajit admitted.

"Some," Fix said.

"Let me simplify." Holy-Pot cleared his throat, emitting a soft whistle from the veiled face. "An important party has an interest in a certain person. They have hired joppers to protect her for the next eight days. And they have taken out a risk-selling policy, which means that they pay a risk-merchant, and if the person is killed or kidnapped, the party will pe paid py the risk-merchant."

"Someone paid this party?" Indrajit asked. "What did they sell?"

"Ah, no. A person is said to *sell* risk when he pays another person to take the risk in his place. The risk-merchant on the other end of the transaction is said to *puy* the risk. The risk-seller is only paid if the risk is realized, if the feared event comes to pass. A curious terminology, put one grows accustomed to it."

"That's you," Indrajit said, looking for a shortcut. "You sell . . . no, you *buy* the risk." He thought he had it right.

"No. The risk-puyer involved in this particular transaction wants to protect herself from what she regards as a high-risk contract, so she has entered into a risk-*reselling* contract with me."

"So she pays you part of the fee she earns," Fix said, "and if she has to pay out to the risk-assured, she collects some of that amount from you, instead."

"My head hurts," Indrajit said.

"Correct." Holy-Pot's face became decidedly unexpressive.

"What do you need from us?" Fix asked.

Indrajit nodded. That was the right question.

"I worry that the original risk-merchant might pe cheating. I do not *think* she is, put she *may* pe. Perhaps she will kidnap this person herself, take my risk-repurchasing payment from me, and then hold the person for ransom."

"Or the risk-assured party might do that, too," Fix suggested. "Risk-merchanting fraud."

"That is also a possipility, correct."

Indrajit was beginning to understand. "So we are going to watch the situation for the next eight days. And if anyone tries to mess with this . . . risk-assured? Or is the risk-assured the . . . who is the risk-assured?"

"You will watch the opject of the risk-contracts," Holy-Pot Diaphernes said. "If anyone tries to interfere with her, you will stop them."

"Does the risk-merchant have jobbers at work, too?" Fix asked.

Holy-Pot nodded. "Mote Gannon's crew."

"The Handlers," Fix said.

Indrajit nodded, though he didn't know anything about Mote Gannon or his crew. "Why only the two of us?"

Holy-Pot shrugged. "I do not think it is likely anyone is cheating. Only possible. So I do not wish to spend too much money. Also, I want you to keep out of sight of the Handlers, so I do not wish to hire a large company with a distinctive uniform. The contracts start at sunset tonight and continue until the seventh sunset thereafter, so I wish you to pegin opserving the opject immediately." He reached under the table and produced two small purses, dropping them in front of the two jobbers. "Partial payment in advance. A similar amount upon completion for Fix, and for Indrajit, upon completion, the forgiveness of all debts."

They took the money.

"We'll need to get close to the object right away," Fix said.

"Who needs guarding?" Indrajit asked. "Who is the . . . object?"

"Ilsa without Peer," Holy-Pot Diaphernes said. "The actress."

Chapter Three

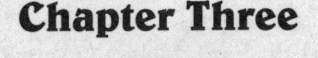

"I HEARD SHE'S A WEREWOLF," INDRAJIT SAID.

"Oh, I heard she was an illusion," Fix murmured. "She doesn't exist at all. She's a figment of the public's imagination."

"No, she changes into a wolf. On the full moon. Or the new, I can't remember."

"Maybe you heard that she's Orem Thrush's secret daughter. Maybe that's why someone wants to kill her."

"One of the other great families, you mean? The Lord Marshal? I heard he's a real bastard. Killed a servant for boiling his tea too long. When one of his horses came up lame at the Racetrack, he had a nail pounded into the groom's heel."

"Perhaps she's a priestess in the entourage of the Vin Dalu Rao."

"The Dismemberer? He's terrifying. I heard he's incapable of feeling pain, and that he runs a foundling house entirely to care for the children of the enemies he's killed, raising them as his own sons and daughters as the ultimate act of revenge."

"I've also heard she's a Xiba'albi spy. And that she's part of a burglary ring, and while theatergoers watch her perform the part of Zolit in *The Wanderers of Love*, her accomplices are burgling their homes."

"Now you're making fun of me."

"A little bit."

"Still, the burglary thing sounds like a good idea. Maybe we should suggest it to her."

Indrajit and Fix moved laterally across the Crooked Mile, up toward the Crown. They walked alleys and secret staircases and through the cracks between stores, taking a winding route free of sedans and retinues from one zig of the Crooked Mile to the next zag and on to the next. In their shortcuts, they scattered pecking flocks of long-plumed red Kishi Fowl and hunched-over, scurrying rats.

At a wooden post supporting the sagging corner of a plastered building Fix abruptly stopped. Leaning closer to the column, he examined a sheet of parchment pinned to it with a brass nail.

"What are you doing?" Indrajit asked.

"This notice is outdated." Fix collected the scrap of writing material, secreting it inside his tunic. "So I'll reuse the parchment."

Indrajit snorted.

They were headed for the Palace of Shadow and Joy, a theater in the Crown, where Bank Street with its guildhalls collided at an oblique angle with the Street of Fallen Stars, lined with old-money villas and foreign embassies. The Palace was one of Kish's grandest theaters, the sort where only the highest of high opera could be performed, and where only residents with good taste, spare money, and lots of leisure time attended.

The sort where actresses like Ilsa without Peer performed.

"So are you part fish?" Fix asked. They skipped across another stretch of the Crooked Mile, briefly exposed to the bright blue sky, and then plunged again into narrow, brick-lined darkness. He made fish lips and mimed blowing bubbles.

"I'm Blaatshi," Indrajit said. "We're an ancient and noble people, but in recent years our numbers have dwindled."

"Everybody is an ancient and noble people," Fix said. "But my question is, since you're green and you have eyes on the sides of your head, are you descended from fish? Also, that bony ridge you have for a nose...it would look good on a fish."

"That's ludicrous. In the first place, I'm not green. I'm mahogany, with hints of green."

Fix considered this. "Mahogany is brown with red in it."

"I know what mahogany is."

"So you are brown and red and green."

"You see why I use the word *mahogany*? It sounds much more elegant."

"But don't red and green cancel out?" Fix asked. "Wouldn't that make you brown and white? Or do you see yourself more like a Bonean stripehorse, but with three colors? Or spotted, like a leopard?"

"My complexion is a rich brown." Indrajit felt he should be losing his patience. Instead, perversely, he was enjoying the banter. "When viewed at different angles and under different lights, it may appear to contain shades of a dark red and a dark green."

"Ah." Fix nodded. "You are complex."

"All Blaatshi are. And in the second place, none of the thousand races of man is descended from fish. We are all descended from the original men. Naturally, the Epic suggests that the original men looked like contemporary Blaatshi do, but I am willing to entertain the possibility that that is an embellishment of one of my predecessors. In any case, my eyes are set farther apart than yours, but that doesn't make me the child of a trout. Does your large nose make you the child of a hawk, or an elephant?"

"My nose isn't large. It's prominent."

"*Prominent* is such an excellent word. It's almost as good as *fascicle*."

"I'm glad you appreciate my vocabulary. It's so hard to find peers who are men of letters."

"Oh, I'm not literate," Indrajit said. "Reading makes you weak."

"Weak?" Fix smiled faintly.

"But instead of *fascicle*, couldn't you have said *book*?"

"It's not a book. Too small."

"What about *pamphlet*?" Indrajit suggested.

"Wouldn't that rather imply that someone published the papers, with, for instance, a political or an informative objective?"

"You are indeed full of large words, Fix. And by the way, isn't that name rather . . . inadequate . . . for such a literary man?"

"What do you mean?"

The stink of camels and goats briefly choked Indrajit as they crossed the Crooked Mile again. Shouted sounds of haggling suggested the presence of an impromptu livestock market, the sellers likely being nomads from the Endless Plain. Beneath the beasts' reek lurked a dark stench of blood and offal that oozed from the butchers' shops on this stretch of the street.

Better the butchers than the tanners, anyway.

"Men who read and write have long and ridiculous names, don't they?"

"Like *Indrajit*?"

"*Indrajit* is a proud and ancient name, a name for poets. *Inder* is a name given to the storm-god Hort in the oldest parts of the Epic."

"And *jit*?"

"It's a grammatical termination of unknown origination." Indrajit sniffed. "It may be a diminutive."

"You're telling me that you're Little Hort?"

"As I was saying, literate men have long names, and also strange titles. Like Lucius Stratographos Kallipygian, Keeper of the Fourth Decan."

"You made that one up."

"True. But you know what I mean."

"Well, I learned to read in a discreet fashion. Probably the other readers just haven't heard of me yet, or haven't gotten around to giving me my longer name."

"I expect it will be Fiximon Nasoprominentus Fascicular."

The gate connecting the Spill and the Crown was narrow and guarded. Indrajit and Fix fell quiet. Indrajit adopted a facial expression that communicated that he was minding his own business, and wouldn't everyone else like to mind theirs? He noted with pleasure that Fix wore a similar mask.

He didn't recognize the jobbers minding the gate. They were lavender-skinned Zalaptings and slate-blue Luzzazza, tall and with down-turned ears, and they wore the hammer and sword device of House Miltric; the Lord Farrier had the contract for the city's gates.

Having passed through, he nodded back in the jobbers' direction. "Those guys don't have to waste any time today thinking about the insane and unwholesome details of risk-merchant arrangements."

Fix nodded. "On the other hand, if a riot breaks out, they'll have to put their bodies between the rock-throwers and the rich."

"You don't look like a man scared to skin his knuckles."

"I'm not."

"Maybe, if this thing with Ilsa works out, you and I could look for a gig like that."

"What? Become jobbers?"

"Well, we *are* jobbers, aren't we? Only as individuals there aren't many things we can do, so you and I alone are never going to be contracted to dig out a well, or collect taxes, or lead a sacred procession at midwinter from the Sun Seat to the Stone of Winter."

"Priests aren't jobbers."

"*Guard* a procession, then."

"You're suggesting we form a jobber team. A squad."

Indrajit hadn't really intended to suggest that, but as Fix said the words, it struck him as an interesting idea. He paused for a moment...but this was, after all, just talk, and if something came of it, he *could* use the money. "If this works out. I wouldn't mind working for myself a bit. Be hired by someone more important than Holy-Pot Diaphernes."

"Would we have to form a joint-stock company? Or a registered partnership?"

"What? Surely not."

"Put up a bond?" Fix pressed. "Enter a risk-merchantry contract to cover damages we might cause?"

"Ugh. You say *risk-merchantry*, and I lose all my enthusiasm." Indrajit turned onto Bank Street, Fix close on his heels. Above them rose high minarets, crenellated walkways, and arches that reached over the streets below to join building to building. They passed the Imperial Library, with its virtual palisade wall of statues of sages and teachers, their history stretching back centuries, into the years of Imperial Kish and beyond.

The scholars probably all had long names. And titles.

"And I assume you're imagining that you would be captain," Fix added.

"Forget it," Indrajit said. "It was a terrible idea."

"I'm not saying no. I'm just thinking out loud. You'd want to talk to a notary first, at the very least."

"This sounds worse the more you say. I guess I'll just keep working alone, at the crummy little jobs."

"This job doesn't seem so crummy." Fix shrugged. "We're backup bodyguards for an actress. The hard part will be figuring how to get close to her without making her nervous. Probably, nothing will happen, and we'll get paid. And if anything does happen, probably Gannon's Handlers will take care of it. We're being paid to be there, out of sight, just in case."

"I'll congratulate myself afterward, when the week has gone by uneventfully. Maybe I'll ask you to write the congratulations in a fascicle."

Bank Street was not cluttered with shops like the Crooked Mile, but merchants' carts did rattle slowly along it, or stood with their windows open to display wares. Trees were planted at regular intervals here, banyan and pipal and sweet-smelling ketaka. Indrajit stopped at the sight of a tailor's wagon, his eye lighting on a red cloak with elaborate patterns embroidered into the shoulders.

They would need some way to get close to Ilsa. He fingered the cloak, and when the tailor, a man with a trunk like an elephant's and no chin whatsoever, told him the price, he opened Holy-Pot's purse.

Delighted to find that he had enough money for the cloak and to spare, he bought it. Fix watched the entire exchange with narrowed eyes, but said nothing.

They continued.

"That's the Palace at the end of the block." Fix pointed with his square chin. "We should find a discreet place to observe it for a few minutes."

"There's a coffeehouse across the street. They charge way too much for something they call Burning Sea Blend, so I'd never ordinarily buy it. But if we pay for a couple of cups, they'll let us sit for a while and we can watch the opera house."

"I suppose if their beans come all the way from the Burning Sea, they'd naturally be expensive. You'd have to factor the costs of the caravan merchant who brought them, including his reasonable profit, into every cup."

Indrajit led them toward the coffee house, an elegant, two-story building with a fountain in front. "They grow the beans about thirty miles from here. And they taste like mud."

"Why would anyone buy their coffee, then?" Fix scratched his chin.

"They don't really sell coffee. They sell the illusion

of being the kind of person who buys expensive coffee and a place to sit and drink it. Mostly aspiring poets, is my understanding. And, in our case, they sell a good view of the Palace of Joy and Shadow."

"Shadow and Joy."

"There's only the one opera house, anyway. You knew what I meant."

They bought two coffees in two wooden cups and then climbed to the second story. They sat at a round table on a balcony looking across at the Palace, which was four or five stories tall, though it was hard to tell exactly, since the front was occupied by a single pillared facade that made the Palace look like a temple. Over the top of the building rose an immense dome shaped like an onion and gleaming like copper. Through three open doors, a desultory stream of theatergoers trickled into the Palace. They wore the impractical togas and gowns of the great families and their near allies.

To the immediate left of the Palace, almost out of Indrajit's sight, stood the nearly featureless stone block that was the Auction House. At a mere two stories tall, with zero decoration, it might be the smallest building in the Crown, and it sat in the center of a plaza with no statue or other monument to mark the building or its importance.

"I guess we'll have to buy a ticket," Fix said. "What if they're sold out?"

"We can always bribe a doorman to be allowed to stand in back. We don't need to sit, anyway. After the show it will get more complicated."

"We could introduce ourselves."

Indrajit shook his head. "I don't think so. I don't think she knows we exist. I don't think she even knows about the whole...about the underlying...about all the risk-merchanting going on over her."

"In that case, we'll have to tail Ilsa back to her apartment and watch her there."

Indrajit nodded. "Sit across the street and watch through the windows. Take shifts."

Fix sipped his coffee. "So, do your people have fish gods?"

"A fish god. Goddess, actually."

"Named Blotto or Bluto or something similar, I imagine."

"Blaat." Indrajit's eyes narrowed. "Why do you ask?"

"Well, you know. Sometimes in the old stories, gods...and goddesses...mate with some of their followers, and so you get the blood of gods flowing in the veins of men."

"I'm not a fish, Fix. I'm not even a little bit fish."

Fix shrugged. "So there are no stories among your people about...weddings with the goddess? Or rituals of marrying the sea?"

"As it happens, I know all the stories of my people. They are contained in the roughly thirty thousand lines of the Blaatshi Epic, which I can perform in its entirety at any moment. I learned it from my master, I perform it, and one day I will pass it to my apprentice, who will be the four hundred twenty-eighth Recital Thane of the Epic."

"Recital Thane? Isn't a *thane* a kind of warrior?"

"It's a warrior of high status. Or in my case, a person with the status of a high-status warrior, though my role is to perform and pass on the Epic, rather than to fight. I am a warrior of poetry."

"Wouldn't it be easier to write the Epic down?"

"Then it would be susceptible to wrong performance. Wrong intonation, wrong emphasis. Many of the scenes are incomprehensible except in the light of the accompanying gestures, which I have also committed to memory and perform."

"I think I would still write it down."

"That would also be impious."

"And no marriages with the goddess?"

"The goddess does not marry her children. She blesses them with fish, and favorable weather, and good health."

"Her *children*?"

"That is *figurative*."

"Huh." Fix sipped his coffee. "So you swam to town to find people to hear your epic."

"I *walked*. I am here to recite, as I am sworn to do, to any willing audience. And also to gain experience of life, which shall inform the additional narrative that I must one day add to the Epic, and also to make a living."

"Your mother-goddess couldn't just send you fish?"

"I grew bored of fishing, as it happens, and I don't particularly like the taste. What about you?"

"I like fish."

"Indeed, I would say you're obsessed with them. But where are you from? How does such a well-armed man come to be a reader? Where did you get your fascicle?"

"Nothing to say about me. I was born in Kish, and unless I catch a lucky break, I'll probably die here."

"Xiba'albi? Free Cities? Bonean?"

Fix shrugged. "I don't know. Just a man, I guess. I never knew my parents, and I was raised in an ashrama of Salish-Bozar the White."

"Wait, I know this one. His followers are called the *Useless*."

"His *initiates* are called *Trivials*. His *priests* are called *Selfless*."

"I was close."

"To qualify as a Selfless, an adept must demonstrate that she retains in her memory ten thousand pieces of information that are completely useless. That is the great commandment of Salish-Bozar, that no knowledge shall perish, no matter how impractical, and his adepts seek to fulfill the commandment."

"And with your feeble memory, weakened by the pernicious habit of reading fascicles, you were unable to remember the necessary number of things."

"No, I have a pretty good memory. But I could never be persuaded to waste my time on anything that was genuinely without practical application. I would spend all my money on scrolls, borrow codices, and even stand for hours to read the pamphlets being sold by street sellers; they couldn't stop me from reading, but I wanted to know things that mattered."

"Like what?" Indrajit pointed at Fix's spear and then his falchion. "Fighting skills?"

"Of course. And crafts."

"Ah ha, so you *can* fix things!"

Fix ignored him. "And trades, and geography, and politics, and history."

Indrajit finished his coffee, pleased that the last sips were still warm. "Really, what kind of knowledge is totally useless?"

Fix raised his eyebrows and cocked his head to one side. "Well, if I'd known of the existence of the Blaatshi Epic, I might have memorized *that*."

"I am immune to your japes. The Epic contains history, politics, and geography, as well as liturgy, leadership advice, meditative techniques, tools for consoling the bereft, and, some say, hints to the location of a great treasure, buried in the earth in the days when we fled our first homeland."

"You don't look like a man in possession of a great treasure."

"It would be impious to dig it up."

"The Selfless at whose feet I served had memorized the entire contents of ten large codices."

"Yes, but of what? *That's* the question."

Fix shrugged. "No one knows. The codices are written in a script no one can decipher. My master could reproduce it perfectly, every line, scoop, and dot on every page, and could order all the pages correctly if shuffled, and could point out recurring patterns and correspondences not only across multiple pages, but across all ten volumes."

"But he had no idea what any of it meant."

"Not a clue."

Indrajit Twang laughed. "That's genius. So they threw you out, for not wanting to memorize patterns of blots and squiggles. *That's* what you get for learning how to read."

"They asked me to stay. They said that I should give up other hopes, that I'd grow accustomed to the idea in time, and that I would one day do great work, preserving the heritage of the thousand races of man. But I couldn't do it, so I left."

"Admit it," Indrajit said. "This is all about women."

Fix blinked. "The Selfless of Salish-Bozar are not required to be celibate," he said slowly.

"No, but what woman worth having says, 'Hey, that guy over there who can vomit up ten volumes of writing no one can read, not even him, that's the guy for me'?"

"Not very many say that."

"None. None is the answer."

"I take your point. But are you saying you learned the Blaatshi Epic to impress women?"

"I'm not saying it's the *only* reason." Indrajit grinned. "But it doesn't hurt."

Fix finished his coffee and looked at the sun, a hand's span over the western horizon. "Time for us to go buy tickets."

Chapter Four

‹‹‹‹‹‹‹‹‹‹‹‹‹‹

THERE WERE NO TICKETS TO BE HAD, BUT INDRAJIT was proved right—for six bits from the purse Holy-Pot Diaphernes had given him, he bought his entrance and Fix's.

"Technically, we've sold all the footling tickets." The ticket-taker, a squat woman with faceted eyes like those of a fly crowning her lime-green head, looked left and right as she spoke to them. "But you can squeeze in at the foot of the stage anyway, if you don't like the view from the back. There's always room."

The six bits didn't go into the cash box, but into the ticket-taker's pocket.

She insisted that Fix check his spear. She didn't try to take his other weapons; this was Kish, and a man went armed. The spear disappeared into a closet of polearms and missile weapons.

Fix took a chit in exchange.

The two jobbers waited in the back, trying to look inconspicuous as the lamps were dimmed, and then crept up along the side of the theater. Above and behind them, the seats rose in five tiers, the chairs of each tier more deeply cushioned than the one below. The floor was of a pinkish marble; Indrajit didn't know where it came from, but it wasn't quarried at Kish, or anywhere especially close. Maybe Ildarion? The Epic contained an epithet, a formulaic repeated line, about *red stone of Ildarion*. In any case, the marble of the floors and walls and columns and the polished tamarind wood of the seats suggested serious wealth.

"They don't use jobbers to sell tickets, or guard the Palace of Shadow and Joy, do they?" he whispered.

"No, they have their own staff, like the temples and the great families and the Hall of Guesses and the library. It's the city functions that get farmed out to jobbers. Well, or any other job regular employees and servants aren't dumb enough to do."

"Everyone knows that. That's what the Auction House is for. Half an hour to sunset. Once the play starts, I'll talk my way backstage, to watch Ilsa from there."

"How will you recognize her?"

"She has no peer, right? It should be easy. If in doubt, I'll ask. You watch from the space below the stage."

The curtain swept open, revealing a stage lit by oil lamp and a painted backdrop of blossoming rose-apple trees.

"Look." Fix pointed with a shoulder. "There are some of the Handlers."

For a moment, Indrajit thought the other man was pointing at the theater's own guards, four men who stood, two at each side of the stage, in front of the curtain. They wore red silk from head to toe, including red masks, and the handles of the yetz-wood swords were lacquered red, so that in front of the curtains they were nearly invisible.

But then he saw the jobbers. There were four of them, spread among the footlings. They wore matching gray tunics with a circular glyph on the breast, and they stood with their backs to the stage, staring at the crowd.

The uniforms gave them an air of professionalism. One more thing Indrajit had to think about, if he and Fix were to organize.

On the far side of the footling mob was a Luzzazza, tall, with slate-blue skin and long ears that drooped downward. In the middle stood a broad-shouldered man with the fair skin of an Ukeling or a Karthing from the north, hair red as a pepper from Thûl, and a confident, wide stance that looked as if he were prepared to fight hand to hand that very instant. At the near end stood a pair of people who looked like dull yellow frogs standing on their hind legs, one a cubit shorter than Indrajit and thin, the other two cubits taller, and built like an ox.

"Look at the way that Karthing is standing," Indrajit said. "He's a fighter."

Fix nodded. "A Sword Brother, maybe?"

The skinny frog leaned toward the big one and whispered something.

"We've been noticed." Indrajit smiled and nodded at the froglike jobbers. "That makes me uncomfortable. I'm not sure why."

"Because the Handlers might take us for kidnappers if we're not careful, and attack. Or if Holy-Pot's suspicions are well-founded and the original risk-seller plans to cheat, they might intend to kidnap Ilsa without Peer, and they might decide they should kill us first, just in case."

"Yeah," Indrajit said. "Those are good reasons."

"But they don't necessarily know who we are, they just see us looking at them. Pretend to watch the play."

They slowed their pace and Indrajit pretended. The worst thing about Kishite high opera was its traditionalist insistence on using just the one instrument, the Imperial harp. The Imperial harp had five strings, which meant it played extremely simple melodies in a pentatonic scale.

The music of high opera was dull.

"Be careful around the big Grokonk," Fix said. The two men stopped walking. The chorus came onstage and began to shout together over the pentatonic crash of the unseen harps, a prologue about the twenty-year-long war between two kingdoms that preceded the moment the audience was about to see onstage. "That's the female. Does your epic tell you much about Grokonk?"

"It's not *my* epic, it's the Blaatshi Epic. And yes, the standard short epithet for the Grokonk in the Epic is *fierce-fighting Grokonk, who smell attackers coming*, and the long one is *Grokonks the dreamers, who fight all battles twice, once in their dreams and the second time more deadly*. Both epithets refer to their inborn psychic gift that warns them of approaching danger. They are much prized as sentinels and bodyguards, as a result."

"What do you mean by a *psychic gift*?"

"A magical power they all possess. Like the third eyes of the Yifft, for instance."

"That's nonsense," Fix said.

"Not so. The Grokonk are indeed prized as sentinels, as the Luzzazza are often committed to mystical pursuits, and the Blaatshi are irresistibly attractive."

"Yes, the female Grokonk is highly valued as a guard. But that's because her mates warn her of approaching danger."

Indrajit wanted to scoff, but Fix had shown himself to be surprisingly knowledgeable. "The skinny one is the big one's mate, is that what you're saying? And he watches for her?"

"Not quite. The skinny one is a Third."

"So where is the mate, then? Somewhere else, exercising his psychic gift?"

Indrajit caught himself scanning the audience, looking for more Grokonk. The chorus shouted a final warning, and then three women in old Imperial-style armor of lacquered wood and bronze disks strode purposefully onto the stage. Their faces were hidden by masks, so he couldn't tell which of the three, if any, deserved the appellation *peerless*.

"They're on her back."

Indrajit snapped his attention back to the Grokonk. The big one—the female—was looking right at him with domed, bulbous eyes, a big yellow hand resting casually on her leaf-bladed sword.

"If so, they're tiny. I think your fascicle is tricking you, Fix."

"I didn't read this in the fascicle. I sneaked into a lecture at the Hall of Guesses and saw it there."

"There's a reason they call it that, you know. Scholars know nothing. They just guess, and there's not even a penalty for guessing wrong."

"This was an anatomy lecture. Before the Vin Dalu cut the pickled female Grokonk open, the lecturer and her assistant pried off the male Grokonk one by one."

"The Vin Dalu . . . Rao?"

Fix hesitated. "It might have been one of the other ones. The Vin Dalu Diesa or the Vin Dalu Nikhi."

The Vin Dalu were the city's three priests of a god whose name was so sacred it was never spoken aloud, and consequently unknown. Instead, the deity was called simply the Dismembered One, and his priests, the Dismemberers, presided over torture, dismemberment, dissections, and, if rumors could be trusted, even darker scenes. The Dismembered One was not one of the city's five gods.

"One by one?" Indrajit asked. "How many male Grokonk can fit on a female's back?" He felt as if he was reciting a bad joke, and possibly a dirty one.

"The one I saw had twelve. Apparently, that's not an extraordinary number."

Indrajit swallowed, finding his mouth dry. "I'm going to leave aside, for the moment, the question as to why you were sneaking into a lecture on Grokonk anatomy. You're saying that if I looked at that female Grokonk's back, I'd see—"

"You'd see a jellied, mucus-like mass, easily mistaken for a slime-covered, hunched back. In fact, it is a swarm of male Grokonk, who are much smaller than the females, each attached by his mouth to a sort of nipple on her back. Through that nipple he receives nourishment from her, and he also fertilizes her eggs."

"His . . . *fertilizer* . . . is in his . . . mouth."

"Yes. Or rather, deeper back in his throat. The slime on her back is generated by her, and it protects him.

In turn, he protects her. His eyes are open under the mucus—if you look very closely in good light, you might see them—and when he spots a threat, he trembles."

"I feel ill."

They both pretended to be watching the action on stage.

"To be fair, she'd probably feel ill if she knew how *you* . . . fertilized."

"Well, then I won't tell her. What's the skinny one, the . . . Third? Not male or female?"

"Well, that was the real subject of the lecture at the Hall of Guesses."

"I'm all ears."

"I've seen a race of man that was all ears. It wasn't pretty."

"But I bet it had good hearing."

"Here's the lecturer's hypothesis: When the males fail to find a female to mate with, or fall off their mate sufficiently early and can't reattach—"

"Because of the slime?"

"I guess so. Those males grow bigger. And their . . . fertilizing apparatus . . . dries out and becomes hollow, and they learn to speak with it."

"Uh . . ."

"So the males can't speak at all, because they're attached, feeding and fertilizing. The females can only speak Grokonk, which is unintelligible to you and me, because it just sounds like croaking. But the Thirds develop something like vocal cords, and learn to use them to speak the other languages of man. So they are sexless, and you always see them in the company of a female. She acts as his . . . or *its* . . . protector, because she's bigger than the Third, and it acts as her translator."

"Talking through his dried-out...fertilizing apparatus. Which is in his throat."

"The dissection seemed to bear that out."

"Right." Indrajit took a deep breath. "I'm going backstage."

The women onstage were in full song, one throwing a high descant over the harmony generated by the other two as a fourth person came onto the scene, dressed all in black, face again covered by a mask. How was Indrajit going to figure out which actress was Ilsa without Peer if everyone in this production wore masks? The backing Imperial harps shifted mode and rhythm to something jarring, jumpy, and harsh.

Indrajit exited into the lobby, smiled at the ticket-taker, and then exited the Palace. Outside, the glow of sunset began to pink the inward-leaning spires of the five temples on the Spike, the rock peak above the top of the Crown, as well as some of the tallest of the Crown's buildings, including the Palace.

Holy-Pot's contract was about to start. Time to find Ilsa without Peer.

Indrajit straightened the cloak where it hung over his forearm. He circled the Palace at a jog, and in an alley behind, found what he was looking for: the tradesman's entrance. Breathing harder than he needed to, he rushed up to the nondescript wooden slab and banged on it. He was rewarded with a prompt opening, and a wide pink face, blinking hostility.

"The play is in progress," Pink Face said.

Indrajit panted, pretending to catch his breath. "First act?"

"I suppose." Pink Face squinted quizzically.

"Then I'm...in time!" Indrajit held up the cloak,

keeping it carefully out of Pink Face's reach. "For Ilsa...without Peer! Second act!"

Pink Face frowned. "You're a tailor?"

Indrajit shook his head. "Errand boy." And wasn't that the truth? Everything was for sale in Kish, including Indrajit Twang. He'd become distracted from his real purpose, and instead tried to merely make a living.

Pink Face reached for the cloak and Indrajit yanked it away. He took a deep breath and steadied himself. "I was told only to put it into Ilsa's hands. On pain of beating."

Pink Face frowned.

Indrajit leaned in to whisper. "Is it true she's a werewolf?"

Pink Face sucked his teeth, then came to a decision. "Leave that pig sticker here at the door."

"More of a pig chopper, really." Indrajit unbuckled the knife with a little unease—he hated to go unarmed in a city where people wore swords even to the opera—and handed the weapon to the doorman. "Which way?"

Pink Face, whose body was wrapped in blue-dyed leather, pointed down a hallway toward a narrow staircase. "Up those steps and left. You delivered here before?"

"No."

"You read?"

"No."

"Picture of the sun on the door. She might still be inside there, so knock first."

Alcoves lining the hallway rang with sonorous declamation as spear-bearers, swordsmen, nobles, courtesans, and magicians with stars spangling their robes paced up and down, hurling their lines at each other. A heavy bald man, tattooed on every inch of his body below the clavicles, stood weeping as a tailor adjusted his purple tunic. Two carpenters and a painter worked feverishly at what seemed to be a banyan forest.

A short man, so narrow as to appear almost to be a pole, dark red in color and bearing four walrus-length tusks in his mouth, so huge that the tips of the upward-pointing tusks rose over the bald crown of his head, strode toward Indrajit. As he walked, he bellowed scene numbers and names. "Act one, scene four! Stoolish! Katrang! Yatterino! Act one, scene four!"

Opposite the bottom of the stairs opened an alcove containing wooden racks. Costumes hung there: capes and mock weapons, robes, and long tunics. Ducking behind the racks, Indrajit climbed into a brown tunic, threw a gold cape over it, and grabbed a long brown spear. The weapon was so light, it must be made of balsa; the tip was painted with bronze, to appear to be a spear head.

It felt like low art, all this costume-craft and scenery. Cheap makeup on an ugly harlot. An audience paying attention, an audience that cared, would know from the dialogue and from the skilled gestures of the performers what clothing and scenery and props to imagine. A true performer could travel and perform naked, and astound.

Indrajit hung the red cloak on the rack and climbed the stairs.

What would he say if spotted? The cast of the opera seemed large enough that most people involved could probably not look at him and say for certain he was an interloper, but if he hung around Ilsa too much, he would attract attention.

He should take the costume with him after the play, and sneak back in disguised as a cast member again the following night. It had been surprisingly easy so far.

In the meantime, he and Fix would have the problem of following Ilsa without Peer around and keeping an eye on her during her night and morning.

But at the moment, he needed to find her and start his watch.

On the second story, the hall went left and right. To the right, Indrajit saw red curtains at the end of the hall, which must be the wing of the stage. He found the door Pink Face had indicated, marked both in brushscript and in bannerscript with several words and a neat little sun-glyph.

There were no alcoves on this floor, but there was an open door with an empty dressing room behind it, so he stepped in.

Pots of face paint huddled before an ornate bronze mirror, and several costume changes hung on a bronze rack against one wall. Against another stood a reclining couch, the sort decadent upper-class Kishites used at their eating-smoking-drinking-and-vomiting parties. There was a word for such parties, but Indrajit had forgotten what it was.

He was not invited to such events.

The actor—a man, guessing by the size of the boots standing behind the door and by the breeks hanging on the rack—must be on stage. Indrajit closed the door most of the way and stood in the room, facing so that someone passing by might think he was conversing with the room's occupant.

Thanks to his wide peripheral vision, he could still see the door to the dressing room of Ilsa without Peer.

"Act one, scene five! Ilsa without Peer!" Walrus Tusk bellowed in the hall. Apparently, Ilsa was special enough to get additional notice, because Walrus Tusk then rapped on her door and cried again, "Act one, scene five! Ilsa without Peer!"

Walrus Tusk disappeared. Indrajit tightened his grip on his spear, but forced himself to retain a relaxed stance.

Ilsa's door opened, and she emerged.

Ilsa without Peer was hideous.

Chapter Five

—⁓⁓⁓—

SHE HAD EYES AS BIG AS INDRAJIT'S PALMS, PER-
fectly round, with ice-blue irises. They appeared to have
no eyelashes or lid, but nictitating membranes that slid
up from the underside of the eyes to moisten them.
Ilsa's forehead rose a thumb's width above the top of
her eyes and then turned back at a ninety-degree angle,
becoming the perfectly flat disk that was the top of
her skull. She had fewer hairs than she had fingers,
each coarse and white and reminding Indrajit of wire.
Her mouth was wide and lipless, her nose mere slits.
Her fingers had one more bone than Indrajit's, and
each bone was longer, which made her hands resemble
large nets, or the wire scoops Indrajit had seen used
in Bonean variants of Rûphat. Her skin was pale, so
pale it almost seemed to shine.

With great effort, Indrajit caught the involuntary
gasp that came erupting out of his stomach, grinding
it to death between his teeth.

There were a thousand races of man, and Indrajit
had seen his share. Many were stranger-looking than

Ilsa without Peer, so it wasn't ugliness in an absolute
sense that stunned Indrajit.

Rather, it was *relative* ugliness. He had been expecting great beauty, and instead encountered a creature
that looked like a wide-mouthed troglodyte lizard.

Ilsa swept past, trailing a train and shoulder cape
the color of lightning, and leaving behind a sweet scent.

Indrajit caught his breath. What was that smell?

Some flower, and it provoked distant memories of
paddling in the warm waters of a calm sea, catching
eels with his bare hands, and lying on a warm rock
at sunset, basking in the sun's strength. Deep in his
heart, Indrajit felt he was waiting to hear the voice
of his mother, calling him home.

When the sensation faded, Ilsa was at the end of
the hall, beside the red curtains. Cursing six or seven
random divinities—carefully chosen impotent godlets
from the Epic, and certainly not any of the city's
cobbled-together pantheon—Indrajit rushed after her.

Two burly stagehands wrestled a crowned helmet
over the singer's head. Not only did it hide her features, it made her a cubit taller, transforming her
flat-domed stump of a noggin into a temple of spires
and buttresses, with filmy cloth of gold covering a
projecting cone over Ilsa's mouth.

Ilsa moved to the edge of the stage between two
red curtains as a round of polite Kishite applause—
stomping and whistling—erupted from the audience.
The stagehands, one a burly Xiba'albi with his hair
in a topknot and the other a bright red fellow with a
lower half like a crab, came toward Indrajit. The sight
of the stagehand's crustacean-like legs scuttling across
the hard wood toward him reminded Indrajit that he

hadn't eaten in two days, and the last horngrass he'd chewed to numb his stomach had been three hours before going to the Blind Surgeon.

He was starving.

"No spear carriers this scene," the Xiba'albi said.

Indrajit shrugged. "I was told to come stand right here and wait for my cue. Something about Sigil Hoazza not liking what he saw, last time."

Whether conjured by the name of the Lord Usher or out of indifference, the stagehands shrugged.

"Don't get in the way," Crab Legs said.

Indrajit squeezed himself forward to the edge of the stage. From here he had a clear view of the entire stage, and he also found a fold of curtain within which to stand, where he was invisible to the rest of the backstage area.

Ilsa without Peer drifted gracefully to the front of the stage. The footlings stared up at her, mouths open, eyes gaping.

From where he stood, Indrajit could smell the flowery scent again. What was that? Some rare Bonean flower, or a Pelthite fragrance, but it reminded him of warm times and safe joys. He felt that a place of beauty and safety waited for him just around the corner, if only someone would show him the way.

Ilsa without Peer began to sing. Her voice was loud, and the amplifying cone built into her mask raised its volume even further; her tone was sweet, her vowels open and golden, her vibrato subtle and erotic. Indrajit staggered from sheer surprise, and almost sat down.

She *was* without peer.

Her voice was enough to make him forgive the harsh racket of the Imperial harps that accompanied her.

The footlings swayed back and forth together, eyes

closed, as Ilsa sang of love and forgiveness. Across the stage, a man in a green costume and mask, surrounded by four actors in green loincloths with green skin-paint (or skin) and green swords hanging from their belts, took up the other half of the duet, lamenting the necessities of statecraft and praising the lord wise enough and strong enough to make the sacrifices his people called for in ringing stentorian tones.

Indrajit shook his head, dragging himself out of the spell of the story. It was slow and dull and shallow compared with the Blaatshi Epic, anyway.

Then he noticed that Gannon's Handlers were no longer among the footlings.

He scanned the audience. The stage was lit by oil lamps and candles set into reflective silver dishes, but the audience was darkened. Still, he thought he would notice a big yellow frog-woman in a gray tunic, if she were out there.

He didn't see her.

He couldn't see Fix either, though his fellow jobber was much more nondescript.

They would need a name, if they were going to form a jobbing company. The *Fixers* had a kind of ring to it, but it did rather imply that Fix was the company captain.

Also, it sounded a *lot* like the *Handlers*.

Where *were* the Handlers?

The green singer knelt center stage, bellowing a series of high, leaping notes that were surely very hard to sing, and which Indrajit found annoying. Behind him, his five green swordsmen drew their weapons and raised them in salute, chanting a bass line underneath the lead's tenor.

Only...hadn't there been *four* of them?

Indrajit looked closely: four of the men had matching long, straight blades, painted green.

The fifth man's weapon was leaf-bladed, and glinted like steel.

Indrajit sprinted onto the stage.

The audience gasped in delight.

The man with the leaf-bladed sword darted forward, swinging for Ilsa.

Indrajit was too late—

But the swordsman's aim was too high. His weapon sliced neatly through Ilsa's mask, scattering all the horns and buttresses and possibly slicing off a few of her wirelike hairs, but not touching her scalp.

Then the attacker stopped, looking at Indrajit with a delighted expression.

Indrajit stabbed the man in the forehead with his spear.

It was only after he thrust the weapon at the man's face that he remembered that he was holding a balsa-wood prop, and not an actual killing implement. The painted spear head and the top third of the shaft shattered, snapping into half a dozen bits of wood that exploded out in all directions.

The force of Indrajit's charge still carried him forward, so as the would-be assassin raised his arms defensively, a stupid expression on his face, he sprang forward, twisting and channeling the energy into his shoulder.

The swordsman was shorter than Indrajit. Indrajit's shoulder slammed into the man's nose and sent him flying into the footlings.

Indrajit caught himself at the edge of the stage.

He flapped his arms wildly, as if they were wings and by sheer force of motion he might be able to take flight, and managed to regain his balance. He shook his head, clearing it of persistent memories of the sunlight on the sea and mild breezes, and looked up to see a Luzzazza in a gray tunic, charging toward him across the front of the stage. The man's flopping blue ears would have been comical, if he weren't a head taller than Indrajit and attacking.

The yelling from the audience was no longer an indication of delight.

The actors stood still, stunned and uncertain. From behind the curtain came yelps of surprise and anger.

The Luzzazza had a long straight sword in one hand. Catching Indrajit's gaze, the slate-blue man slowed, raising his arms to the side in a pacific gesture.

He was still armed, though.

Indrajit saw the leaf-bladed sword at his feet. Kneeling, he picked it up, and pointed it toward the Luzzazza, tip low.

"You're one of Mote Gannon's Handlers, right?" he asked.

"Step away from the actress," the Luzzazza said.

"Right, you're here guarding her," Indrajit said. "So am I. Didn't you see that guy?" With his left hand, he pointed down into the mass of the footlings. He was afraid to look for the assassin, keeping his eyes fixed on the advancing Luzzazza. The man had a sprig of some flower worn on his clavicle, bright green with a splash of yellow, hanging from a short string.

The Luzzazza sheathed his long sword and spread his arms wide. "I mean you no harm, Twang." He stepped closer.

"Good." Indrajit raised the tip of his sword, pointing it at the Luzzazza's sternum. "So just stop right there."

The Luzzazza nodded and smiled.

"Hey," Indrajit said. "How do you know my name?"

An unseen power slapped the leaf-shaped blade aside and the Luzzazza swept in. Trying to stab but with his weapon abruptly out of place, Indrajit lurched forward, and an invisible force grabbed him by his tunic, raising him off the floor and drawing him in close to the Luzzazza.

With one hand, the Luzzazza seized the wrist of Indrajit's sword hand, pinning it. With the other, he drew his long sword again.

Over the Luzzazza's shoulder, Indrajit saw the two Grokonk come lumbering along the stage. The female really *was* enormous. He grabbed at the force gripping his tunic, patting it and finding it was shaped like two hands. The hands flowed into wrists, which became arms, which seemed to be attached to the Luzzazza. The blue man had a second set of arms, right underneath his first set, and they were invisible.

"What in frozen hells?" Indrajit muttered.

"I seek the path." The Luzzazza's face was calm, expressionless. He raised his sword over his head, angling his point down as if he planned to skewer Indrajit through the neck.

"Hey!" Indrajit squirmed and kicked, but the Luzzazza was stronger than he was. "Hey, I was *rescuing* her!"

At that moment, Ilsa without Peer, her theatrical helmet dangling around her head in a splintered ruin, darted forward. She had to jump to do it, but she flung herself upward and grabbed the sprig of flowers at the Luzzazza's neck.

The string broke and the flowers came away in Ilsa's hand.

And the Luzzazza froze.

His face, serene and expressionless a moment earlier, was taken over by a glazed, vaguely ecstatic expression. He breathed deeply and smiled.

His heart hammering in his chest, Indrajit again felt warmth and smelled the salt sea. But he also saw the blade hanging over his head.

With a grunt and a heave, he managed to swing his knees up and get his feet between him and the Luzzazza. The Luzzazza resisted, but only barely, as if he were half asleep.

Indrajit kicked, and he flew away from his attacker.

The Luzzazza staggered back, crashing into the female Grokonk.

Indrajit fell to the stage. He landed hard, lost most of the air in his lungs, and found himself staring up at Ilsa without Peer.

"There's something about you," he murmured. "I just want you to . . . I just want to know . . ."

She reached down and grabbed his unresisting hand, then hoisted him to his feet. "Hold this," she said to him in a rasping voice in the low bass range, and she pressed the bundle of flowers into his palm. "Sniff it."

Warm waves, warm air. And he felt an irresistible urge to do as Ilsa had told him.

Indrajit sniffed the flowers, and his head cleared. Where was Fix?

"There's a trap door," the singer growled. "We can get beneath the stage."

Indrajit shook his head. "Time to get you out of here," he said. "I think these guys are trying to kill you."

"They are only men, after all." She shrugged, nictitating membrane fluttering, the tops of her eyes just visible from this angle through the ruins of her singing mask. "Did Orem send you?"

"No, I work for the risk-seller. Or the reseller, rather. Repurchaser? I think."

Ilsa without Peer laughed, and her golden vocal tones returned.

The Luzzazza and the Grokonk female were trying to climb each other to stand, and getting in each other's way, instead.

"This way!" Indrajit whispered, and dragged Ilsa with him.

"Beneath the stage," she said again. "There's an exit that only *I* know."

Indrajit had already picked his way out, and didn't want to risk getting lost. He dragged the singer along by main force. "There's an exit this way!"

"To my dressing room, then!" She pointed.

"No time!" he panted.

"If you want to hide me," she rasped, "I can't go outside looking like this."

Good point.

Indrajit stood in the door of her dressing room for just ten seconds while she tore off her stage helmet and glittering train and threw on a black hooded robe. He noted a pair of windows, open and facing out onto the street. Cool night air, painted yellow by torches and oil lanterns, drifted in from the Crown.

"I hope you're good with that sword," she croaked. "I'm unarmed."

"I'm excellent," he lied. "Positively heroic."

He also had no idea where to go. The shared garret

where he'd been sleeping on a pile of rags in the corner? Though he was in arrears there, and the landlady, a three-legged woman with a bloblike, trembling knob of flesh on a long stalk that hung before her like an esca, might not let him in. The Blind Surgeon, where apparently his credit had been restored? Holy-Pot's office?

The last idea seemed to be the most commonsensical—Holy-Pot had resources and knowledge—but he wouldn't be in his office at night, would he? And Indrajit had no idea where the risk-merchant lived.

"This way!" He grabbed her hand again and they ran down the stairs. He was leading their charge toward the tradesman's entrance when a man in a gray tunic leaped into his path. He emerged from a hall that reached the door at right angles to Indrajit's. He was the fair-skinned man—Ukeling or Karthing, or maybe Ildarian, since those river-valley dwellers of Ildarion had northern blood in their veins—and he held a long, straight sword in each hand.

Pink Face the doorman shrieked and ran.

A Sword Brother, indeed. Indrajit groaned.

The Sword Brotherhood's name made it sound like a monastic order, but in fact it was a martial art. The warriors who mastered it were sworn to ancient ideals of justice and poverty, or maybe they had secret masters directing them from an underground kingdom, or perhaps they were mere mercenaries.

Sword Brother or not, the pale man standing in front of the door looked grimly competent in his stance, and he wasn't budging.

The Sword Brother growled. Lowering his chin to his own sternum, he inhaled deeply, and Indrajit saw a sprig of the same flower he held in his hand, pinned to the top of the man's linothorax like a blotch of yellow and green paint.

Ilsa without Peer dropped her hood.

The Sword Brother flinched and Indrajit attacked.

For a moment, he had the upper hand. He knew his own limitations as a fighter, and kept to strictly utilitarian strokes, aiming for the center of the man's mass, putting his weight behind blows that would, if he landed them, be fatal.

But the Sword Brother twisted aside, so the blow that should have stabbed him to the heart skidded along his ribs instead, and then he battered aside Indrajit's second attack, and then suddenly both longswords were flashing for Indrajit's head.

Indrajit stepped in front of Ilsa. After a couple of deflected slashes, he found he barely had the speed and energy to parry the blows that came at him and keep his body between Ilsa and the Sword Brother, and no capacity to attack.

It was a matter of time before one of the Sword Brother's blows got through.

And then the Sword Brother caught Indrajit's leaf-shaped blade between his two swords. Stepping forward and cranking his blades in a circular motion, he ripped Indrajit's sword from his hand and to the ground.

Then the Sword Brother lunged forward—

And a spear hit him in the side.

The spear was thrust, not thrown, and Fix followed through his attack. The short brown Kishi emerged from the same hallway from which the Sword Brother had come, at a full sprint.

A man with slower reflexes would have been impaled through the gut and died horribly. The Sword Brother, caught by surprise, still managed to turn and avoid the worst of Fix's blow. Still, Fix's onslaught was so fierce that it knocked him to the ground and tore both his weapons from his hands. As the Sword Brother fell, Fix kneed him in the groin, elbowed him in the throat, and then punched him repeatedly in the face.

The Sword Brother groaned and passed out.

Indrajit picked up his leaf-bladed sword.

"Where did you leave Ilsa?" Fix asked.

"I'm Ilsa," Ilsa croaked.

Fix frowned and cocked his head quizzically.

"*I'm Ilsa*," Ilsa sang in her golden voice, and Fix's eyes grew wide.

Indrajit snatched the sprig of flowers from the Sword Brother's linothorax and clapped it over Fix's mouth. "Come on," he said. "Let's get out of here."

Chapter Six

~~~~~~~~~~

"I GUESS ONE OF THE THINGS YOU STUDIED THAT got you thrown out of the Trivials was martial arts," Indrajit said.

They stood looking around the corner of a building, back at the Palace of Shadow and Joy. In any other district of Kish, the street they stood on, passing between two tall, square buildings, would have been a filth-flooded alley, ringing with the calls of prostitutes and the heavy steps of footpads. Here in the Crown, it was a lane paved with cobblestones and wide enough for a carriage. The buildings were both residences, three stories tall, with the upper stories reveling in a profusion of balconies and broad windows. From one of those balconies, a narrow arch leaped over the lane, fusing with a balcony on the other side.

Ilsa without Peer looked intently at both men. Her hood was up and Indrajit and Fix each had a sprig of the Handlers' flower pinned at the top of his tunic, so it was easy to think of the short, cloaked figure with extra-long fingers and gleaming eyes like pools of ice shining from the depths of her hood as a goblin.

But Indrajit couldn't shake the memory of her haunting singing voice, or of the strange effect she'd had on him, evoking memories of his childhood.

Or of the strong desire he'd felt to obey her.

"I wasn't thrown out." Fix's voice was gruff. "I quit."

"What the Sword Brothers do is all based around bladed weapons. The Boneans have unarmed fighting styles." Indrajit considered. "And I've heard that at the end of the Endless Road, there are strange kingdoms where no one uses any weapons at all, and they even fight their wars with kicks and punches."

"You know what I've heard is at the end of the Endless Road?" Fix countered.

"What?"

"Nothing. It's endless."

Indrajit scanned the street. Men in gray tunics had come running out of the Palace, but they had all run in wrong directions. He was waiting just a few moments more to be certain they weren't followed, and then he'd lead them off.

Really, the jobber company couldn't be named the *Fixers*.

"So what do you call your fighting style?" he pressed.

"I call it *knock them down and kick them*. Advantages of reach and size go away when the other fellow is lying on the ground."

"I'm glad you arrived in time." Indrajit was teasing, but he was grateful. "How long did it take you to go turn in your chit and get your spear back?"

Fix grunted and hefted the weapon in question.

"The Handlers were armed. I took the spear from one of them, Little Hort."

Ilsa without Peer spoke in her grinding voice. "I'm grateful for the rescue. Can I know your names?"

"I'm Indrajit Twang. This is Fiximon Nasoprominentus Fascicular."

"Oh, a literate man?" the singer asked.

"Fix," Fix said. "Just Fix."

"Fix, then. And Indrajit. But if we stand here in the street, sooner or later someone is going to find us."

Indrajit and Fix looked at each other.

"I'm not sure who attacked me," she continued, "but if they knew where to find me on the stage, they might just as easily know where to find me at home. So I'd like a safe place to spend the night."

"The thing is," Fix started to say.

"Yes." Indrajit cut him off.

He led them directly away from the Palace of Shadow and Joy in a straight line, as fast as they could walk. He didn't want to hail a sedan or a carriage, for fear of who might already be inside. Ideally, he'd have liked to walk toward the Spill, and hide somewhere near Holy-Pot Diaphernes's office, but that would have required passing the Palace again, and the thought made him nervous.

So instead, they went the opposite direction, toward the Lee. The Lee housed the city's second-tier wealthy, as well as some of its more popular civic institutions— racetracks, ball courts, and markets. Beyond its gates lay the Caravanserai, the great bazaar facing the landward side of Kish, where horses and camels were traded and provisioned, and where the most exotic goods were bought and sold.

Not too bad. Much better the Lee than the Dregs, given the chance.

They passed under the Spike, with its five temples. Indrajit didn't love the silence, so he broke it. "Which of the five gods shall we pray to, then?"

"There are far more than five gods," Fix said.

"Pedant. I know that. Ten thousand or a hundred thousand, depending on how you like your proverbs. But of those five," he pointed at the temples clinging to the Spike, "which?"

"I grew up singing the songs of Machak," Ilsa growled.

"So did I," Indrajit agreed. "He is Blaat's favorite consort. But we're about as far from the sea as we can get and still be in Kish. I was thinking maybe Hort Stormrider?"

"Or Spilkar the Binder," Fix countered.

"Ah, that's the one. May the Lord of Contracts ensure that we poor contract-men may fulfill our obligations tonight."

"You said you work for a risk-merchant," Ilsa reminded him.

"True. Holy-Pot Diaphernes, though there's probably no reason you should know who he is."

"I do not."

"Do you know Mote Gannon?" Fix asked.

"I've heard the name. Were those his men, the jobbers in gray? The men who attacked me?"

"Yes."

"What kind of name is *Mote*, anyway?" Indrajit snorted. "What, is he tiny?"

"I understand that it means something different in his race's tongue," Fix said.

"Oh? You learn languages from your fascicle, too?"

Fix was silent.

"What's a fascicle?" Ilsa asked.

"Go on, impress us, what does it mean?" Indrajit was relieved to see the city's wall and gate leading into the Lee rising out of the darkness ahead of them.

Fix shrugged. "*Throw*, I believe. Also perhaps *vomit*."

"That sounds like a delightful language," Indrajit said.

At the gate, three squads of bravos waited. They didn't wear uniforms as such, but instead were dressed in consistent colors of clothing that was elegant and stylish, without getting in the way of practicality. There was a squad in blue, and one in white, and a third dressed in fuchsia. The men waiting at this gate hired themselves out as bodyguards to residents of the Crown who had business in other districts, especially at night.

The three companies here stood in a loose line, waiting more or less politely together for potential clients.

They said nothing to Indrajit and his companions— unsurprising, given how they were dressed. The leader of the first company, a man with blue puffed sleeves, a completely bald head, and skin the color of copper, hesitated as if he might speak to Ilsa, but then said nothing.

"Would you feel more comfortable if we hired a company of these men?" Ilsa croaked. "I have the money, and they are only men, after all."

"Would *you* feel more comfortable?" Indrajit asked.

The singer looked at Fix. "No."

The buildings on the far side of the gate were shorter, two stories tall at most. This street was lined with shops now closing for the evening.

"Speaking of delightful language," Indrajit continued, "you seem to have two voices."

"And one of them is delightful." Ilsa threw her head back, her mouth opening unnaturally wide, and guffawed.

Indrajit was grateful for the darkness, which hid his blush. "My observation was more to the point that they are very different."

"A scholar from the Hall of Guesses claims I have two voiceboxes. One works when I speak, and the other when I laugh or sing."

"In your...throat?" Indrajit ventured.

"She's not Grokonk," Fix muttered.

"Yes," she said.

"And they're both...*supposed* to be voiceboxes?"

Ilsa fixed him with a cold stare. "What else would they be?"

Indrajit shrugged. "Just asking. Do all your race have two voiceboxes like you do?"

Ilsa was silent for a moment. "I don't know anyone else of my people. They all died when I was a baby, and I alone was saved."

In their short time together, Ilsa without Peer had led Indrajit to feel many things. Her words now added a deep and poignant sorrow to the list. "Rescued by whom? By the Palace of Shadow and Joy?"

"Yes," Fix said. "Because in the off-season, opera house employees and unemployed actors wander the wild, trying to perform good deeds."

"Why not?" Indrajit asked. "That's *exactly* what Recital Thanes of the Blaatshi Epic do."

Fix snorted.

"By Orem Thrush," Ilsa said. "Who is one of the

Palace's more generous patrons, so you are not entirely wrong. He was a younger man then, a hunter and a warrior, and not yet Lord Chamberlain."

"Interesting that he should be your rescuer, and also a patron of your art," Fix said.

"My people were killed by a folk I had never seen before. Tall men, with thick hides and tusks like elephants. They were on the move, a race that had lost its own home and was intent on stealing someone else's."

"They stole yours." Indrajit tried not to think of his own people.

"We lived in a valley above the sea. Hidden, we thought, from all other peoples, drinking fresh water from our rivers and eating the fish that swam in them. The attack came by night, and with fire, and in the morning my people were dead. I alone survived—my mother tossed me out the back window of our hut and then made a great commotion at the hut's front door to draw attention. She was impaled with a spear, and then hurled, still alive, into the flames. I ran."

Indrajit imagined the river valley of his own people, burning. He touched the sprig of yellow flower to make sure it was still in place and wiped a tear from one eye.

"Orem Thrush found me in the morning. He was returning from a journey to Ildarion, or perhaps he had some business on the steppes of the Yuchak, and he saw the smoke. He and his men killed the tuskers, but I was the only survivor."

"You were a child," Fix said. "How old were you?"

Ilsa shrugged. "Too young to remember, and my people did not use the Kishite calendar, in any case. We counted seasons. I am in my thirties now."

"Ilsa without Peer," Indrajit murmured. "Unique in the world."

"Destruction is one way to render a thing unique," Ilsa said.

"Not our way, happily," Indrajit said. "We are men of letters."

"Only one of us can actually read, of course," Fix said.

"Fine. Men of ideas." He hesitated, because he had heard rumors, and didn't want to give away the fact that he had heard them. "Is the Lord Chamberlain still involved in your . . . is he your patron?"

Ilsa chuckled, a sound like chains being dragged over a sheet of iron. "What have you heard? That I am his lover? His daughter? That I myself am in fact Orem Thrush, who secretly sings opera, but can only do it wearing a mask?"

"Well . . ." Indrajit said. "Yes."

"This morning, if I had gotten lost on my way to the Palace of Shadow and Joy and you had offered to take me to the Lord Chamberlain, I would have accepted with gratitude. But tonight, someone tried to kill me, and I don't know who."

"And you can't be certain it isn't the Lord Chamberlain himself," Fix added. "Do you have some cause of disagreement with him?"

"I have told him I will retire after this season." The singer's voice was hollow.

"He's that attached to your singing on stage?" Fix pressed.

"He has an interest. He acts as my patron socially, but he is also my . . . you might call him my business manager. He and I share in the proceeds of ticket sales. When I quit singing, he will lose money. The Lord Chamberlain is very good at making money, and he is very attached to the money he makes."

"You think he'd kill you?"

"I'd kill *him*," Ilsa rasped. "If I *had* to."

"Whoa." Indrajit had not expected to have to unravel any mysteries, but he couldn't protect Ilsa if he didn't know whom to trust. "The Palace of Shadow and Joy also wouldn't want you to quit, for much the same reason."

"Correct."

Fix's face was screwed into a mask of concentration.

"Well don't worry." Indrajit turned his best grin on the singer as they passed through a puddle of torchlight. "I'm taking you somewhere safe from all those people."

"One of Orem's rivals?" Ilsa asked. "Perhaps the Lord Marshal or the Lord Farrier would be willing to take me in, to spite Orem."

"Better than that," Indrajit said.

"A temple?" she asked. "The Hall of Guesses? A waiting ship?"

"A bordello."

After a moment's hesitation, Ilsa without Peer laughed, and her voice shifted into its sweet register. *"Well, it's surely true that men don't go to bordellos seeking women who look like me."*

"There are a thousand races of man," Indrajit said. "You'd be surprised. But this is a bordello that caters to men who live in the Crown. It's just ahead of us, on the Avenue of the Occluded Moon. Discretion, and therefore security, are everything to that business. We're going to rent a room for the night."

"We need to find out who bought the risk-contract," Fix said.

"What?" Indrajit and Ilsa answered at the same moment.

"The risk-contract," Fix said. "It's a bet."

"Brace yourself," Indrajit whispered to Ilsa. "I think this is the fascicle talking." Still, the fact that Fix, who seemed to know so much about risk-merchanting, referred to it as betting, made him feel good. It made him feel that he almost understood the subject.

"I still don't know what a fascicle is," Ilsa whispered back.

"A risk-contract is a kind of bet," Fix said. "Usually, it's the bet you place on the thing that you *don't* want to happen. So if you're a merchant sending a caravan off down the Endless Road to buy silks, you sell the caravan's risk. The policy says that if the caravan is lost, the risk-merchant will pay you. That way, you get a kind of protection against downside risk. *Either* the caravan is successful and you make lots of profit, minus what the risk-contract cost you, *or* the caravan is lost and you make a profit on the risk-contract instead, so you're not as bad off as you would have been."

"Yes, yes." Indrajit waved a hand to hide the fact that his nonchalance was pretended. "Everyone knows that."

"But you could cheat." Fix's eyes glittered in the darkness. "You could buy a risk-contract on your caravan, but then, for instance, stuff the caravan's chests with worthless filler and hire bandits to destroy the caravan yourself."

Ilsa's back stiffened. "Why would you do that?"

Fix shrugged. "Maybe cheating the risk-merchant is easier than leading a caravan down the Endless Road and back. Or maybe . . . you've decided it's time to get out of the caravan business, and there's one last big profit to be had."

"You're saying the Lord Chamberlain makes the risk-contract," Indrajit said, thinking out loud, "and then has Ilsa killed himself. Because she's done singing, anyway, so why not squeeze out a few last coins?"

"Or the Palace." Fix turned to Ilsa. "Do you think either of them is capable of such a ruthless act?"

They turned onto the Avenue of the Occluded Moon, a street famous for the subtlety of its vice shops, all of which catered to the wealthy of the Crown. The building fronts might have been warehouses or dry goods shops, they were so nondescript, and they weren't even identified by numbers.

"My peaceful people were destroyed for their grass huts." Ilsa's voice was deeper than ever. "I think anyone is capable of ruthlessness. There are a thousand races of man, and they are all wicked."

"Or," Indrajit said, struggling to think through this risk-merchanting idea, "one of them gets wind that some third party is trying to kill you, and enters the risk-contract to cover their possible losses. Could anyone else want you dead?"

She shook her head, a gesture mostly hidden by the cloak's hood.

"In the morning," Fix suggested, "we'll go talk to Holy-Pot Diaphernes. We'll find out who sold the risk, the original contract, the risk he's repurchasing. He must know the details of the underlying contract—otherwise, how could he calculate his own odds? If it wasn't the Lord Chamberlain, then ... maybe we can turn to him for help."

Something bothered Indrajit, but he couldn't quite identify what it was. "Is there somewhere outside Kish we can take you?"

"No. My only life is in Kish."

"Okay." Indrajit smiled. "So if we find out that Orem Thrush sold the risk on you, then the three of us will take to the road together, singing and reciting poetry."

"I neither sing nor recite poetry," Fix said.

"I bet you're a great dancer, though," Indrajit told him.

"I'm really not."

"Here we are." Indrajit stopped. The bordello was called the Fountain, but there was no sign out front. Indrajit knew that this was the Fountain because the silk ribbon hanging in its doorway was green, and knotted around long, pointed tower shells. "Wait here a moment."

The bouncer lurking in the doorway was twice Fix's size in all dimensions, which made him—Indrajit tried to do the math in his head—*much* bigger than Fix. His knuckles were wrapped in dully glinting brass and a broad, red leather belt was thick with knives of all shapes and sizes.

"I need to rent a room," Indrajit said to the guard.

The bouncer looked Indrajit up and down. "You've got the wrong place. We sell beans."

"Okay." Indrajit grinned, realizing now that he and Fix were both dressed like lowlifes. Under her black cloak, Ilsa wore a theatrical costume, which was impressive, but didn't necessarily communicate wealth. "I will happily pay a bean for a full night of her time, provided that that comes with a room."

The bouncer chuckled. "You're so funny, I almost want to say yes. But no."

Indrajit was about to try again when the bouncer's jaw went slack. Indrajit turned and found Ilsa and Fix at his elbow.

"*We're going in*," Ilsa sang to the guard.

He nodded, and they passed through the ribbons into the bordello.

"Oh yeah," Indrajit said, "I've been meaning to ask you about that."

Chapter Seven

THE FOUNTAIN'S PARLOR HAD LURID RED WALLS and dim light, spiked with a hint of the smoke of yip and several of its derivatives. The narcotic and the alcohol served at the dark wood bar in the corner were doled out in small amounts, so the patrons were lucid.

They didn't aim for drunkenness at the Fountain; that was for cheaper establishments, where you didn't really want to see your companion too clearly, and you certainly didn't want to see yourself. At the Fountain, the clientele wanted their senses heightened, just a bit. They wanted to be offered exotic entertainments they couldn't have in their own palaces in the Crown, and they wanted to experience every moment.

The light in the sitting room was dim, but before a client was taken upstairs by an employee, they could examine each other in well-lit viewing alcoves. Upon request, a client could sit in such an alcove and inspect a parade of possible entertainers.

A flautist played in the corner, seated on a round

cushion, Xiba'albi-style. Indrajit stepped around another heavily muscled bouncer to speak to the pander. She stood behind a red wooden lectern, a tall, thin woman with subtly blue skin and eyes that were entirely a vivid purple, with no whites. Her hairless skull was dotted with large bumps, as if a crown of horns was on the verge of sprouting through the skin.

She squinted at him. "Do I know you?"

Indrajit had only been to the Fountain once before. "I . . . I came here one time looking for work."

The pander looked baffled for a moment, but then laughed. "Oh yes, the poet. We still don't have a need for . . . your art."

Indrajit was pleased by her tact. "I'm not here for that, I'm here as a customer." The sight of her blue skin reminded him of the Luzzazza who had grabbed him with invisible arms. "Are you Luzzazza?"

"No." Her voice managed to be soft, but firm as iron. "And *I'm* not available." She looked back at the singer, hidden in her black cloak, and Fix, who looked about with open curiosity on his face. "How much companionship do you need?"

"I need a room until dawn. I'll pay for however much companionship I need to get the room, and your people can take the night off." Suddenly Indrajit wished he had counted the money in Holy-Pot's purse—it might not be enough.

He could probably talk Fix into chipping in.

"Who wants to take nights off?" The pander raised her eyebrows and blinked in mock innocence. "You don't take the night off from a *party.*"

"Right. Then I guess they can keep partying and just earn double."

"I have just the room for you. Discreet. Near a back entrance, in case you should want to take a late-night stroll." The pander looked closely at Indrajit, then made a notation with a wedge-pen in a thick ledger. "That will be three Imperials."

Indrajit took out his purse and opened it, but before he could count the money, the unnervingly long fingers of Ilsa's hand caught him by the wrist. With her other hand, she pressed coins into his palm.

Fair enough. Indrajit paid and the pander handed over a key. "The Twins room," she said, and the three of them climbed the indicated spiral staircase in the corner.

"So," Ilsa without Peer croaked. "What sort of man frequents a place like this, that is so decadent, and so far above his station?"

Indrajit only chuckled. At the second story, he stopped and faced the singer. "You gave me nine Imperials. I'm pretty sure you heard the price that woman quoted."

"We all did," Fix said. "Why do you care if she's Luzzazza?"

"Because I . . . hold on, let me come back to that. Ilsa, the price was three and you handed me nine. Did you want me to get this Twins room for three days?"

Ilsa was silent while two men wrapped in long blue towels tiptoed past. Then she lowered her hood. The gleaming skin, the flat head, the lipless mouth, the thick hairs, and the icelike eyes were still shocking. When she spoke, it was in a singsong, with her golden voice. *"I am alone in this city. I am alone in this world, and someone is trying to kill me. I don't know for sure what your contract with Holy-Pot Diaphernes is, or even if he is your master."*

"I wouldn't say *master*," Indrajit muttered.

"*So if Holy-Pot, or anyone else, offers to pay you to kill me or to give me up . . . I just want you to know that I can pay.*"

"Ah," Indrajit said.

"Ah." Fix raised his eyebrows. "Ah . . ."

"Forget it." Indrajit handed the six Imperials back. "We're on your side. Right, Fascicular?"

Fix nodded.

"*And if Holy-Pot tells you to kill me?*"

"Pretty sure he won't," Indrajit said. "If you die, he has to pay up. The whole point of hiring us was to protect you."

"Good thing he did," Fix added. "Gannon's Handlers failed spectacularly."

"Yeah, and they think I'm the assassin." Indrajit hung his head, chagrined. "Anyway, I've crossed Holy-Pot before, I'll do it again. But tell me one thing, before I get distracted."

Ilsa without Peer nodded, waiting for the question.

"You have some kind of magic power," he said. "You make people feel . . . calm. Peaceful. You made me think of my childhood, and I lost the will to do anything but sit and remember." He touched the sprig of flower pinned to his tunic and deliberately *didn't* say that something about Ilsa made him want to obey her. "And this plant blocks your magic."

"My magic is in my scent," Ilsa growled.

Indrajit sniffed. "I smell . . . lemon, I think. A hint of vanilla bean."

"Not that," she said. "That's just a Pelthite perfume that Orem gave me. But females of my race have power over men's minds."

Indrajit searched the Epic in his memory, trying to find a description of this phenomenon and failing. "All men? Men of any of the thousand races?"

"Maybe not," she said. "But I can tell you from experience that it works on *most* men. That flower that you're wearing produces a very faint scent that neutralizes my power. We called it the Courting Flower."

"Men wore it to go courting?" Indrajit grinned. "To keep them rational?"

"A woman sent it to a man she planned to court," Ilsa said. "As notice of her intent, and so that he could keep himself rational."

"Fascinating," Fix said. "Very...thoughtful."

"Write it in a fascicle," Indrajit told him. "Not very romantic, though."

"Poets and madmen and those already in love with the woman accepted the notice but didn't wear the flower."

"Go on, then," Indrajit said to the singer. "Which one of us are you courting? It's me, isn't it? You gave me a flower first."

"*Poets and madmen* certainly sounds like you." Fix looked around with some skepticism at the blue marble floors and the gilded molding at the tops of the walls. "This would be the place for that sort of thing, I suppose."

Ilsa laughed, then batted her nictitating membranes. "We'd better find this room, don't you think?"

The rooms weren't numbered, but identified with the signs of the seven planets and the twelve celestial houses. Apparently not all of the wealthy of Kish could read. Indrajit's key was engraved with the sign of the Twins, and he easily found the Twins room.

He entered first, scanning quickly and noting the divans, the cushions, the hanging benches, the flagons of wine, and the open door to the balcony. Oil lamps resting in niches in the walls gave a warm, yellow light. From outside, the smell of sweet pepper trees wafted in on a cool breeze.

"Come in," he said, and then locked the door again behind them when they had done so.

"Indrajit Twang." The voice came from the balcony, and it was followed by the appearance of a man, stepping into view from the unseen edge of the balcony. His face was shadowed, but the outline was vaguely familiar.

Ilsa without Peer pressed back against the wall, sucking in breath.

"We're armed," Indrajit warned the man.

"I can see that. Especially your friend."

"He likes to be called *Fascicular.*"

"I do not."

"Step forward," Indrajit adjusted his grip on the hilt of the leaf-bladed sword. "Let us see you."

The man stepped forward, and Indrajit cursed.

"You remember me." The intruder was the Yifft Indrajit had met earlier in the day. He had to be the same one; the flesh around his forehead-set third eye was swollen and puffy.

Also, Indrajit noticed that he had a sprig of the Courting Flower pinned to his turban. So the man knew what he was dealing with.

"I see I didn't hit you hard enough. You had enough vision left to know we would come here."

The Yifft smiled. "We don't see the future. We see . . . other things."

"So if I'm going to punch you again, say, in two minutes, you don't know that now?" Indrajit shifted his weapon to his left hand.

The Yifft raised his hands, showing that they were empty. "You attacked me before, without warning, when I was unarmed. You'll be hitting a defenseless man again this time."

Indrajit shrugged. "You were following me. I'll punch you again next time I catch you, and the next, every day of the week."

"I'm just here to talk," the Yifft said.

"I'm listening." Indrajit didn't lower the sword.

"To her."

Fix moved to put himself between the singer and the Yifft as well.

"Who are you?" Ilsa growled.

"I'm Grit Wopal," the Yifft said. "I serve the Lord Chamberlain."

"I don't recognize you," Ilsa said.

Wopal smiled. "I'm one of the Lord Chamberlain's Ears."

"Funny," Indrajit said. "I would have sworn you were going for *Eyes*. In fact, all things considered, I'd still say the *Lord Chamberlain's Eyes* makes more sense than his *Ears*. More aesthetically satisfying."

"More thematic," Fix added.

"Unless maybe the rest of his people have a third ear." Indrajit scratched his chin. "What would that look like? Kind of, the only place to put it is the forehead, in a commonly ordered face. An ear that opened in the middle of your forehead and let you hear special things, yeah, that would make sense for the Lord Chamberlain's Ears."

Fix grunted. "How do we know that slit in his face *isn't* an ear? Maybe it opens up and there's an eardrum inside."

"I've seen it," Indrajit said. "It isn't pretty, but I'm quite sure it's an eye."

"The Lord Chamberlain gave us the name," Wopal objected. "Most of us are not Yifft."

"*What does Orem want?*" Ilsa asked her question singing, and the musicality of her voice shut them both up.

"He asked me to bring you home." Wopal smiled. It was at least a good simulacrum of a warm smile. Indrajit watched the third eye carefully, prepared to leap forward and pummel it again if it began to open. People had tried to kill him tonight, and he had no idea whether Wopal might be in league with them. "All is forgiven."

Ilsa snorted. Coming from her, this was a truly fearsome sound, like a horse clearing its throat. "Meaning, I am forgiven for wanting to be free?"

The Yifft spy shook his head. "I don't know the details of your life, my lady. But I was told that you are in no danger, and you will be given anything you want."

It was Indrajit's turn to snort. "*No danger* seems like manifest nonsense. I just had a heaping helping of danger, earlier this evening."

And something nagged at him about it.

Wopal frowned. "No danger *from the Lord Chamberlain.*"

The words certainly sounded like forgiveness and safety, but every time the Yifft spoke, Ilsa without Peer edged back. She was still convinced Orem Thrush had tried to have her killed. Or at least she feared that it was possible.

"I guess I'm still skeptical," Indrajit said. "Probably comes from having a bunch of jobbers attack me onstage at the opera."

"Was any of those jobbers the Lord Chamberlain?" The Yifft secret agent spread his hands and smiled.

Indrajit turned to Fix, brow furrowed. "This guy has a mouth on him."

"Does it make you want to punch him again?" Fix asked. "Or are you thinking of offering him a job?"

"Both."

"I have a job," Grit Wopal said.

"Come to think of it," Indrajit said, scratching his chin, "I'm not sure I would recognize the Lord Chamberlain. I don't suppose he actually looks like his device, does he, Wopal?" The rumors that the Lord Chamberlain was a shapechanger who could walk unseen in any crowd were surely nonsense.

"A horned skull?" Grit Wopal briefly covered one eye, the gesture of piety used by followers of the city's god of seers. "In a life of travels, mercifully, I have never seen a race of man whose face resembled an actual horned skull."

"I don't know that it would be so bad," Fix murmured.

"You'd be distinctive," Indrajit added. "Anyway, I guess the point is that the Lord Chamberlain has never hurt me."

"Correct." The Yifft smiled.

"He *did* send you to follow me, though," Indrajit said. "Why was that? And how did you get here ahead of us? I chose this place, and I didn't tell the others until we were practically here. Wait—can you read my mind with that thing in your face?"

The Yifft looked overwhelmed.

"Okay," Fix said. "Take the questions in reverse order. Can you read minds?"

"Not really," the Yifft said.

"They are only men, after all," Ilsa said.

"What?" Indrajit asked. "So . . . you can *kind of* read minds?"

"I can see emotional states. I can see certain other kinds of energies. I cannot see *thoughts*."

"How did you get here ahead of us, then?" Fix asked.

"I didn't. I got here after you, and listened to your conversation with the pander, and then ran around back, climbed the fence, and scaled the wall to get here just as you did."

"How did you pick the right room?" Ilsa asked.

Wopal smiled. "It's the balcony with Twin devices carved into it. It stood to reason it would be the Twins room."

"Pretty good spy-work. I guess I'd hire you," Indrajit conceded. "So, the energies you see . . . can you see invisible limbs?"

Wopal smiled. "Such as the Luzzazza possess?"

Ah-ha. "Did you read about that in your fascicle, Fix?"

"No. Many of the Luzzazza follow a mystical path that involves search for, then denial of, then complete annihilation of the self. I read *that* in my . . . papers."

"That doesn't really sound like *invisible arms*."

"My point exactly."

"Yes," Wopal said. "With my inner eye open, I can see the additional limbs that the Luzzazza possess."

"And Grokonk?" Indrajit pressed.

"Grokonk aren't invisible," Fix protested.

"But can you see the males?" Indrajit clarified. "Separately? All huddled there in the slime?"

"Yes." Wopal nodded.

"And what do you see when you look at me?"

"He means, does he look like a fish?" Fix said.

"Really?" Wopal asked.

Indrajit chuckled. "Not do I look like a fish, but what do you see when you look at me with your third eye?"

The Yifft nodded and took a deep breath. As he exhaled, the lid of the eye in his forehead lifted, revealing an oversized pupil and iris, streaked red and gold. The Yifft blinked twice, gazing on Indrajit's face.

"I see a man who has lost his way," the spy said. "A man who has very nearly forgotten his quest, and who is in danger of forgetting his soul."

Indrajit punched him in the eye again.

He had been attacked, the Lord Chamberlain might be behind the men trying to kill him, he was tired of being followed, and the Yifft had insulted him. Punching Grit Wopal might not have been a good decision, but in the moment, it felt right. The spy dropped to the floor with a high-pitched shriek, clapping both hands over his forehead.

"I warned you," Indrajit said. "Kind of."

"Wow," Fix said. "That guy made you sound romantic. Like the hero in a cheap tale."

"A cheap tale, such as might be written in a fascicle?"

"Or sung in an epic."

Indrajit turned to Ilsa. "I take it you don't want to go with this guy." For emphasis, he kicked the Yifft in his dirty yellow turban.

"Knock them down and kick them," Fix said. "You're learning."

"I do not," Ilsa said.

"Last chance," the Yifft gasped from the floor. "This doesn't have to get ugly."

"Way too late for that, I'm afraid." Indrajit unlocked the door. "You see, you made a rather simple mistake. This was a job for a strong jobber *company*. You never should have come alone."

He opened the door, and found himself looking into the copper face of the bravo with puffed sleeves. The man had a curved saber in his left hand and a hooked dagger in his right. Behind him, crowding the hall, were the rest of his bravos dressed in blue.

Grit Wopal staggered to his feet.

"I never told you I came here alone," he said.

Chapter Eight

~~~~~~~~~~~

INDRAJIT SLAMMED THE DOOR SHUT.

Copper Face lurched into the gap and the door cracked him in the head.

The leader of the bravos staggered backward, but the door shivered in Indrajit's hand and pushed him away. By the time he could catch his balance and hurl his shoulder into the wood, one of the bravos had shoved a shield against the door jamb. Indrajit grunted and pushed and swore, but couldn't force the shield from the door.

The Yifft was on his feet, keeping an eye on Indrajit and Fix both. He picked up a wine bottle, holding it like a club. "You can still surrender."

Fix stepped smartly to the side of the crack between the door and its jamb. Two sword blades poked awkwardly into the room, beneath the shield. Fix raised his spear over his head, angled the blade sharply down, and stabbed.

A sharp scream on the other side was followed

immediately by the disappearance of the shield and the two sword blades, and then a loud clatter. Grimacing, Fix wrenched his weapon back.

The door fell shut and Indrajit slid to the floor. Reaching up, he turned the lock again.

"Thank the Stormrider that the patrons of the Fountain enjoy their privacy, and that the management protects that privacy with doors that actually lock." Indrajit rolled to his feet and found his leaf-bladed sword. "If these were strings of beads, we'd be dead."

Fix crossed the room to the balcony. "We already know the wall outside can be climbed."

The door shuddered as men tried to break it down from the outside.

"That's our exit," Indrajit said. "Just give me a moment to kill this fellow."

"No!" The Yifft shrank. His third eye was shut again, but Indrajit couldn't tell whether that was on purpose, or the result of swelling.

"Drop the bottle and you live." Indrajit was bluffing, but Grit Wopal dropped the bottle.

"Why let him live?" Ilsa asked. "He can hurt me! He'll tell Orem Thrush where I am!"

"Mercy is scarce enough in this world," Indrajit murmured, "and you may want it yourself someday."

Ilsa's eyes held a curious expression, but Indrajit couldn't read it.

"I won't let them in, I swear."

"Correct," Indrajit agreed. "Now crouch in the corner there."

He was worried about more than just the Yifft letting the men in. He also didn't want the Yifft to see and report the true direction of their exit.

Grit Wopal crouched in the corner.

"The garden below is clear," Fix reported. "Other than of revelers, of course."

Indrajit handed the sword to Ilsa. "If Wopal moves, stab him."

The divans in the room were heavy, but Indrajit was tall and strong. He slid one across the room and penned the spy into the corner, then tossed a second on top, squashing the little man across his shoulders.

Wopal let out a soft groan.

"You can still breathe, right?" Indrajit called to him under the pile of furniture.

"Barely."

"*Barely* breathing is breathing," Indrajit told him. "Just be glad you're not *almost* breathing." For good measure, he tossed a silk coverlet over the top of the mound, blocking off the last of the Yifft's vision.

"Down we go!" he called to the others.

The door thudded.

Indrajit stepped to the balcony. There, he put a finger over his lips to urge his companions to silence. Then he mimed the action of climbing with both hands, and pointed up.

Fix grinned.

Ilsa's nictitating membranes fluttered rapidly. She nodded.

The climb turned out to be easy. The thighs of a winged and wanton maid on one side provided a good foothold, and an ithyphallic man with goat's legs and a cob of maize for a head gave an excellent handhold on the other. From there, a stone vine bearing strings of sex organs as fruit was almost as good as a ladder, and led right to the rooftop.

Fix lumbered up first. Then Indrajit hoisted Ilsa without Peer; once up to the vine, she climbed easily to Fix's extended hand. Indrajit managed not to think too much about how nice the opera singer smelled.

He looked back quickly; the furniture pile was unmoved. The door's hinges were straining, and close to a rupture.

He threw himself up the wall as quickly as he could, and onto the roof.

The roof was tiled with baked red clay, at a gentle slope. Indrajit spread himself on his belly with his face at the edge of the rooftop, looking down into the private garden. The garden's walls were two stories tall, as tall as the buildings around it, and had several gates. Porters stood inside each gate; Grit Wopal must have bribed or bullied one of those men to let him in. The wall was wide enough that a person with good balance—which Indrajit was—could jog around it all at a quick pace.

The garden itself contained pools and fountains and ornate sculptures depicting mythological scenes. Clusters of winsome amalaki trees and sweet-smelling ketakas around the outside downplayed the presence of the wall, and gave the garden the feeling of being a forest. In a cleared space surrounded by statues, a play was being staged, in which all the actors were nude—it looked like the unholy offspring of high opera and low bawdy theater. The audience sat on other undressed people, crouched on hands and knees to make their bodies into seats. Yip smoke wafted up to Indrajit on the breeze, and Indrajit smelled the bitter, honeyed scent of soma.

He heard the splintering crack of the door below

giving way, and within seconds two of the bravos stood on the balcony. Out of natural impulse or curiosity or because they had heard and believed Indrajit's misdirection, they looked down into the garden.

"No, don't stab!" He heard Grit Wopal's voice, muffled. The words became clearer, presumably as the bravos pulled the furniture away. "Don't stab, if you want to get paid! It's me! Get these divans off me! They went down the wall—they're probably already out one of the gates!"

Several bravos jumped over the edge of the balcony and rushed across the garden to the porters. They'd get no answer, or a confused answer. They would attribute that to the staff's discretion, or to the drugs and the wine. And they'd scatter, to search the city.

Smiling in satisfaction, Indrajit eased himself back away from the edge of the rooftop.

Ilsa without Peer was smiling. Fix looked more thoughtful.

"We wait here," Indrajit whispered. "Then we get the Fountain to arrange a closed sedan for us, and our own set of bravos."

"They'll do that?" Fix asked.

Indrajit shrugged. "Surely they must have some way to deal with the situation where, say, the young heir to one of the great families passes out drunk on their premises."

"I'll pay," Ilsa said. "Where do we go? Back to the theater?"

"No," Indrajit said. "We'd be seen there."

"Maybe she's right," Fix said. "After all, there are now two different jobber companies searching the city for us. Maybe moving around just increases our chances of running into them. We could go to the theater—they won't look for us there. Or maybe, we should just stay right here, for the same reason."

"Right here is going to be pretty chilly by the time the night is up," Indrajit pointed out.

Fix nodded. "Fish are cold-blooded."

Indrajit sighed. "Besides, we need to find out who sold the risk on Ilsa. That means going to the Paper Sook and, unless you've got some other source of information, it probably means asking Holy-Pot Diaphernes to tell us about the contract."

"Will he break a client confidence like that?" Ilsa asked.

"I doubt he sees it that way," Indrajit said. "He's not a priest or a notary. And besides, we're trying to protect his interest, keeping you alive. He'll tell us. Let's give our friends a couple of hours to give up. Try to sleep a little, if you can."

The night fires of Kish were low enough that Indrajit could see the stars. He marked the position of the Snake-Charmer behind the silhouette of one of the few nearby buildings that was taller than the Fountain, a jagged row of chimneys and a dome-topped tower to the southeast. Then he waited to watch the constellation move two handspans.

The rooftop air was cool, but he didn't dare climb down into the Twins room for a coverlet. Ilsa without Peer, fortunately, wore her cloak. Her breathing soon dropped into deep rhythms, and while Indrajit was too chilly to sleep, he was able to stretch out flat, and thereby relax.

What would he do if Orem Thrush, the Lord Chamberlain and one of the most powerful people in Kish, turned out to be behind the attempt on Ilsa's life? And Indrajit had punched his spy in the face, twice.

Though he had spared the man.

But he had stayed true to his contract. He had watched Ilsa without Peer, and had in fact saved her life. Twice. His debt with Holy-Pot was squared, now.

Or would Holy-Pot see it that way? Maybe Holy-Pot would require him to keep protecting the singer until the contract period was up, which was a whole week. Or maybe the contract had an out clause of some kind, or maybe Holy-Pot would prefer a larger jobber company to take over now.

More good reasons to talk to Diaphernes.

The Snake-Charmer's arrival above the silhouette of the adjacent roof told him an hour has passed.

"It's been an eventful day," he murmured.

"Hmm," Fix said.

Ilsa breathed deeply.

If Orem Thrush decided he wanted Indrajit dead, there was nothing for it but to get out of Kish. The Lord Chamberlain was wealthy enough that he could send assassins anywhere on the Serpent Sea to kill the Blaatshi poet, so maybe Indrajit would have to take the Endless Road and find out for himself what, exactly, lay at its eastern end.

He certainly couldn't go home.

And his quest—the reason he'd really come to Kish—would be effectively destroyed.

Maybe, as an alternative, he could seek patronage among the other great families. The Lord Usher or the Lord Gardener or the Lord Stargazer, or one of the other heirs to the seven servants of Kish's last emperor who had picked up the reins of power when the emperor's hands had fallen cold, hired jobbers for all manner of reasons. Maybe being the man who had thwarted Orem Thrush would be a good qualification for a job working for one of Thrush's rivals.

As what, though? Bodyguard? Assassin? Thug?

Not as Recital Thane, that was for sure.

Indrajit sighed.

The second hour had passed. "Come on," he said. "Let's make our way back to the Spill."

Dawn was still hours away, and the night had grown cold. Even here in the Lee, where the height of the hill on which the city stood sheltered the air from the worst of the sea's excesses, the breeze was wet and salty. Indrajit's bones ached as he rolled over.

Fix sat up.

Ilsa without Peer came instantly awake when Indrajit touched her shoulder.

"I'll go first," the former Trivial of Salish-Bozar the White offered.

Fix lowered himself to the balcony quietly, and Indrajit dropped him his spear. The garden party continued, at a slower, quieter pace. Fix signaled that the way was clear, and Indrajit and Ilsa followed.

Just in case, they dropped down into the garden and then Fix and Ilsa stood in a shadowed corner while Indrajit, Ilsa's bag of coins in his hand, approached the pander.

The same woman occupied the station. She smiled at Indrajit. "Your friends came looking for you."

Indrajit grinned back. "Not my friends."

"Then it's good they didn't find you."

Maybe he could get a job working at the Fountain. They'd already rejected him as a poet, but they might be willing to hire him as a bouncer. Would such a job protect Indrajit from the wrath of the Lord Chamberlain?

"I'm hoping to hire a sedan chair from you," Indrajit said.

"For three?"

Indrajit considered. "Do your bearers and guards wear uniforms?"

❖   ❖   ❖

Indrajit and Fix wore the Fountain's livery and Ilsa without Peer reclined inside the sedan chair, curtains closed. In addition to the six bearers, four armed guards accompanied the sedan, two before and two behind.

The livery was a red tunic emblazoned with a blue fountain. Obvious, clear. If he were to organize a jobber company—if Orem Thrush didn't kill him—Indrajit would want a similarly clear, memorable insignia for his company. Another strike against the *Fixers*—there was no obvious symbol that went with that name.

Maybe the *Leafblades*? With crossed leaf-bladed swords for the heraldry? But that only occurred to him because he had by chance acquired such a sword for himself today. But then, perhaps what he took to be chance was in fact fate, or a sign. The Epic was full of signs and omens, and the interventions of fate.

The guards wore the same livery, but over thick leather breastplates. Leather skirts studded with bronze disks and bronze greaves rounded out their armor. The bearers had a short sword or dagger each, other than Fix. His ability to hold a long spear in his right hand while steadying the sedan chair pole on his shoulder and still trot along, keeping pace with the unencumbered bearers, was impressive.

Only one gate connected the Lee to the Crown, and that would be easy to watch. There was no guarantee that *all* the gates out of the Lee wouldn't be watched, but Indrajit thought it unlikely. So they took the longer road, exiting the Lee by the south gate into the Caravanserai. The sleeping camels, the merchant trains coming and going, the tents of the spice-men and the jewelers and the wandering smiths ignored their flight as they rounded through the big trading-ground and dropped down onto the East Flats.

Both the East and West Flats lay down close to sea level, so a bluff separated the Caravanserai from the East Flats, but it was a slope with many trails down. The bearers appeared to know the way, and were sure-footed as goats. Fix also navigated the footing easily, but Indrajit cursed and tripped and caught himself and cursed again, several times over before they'd reached the flats.

Small creatures scattered before their approach. Indrajit caught just a glimpse of one, a six-legged rodent gnawing on a small limb that looked like it might—hopefully—have come from a reptile.

The stink of fish climbed to meet them, like the rising, inchoate din of an orchestra tuning up. The huts of fishermen and smugglers and sailors, and the net-shops and provisioners and taverns that catered to them, lay scattered in such chaos that it was barely possibly to identify any strip of ground between them to call a road.

Indrajit barked his shin on the corner of a porch that sagged off one end of a tavern called the Alewife. "Hort's ribs!"

"Think of all the lovely experience you're getting,"

Fix muttered to him. The stocky man didn't even seem winded. "Perhaps you can compose an epithet to the Alewife, with her apron of tree's bones."

"Hey, that's almost like a kenning," Indrajit said.

"It *is* a kenning," Fix insisted. "Like the *dolphin highway* instead of the sea, or *sheep in the pastures of the sun* instead of the clouds. I read about your people's poetics, you know. Before you ask, not in a fascicle. In a codex, as it happens."

"Well . . ."

"Well, what?"

"Fine, it's a kenning. It's just not a very good one."

The Fountain's bearers said nothing.

The section of the East Flats contained within the city's walls was called the Dregs. Zalaptings wearing the House Miltric hammer and sword didn't even bother to wave them through, but slouched, half-asleep, as the sedan chair passed through the gate. Only three main streets were discernible in the Dregs, one running from the East Flats Gate to the Crown Gate, steeply uphill and zigzagging, and a second running downhill, breaking off from an early turn of that zigzag and connected the Crown Gate with the Spill Gate. The third street ran level, just inside the wall, turning right from the East Flats Gate and connecting to the Spill.

Dawn was close now. Fatigue hung around Indrajit's shoulders and made his head heavy, and the soles of his feet ached. They carried the sedan chair through the Dregs and into the Spill.

Once through the gate, they were within a few minutes' walk of the Paper Sook.

"Okay, right here is good," he said. He and Fix

both had to grip the sedan chair poles and slow the forward momentum by main strength, the bearers were so intent on their task and so insistent in their pace.

Ilsa without Peer climbed out of the sedan chair. While Indrajit was still wondering whether it was customary or appropriate to tip the bearers, she went ahead and did so, producing one Imperial for each of the men. She also said *bless you* to each in a singsong voice, as if she were a priestess or a queen.

The men had beatific expressions. When Ilsa released them, the bearers still stood there, staring at her with idiotic smiles on their faces.

Ilsa finally had to order them to return to the Fountain.

With the sky turning gray in the east, the three entered the Paper Sook. Burning lamps and candles indicated that the workers in money had been at it for some time already, tallying the results of the previous day's shouting, making certain of the amount of liquid wealth and the status of long-term bets, and drinking tea and liquor to fortify the throat for another twelve hours of shouting today.

"Okay," Indrajit said. "Time for Holy-Pot Diaphernes to tell us the whole story."

Chapter Nine

~~~~~~~~

APPRENTICES WHO LOOKED LIKE PRAYING MANTISES with fur on their shoulders and about their midsections were stoking the blacksmith's fire with more fuel and pumping air into it with a two-man bellows as Indrajit and his companions approached.

"Do you think he's in there this early?" Indrajit asked. "There's no noise to hide his private conversations."

"He's in there," Fix assured him. "He's doing the paperwork and writing letters, the stuff that doesn't require talking."

"You understand his business much better than I do." Indrajit led the company toward the alley behind the blacksmith's.

"I was sort of studying the industry," Fix said. "Trying to figure out how he worked. Thinking maybe I might go into it myself."

"Yeah? What's so attractive about it?"

Fix looked at Indrajit in surprise, but then began

the explanation. "Well, in theory, you can start the business with no capital at all, since the risk-assured pay you up front. As long as you can calculate the risks right and recruit a large enough pool of initial policyholders, you can start the business with no cash of your own. I'm a little capital-poor, so—"

"Stop!" Indrajit raised a hand. "I thought you were going to say *because I'm sick of physical labor,* or *because I want a job where people aren't trying to kill me,* or *because it will make me rich.* Whatever it is you're saying instead, it's making my head spin."

"Fine," Fix said. "I wanted to get rich."

"Good. *That* I understand."

"And I want to impress a woman."

"I understand *that* even *more.*" Indrajit thumped Fix on the back. "Wait...do you mean a *particular* woman?"

Fix shrugged and look at his feet.

"Huh. So you too are complex, my friend."

They had arrived at Holy-Pot's door. Indrajit sucked his teeth.

"Should we knock?" Ilsa without Peer asked.

"Considering it. On the other hand, I've always wanted to just kick a door in and make a dramatic entrance. Some of the best scenes in the Epic involve kicking doors in, and it's great fun to pantomime the action."

"That door might be more solid than you think," Fix pointed out.

"Yeah," Indrajit agreed. "Also, it feels as if we're not in quite the right dramatic moment. I mean, we've been pursued, it's been an exhilarating and dangerous evening, but we're not being chased *at this second.* Also, we're not trying to catch Holy-Pot red-handed. So..."

He knocked.

No answer.

"Maybe you'll get to knock the door down after all," Ilsa said.

"Diaphernes!" Fix bellowed. "Holy-Pot Diaphernes!"

Indrajit looked up and down the alley nervously. "There *are* still two different jobber companies trying to find us right now."

"Holy-Pot!" Fix bellowed again and hammered on the door with the bronze pommel of one of his knives.

Indrajit began looking for ways to escape, if the bravos suddenly arrived. The route through the blacksmith's shop looked promising. Also, the building opposite the alley from Holy-Pot had a low enough roof that he thought he could pull himself onto it in a pinch, though that would probably mean abandoning Ilsa.

"Holy-Pot Diaphernes!"

The door opened. Diaphernes trembled in the doorway, a mere sack pulled over his second face, a sheet wrapped around his waist and held against his hip to keep it in place.

"Spilkar's darts!" the risk-merchant hissed, and his eyes grew wide. "What are you doing in my place of pusiness?"

"Spilkar's darts, indeed," Indrajit said. "It is to avoid Spilkar's darts that we've come." He pushed Ilsa without Peer forward, and she dropped her hood.

Holy-Pot's visible jaw went slack.

"We should probably collect more of this flower, if we're going to continue working with Ilsa," Fix said.

"It isn't hard to come by," Ilsa told him. "It's a weed that grows wild in Ildarion. With my people dead, no one else has any use for it."

"We have a use for it," Indrajit said. "Here, let's experiment."

He tore his own sprig into two pieces, making sure that each half had both some yellow flower and some green leaf in it, and pressed one of them against Holy-Pot's jaw. Two breaths later, the risk-merchant's eyes cleared, and a wave of astonishment crossed his face. "What is that?"

"By *that*, do you mean Ilsa's magical power of fascination, or the herb that prevents it?" Indrajit grinned.

Holy-Pot raised his visible eyebrows. "*You* are Ilsa without Peer?" He frowned as if in furious thought, then opened the door wide. "Come in, and quickly."

They filed inside. Holy-Pot took Indrajit's half-sprig and pinned it inside the sack over his second face, and Fix locked the door behind them. Holy-Pot sat at his desk; as Fix had predicted, he had correspondence in front of him. Indrajit didn't write, but he recognized the mechanical device with two pens and two inkpots, whereby Holy-Pot could write a letter on loose paper, and the machine simultaneously wrote out the same letter on a page in a copybook.

"Something has gone terribly wrong," Holy-Pot said.

"What do you know about it?" Fix pressed him.

Holy-Pot spread his hands. "I only know that you are here. If things had gone well, you would have shown up six days from now, having completed an uneventful contract, and I'd have paid you the rest of your wages. Instead, you are here, with the opera singer. Something went wrong." His eyes narrowed, and he looked at Ilsa. "Did someone make an attempt on your life?"

She nodded.

Holy-Pot leaned back in his chair and exhaled. "Do we know who?"

"An assassin," Indrajit said. "That's what we know. And Mote Gannon's Handlers, at least, seem to believe that I'm in on the plot."

And something else that niggled at the back of his conscious mind, but didn't quite come forth.

"We want to know more about the contracts," Fix said.

Holy-Pot started, as if bitten. "I don't share my contracts. Not with anyone, even employees. Or *hirelings*, as the case may pe." He glared at Fix. "Like I don't share my client lists."

"We can't protect Ilsa," Indrajit said, "if we don't know who we're protecting her *from*."

"What do you mean?" Holy-Pot looked shocked.

"Who would want to kill her?" Indrajit asked. "Other than whoever sold the risk?"

Holy-Pot laughed. "No, no. You're confused. It's your poetry, Twang, it's gone to your head. The risk-assured party on the underlying contract would pe *harmed* py Ilsa's death, and therefore they sold the risk to protect themselves. Propaply because so much depended on her."

"What do you mean, so much depended on her?"

"Well, the Palace of Shadow and Joy has peen struggling. It hasn't had a hit in years, other than the shows starring Ilsa." Holy-Pot Diaphernes smiled at the singer. "Maype they signed the underlying contract, pecause they're worried about the possipility she might simply get sick or have an accident."

"I don't see how that makes any sense at all for a contract that lasts only seven days," Fix said.

Holy-Pot shrugged. "Maype the Palace wished to protect certain performances."

"What do you mean, *maybe*?" Indrajit asked. "Do you mean that you don't know who signed the contract?"

"Or is this some way to speak hypothetically," Fix asked, "without committing to who sold the risk?"

"I know who signed the contract. I read the underlying risk-selling contract very carefully, and I had a copy made. Look, I can't just send you to the merchant who pought the original risk," Holy-Pot said.

"Why not?" Indrajit smiled. "We're friendly. Look how friendly we are."

Fix put away his knife.

Holy-Pot leaned forward. "People come to me pecause they trust me. If they thought that at the first sign of things going funny, I might send thugs after them, I'd lose customers."

"Thugs?" Indrajit protested.

"The *first* sign?" Fix objected. "Since we last saw you, we've been in two pitched battles, spent the night huddled on a rooftop, and then run nearly a complete circuit around Kish, carrying a sedan."

"Which was very light," Indrajit added, "because the occupant inside is such a delicate flower."

Ilsa without Peer snorted.

Holy-Pot shook his head.

"Look," Indrajit said. "We're not thugs. And don't you . . . I don't know, have an obligation to notify the risk-assured? Or the other risk-merchant—isn't there another risk-merchant involved? Don't you have to tell that person what happened?"

Holy-Pot leaned back. "I don't *have* to. I don't have to do anything, unless I want to make a claim, and I can't make a claim unless the risk-assured makes a claim under the underlying contract. Which he would make to the original risk-merchant, and yes, there is another risk-merchant involved."

"Okay," Indrajit pressed. "You don't have to, but you could, right? As a courtesy, you could let the risk-merchant and the risk-assured know about the night's developments."

"I could," Holy-Pot conceded.

"In fact," Indrajit continued, "maybe, if you did that, your reputation as someone who keeps his business partners fully informed would help you attract future customers, right? And the fastest way to inform those people would be to send a messenger. Right?"

Holy-Pot nodded to both propositions.

Indrajit spread his arms. "There it is. You send us as messengers."

Holy-Pot snorted. "So that you, as messengers and not ruffians, can peat him up?"

"Hey," Indrajit protested.

"Say the risk-assured isn't to blame," Fix said. "If that person tells us why they were particularly concerned about the next week, couldn't that give us useful information, information that would help us protect Ilsa over the next week? I assume your risk-repurchase obligation hasn't ended, just because one attempt has been made, right? You're still on the hook, your money's at risk? And in fact, if you try to wiggle out now, after Ilsa has been attacked, won't that be bad business practices on your part? Won't that look like a merchant who wants to renege on his obligations?"

Holy-Pot sighed. He looked up at Ilsa and nodded. "The man who signed the risk-contract was a high-placed servant of Orem Thrush."

"When you say *high-placed*," Indrajit began.

"His majordomo," Diaphernes said. "The man who runs his household and manages most of his domestic affairs."

"Orders his wine," Indrajit said. "Deals with his tailor. Hires and fires maids and footmen. Has the coachman whipped when he gets the coach painted the wrong color."

"Yes," Holy-Pot agreed. "I suppose."

"Sells risk for the Lord Chamberlain?" Indrajit asked.

Holy-Pot shrugged. "If you're asking whether Orem Thrush is the real peneficiary of this risk-contract, I can only say that it seems likely."

Fix looked at Indrajit. "Are you sure you want to go ask?"

Indrajit hesitated, looking at Ilsa. She seemed nervous. "Well, I am definitely uncomfortable," he said.

"*Orem Thrush is a cruel man.*" Ilsa's singing was soft, her voice like the bleating of a frightened lamb.

"But if it wasn't Thrush who tried to kill you," Indrajit said, "there's no one better positioned to keep you safe."

"That's true." Holy-Pot looked pleased with this line of reasoning.

"What's the majordomo's name?" Indrajit asked.

"Thinkum Tosh," Ilsa said. "He's a Zalapting. Maybe you can talk to him and avoid seeing the Lord Chamberlain at all."

"That sounds like a good objective," Fix agreed.

"Zalapting," Indrajit murmured. "Those guys don't usually rise above menials, do they? I thought they tended to have limited brainpower."

"The smart ones can pe as intelligent as you or I,"

Holy-Pot said. "Or anyway, they're as smart as *you*. And their opsessive attention to detail makes them good managers. Some of the pest clerks here in the Paper Sook are Zalaptings."

Indrajit nodded. To Ilsa he asked, "Does Tosh live in the Lord Chamberlain's palace, then, do you know?"

"His room is directly below the Lord Chamberlain's," Ilsa said.

"Is it a nest?" Indrajit frowned. "According to the Epic, Zalaptings are stupid and live in nests."

"It's a *room*," Ilsa said.

"If we go try to talk to the Zalapting," Indrajit said, "take him a message, see if he knows anything, definitely not beat him up, what about Ilsa? Is there a place here she can stay?"

"She'll stay with me," Holy-Pot said. "I'll get more joppers for the door."

"Maybe shut down business for the day?" Fix suggested. "Give us a chance to see if we can find anything else out?"

Holy-Pot nodded, but didn't promise anything.

Fix sighed. "Back to the Crown it is."

✦ ✦ ✦

Indrajit and Fix bought a couple of bright green cloaks and threw them on, hoods up to cover their faces. With only the brown skin of their arms and legs showing, they looked like fifty thousand other people in Kish, at least.

They hiked up the Crooked Mile. Fix walked with his free hand resting on the hilt of his falchion. Indrajit tried to figure out what he was forgetting, what little detail was right on the edge of his mind and never quite materialized. The sight of crested Kishi Fowl, pecking at dropped grains of maize between the cobblestones, made his stomach rumble.

"What did you mean, the *last* Recital Thane?" Fix asked.

"Hmm? Oh, just that there isn't one appointed to follow me. Yet."

"But there will be." Fix stopped, again examining a piece of paper nailed to a wall.

"Exactly. Collecting more writing material? Are you going to make your own fascicles?"

"Yes, in fact, I *do* make my own fascicles. It's a poor man's solution, and it works. Making ink is much harder, so I buy that. But this notice isn't outdated yet, and I'm a good citizen, so I'll leave it here."

"What does it say?" Indrajit squinted at the letters, as if they would thereby become intelligible. He recognized the seal of the Auction House.

"There's an Auction in two days. Jobber companies with capacity over the next season are invited to register with the Auction House. How do you propose to get information out of this Thinkum Tosh?"

Indrajit took a moment to answer. He was breathing hard, from a combination of sleeplessness and the exertion of hiking up the Crooked Mile. Hunger gnawed at his belly. If he couldn't eat soon, he at least wanted another mouthful of horngrass. They were approaching the gate into the Crown, and he looked forward to being able to stop walking.

"I say we tell him just what we said to Holy-Pot. That we're messengers from the risk-merchant Diaphernes, messengers only, and that we've been sent to tell him there was an attempt to take Ilsa's life last night. Assuming he doesn't already know."

"The whole thing was pretty public," Fix agreed.

And then Indrajit realized what had been nagging him all night. "The Luzzazza," he said.

"Which one. At the gate?"

There were indeed again Luzzazza at the gate, along with Zalaptings, all in the livery of House Miltric. Indrajit and Fix nodded, looked harmless and uninteresting, and were waved through.

"No. On the stage last night."

"The one who attacked you with invisible arms."

"Yeah. Good trick, that. But also, he called me by name."

Fix considered this intelligence. "Are you asking whether mind reading is also a secret power of the Luzzazza mystics?"

"Yeah, I guess so."

"I have no idea."

"That is *not* reassuring."

"What's the reassuring answer?" Fix asked. "That they *can* read your mind, or that they *can't*?"

They had arrived at the Lord Chamberlain's palace. The building was the palace in the same sense in which the Palace of Shadow and Joy was a palace, or in which many of the wealthy of Kish and its seven great families were said to have palaces; a *palace* within the city walls was a rectangular building, three stories tall or more, without windows on the ground floor. A palace generally occupied an entire city block by itself, with streets or at least alleys on all four sides.

The Lord Chamberlain's palace was four stories tall and had two doors. At two of its corners rose tall towers, ringed with balconies that resembled the knees of giant insects. The front entrance was a double door recessed into the wall, with a portico in front. Men in livery stood on the portico, and the horned skull banner of House Thrush flew above.

Indrajit kept walking.

On the lane behind the palace, there was a plain door, with no recess, portico, or marker of any kind, and a peephole shut with a sliding iron panel.

"We're going to pose as tradesmen?" Fix asked.

"We *are* tradesmen," Indrajit said. "Here with a message for a servant. This is the right door for us."

He knocked. The iron panel slid sideways, revealing four eyes set in a horizontal line into a single pale face.

"We're here with a message for Thinkum Tosh," Indrajit said.

"Written?" the person to whom the eyes belonged asked.

Indrajit shook his head. "Verbal. We need to give it to him in person, please."

The panel shut.

Moments later, the door opened. Four Zalaptings armed with swords filed out and arrayed themselves in a loose circle around Indrajit and Fix.

Standing in the doorway was a pale-skinned man with no nose or teeth, and four eyes set close in a row. "You'd better come inside," Four Eyes said.

"Is one of you the majordomo?" Fix asked the Zalaptings.

They chittered to each other.

"No offense," Indrajit said. "We just can't tell you apart."

"Thinkum Tosh is dead," Four Eyes said. "And the Lord Chamberlain would like to speak to you."

Chapter Ten

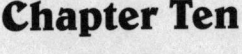

WITH HIS EXCELLENT PERIPHERAL VISION, INDRAJIT saw more Zalaptings appear, blocking off both ends of the street.

"You're a pretty impressive fighter," he murmured to Fix, hoping Four Eyes and the Zalaptings couldn't hear him. If they were really going to set up a jobber company, they should have a secret language. Maybe he could teach Fix some phrases in Blaatshi.

"Not *that* good." Fix had seen the new Zalaptings, too.

"It's just that I think that if we're going to fight, now is the time to do it. Once we go in there, we can only be outnumbered more, in terrain we don't know. It could be complicated. It could be a literal labyrinth."

"True," Fix whispered back. "But we came here to talk."

The Zalaptings muttered to each other, gripping spears and scimitars with looks of discomfort on their faces.

"I imagined speaking with Thinkum Tosh. But he's dead, and Orem Thrush thinks we did it."

"That's not what the man said. He said Thrush wants to talk with us. And besides, we're innocent."

"Of *this*," Indrajit protested.

The Zalaptings all took a step close. All four of the pale-skinned man's eyes narrowed.

"And we have alibis," Fix pointed out. "And at least one eyewitness who can attest to where we were for the last sixteen hours or so."

"An eyewitness we don't want to produce, until we're sure the Lord Chamberlain didn't try to kill her, or until we really, really have to."

Fix nodded. "Yes, but . . . you're pretty good at talking, aren't you?"

Indrajit took a deep breath. "Okay," he said, at a more normal volume. "Let's go meet the Lord Chamberlain."

"You will leave your weapons with me, of course," Four Eyes said.

Indrajit raised his eyebrows at Fix, who nodded. They handed over their weapons, and then Zalaptings with spears herded them into the building.

Indrajit had seen wealth before, but never in its own home. Every wall on the inside of Orem Thrush's city palace was a bright mural commemorating some event in the history of House Thrush. There was the first Orem Thrush, the original Lord Chamberlain, taking up the scepter from the emperor's dying hand and then presenting it to the assembled imperial servants who would become the first Lords of Kish, post-Empire. There was the spurned Bonean princess, her father endlessly following the ceremonial path of the moon in his monumental palace, and the marriage with the Xiba'albi princess that violated agreements on all sides, leading to the War of the Night Sky and the Sinking; in that series of murals, an Imperial chamberlain stood in each scene, prominent among other onlookers and participants by being smaller than the emperor but larger than all the rest, and wearing somewhere on his clothing the skull and horns device of the future house. Later, a Lord Chamberlain struggled to exterminate, and then finally came to terms with, the House of Knives; another fought off barbarians during the Winter of Blades; and a third confronted the Mad Duke. Stylized Lords Chamberlain who seemed to represent all the holders of the office simultaneously appeared in ceremonial scenes, leading the Dawn Gate Procession or bidding in the Auction.

Some of the furniture was of polished yetz-wood, which shone a dark red and which could be cured to be so hard and so flexible, swords could be made of it. Other pieces were made of green- and red-swirled stone, or simply of silver and gold. A servant stood at every door, opening it as Four Eyes and his captives approached, and shutting it after; double doors were opened by pairs of waiting servants. The servants wore matching livery, kilts and tunics and sandals, and on their tunics, front and back, was embroidered the horned skull.

Scents—citrus and sandalwood and tree resin—wafted through the palace on air that circulated through unseen vents. Carafes of wine stood ready on every table they passed, and the cold marble of the floors was frequently covered by thick red carpets.

Fix whistled low. "This is what comes of being the shrewdest Lord at the Auction."

"And this is what he *permits* us to see," Indrajit

whispered back. "If this is the wealth that lies around in the open, what untold treasures must he have secreted away in his vaults?"

"Unless he doesn't," Fix said. "Unless perhaps this is everything, and he puts it on display to make us think he has even more at his disposal than he does."

"That's insane."

"Is it? Power is determined by how other people react to you. At least, political power is. A palace like this exists to communicate wealth and influence, in order to create power. If you were Orem Thrush, wouldn't you want to communicate more wealth than you actually have? You attract talent, you win loyalty, you frighten off competition."

"Everyone knows Orem Thrush is the richest of the seven Lords of Kish."

"Yes, everyone *knows* it."

Four Eyes turned and frowned at the two jobbers.

"You know," Indrajit said to Fix, "you really ought to learn to speak some Blaatshi, if we're going to spend much time together."

"You're probably right. Do you know a good textbook, a grammar? Something with a nice chrestomathy?"

"*Chrestomathy?*" Indrajit laughed out loud. "Frozen hells, I think I've finally heard you say a word that is more mockable than *fascicle.*"

"I don't think *mockable* is a word."

"Hmm, let's see. You are mockable. The word *fascicle* is more mockable. The word *chrestomathy* is most mockable of all. Yes, *mockable* is definitely a word."

"*Chrestomathy* just means a collection of texts for learning a foreign language. You know, for reading practice."

"Texts? The only text there is in Blaatshi, at least the only one worth learning, is the Epic. Which means that *I* am your chrestomathy, you fool!"

Fix frowned. "I'd prefer a written version."

Indrajit laughed, entering the next room. He laughed so hard, he barely noticed the room's only occupant, a bland-faced man standing against one wall with his hands behind his back. The man wore a simple red tunic and red breeks, with a knife on his belt so small, it might be for cutting fruit. Indrajit was laughing when someone struck him in the head from behind and knocked him to the floor.

Fix hit the stone beside him. Indrajit put his hands behind his neck to try to soften any additional blows, but none came. His vision swam briefly, and when it cleared, Four Eyes had disappeared. Six Zalaptings still stood surrounding the two of them; their spears were gone, and in their hands they held cudgels.

The plain-faced man looked subtly different than he had moments earlier. Indrajit tried to figure out exactly what had changed; he still wore the same simple, severe clothing, with the tiny knife his only visible weapon. He still had the same bland, mild expression on his face.

Had he changed color? Just a little?

"We came bringing a message from Holy-Pot Diaphernes," Fix said.

Oh, right. "Yes, we just came to talk. To notify your majordomo. Thinko. Tosho." Indrajit found he couldn't quite remember the name, probably because of the trauma of being knocked down.

"Thinkum Tosh," the man said. "Who is Holy-Pot Diaphernes?"

"He's a respected merchant in the Paper Sook," Indrajit explained. "Risk-selling. And also risk-reselling." He still wasn't entirely clear on the difference.

"Purchasing," Fix murmured.

The stranger frowned, slightly.

"Are you...the Lord Chamberlain?" Indrajit asked.

"You're surprised I don't have a face like a skull, and horns?" The man smiled.

"Well, I didn't want to overliteralize your family heraldry," Indrajit said, "but there are a thousand races of man. It seemed a possibility."

"Yes, I'm Orem Thrush. The seventh of that name. This is my house. Thinkum Tosh was my servant. And in public, and for special occasions, I do indeed wear the mask of the horned skull."

Orem Thrush's skin had definitely grown slightly darker. Was he light-sensitive?

Information. They had come seeking information, and not about the peculiarities of Orem Thrush's complexion, or on what occasions he might wear a skull and horns mask. "Does that mean that he... that you..." Indrajit shook his head and tried to organize his thoughts. "Thinkum Tosh sold the risk on the life of the opera singer, Ilsa without Peer. We came to give Tosh a message from Holy-Pot, who is the risk-repurchaser. Or reseller, maybe. I can't keep the terms straight." Indrajit sighed. "But maybe, since Tosh was your servant...was the policy actually for you? Should we talk to you?"

"Yes," Thrush said. "You should give me your message. But not until after I've had you beaten."

A rain of cudgels fell on Indrajit and Fix.

Indrajit tried to stand, got knocked down, tried to

stand again, and was beaten to the floor. Through the blinding flashes of light that came with each blow, he saw that Fix did only slightly better: he managed to yank the club from the hands of one Zalapting before three others pounded him down and disarmed him.

The blows ceased and the Zalaptings stepped back.

"Ouch," Indrajit said.

"That was for attacking my man." The Lord Chamberlain's voice held not a hint of emotion.

He looked different still. His skin was darker, and had taken on the underlying green of a Blaatshi complexion. His stature and body were unchanged, but in color and in the shape of his head, the Lord Chamberlain was transforming before their eyes.

"Wopal? He was tailing me. I didn't know he was your man."

"The first time, that was true." Orem Thrush nodded. "But the second time, you knew full well who he was."

"An eye for an eye," Fix muttered. His jaw didn't seem to want to move. "Isn't that what they say? Shouldn't you just punch Indrajit in the face? An eye for an eye?"

"*An eye for an eye* is a fine maxim," Orem Thrush said. "It promotes fairness. If you cause an injury, you will receive an equivalent injury. That's fair."

"So who did I beat the frozen hells out of?" A tooth in Indrajit's mouth wiggled. "Some other hireling of yours?"

"I am not interested in fairness," Orem Thrush said. "I want peace. I want docility. I want *cooperation*. So I require you to understand, right now and forever, that I do not practice an eye for an eye. I have been merciful to you this time. If you punch my servant in the face again, know this: I will have you killed."

Indrajit coughed, and the loose tooth flew from his mouth and clattered across the floor.

"We understand," Fix said.

Indrajit nodded.

"Good." The Lord Chamberlain motioned with one hand and the Zalaptings stepped back. They still held their cudgels ready. "You can rise, if you like. Or lie on the floor, if it hurts less."

Gingerly, wincing, they stood.

Orem Thrush nodded his approval. "Now tell me, what is the message that you were prepared to give Thinkum Tosh, from the risk-merchant Holy-Pot Diaphernes?"

"Risk repurchaser, in this case," Fix said.

"True," Indrajit said, "I think. If somewhat pedantic."

"I can have you beaten again." The Lord Chamberlain did not look amused. Also, his eyes were slowly drifting apart in his face.

"Ilsa without Peer was attacked at the Palace of Shadow and Joy last night," Indrajit said.

Orem Thrush's nostrils flared. "The whole city knows that. I know myself, since I was in the audience."

Fix was staring at the Lord Chamberlain.

"She lived," Indrajit added. "I . . . *we*, rather . . . saved her. We were hired by Holy-Pot Diaphernes as a backup protection, in case any attempt to hurt her got past the jobbers the risk-merchant hired."

"The Handlers," the Lord Chamberlain said. "So you're not just messengers."

Oops.

"You've given nothing away I didn't already know," Thrush said. "I saw you on stage last night. I especially enjoyed your attack with the balsa-wood spear."

"Yeah. So, I guess Holy-Pot wants her protected because otherwise he has to pay out...I think."

"I understand how risk reselling works," Thrush said. Fix nodded.

Indrajit silently cursed them both. "She's alive and in a safe place. Our message is to tell you that. But also, since Holy-Pot is on the hook for another six days, he wants to know what made you sell the risk in the first place. So we know what to protect her against. What threats did you see that made you enter into that agreement?"

"I understand. Only I can't help you with that, because I didn't sell the risk." The Lord Chamberlain raised one eyebrow.

"But..." Indrajit felt stupid.

"I lied earlier," Thrush said. "It will not be the last time I lie to you. I do not suggest that you consider lying to me."

"Do you have any idea why someone would want to kill her?" Indrajit asked.

The Lord Chamberlain laughed out loud. "Oh, any one of the six families."

Indrajit frowned. "Because of the money she made you?"

A brief flash of a reaction crossed the Lord Chamberlain's face, and then the steel visor of his expressionless demeanor dropped down again. "What do you mean?"

"Singing? At the opera?" Fix said.

Orem Thrush shrugged. "Yes. And also, the prestige. She was indeed without peer. For me to lose her would be...a blow. My rivals are always acting against me, of course. It is likely they are acting against me now."

Indrajit struggled to think through the moving

parts, many of which were new to him. It was certainly possible that the risk-contract was not what had motivated the attack, but was only coincidental.

"If you didn't order him to do it, why would Thinkum Tosh sell the risk on the singer?" Fix looked puzzled. "Did he have some interest in her? I mean, a financial interest?"

The Lord Chamberlain shrugged. "Not that I'm aware. Perhaps"—he looked reflective—"perhaps he had information that an attempt was to be made on her life. He told me nothing of it, but then he wouldn't have told me, if he hoped to profit."

"Is it possible that Thinkum Tosh was working for one of the other families?" Fix asked. "That you had a traitor in your house?"

Orem Thrush fixed them both with a stare that would have penetrated brick.

Indrajit raised his hands. "Our only interest is to protect Ilsa. That's how we get paid. We do not want to get into your affairs, unless doing so helps us understand how to protect her."

"It is possible," the Lord Chamberlain conceded. "If he was a traitor or a spy, I didn't know about it."

"Maybe he was spying for another house, and threatened to confess, and they killed him for it?" It was only a suggestion, but it wasn't the craziest idea Indrajit had ever had.

"Rank speculation." Orem Thrush frowned.

"Is there anything else you can tell us...or show us...that might help? Maybe, the manner of his death? Was he poisoned or garroted?"

Orem Thrush smiled. "Or killed in some other lurid fashion characteristic of one of my enemies, or of the House of Knives? Or was he killed by trained venomous snakes, such as Pelthite assassins are said to employ?"

Indrajit shrugged.

Orem Thrush shook his head. "The body is destroyed. Tosh's throat was cut with his own dagger. We found him yesterday morning on the floor of his room. There was no other sign of violence, and no sign of any forced entry."

"Are you having anyone look into the death?" Indrajit asked. Kish had no police force as such, but Thrush clearly had the wealth to hire jobbers to investigate a crime against him. A thought occurred to him. "Was that why Grit Wopal was tailing me yesterday?"

"I'll show you his room." The Lord Chamberlain stepped through an open doorway. Indrajit and Fix lurched to follow.

Orem Thrush hadn't answered his question. That seemed like an admission in the affirmative.

The room was ascetic and spare. A cot, a trunk, and a niche in the wall.

The Lord Chamberlain stood against the wall beside the niche. "This is one way I communicate with my majordomo." He pointed at a hole in the ceiling of the niche. "At night, I drop messages down this shaft to him. He rises—he *rose*—before me, and attended to those tasks first."

Orem Thrush's facial transformation seemed to have come to a rest, or at least to a pause. Indrajit shuddered, looking at the man. He was still recognizably Orem Thrush, the man they'd been speaking to all along. But he also looked like a native-born Blaatshi, wide-set eyes, mahogany-green skin, and all.

"The chest?" Fix pointed.

"Clothing. Feel free to look."

Indrajit rifled through the chest: tunics and kilts, nothing more.

"Where does that leave us?" Indrajit asked. For his part, he was left with more information, none of which he was certain he could trust, and more questions.

"You're not going to tell me where Ilsa is, are you?" The Lord Chamberlain said.

Taking a deep breath and preparing to be beaten again, Indrajit shook his head no.

"Then you should leave now," Orem Thrush said. "You will try to protect Ilsa in your fashion, and I will protect her in mine."

Chapter Eleven

"WE'RE BEING FOLLOWED, OF COURSE," FIX SAID.

Indrajit nodded. "We can't go straight back to Holy-Pot's. We need to lose our tail."

"Did you see how he looked at the end?" Fix asked. "He could have been your brother. What race of man is *that*?"

"It's not one I know an epithet for." Indrajit shook his head. Had Orem Thrush deliberately chosen to look like Indrajit? Could he have done the same thing quickly? Was it an instinctual transformation? Did the Lord Chamberlain experience a physical change, or was it pure illusion, magic?

And how many people knew about it?

Perhaps the Lord Chamberlain did, after all, wander the streets of Kish unseen.

Four Eyes had given them their weapons at the door and shown them out, with clouds gathering on the northern horizon. Now the Yifft, Grit Wopal, trailed brazenly a dozen steps behind them. Indrajit and Fix were both limping; Wopal whistled a cheerful tune that Indrajit thought he recognized, though the words eluded him. Something about the wedding of a fisherman and a seamstress.

"I hurt too much to outrun him," Fix said.

"Punching him in the face is no longer an attractive option," Indrajit added.

"We could hire horses," Fix suggested.

"I don't know how to ride."

Fix stared. "Really?"

"My people are fishers. On the other hand, I can handle a boat of just about any kind."

"Oh, good. In that case, let's jog down to the East Flats and rent a tidy little yacht. We can sail out to the Paper Sultanates, lose him in all those islands, and then sail back."

"You're bitter."

"I just got beaten to the floor, apparently because you punched Wopal."

Indrajit shrugged. "Thrush would have had us beaten in any case. That was about showing his power, not about punishing me. He as much as said so. He would have found another pretext."

Fix grumbled wordlessly.

"Still hurt," Indrajit added.

"Well, let's find a crowd of people where we can lose the bastard. What do you think, the Racetrack? A nice, crowded game of Street Rûphat?"

"The Caravanserai, I think. Or the Necropolis."

"They're both the wrong direction. But if you insist on one of those, the Caravanserai is closer."

"Good. It'll throw him off the track."

They descended through the Lee and out the South

Gate, into the Caravanserai. There were crowds here, scattered haphazardly across the flattened ground, clustering into evanescent markets for exotic goods or caravan supplies, knotting up to launch or receive actual caravans, and trembling to announcements of foreign doings and surprise shifts in prices.

There were also tents.

Indrajit stepped into a blacksmith's tent at one end, crossed it to the protest of two bleary-eyed apprentices, and exited the back, dragging Fix in his wake. Accelerating as much as he could with his battered legs, he ducked into and out of, in quick succession, a leatherworker's tent, an armorer's, an oil merchant's, and a seller of long colored feathers pronounced enthusiastically to be from distant Fasha and Ngharâdu-Isst.

Stepping out of the feather merchant's shop, he grabbed Fix to be certain he didn't leave the other man behind and then turned ninety degrees to his left, plunging immediately into the tent of a seller of flavored ices. With snow brought down from Karth and Ukel, and flavor syrups in a dozen varieties, the rotund and pale green merchant was doing a brisk business.

"Free sample?" the merchant called out to the two jobbers.

"Only if it's large enough to cover my entire body!" Fix's retort triggered a laugh in response.

Indrajit turned his head slightly, his peripheral vision good enough to be certain that the tent flap behind them shut entirely before their Yifft tail appeared.

"Faster, now," he murmured to Fix.

Another ninety-degree turn sent them marching straight back toward the walls of Kish. Most likely, Grit Wopal would realize what they'd done and come after them. Hopefully, he wouldn't realize it in time to actually catch them, and they'd have lost him.

Also, hopefully, his third eye didn't give him any sort of ability to follow them, regardless. Indrajit imagined Wopal seeing through walls with the eye, or seeing visible spoor on the ground where they had passed, like a dog smelled scent, or seeing backward and forward in time to know where they were going.

But no, if the Yifft could do any of those things, they wouldn't have been able to shake him at the Fountain the night before. The Yifft saw other kinds of visions.

What had he said about Indrajit? A man who was failing at his quest, had lost his way? How could he possibly see anything of the kind?

Even if it *were* true?

"I think we lost him." Fix looked over his shoulder as the two jobbers reentered the Lee through the South Gate. "If you don't know how to ride, we could rent a sedan chair. Get off our feet, move a little faster."

"If it's all the same to you, I need to keep the money."

"It's *not* the same to me," Fix said. "But I'm pleased to see you learning a little financial discipline."

"It's not discipline," Indrajit said. "I'm starving. I almost stopped and ate those feathers, I'm so hungry."

They climbed the Crown and descended into the Spill, Indrajit muttering every prayer he knew to Spilkar, Lord of Contracts, begging for the power to protect Ilsa without Peer. For good measure, he asked Yispillin, seer of the gods, to blind the Yifft spy Grit Wopal, and anyone else looking for Indrajit and Fix, and to hide their passage from all hostile eyes.

Which was a lot to ask. Kish was full of hostile eyes.

Nothing stays secret in Kish, they said.

As they approached the Paper Sook, Fix jogged his elbow. "What's that?"

That was a column of smoke, rising from the vicinity of Holy-Pot Diaphernes's office, and a bustle of activity, including cries for water and yelps of panic.

"Holy-Pot works behind a blacksmith's shop," Indrajit said. "An accident?"

They slowed their pace and circled around the risk-merchant's office, squinting down the alley.

The smithy, and the risk-merchant's office with it, were gone. Fire had been only part of the cause of destruction; splintered timbers and furniture lying in the alley, smashed and upended, suggested that someone had deliberately destroyed the building. Jobbers in orange tunics hulked in the alley and stalked the Paper Sook, squinting in all directions.

"Any chance those fellows are carrying out the city's fire prevention contract?" Indrajit murmured.

"I don't see any buckets of sand or water pumps," Fix answered. "Do you?"

Rattled and nervous, the Paper Sook nevertheless continued its business. Indrajit and Fix filtered across the square of men shouting and waving papers, and stood behind the corner of a stationer's shop, looking back toward Holy-Pot's former premises.

"Coincidence?" Fix asked.

"Frozen hells, no. Who do you think did this?"

"The Lord Chamberlain. As soon as we left, he sent men down here to wreck the place."

"If we'd come straight here, maybe we could have warned Ilsa. Instead, we spent precious time trying to lose a tail."

Fix slammed a fist into the wall. "Wopal didn't care if we lost him or not. He wasn't really tailing us at all, he just wanted us to delay our return, so this could happen."

"Frozen hells."

Fix's nostrils flared. "I've been meaning to ask you about that."

"About what? About Wopal?"

"Your hells are always frozen. Why is that?"

Indrajit thought about it. "Well, a hell with fire might be okay, I guess. You could fry fish there. But a hell where all the water is frozen is a hell where you can only starve."

"Huh." Fix stared up the Paper Sook, squinting in thought. "So the hells in the Epic are all frozen."

"Yes. What about your hells? Are they fiery?"

"I don't have any hells. Don't have any gods, either. The Selfless of Salish-Bozar determined over a century ago that all detail about the afterlife is useless, so there are various adepts who have memorized reams of description of heavens and hells known to every race and cult. I could never bring myself to care much."

"Not useful enough?"

Fix shrugged. "I'll do what I need to do in this life. I know how to be a good man, and when I fall short, I can try to do better. I don't need someone to tell me that if I steal, I'll have my hands roasted, or if I sleep with my sister, I'll be forced to eat my own children for all eternity, or if I don't memorize enough lines of the Epic, I won't be able to catch fish. That's for children, or fools."

"Ouch, that's a little personal." The orange-tunicked jobbers were poking their heads into various stalls along the sook and asking questions. "I do like saying *frozen hells*, though."

"I'm not stopping you."

"Also, I'm hungry."

"We should have bought some of that flavored ice. I don't think the feathers would agree with your digestion."

Indrajit nodded at the jobbers in orange. "Those guys are looking for something. I bet it's Holy-Pot and Ilsa."

"That suggests that our employer and our charge were not captured in the attack that destroyed the building."

"Which in turn means we still have the opportunity to complete this contract and earn the second half of our wages." Indrajit nodded. "Which, at the risk of repeating myself, I could really use."

"That makes our course of action obvious."

Indrajit cocked his head to one side. "It does?"

"We go talk to the risk-merchant. The merchant who signed the underlying contract, the agreement whose risk Holy-Pot is only repurchasing."

"Because that person would be willing to help Holy-Pot, because they both have an interest in keeping Ilsa alive?"

"That's my thinking. And if not, then perhaps as colleagues, he'll have some idea where Holy-Pot might go to ground in an emergency. I mean, unless you know some secret address where Holy-Pot might be hiding."

Indrajit frowned. "No, I don't. But I don't know who the risk-merchant is, either. Holy-Pot wouldn't tell us that. Although I think the risk-merchant is a woman. Didn't Holy-Pot call her *she*?"

"Holy-Pot didn't identify the risk-merchant. But the contract was probably registered."

Indrajit already had a slippery grasp, at best, on this whole risk-selling concept. Risk reselling was foggier still. Now Fix was suggesting something that sounded like an additional layer of complication. "What are you talking about?"

"The risk-merchants of the Paper Sook are a kind of guild. What's the basic function of a guild?"

There were no guilds in the Epic. "Uh...to provide training for its members?"

"The basic function of a guild is to limit the number of people practicing a trade, so you can keep prices up. Keep out foreigners and new people, make any one who joins pay their dues."

Indrajit struggled. "Why...you have to have *some* people in the trade, don't you?"

"You have to have *some*. But too many people, and they compete, and bring down prices. So the guild limits the number of risk-merchants."

That made a kind of perverse sense. "So they must have a list of all the guild members."

"Yes, but that won't help us. How would we know who we're looking for? But even better than that list is the registry of risk-merchantry contracts. About twenty years ago, the Paper Sook pressed the great families really hard, and got a law passed that the only risk-merchanting contracts that are enforceable in the courts of Kish are those that are written down in the registry. And the rules of the Paper Sook provide that anyone who enters into a risk-merchanting contract that is not registered can no longer buy and sell in the sook."

Blurred and fog-shrouded though it was, a light began to appear at the end of Indrajit's mental tunnel. "So Holy-Pot's risk-reselling contract and the underlying contract should both be written in the registry."

Fix nodded. "Should be. Including the name of the risk-merchant who entered into the underlying contract."

"Where is the registry?"

Fix nodded, indicating a stall that the jobbers in orange tunics had already passed. Indrajit took the opportunity to scan the Paper Sook for any sign of Grit Wopal, and saw none.

"You really learned Holy-Pot's trade well," Indrajit said.

"I think he was unhappy about that," Fix said. "He had stopped giving me work for several weeks, before this job came up. But what I don't know is how to convince the Registry Clerk to show us the information."

"Oh, that's easy. That's just *talk!*" Indrajit waved a hand in a theatrical flourish. "Show me the clerk!"

The Registry Clerk of the Paper Sook was a woman with a head like an inverted cone, bright yellow skin, and hair that resembled ferns or the branches of an amalaka tree and rustled when she moved. She wore a dark fur wrapped around narrow shoulders and shivered, though the day had become warm. She stood at the back of a stall behind a broad counter on which sat three large codices; on shelves behind her stood more stacks of books.

"My name is Thinkum Tosh," Indrajit said, resisting the urge to wink at Fix.

"Yessss?" The yellow Registry Clerk turned out to have two forked tongues.

"I'm a servant of the Lord Chamberlain, Orem Thrush. He bids me thank you for your trouble." Indrajit put the last of his full coins, a recently minted Imperial with its milled edges whole and toothy, onto the table in front of the woman. It was a bribe if the clerk wanted to take it as one, and a tip otherwise.

The clerk tilted her head to one side to look out into the sook. Indrajit turned his head just slightly, enough to see that a man in an orange tunic was passing by. "Many of the Lord Chamberlain's sssservants are in the ssssook today."

Indrajit waved dismissively. "Jobbers. Muscle, for a simple task. I am here because I'm entrusted by my master with more serious, complicated transactions. Such as merchanting his risk."

The clerk eyed the coin but didn't touch it. "Tell me more."

"It's quite embarrassing, and I hope you can spare me another beating." A deep purple bruise was showing on Indrajit's forearm, and he pointed it out.

"I'll ssssee what I can do."

Indrajit nodded. "I was entrusted by the Lord Chamberlain to merchant some risk of his—oh, I hope I am using the terms correctly—and I did so. On the Lord Chamberlain's behalf, I entered into a contract that started yesterday. Only I've misplaced my copy of the contract, you see. And I'm not accustomed to the ways of the Paper Sook, and I can't seem to retrace my steps."

"You've forgotten who you ssssigned the deal with." The clerk's fronds trembled.

"Spilkar's fine print, that's exactly right." Indrajit wasn't totally sure what *fine print* was, but he thought the words fit. He jerked a thumb at Fix. "And this fellow, who has some knowledge of how the sook works, told me that you might be able to help me."

The clerk hesitated, eyeing the coin. "Asssuming it was a regisssstered contract of risssk-merchantry."

Indrajit shrugged. "Well, I didn't register it. But the merchant seemed reliable and honest, so I assume she did the things that are supposed to be done."

The clerk took one of the codices in her hands and began thumbing through its pages. "Would the contract have been in the Lord Chamberlain'sssss name, then?"

Indrajit resisted looking at Fix, and hoped his information and his guess were correct. "I signed it myself, so I assume the entry in your book should say my name."

"*Thinker*, did you say?"

"Thinkum Tosh." If the entry had any significant detail, such as, for instance, *Thinkum Tosh—Zalapting*, the deception might come to an immediate halt. But that was one purpose of the bribe, to ease the transaction over any such bumps, provided the jostling wasn't too large.

"Oh yes, here it is." The clerk swiveled the codex around and pointed it at Indrajit. "Name and address."

"Ah, yes. Could you, perhaps, write it down?"

"I'll take you there," Fix said.

Indrajit nodded. Without his noticing, the Imperial had disappeared.

Indrajit followed Fix out into the sook. Avoiding catching the gaze of any of the men in orange, they threaded their way through the shouters and the paper-wavers and then down a street that turned three times at right angles in quick succession, until

Indrajit thought it was tracking back parallel to the sook itself, in an uncobbled, muddy lane bordered with square brick buildings, shoulder to shoulder with only an occasional crack of an alley breaking the monotony, like so many dusty yellow crows waiting for something in the alley to die so they could feed on it.

"Seventeen." Fix pointed. "The risk-merchant is named Frodilo Choot."

"Do you know him?"

"Her. You were right, she's a woman. I recognize the name, but that's all."

They knocked on a heavy wooden door, and were quickly admitted. This shop resembled the Registry Clerk's stall more than Holy-Pot's place, with a front counter before which stood two stools. The doorman who had let them in was heavily muscled, covered with coruscating purple scales, and appeared to have no eyes whatsoever. After shutting the door, he shuffled into a corner.

A squared-off, broad-shouldered woman swathed in bands of densely tooled, green-dyed leather, stood behind the counter. The tooling looked astrological, and heavy on the moon signs—Bonean, maybe, and the woman's face, pleasant, slightly yellow, and devoid of any makeup, could be from Boné as well. As they entered, her tongue crept out between her lips and briefly probed the air, as if she were a reptile, sniffing with it. Behind her, strings of beads formed a curtain in a doorway leading into the back half of the building; on the counter in front of her were an ink pot, a pen, and a few sheets of paper, bound together.

"Look," Indrajit said. "It's a fascicle."

Fix chuckled, but Frodilo Choot only smiled.

Her smile was pleasant. Distracted. Unengaged. It didn't have the piercing quality that Holy-Pot's did, when he was negotiating a contract or haggling over a fee.

"Is she stoned?" Fix asked.

Choot smiled more broadly and tongued the air again.

"It's Ilsa," Indrajit said. "She's under Ilsa's spell. Ilsa!"

There was a moment's hesitation, and then Holy-Pot Diaphernes peered through the beads.

"Oh, thanks pe to Spilkar!"

Chapter Twelve

HOLY-POT EMERGED FROM THE BACK ROOM. BEHIND him, partially revealed as the strings of beads swung back and forth, stood Ilsa without Peer, last of her kind, bizarre of appearance but potent of sound.

And scent. Indrajit checked the sprig of Courting Flower at his throat and looked to see that Fix's was also in place.

"How are you not dead?" Holy-Pot's limbs trembled. He had replaced the morning's black sack with a proper veil and was now properly clothed in a kilt and tunic. "Those joppers."

Indrajit sighed. "Yeah, sorry."

"Probably in the pay of Orem Thrush," Fix said. "At least, that's what the people in the Paper Sook seemed to think."

"And we probably tipped Orem off. We went to talk to the Zalapting, Thinkum Tosh, and we got taken right into the presence of the Lord Chamberlain."

"Was he the one who had you beaten?" Ilsa croaked. "Or was that done by the jobbers in orange?"

Indrajit grinned in what he hoped was a reassuring way, remembering at the last second that he had lost a tooth today. "The meeting with the Lord Chamberlain was preceded by some unconventional preliminaries."

"He had us beaten," Fix explained.

"Is there any food?" Indrajit asked. "I'm starving."

"Frodilo?" Holy-Pot asked. "May we have pread?"

"Of course," Frodilo Choot murmured. She twisted slowly, then gestured indistinctly toward a space behind the shop.

Diaphernes disappeared into a back room and emerged with a loaf of bread and a chunk of cheese. Fix quickly cut both in half with one of his knives, and he and Indrajit wolfed the food down.

"Orem Thrush had you peaten," Holy-Pot said. "Put not killed."

"I need to leave town," Ilsa croaked.

"All things considered, that sounds like a terrific idea," Indrajit said.

"May I suggest a boat?" Fix added. "We're close to the docks; we can easily buy out some fisherman's rig, and Indrajit actually knows how boats work. Unlike horses."

"*Agreed.*" Ilsa sang, and the contrast with her speaking voice sent tremors up and down Indrajit's spine. "*But I need to get something from the palace first.*"

"Uh." Indrajit ground his eyes with the heels of his hands, feeling exhausted. "I hope you don't mean the Lord Chamberlain's palace."

"*The Palace of Shadow and Joy.*"

"Oh, good. That suggestion is only *moderately* insane, as opposed to suicidal."

Ilsa shot Indrajit a look so poignant, he lowered his head in shame.

"Really, Ilsa," Holy-Pot said, "is there anything you can't do without? I mean, you have money, and you know I'll pay to...keep you alive, too. Let's get you passage to Pelth or Poné and just replace whatever you leave pehind when you get there."

"There are things in the Palace of Shadow and Joy that I cannot replace," Ilsa sang. *"Not in Pelth, not in Boné, not anywhere in the whole wide world."* She looked into Holy-Pot's eyes and her nictitating membranes fluttered.

Holy-Pot met her gaze briefly, then looked away. "Yes," he agreed. "We need to take her to the Palace of Shadow and Joy."

Indrajit checked the risk-merchant's veil to be certain there was still a sprig of the Courting Flower pinned to it. There was. So Holy-Pot's mind wasn't being bent by Ilsa's weird power, he was just...persuaded.

By what?

Some confidence existed between Ilsa and Holy-Pot. What had they talked about, while Indrajit and Fix had visited the Lord Chamberlain?

"As dangerous as it is for me and Indrajit out there," Fix said, "it's more dangerous for you. Indrajit's already proven he can talk his way into the opera house without trouble. Why don't you tell us what it is you need, and we'll go collect it?"

Ilsa shook her head vehemently, a motion which surprised Indrajit, since he hadn't realized she had a neck. Holy-Pot, more hesitantly, also shook his head.

"Well, Diaphernes," Indrajit said, "you at least should stay here. No sense attracting any more attention than we need to."

Holy-Pot again shook his head.

"How did you get out of your shop, anyway?" Fix asked. "It looked completely demolished."

"It did?" Holy-Pot looked surprised at the news, but not outraged. "Well, I had a pack way."

"A secret door through the blacksmith's?" Fix looked surprised.

"A tunnel." Holy-Pot sniffed with both noses, his veil lifting enough to reveal a receding chin on the second face before it fluttered back into place. "If you must know. Not that it's any of your pusiness."

"You don't seem as put out as I thought you'd be," Indrajit said, studying his two-faced employer.

"Apout the place of pusiness?" Holy-Pot shrugged. "That's not really where my value is stored. I can rent a new office in five minutes' time."

"Where is your value stored, then?" Indrajit immediately regretted asking the question, knowing he would either get rebuffed, demonstrating again his insignificance in Holy-Pot's eyes, or he'd get a baffling mini-lecture on risk-merchantry, which would make Indrajit feel stupid.

In the event, it was the latter.

"In my receivaples, mostly, also represented py the large surplus I've accrued on my palance sheet." Holy-Pot looked down his nose at Indrajit and snorted. "Premiums receivaple and claims receivaple under risk-merchanting arrangements in which I hold the underlying contract."

"Okay," Indrajit said.

"And bank deposits," Fix added.

"Yes, some cash, of course," Holy-Pot Diaphernes agreed. "Mind you, cash in the form of cash generates a very low return, put of course I have to maintain enough liquidity at all times to meet my payaples when they are due."

"Naturally," Fix said.

"Forget I asked," Indrajit said.

"I didn't even lose my petty cash." Holy-Pot reached inside his kilt and produced a sack, shaking it to evoke the jingle of coins. "I grapped that on the way out. And I have a spare copy of all my records at an off-site location, so all I lost was the correspondence from this morning. And it's pretty likely that even that is just lying on the ground in the wreckage."

All Indrajit's bruises stung him at the same moment. "Well, I'm glad to see you're getting off so lightly."

"In fact . . ." Holy-Pot laughed, his voice suddenly light. "I had sold the risk on my own office space, too. So I'll collect on that and come out ahead."

Indrajit took a deliberate step backward, so as not to be tempted to punch Holy-Pot in both his faces.

"Tell me about these tunnels," Fix said. "Can we take them to the Palace of Shadow and Joy?"

Holy-Pot took a sudden step back and straightened his spine. "Oh, that would pe . . . a pad idea. Propaply not possible. Put certainly very dangerous."

"Why?" Fix furrowed his brow. "How far down do your tunnels go? Are we talking about some cellars and maybe sewers of Imperial Kish, or did you escape your shop by crawling all the way down to the Druvash levels?"

"Well . . . I don't know for sure. Put Kish is very, very ancient. And the Paper Sook is puilt on top of old levels of occupation, so peneath the sook there are tunnels. And champers, and caverns. Several levels of them. Maype many levels."

"Yes," Fix said. "That's true of the whole city. Kish is the world's first city."

Indrajit snorted. "Please. The Epic records the building of Kish, long after mankind had separated into the thousand races. Kish is old, but there were cities before her. Many cities, some of which lasted a thousand years."

"Fine." Holy-Pot shrugged. "Put the registered merchants of the Paper Sook—"

"The guild," Indrajit said, looking at Fix.

"The guild, if you will," Holy-Pot agreed, "years ago walled off a section of those tunnels peneath the Paper Sook and the surrounding streets. We used to deal with strange disappearances at night, and unnatural noises peneath the floors, and queer peasts tunneling into our cellars. So we walled off the area peneath the Paper Sook as a protective puffer against the larger, wilder lapyrinth peneath the city. And it turned out we could also use that space for . . . discreet passage from shop to shop, when necessary."

"Someone patrols this buffer?" Fix asked.

Holy-Pot shrugged. "From time to time. Not constantly."

"So we could at least get to the edge of the Paper Sook unseen." Fix nodded his approval.

"But are there exits?" Indrajit asked. "Underground, I mean. Can you leave the sook's cellar and get into the larger catacombs beneath the city?"

"There are gates," Holy-Pot admitted. "They are locked."

"Do you have keys?" Indrajit asked.

"The locks are arcane," the risk-merchant said.

"Magic," Fix murmured.

"Yes, I know what *arcane* means." Indrajit growled. "But that doesn't answer the question. Do you have the passwords, or the secret gestures, or whatever we'd need, to get past the gates? If we can get from the Paper Sook to the Palace of Shadow and Joy entirely underground and therefore unseen, I'd say that was ideal."

"You're insane," Holy-Pot said.

"The risk-merchant is right," Fix added. "Look, say we walked to the northernmost point of the catacombs beneath the Paper Sook and exited there. We'd have, what, a mile as the crow flies to go? Or more? Through unmapped caverns, with who knows what strange races of men or beasts waiting in ambush to eat us?"

"I'm not sure I believe in vast hordes of unknown monsters living beneath Kish." Indrajit shrugged. "I mean, *some* monsters. But, you know, even monsters have to eat. So if there's some beast that eats men, there can't be all that many of them, or we'd know about it. But you're probably right. We'd get lost. Let's call the underground route our backup plan, then."

"It can only pe our *desperation* plan," Holy-Pot grunted.

"So we take the sook's tunnels as far as we can, then we get out and walk." Fix nodded. "I wish we had a little more disguise than that, but with luck, we'll be fine."

Indrajit grinned. "I know where we can get a bit of disguise."

Fix waited for more explanation.

"How many of those orange-tunicked jobbers did you see?" Indrajit asked him.

"A dozen, maybe more."

"A big jobber company, right? And were they all Zalaptings, or Ildarian?"

"It was a mixed company." Suddenly Fix smiled. "You know, if you're a jobber in an orange tunic, looking for a runaway risk-merchant, the one person you don't look twice at—"

"—is another jobber in an orange tunic."

"Stay here," Fix said to Holy-Pot Diaphernes.

Frodilo Choot continued to smile, as if sunk deep into a yip-induced trance.

Indrajit and Fix emerged into the warren around the Paper Sook, and in short order found two of the jobbers in orange. They were swarthy Yuchak tribesmen, an unusual race to see working jobs in Kish, and they seemed to be searching the sook by sense of smell, stooped and snuffling at the ground from time to time.

Indrajit smiled at the Yuchak and passed them, taking a good hard look at the glyph on their tunics. Then it was a short walk to a cloth-merchant Indrajit knew on the Crooked Mile, where a few small coins purchased orange cloth. At a bookstand nearby, they acquired a bottle of black ink, and then they hid in an alley and fashioned two rough tunics of the orange material, with an imitation of the jobbers' glyph inked onto the front.

Fix dropped the empty ink bottle and the surplus scraps of orange cloth down the seat-hole of a cramped latrine in the alley corner.

Indrajit stuffed both orange tunics inside his own tunic to conceal them, and looked down the hole of the latrine. "I guess while we're down there, we should avoid walking beneath any shaft of light."

Fix shuddered. "That's why I never use latrines. You just don't know what's beneath you. It doesn't have to be man-eating beasts; I don't want some risk-merchant out for a stroll looking at my nethers, either."

"So, what? You just use the ground?"

Fix nodded. "Rain takes it out to sea in time."

"*You're* the reason Kish smells so bad."

"Kish smells bad for all *sorts* of reasons. My tiny contribution goes unnoticed, and gets washed away on a regular basis."

They returned to Frodilo Choot's office, and Holy-Pot and Ilsa each donned one of the improvised orange tunics, Ilsa putting it on over her black cloak. Then, with Choot waving a torpid goodbye, they lit two oil lamps and descended.

They accessed the catacombs by walking down stairs at the back of Choot's shop, stairs that ended in a heavy door. This was, if anything, even heavier than the door that opened onto the street, and it had a lock as well as two iron bars. On the other side, the lamps of Choot's basement revealed an unsteady and irregular world of ragged brick columns, putrid streams trickling across time-eaten cobblestones, and walls thick with multicolored lichens.

They took lamps with them.

Something, Indrajit would have sworn, scurried away into the darkness as he stepped out of Choot's building. Something at least as long as Indrajit's arm, with a white tail and many legs.

Holy-Pot shut the door. "When Frodilo recovers herself," he asked Ilsa, "will she realize that she has to come down here and lock the door?"

Ilsa nodded. "Probably."

Indrajit looked to his left, seeing staggered ranks of decayed walls that formed a maze. "I know right now that north is that way. But I also know that once we've turned around a couple of those walls, I'll have lost track of north completely. Does anyone have a lodestone?"

"Apsurd." Holy-Pot snorted dismissively. "I don't need a lodestone. I'll take us to the northernmost exit."

"You spend a lot of time down here?" Fix asked.

"It's not that large, and it's not that complicated." Holy-Pot led them in a meandering line that for a brief while followed a stream of thick, dark liquid gurgling in a channel it had carved into the stone, then turned away and instead marched alongside a length of wall that, instead of orange brick, was made of black stones, each as large as a man, and finally wove left and right through a field of leaning brick columns. They spoke little, because every word came back to them as a whisper from the void, and their footsteps bounced off unseen surfaces and created phantom stalkers for Indrajit to imagine.

Finally, Holy-Pot Diaphernes stopped at a door. It was indistinguishable from Frodilo Choot's in being a large, iron-bound wooden slab, with a heavy knocker in the center, but it was wedged into a corner, the walls angling sharply away from it in two directions, both wall sections slimy to the touch, smelling of sulfur, and vaguely green.

Indrajit tried not to gag.

Holy-Pot used the knocker vigorously, and was rewarded after a minute with a voice calling from the other side of the door. "Who is it?"

"Holy-Pot Diaphernes. Open up, Feen."

"Eh, how do I know it's really Holy-Pot?"

"You know pecause the last time you and I jointly syndicated a risk-contract, it was a muleskinner off to Ngharâdu-Isst, who claimed to have found a shortcut to the farther reaches of the Endless Road, that avoided poth the pandits and the powder priests. When he left his pones pleaching on the sand and his widow sued, we were aple to avoid payment because the judge ruled that their marriage was never properly formalized and that therefore she wasn't his heir."

"All of that . . . could be found in the public record," Feen said slowly.

"We priped the judge." Holy-Pot shot a harsh glare at Indrajit. "I will deny all this, if it ever comes up."

Indrajit shrugged. On a better day, he might have been bothered by the thought of working for someone willing to corrupt a judge. On this day, he didn't have the time to think about it.

"Also, you've never learned how to pronounce the letter *B*." Feen opened the door. He was a shriveled man with eyes like gleaming yellow coconuts and skin like an old leather bag, wrinkled, cracked, and reddish in the light of the oil lamp he held. "Eh, Spilkar's purse-strings, you've joined a jobber company."

Holy-Pot shook his head, passing Feen and climbing the steps up into his shop. "The men in orange are looking for me. It's nothing, just a contract dispute. This is put a disguise to throw them off the track."

"Eh, it would work better if you didn't have two faces."

Ilsa followed, then Fix, and finally Indrajit. Indrajit nodded and smiled a friendly greeting, and Feen ignored him. Indrajit was almost offended, and then realized that Feen's eyes had settled into the glazed look that suggested he had been overwhelmed by Ilsa's uncanny power.

Feen had no customers at the moment, being apparently engaged in examining and transcribing records at his counter. Indrajit stepped out in the street first, and saw that Holy-Pot had been good to his word; the trip through the underworld had taken them beyond the borders of the Paper Sook proper, and even past the first leg of the Crooked Mile. There wasn't an orange tunic in sight.

"Come on," he called in to the others. "Let's go to the opera."

Chapter Thirteen

~~~~~~~~~~~

"IT'S A CHEST," ILSA WITHOUT PEER SAID. "A CHEST of certain items that I need."

"Rare items, I suppose?" Indrajit asked. "Because if not, we could just replace them in Pelth or wherever."

The singer fixed Indrajit with an icy eye. Courting Flower notwithstanding, he felt daunted, and rocked half a step sideways in his walk. "I am no creature of vanity, risking my own life and yours for makeup or some frivolity. This chest contains...things I need. Things...relating to my race."

Indrajit imagined a chest packed full of mud and rare seaweed, in which the singer had to sleep. Or crawling with juicy little amphibians, that made up her entire diet—despite the gruesomeness of the thought, his stomach rumbled from hunger; the bread and cheese would tide him over, but he was still hungry. Or maybe Ilsa was a symbiote, and the other half of her lived inside a chest. Maybe the top portion of her skull, which seemed to be missing.

"Okay," he said. "I didn't doubt you."

The risk-merchant and the singer wore large orange tunics over their clothing, and all four of them trooped up through the Crown. In the afternoon, many of Kish's wealthy inhabitants took constitutional strolls, and in such strolling exhibited the latest fashion, cut from the finest silks and cotton. In his baggy tunic and linen kilt held up with rope, Indrajit might pass for the servant of one of the strollers, at best.

He avoided making eye contact.

"Since people—lots of people—are looking for Ilsa," he said, "Fix and I will go into the building and bring out the chest."

Then he stopped. The others staggered awkwardly, halting and then regrouping around him. Passing strollers, too important to curse at the inconvenience, shot Indrajit a heavily lidded gaze like sunning serpents.

Indrajit grabbed Fix and Ilsa by the wrists and dragged them onto a less-busy side street. "Something has been bothering me all day." He shook his head. "I finally realized what it was."

"The fact that people are trying to kill you?" Fix asked.

Indrajit shook his head. "I won't say I'm used to that, but you must admit, it comes with the territory."

"Yes, but now people like *Orem Thrush* appear to be trying to kill you."

Indrajit waved the concern away. "If Thrush wanted me dead, I'd be dead now. He wanted me *compliant*."

"I can see he failed."

"I'm stubborn that way."

"What has been bothering you?" Ilsa asked.

"On the stage last night," Indrajit said. "The jobber knew my name."

Ilsa's nictitating membranes flapped twice. "*The man who attacked me?*" she sang.

"No, the Luzzazza. He called me by my name."

"We talked about this," Fix said. "You wondered whether the Luzzazza might be mind readers."

"Yeah, but I don't think they are." Indrajit sucked at the new gap in his teeth. "And I also don't think I'm famous enough that some random jobber should just know me, if I run into him on the street."

"Maybe the Luzzazza wasn't a random jobber," Fix suggested. "Maybe he was a connoisseur of the Blaatshi Epic."

Indrajit hissed. "I should have asked Frodilo Choot. I missed my opportunity. She hired them. Diaphernes, did you tell them about me? Or did you tell Choot?"

Holy-Pot looked stumped. "I might have," he admitted. "When she engaged me to repurchase her risk on the contract, I might have mentioned that I was thinking of having you watch whatever joppers she engaged."

"Is it strange that she would tell them?" Indrajit asked. "I mean, why would they need to know?"

"Maybe so they would know that you were on their side, if your paths crossed on the job?" Fix suggested.

"Only the Luzzazza didn't act like he thought we were on the same side. He acted like he thought I was guilty."

"Heat of the moment?" Holy-Pot suggested. "Mistake? Professional jealousy?"

At the last suggestion, Indrajit laughed out loud. "Yes, that sounds right. A magician-mystic in a famous jobber company is envious of my many accomplishments as a mercenary. So envious, he calls me out by name as he attacks me in hand-to-hand combat."

Indrajit pushed the questions back into a dark corner of his mind, but the mystery remained.

"But the point," he said, "is that I'm known. If Gannon's Handlers are watching the Palace of Shadow and Joy, at least, then they know who I am."

"The Palace is just down the street," Fix said to Ilsa. "Tell me what I'm looking for and I'll go in."

"Yes, this is an excellent idea." Indrajit laughed. "What are you going to do, show them your fascicle? Read to them from a registry so they let you in?"

"I'll say whatever you tell me." Fix's face was earnest.

"No, you're no liar. You don't have the poetry in you to tell an easy lie. If you try to talk your way in, you'll be spotted in a heartbeat." Indrajit took a deep breath. "I'll do it."

Though if Pink Face were watching the door again, Indrajit might have some explaining to do.

"We could just walk in, and ignore anyone who tries to stop us," Fix suggested. "We only have to be in there long enough to grab the chest." He turned to Ilsa. "Is it easy to find? Is it labeled?"

"It's not in my dressing room," she said. "It's hidden under the stage. You're going to have to take me in there with you."

Ilsa had tried to direct Indrajit to escape the Palace of Shadow and Joy the first time by going underneath the stage. Perhaps she had wanted to collect this chest back then.

Indrajit sighed. "Well, that rules out my best plan."

"Which was?" Fix asked.

"Steal a chariot and crash it through the front door. Grab the box, race it out the back door."

"You really *don't* know how horses work, do you?"

"I know how they work in the Epic."

"How's that?"

"Foreigners ride them, and they taste good."

"That's not wrong, as far as it goes."

"Fortunately, I have come up with another plan." Indrajit turned to Ilsa. "Your dressing room has windows...am I remembering that right? Can you tell us from the outside which windows belong to your room?"

Ilsa nodded. "They'll be on the second floor."

"Be nice if we had a saddlebroken Ylakka. We could climb right up the wall. I've seen Ylakka climb walls smooth as glass to get to the dragon eggs at the top."

"Have you *seen* it?" Fix asked. "Or have you *heard about* it in the Epic?"

Indrajit ignored him. "Lacking an Ylakka, or a wizard to lift us up into the windows, or any skill at pole vaulting, I think we can probably make do with a tall wagon."

With a little walking, Indrajit found a Rover wagon. It stood a quarter mile from the Palace of Shadow and Joy, and its drivers—smiths and jewelers and horse tamers, like so many Rovers were—had set up an impromptu stall in a small plaza. Rovers covered their wagons with painted images of clan totem animals, which in this case appeared to be the otter. Armored otters, winged otters, and swimming otters circled in bright colors around an otter swinging a heavy hammer above a forge.

Beside the wagon, a burly, mustachioed man was repairing horseshoes and skillets while the woman at his side plaited hair and sold ornaments to be pinned into it. A younger man hung back, keeping an eye on the tall, arch-backed wagon. When Indrajit whispered

into his ear what he had in mind, and pressed one of
Ilsa's Imperials into his palm, he nodded.

Ilsa turned out to be surprisingly nimble. After
Indrajit climbed to the top of the wagon and lay on
his belly, extending a hand down to help her, she fairly
sprang up under her own power. The cool evening
breeze—the sun was beginning to set in the west,
and on the far side of the Palace of Shadow and
Joy, the evening's audience was filing into the opera
house—blew a wave of her scent into Indrajit's face,
and he was reminded how exotic and potent it was.
Mercifully, he still wore a sprig of the Courting Flower.

"You should wait outside," Fix suggested to Holy-Pot.

He shook both heads in answer. "And pe caught
alone py the joppers who purned down my office?"

The risk-merchant had the most difficulty climbing,
but with Fix's and Indrajit's help, he at last lay, as flat
as he could, on the curving, gold-painted wood, and
the Rover, after introducing himself as Virti, flicked
his horses into motion with a short whip.

The street alongside the tradesmen's entrance to the
Palace was not as quiet as Indrajit would have liked.
Couriers, carpenters, tailors, make-up artists, and the
actors choked up the street, each trying to get recognized at the same time by Pink Face the doorman.

Fortunately, that created something of an obstruction,
slowing the street's traffic dramatically. No one looked
twice when Virti brought his horses to a stop at the
spot indicated by Ilsa. No one looked twice despite
the fact that, under the broad brim of his hat, Virti
was a startlingly handsome young man.

The windows were open. Looking now, Indrajit saw
that they didn't have glass to shut, but wooden slats

that would be pulled over the windows and probably barred in the event of stormy weather. On a cool, balmy spring day like this, leaving the windows wide open would let the air inside circulate.

Ilsa went up first, and quickly.

"Where did she say her people lived?" Fix whispered. "Some mountain pass, or the tops of trees? She climbs like a monkey."

"A valley with a river, I think." Indrajit shrugged, keeping his eyes on the crowd, none of whom looked in his direction. "Ask her, if you're curious."

The two jobbers hoisted Holy-Pot up together. The risk-merchant went up inhaling sharply, and Ilsa dragged him into the window with her apparently powerful arms.

Indrajit made his fingers into a stirrup—he knew *that* much about horses—to push Fix up, and then went up himself. It was an easy climb. Beneath Ilsa's windows ran a ledge, and carved serpentine monsters, four-eyed demons, and lewd groupings of unknown gods arranged their bodies into spouts to send water cascading off the building and over the heads of pedestrians below, into the street proper. The sculptures offered excellent handholds, and Indrajit knew how to climb.

You had to, when you grew up along seaside cliffs, and sometimes the best mussels, or crabs, or fish eggs, were located at the bottom of a steep rock face.

Once inside, he looked down at the street again, to be certain no one was looking up. He signaled with his hand to Virti, who signaled back, and then settled in to wait. This Rover band, apparently, was one of those that knew the secret of Thûlian powder; the

Rover had a brace of pistols tucked into his sash. So much the better, since it meant it would be harder for a hostile party to move Virti against his will.

Ilsa's dressing room door was shut. Indrajit now saw a small bright green bush in the corner of the room, speckled with blotches of yellow, which he recognized as the Courting Flower.

"How do we get to the space peneath the stage, with the show apout to go on?" Holy-Pot asked, fussing with his hands.

"This is the easy part." Indrajit looked at Ilsa and gestured at a rack of costumes. "You dress up to hide who you are, I'll get us some costumes."

He grabbed three spear-bearers' costumes from a rack in the hallway below, just as he had the evening before, but this time with the addition of helmets. Helmets made of balsa wood, with balsa wood face-guards that completely concealed the wearers' features.

When he reentered the dressing room, Ilsa had hidden her own face inside a hood and was draping a crimson cloak about her, Fix and Holy-Pot facing away from her. Ilsa's build was still obvious through the costume, and when her fingers flashed into view, Indrajit thought he could easily identify her himself, but dressed like this, in the hubbub of the opera actually being performed, no one would spot her.

Her black cape and the rough orange tunics lay on the floor—Indrajit picked up the latter and tucked them into the pocket of his kilt, just in case. The orange fabric made his kilt bulge out ludicrously, like a mushroom cap.

Fix and Holy-Pot climbed into their costumes, Fix looking amused and Holy-Pot appearing more distressed by the minute. As Indrajit reached for the door to leave again, Ilsa caught him by the forearm.

"What if they see me?" she asked. "What if they attack me again?"

"Would you rather wait here?" he asked. "Fix can stay with you."

"The chest is heavy," she said. "You'll need him."

"I'll stay." Holy-Pot smiled. "I don't think I'd pe that useful in a fight, in any case, even if this spear wasn't a prop."

Ilsa gave Indrajit directions: down the hallway onto the stage, then behind the curtains and across the stage to a staircase at the far side, then a left turn and look for a door labeled The Queen of All Islands.

"Another reason I ought to be along," Fix murmured.

Indrajit ignored him.

Inside that room, Ilsa explained, there was a large blue leather chest, with the name Ilsa written on it. It should be easy to find, since the theater allowed her to use that room as her exclusive storage closet.

"Large, but light enough that the two of us should be able to carry it?" Indrajit asked.

She nodded.

"Keep the door locked," Fix suggested.

The director and the extras and the other opera personnel standing at the wing of the stage ignored Indrajit and Fix. They slipped behind the red curtains as the Imperial harps banged an improbable chord and two men traded insults in song.

"You know," Fix murmured, "this opera house is named after the city."

"It's not called Kish," Indrajit said.

"No. But the Palace of Shadow and Joy was the

official name of the palace of the Emperor of Kish, for about three hundred years, right down to the last Emperor. It burned down the night he died, and when the Refounders, the first lords of the great families, paid to have this theater built, they named it after his palace. The palace where they had all worked as servants."

"So it's not named after the city." Indrajit found the staircase and they climbed down into shadow, lit only by shafts of light from above. Indrajit thought of the latrine in the Paper Sook and winced. "It's named after the old palace."

"Only back in the day, the palace was so famous, when people would talk about the city, they would sometimes refer to *it* by the name of the palace. *Where are you sailing, Captain? To the Palace of Shadow and Joy. Who will declare war first? The Palace of Shadow and Joy has already sent its heralds.*"

"Hmm." Indrajit was not convinced. He looked for the door Ilsa had described, and had to shove aside racks of clothing and carts piled with props.

"So you see, it makes a kind of neat cosmic statement. The lords are the servants are the actors on the stage, as the city and the palace and the opera are all the same." Fix smiled, a menacing expression in the near-darkness.

"I feel like you have finally discovered the first of your ten thousand useless things."

"I have another thought," Fix said. "It occurred to me while I was climbing into the window a few minutes ago."

Indrajit found a door, but it had no writing on it. "You remember some threat we need to worry about?"

"It occurred to me," Fix said, "that Diaphernes's first name might be Holibot."

Indrajit laughed out loud. Fix joined him in the laughter, his voice gentle and high-pitched even while guffawing.

"And he just can't say it," Indrajit said.

Fix wiped a tear away from his eye. "So you and I—and maybe the whole world—think his name has something to do with *pots*."

Indrajit got his laughter under control. "Now I really want to ask him." He pointed at characters neatly painted onto a second door. "Does this say *The Queen of What Is It*?"

"*The Queen of All Islands*." Fix nodded.

"This was not as difficult to find as Ilsa made it sound, when we were standing outside discussing plans."

"She must not think we're very bright," Fix said.

The door was unlocked. As Indrajit stepped inside, he heard yelling, elsewhere in the theater. "Frozen hells, this place. Do they ever actually finish a production, or are all their shows just the backdrop for mayhem?"

Fix looked left and right. "In any case, we haven't been discovered. Let's hurry this up."

The yelling was quickly stifled.

The only contents of the room behind the door was a large blue chest.

"I guess when you're important enough," Indrajit said, "you get *two* rooms of your very own."

Fix nodded. "Just to hold a box."

The chest was locked with a heavy iron clasp, and between the two of them, they could barely heft it.

They dragged in the largest prop cart they could find and scooped all the helmets, fake weapons, maps, astrolabes, and books from it. Grunting, they levered the chest into the cart and began to wheel it toward the stairs.

At the bottom of the stairs, they stopped. "I'll push from below," Fix offered, but Indrajit shushed him with a finger to his own lips. He heard voices above, and wanted to hear.

Fix held his peace.

"I don't know whose body it is," one of the voices whispered. "But it sure doesn't belong *here*."

"Keep it quiet," whispered the other. "Lock the door. If anyone asks, tell them a patron fainted, and is resting in the dressing rooms."

"He didn't faint, he had his head nearly chopped off. And some of the crew saw it."

"Tell them they didn't see anything, or else they are fired. And let the jobbers know."

Footsteps moved in two opposing directions as the owners of the voices went their separate ways. The sound of the Imperial harps grew louder and changed mode, sounding an angry arpeggio.

"Did you hear that?" Indrajit asked.

"Any chance it was dialogue from the play?"

Indrajit shook his head. "I don't like it."

Fix gestured at the trunk, reminding Indrajit that they had a job to do.

"Okay," Indrajit said. "We use the cart to get the chest to the top of the stairs, but then we'll have to carry it. The cart wheels aren't going to slip by unnoticed behind the curtain."

Fix nodded. Counting together "one, two, three" and hoisting on *three*, Fix pushed and Indrajit pulled, and they dragged the cart up one step, a second, then more, and Indrajit lost count. His arms were beginning to ache as the cart reached the top of the stairs... and his back foot stepped on something, unseen, that wasn't the floor.

Indrajit lost his grip. The cart skewed sideways and then dumped the chest. The chest toppled forward, knocked Fix aside, struck the stairs, and sprang open.

A corpse flew out of the opening chest, along with clothing and shoes and makeup. The body hit the steps and tumbled with a horrendously loud noise, coming finally to a rest at the bottom of the stairs, face up, on its back, head pointing downward.

The corpse was Ilsa without Peer.

Chapter Fourteen

~~~~~~

"FROZEN HELLS!" FIX GASPED.

"That's *my* saying!" Indrajit snapped. "*You* don't *believe* in hells!"

"It can't be her."

It certainly looked like her. Bulbous eyes with the same nictitating membranes, though the eyes were gray in death and the membranes looked dry and brittle. Skin white as white eggshells, with dark-blue veins showing through. Long finger bones and fingers with too many bones in them. Wide, lipless mouth, thin, wiry hair, and flat head.

"Touch her," Indrajit suggested.

The heavy footfalls of several men running in his direction spurred Indrajit into action. He scurried down the steps again, and as his head dropped below the level of the stage, he saw three jobbers charging toward him. One was a slate-blue Luzzazza, the second a pale Ildarian or Ukeling, and the third a man with green skin; they all wore gray tunics with a circular glyph, marking them as Gannon's Handlers.

Something about the three men nagged at his memory, but he wasn't quite sure what.

Fix was trying to shift the box out of the way.

"Forget that!" Indrajit hissed. "We need to hide *her!*"

They each grabbed an elbow and hoisted the corpse up to hold it vertical, as if they were supporting a drunken companion. Rushing pell-mell across the dark space beneath the stage, they found a rack of costumes and stood behind it.

Just behind him, Indrajit realized, was another staircase leading up.

The clicking of heels on the wood in a circular pattern over their heads suggested that the actors were performing some sort of group dance.

"This isn't Ilsa," Fix whispered.

"Are you sure? It looks just like her."

"The corpse is cold to the touch."

Indrajit was about to retort that maybe Ilsa had been cold-blooded, but he had recently gripped her hand, in helping her climb into the opera house, and knew that her flesh was normally warm. "How do you know her race doesn't go cold instantly?"

Fix said nothing.

"Okay," Indrajit said. "It's probably not her. If she sent us down to get the trunk, someone would have to work very hard to kill her, race down ahead of us, and stuff her in the box before we got there."

"And cool her."

"But that means a stranger question remains."

"Why is she carrying around a body?"

"Maybe it's a memento," Indrajit suggested. "Maybe this was a sister or something."

"I thought all her people died when she was very young."

"Maybe this *is* her, but not in the way we're thinking."

Fix hesitated. "What do you mean?"

"Maybe she moves from body to body. Maybe this is a new body she has generated, and she needs it because her old body is wearing out."

"You are completely making this up," Fix said. "Or are you telling me this is in the Epic?"

"I'm hypothesizing. Or maybe this was her old body, and she needs it. Maybe it's the source of her powers. Maybe she uses this to build a new body."

"This is an awfully fantastical explanation."

"Look around you. It's a fantastical world."

"But you have zero evidence. You're just making wild guesses."

"Not *zero* evidence, just not *enough*. Anyway, something has to explain why she was so insistent she needed this ... body."

"Shh," Fix cautioned. "Here come the jobbers."

In the dim light below the stage, they saw the large movements of the three jobbers as shadows, detaching from one pool of darkness, moving through half-light until they disappeared into darkness again. The three congregated first around the chest, prodding at it and digging inside.

"It didn't get to the top of the stairs by itself," the green-skinned man said. Indrajit knew the voice.

"Is this what we're here for?" the Luzzazza asked. "To investigate props that are out of place?"

"These aren't props," the fair-skinned man said.

This was the Sword Brother. "Look at the writing on the chest."

Indrajit found himself unnerved by the cold weight of the body. With his free hand, he began draping scarves from the costume rack over the creature's face and shoulders.

"Maybe Ilsa's come back," the Luzzazza said.

"Why would she be back and not onstage?" the green man asked.

The Handlers drifted across the room, looking into racks of costumes and poking behind pieces of scenery. The green man lit a lamp, and in the greasy yellow light, Indrajit saw that the Luzzazza was doing his poking with a long, bronze-headed spear, stabbing it behind piles of wood and into costume racks.

He stood a little straighter at the thought of being run through. Fix also straightened his spine.

The Luzzazza was creeping closer to Indrajit and Fix, and Indrajit felt cold sweat trickle down the small of his back. In the new light, he saw that he stood beside a bookcase of game props: ten-pins, balls, hoops, darts. Indrajit reached with his spare hand and grabbed a ball.

When the Luzzazza's head was turned to one side, Indrajit tossed the ball across the stage. It thudded into a stack of painted boards, and the Luzzazza froze.

"What was that?" the blue man asked.

"It came from the rack in front of you," the Sword Brother said.

Frozen hells.

The Luzzazza stepped toward them.

"Now!" Fix hissed.

They threw the corpse. Shrouded in scarves, it hit the boards with its feet and then bounced forward, head-first. The Luzzazza raised his spear, but not fast enough, and the corpse barreled into his arms, knocking him back.

For a mad moment, the Luzzazza spun in the lamplight, the dead creature in his arms, trailing lengths of silk. Then they together struck a false stone arch, painted onto a large cheap board, and fell to the floor.

Indrajit scooped three large darts from the shelf. Stepping forward, he jabbed one into the Luzzazza's face. He'd been hoping to get an eye, but the Luzzazza was in motion, and instead, he jammed the dart into the jobber's cheek.

Then he and Fix ran.

Indrajit reached the staircase first. As Indrajit's feet hit the bottom steps, the Imperial harps shifted into a manic sequence. As if they were playing for him, the harpists jumped back and forth across their instruments, high-low-high-low-high-low. The notes *sounded* like sprinting, and Indrajit ran.

At the top of the steps stood the Grokonk Third. The sexless frog-man waved his arms, signaling to someone—probably to his female. Slightly disoriented, Indrajit was aware enough of his surroundings to realize that he was in the wings of the stage nearer to Ilsa's dressing room. They had taken the long way around to get the chest.

They had been *sent* the long way around.

The Third slapped a hand onto the hilt of a short sword hanging at his belt. Indrajit threw his second dart, hitting the Grokonk in the neck. The darts were props, so they weren't very sharp, but apparently they were intended to be thrown, because the balance was right and they were heavy.

The Grokonk backed away, raising his hands to ward off possible additional projectiles. Indrajit bounded past him, stabbing him in the belly with his last dart. Fix, for good measure, rammed his shoulder into the Third's sternum, sending the man reeling through the curtain and onto the stage.

Indrajit heard the angry squeal of theater people, and paid it no mind.

The harp playing ended in a sharp crash. The stage rattled with footfalls that might have belonged to an elephant.

Or to a female Grokonk in full sprint.

Indrajit didn't look back. He didn't want to lead the Grokonk to Ilsa—Ilsa might be manipulating Indrajit somehow, and she certainly wasn't telling him the whole truth, but he was still getting paid to protect her—so he took a sharp left before the stage ended, plunging back behind red curtains.

Cursing, Fix made the same turn. They raced with the plastered wall on their right hand and curtains on their left. Beyond the curtains, confused singing and declamation suggested that some of the actors were still trying to perform the play.

"You and your...long legs...not fair!" the shorter man grunted. But Fix's own legs were muscular, and he kept pace.

The Grokonk apparently missed the turn, because Indrajit heard another enormous crash behind them.

Ahead, in the corner of the stage and hidden from the audience, the Sword Brother stepped into view. He held two long, straight blades, one in each hand, and he assumed a combat stance with one weapon raised over his head and the other extended before him.

Indrajit stopped.

"Twang!" Fix shouted behind him.

The Sword Brother charged.

Indrajit turned and saw that Fix had pulled apart two curtains, creating a gap. He stepped back and then ducked left into the opening. Fix was sawing at a cable—

The Sword Brother lunged—

The last fibers of the cable gave way and, with a *whoosh!*, a bag of sand fell from above and struck the Sword Brother in the back of the head, knocking him to the floor.

Indrajit turned and found he was now onstage. Fortunately, he could make out little of the audience, or their presence might have made him nervous. He looked left, and saw both Grokonk, spears in hand. He looked right, and saw the Luzzazza and the green-skinned man with their spears.

"Frozen hells."

In the center of the stage rose a piece of scenery. From the audience's side, it must have been painted to resemble a mountain or a pyramid or a temple, but from this side, it was a single staircase rising to a platform, all nailed to an enormous sheet of wood. At the top of the platform stood a woman in full costume, face concealed, singing. Judging by her costume, she was singing Ilsa's part, but her voice didn't have a tenth the power.

Indrajit hesitated.

Fix raced up the plank steps.

A gasp of titillated disapproval rose from the audience; they knew this was not supposed to happen. Perhaps they'd come expecting another on-stage debacle, having heard of Indrajit's recent debut.

Indrajit followed. They reached the top together and

the singer turned to face them. Through her opaque wood-and-silk mask, Indrajit imagined a woman glaring at them, but she continued to sing.

"What are you doing?" he asked Fix.

The Luzzazza and the green-skinned man reached the bottom of the steps. Fix pointed up, and Indrajit saw what the other man had noticed earlier—ropes dangled from the rigging above the stage, and hung within their reach.

The platform trembled as the first of the jobbers stepped onto the stairs. It also slid slightly—it must be wheeled. Someone in the wings was shouting, but Indrajit couldn't focus on the words. Looking down the steps, he saw the green-skinned man.

"I know you," Indrajit said. "You're the assassin. You tried to kill Ilsa without Peer last night, only then you didn't have your uniform on."

The green man frowned and moved faster.

"So does Mote Gannon have the contract to protect Ilsa?" Indrajit probed. "Or to murder her? Or both?"

The green man charged.

"Sorry." Indrajit threw one arm around the diminutive singer and tossed her down the stairs into the path of the charging jobber. They tumbled together back down to the floor, landing at the Luzzazza's feet.

The Sword Brother staggered to join the other jobbers, along with a Yuchak encased in red leather, a Zalapting with a spear twice as long as himself, and a man wrapped in linen cloths, hiding even his face. Tucked into the swathed man's waistband was something rare—a brace of pistols.

"Frozen hells," he muttered. "Gannon's got a Thûlian in his company."

Fix jumped and grabbed a rope. When he jumped, the stairs slid to one side. As Fix climbed the rope, hand over hand, Indrajit found himself no longer directly beneath the ropes, but six feet away, and swaying to keep his balance.

The Zalapting and the Sword Brother took the stairs.

For the first time in his life, Indrajit felt the need of a battle cry, but he didn't have one. Backing as far into the corner of the platform as he could, he took one step and then leaped.

The Zalapting stabbed, catching Indrajit on the outside of his thigh with the tip of his spear; the theatrical mountain lunged in the opposite direction from Indrajit, sliding rapidly across the stage, as if it had broken free from some unseen mooring.

A rope struck Indrajit in the face, bypassing his outstretched hands and burning his neck as it dragged across his flesh like a sawblade—

Indrajit flailed at the ropes with both hands—

And caught one.

Hand burning, he swung over the stage, trying not to feel dizzy and focus on the catwalk above him. He climbed, and behind him the prop mountain hit the edge of the stage and tumbled forward, crashing onto the footlings.

Screaming erupted. Indrajit blinked sweat out of his eyes, ignored the pain in his leg, and then took Fix's offered hand. The smaller man hoisted him over a railing and onto the catwalk, and they looked down together.

Chaos reigned. The red-swathed guards employed by the theater itself had stepped in, and were struggling mightily against the more numerous Handlers. The singer, having survived her tumble, lurched away through the scattering clutch of harpists, and footlings threw punches at each other. A heavy man in a gold robe stood in the center, shouting directions at everyone as if he expected to be obeyed, his voice getting shriller with each moment he was ignored.

No one looked up.

Above the stage, a square iron catwalk hung suspended from the ceiling by thick ropes. The catwalk gave access to all the hooks, lashings, weights, loops, and rods that hung and worked the curtains below, as well as painted canvases that could be raised and dropped to provide background imagery to whatever was onstage. Three men, one a Zalapting and the other two stocky Kishi who might have been Fix's cousins except for his hawklike beak, stood on the other end of the rigging, staring at Indrajit and Fix. They must have been the men who worked the curtains; they wore only kilts, and their hands and bare feet were powdered with chalk.

Fix pointed at a doorway, and they both ran.

"I guess any idea I ever had about starting a jobber company is out the window." Before ducking through the doorway and into the hall beyond, Indrajit took one last look back. The three catwalk-hands were still staring at them.

"Really?" Fix asked. "I would have said the opposite."

"Well, anytime some lord of one of the great families, or risk-merchant, or whoever, wants to hire a company for a discreet job, they'll look at us and say, *Oh, aren't you the guys who got into a fight onstage at the Palace of Shadow and Joy, and knocked a mountain over onto the footlings?* And then someone else will get the job."

They found a staircase and dropped down one level.

"I think it was a pyramid," Fix said. "A Bonean Moon-Tower."

"You could guess that from the backside?"

"No, I've seen the play. But think of it this way, instead. Anytime some risk-merchant or lord wants to hire someone for a task that requires courage, boldness to the point of recklessness, they'll look at us and say, *Oh, you guys are the ones who had a hand-to-hand battle onstage at the opera.* And we'll say, *Anything for our clients.* And then we'll get the job."

"That does sound better," Indrajit admitted. "So what do you think?"

They looked both ways down the hall. To their right, the chaos onstage continued. To their left, shouting and darkness.

"About forming a company with you? Oh, you're clever, Indrajit Twang, and you're brave, and you're a smooth talker. I guess that makes up for you being a strictly mediocre swordsman."

"So . . . maybe?"

"Right now, I'm focused on surviving the night."

They scooted across the hall and tried the handle to Ilsa's dressing room. The door didn't open. They knocked, and got no response.

"Ilsa?" Indrajit called. "Ilsa!"

Still nothing.

"I don't like this at all," Fix said.

Indrajit took a deep breath and a step back. Launching himself forward, he cracked into the door with his shoulder and ripped the bolt of the lock right through the wood. The door opened, and the two jobbers stepped inside.

There was no sign of Ilsa without Peer.

Holy-Pot Diaphernes, on the other hand, lay on the floor in the center of the room. His veil was gone, and for the first time, Indrajit saw his second face clearly. It was a mirror image of his unveiled face, only about two thirds the size, and with curiously feminine features—fuller lips, longer lashes, a slightly softer jawline, a receding chin. If Holy-Pot had had a younger sister or a daughter, that might have been her face.

But both faces were frozen with their eyes staring open at the ceiling.

Holy-Pot's throat was cut. It wasn't a neat cut, either; he'd been hacked open with a series of blows that left his windpipe—two windpipes, actually—exposed, and revealed flashes of white bone where the killer had cut all the way to the risk-merchant's spinal column.

Indrajit's mind raced. "Shut the door."

The shouting outside was getting closer.

Chapter Fifteen

~~~~~~~~~~~~~~

FIX SHUT THE DOOR. "WELL, THERE GOES OUR FIRST client testimonial."

Indrajit laughed, and then had a hard time stopping. "Testimonial? There goes our client! There goes our pay!"

"Ilsa could pay us," Fix suggested.

"Good, that's right." Indrajit struggled and managed to get his laughter under control. "We need to find Ilsa, protect her, get her out of town, get paid." He thought a moment. "Unless that was in fact her dead, in the chest."

"Nonsense." Fix snorted. "Ilsa asks us to get the chest, sends us out, and then immediately someone kills her, puts her in the chest before we can get there, and kills Holy-Pot?"

"Or *Holibot*."

"I guess we'll never find out now."

"Could have been sorcery."

"You have no experience with sorcery, I take it."

"None. I mean, I've seen the big lights at parades, and there are lots of stories in the Epic. You?"

Fix hesitated. "Very little. I was healed by a Dru-vash artifact, but I was a child at the time, and my memory is vague."

"Was it one of the Vin Dalu?"

Fix nodded. "This door has no lock."

Indrajit looked around. "Well, if she went into hiding from whoever killed Holy-Pot, she isn't hiding in here." His eyes fell on the Courting Flower. Just in case, he broke off several large sprigs and tucked them into the pocket in his kilt.

"Either she climbed out the window or she went into the building."

The commotion got louder.

"Well, if she's in disguise in there," Indrajit said, "someone will find her, and it won't be us. The whole city, or at least all the rich people, just saw us. We need to get out of here."

"That leaves the window." Fix abandoned the door, crossed the door decisively, and climbed out onto the ledge. "The Rover's wagon is gone."

"Of course, it is. Once trouble broke out, why would Virti stick around? Best to be happy with the Imperial in his pocket and go back to mending horseshoes."

Indrajit's head whirled. Why had Ilsa sent them the long way around? Who had killed Holy-Pot Dia-phernes? Who wanted Ilsa dead? Was Orem Thrush to be trusted, or not? Where had Ilsa without Peer gone?

Feeling slightly dizzy, he climbed out onto the ledge.

"Careful," Fix said. "You're swaying."

"Our company is known for our boldness," Indrajit said.

"If you're going to jump, try to lower yourself as far as you can, first. Lessen the distance."

Indrajit took a deep breath and sat. Fix sat beside him.

Behind them, the door opened.

"The body's still here," said a voice Indrajit recognized. Pink Face? "But who broke the lock?"

"On the window ledge!" someone else shouted.

Indrajit pushed off from the ledge and dropped.

He managed to roll in his landing and stood without injury. Fix hit harder and flatter, and when he stood up, he winced.

"Ankle?" Indrajit asked.

Fix nodded.

"It's them!" a voice above them shouted. Indrajit looked up and saw the Luzzazza with invisible extra arms, the green-skinned assassin, Pink Face, and the man in the gold robes.

"They tried to kill Ilsa without Peer last night!" Green Skin shouted, turning to face back into the building as he yelled.

"Tonight they succeeded!" the Luzzazza bellowed.

For whose benefit were they shouting?

Indrajit fled. Fix hobbled, so Indrajit threw an arm across his shoulders and dragged him.

They staggered together at half-speed down the street. At the corner of the Palace of Shadow and Joy, Indrajit turned, just in time to see Green Skin and the spear-wielding Zalapting drop to the paving stones and climb to their feet.

The Luzzazza was nowhere in sight, but that mystical bastard was probably *teleporting* somewhere to get ahead of them.

"You can outrun them without me," Fix grunted. "And I can take those two."

Indrajit's eye fell on a small placard screwed to the wall of a building across the street. "We're going to outrun them together."

He dragged Fix, accelerating slightly despite the shorter man's grunts of pain, and got around the corner out of the Handler's sight.

Then he pushed left and down an alley, in the direction indicated by the sign.

At the back of the alley, the street took a sharp right, and there was the destination Indrajit was looking for: a latrine.

A man in a simple, but clean and well-cut, kilt stood with his feet apart, preparing to avail himself. "Oh, you don't want to do that," Indrajit said. He pulled Fix into an upright posture and they both smiled.

The man looked Kishi, dark and sturdy. No truly wealthy person would use the public latrine, even up here in the Crown, so this must be a merchant, or someone passing through for the evening, or a servant. His fashionable haircut, thick and shaped like a mushroom cap, suggested the first.

"It's not *broken*, is it?" the Kishi sneered.

Indrajit shook his head. "Rapeworm infestation."

The Kishi paled and took a long step away from the latrine. "You're jobbers?"

Indrajit nodded. "Got the sewers contract, and we're here to investigate."

"You'll want fire." The Kishi backed away. "Oil. And block off the tunnels so the flame doesn't spread."

"You sound like you know what you're talking about, and we're kind of short-handed." Indrajit grinned. "You looking for a job?"

The Kishi ran.

"Don't complain," Indrajit said promptly to Fix. "This is how we're going to survive."

Fix lifted the latrine seat with an effort that produced a grunt. The seat here was made of marble, whereas in the Spill, the seats were of cheap wood. "I'm not complaining. I'm just wondering if there might really be rapeworm down in here."

"There certainly might. In which case, you and I might both be giving birth in a few weeks."

Fix climbed in first, then Indrajit after, and Indrajit lowered the seat above them. They crouched in a space not quite as tall as Indrajit, and only slightly wider—in a pinch, four ordinary-sized men could have stood inside, but no more. Flowing liquid trickled in at one side of their feet and out at the other, through red clay pipes that might indeed accommodate worms, but wouldn't give access to Indrajit or Fix.

"Well," Fix said. "No more running."

Indrajit tried to breathe through his mouth, and quietly. "This sort of gives the lie to the idea that underneath the whole city's bums, there's an immense world of strange creatures and lost treasure, waiting to be found."

"I never said anything about treasure."

"Yeah, but others say it."

Fix nodded, a gesture barely visible in the gloom. "Yes, but remember where you are. This is the *Crown*. If there's any part of Kish where you would want to wall off all the latrines from each other and from the ruins below, to protect the local bottoms from unwanted viewing and pinching, it would be here."

"True . . ." Indrajit said slowly.

"Just try not to think of what might be lurking on the other side of these bricks."

"And watch out for bums." Indrajit scooted as close to the wall as he could without actually touching it. The air reeked of dead things and filth, and the humidity that made the spring evening air on the streets above cool and pleasant made the inside of the latrine feel like a cooking pot.

Torchlight above. A shadow loomed over the latrine seat, and Indrajit saw a bright lavender-colored Zalapting face, with its slightly elongated muzzle and its wide nostrils. Hanging from the Zalapting's shoulders was a gray tunic with circular glyph marking the man as one of Gannon's Handlers. Had the Zalapting seen Indrajit, by the light of the torch?

The Zalapting leaned forward and lanced down through the latrine seat with a bronze-headed spear. The weapon stabbed only empty air, but Indrajit couldn't take the chance that they'd been seen.

He grabbed the spear with his left hand and yanked it down.

The Zalapting had a firm grip on his spear and came forward with it. At the same moment, Indrajit shot his right hand up through the deluxe, Crown-sized latrine opening and grabbed the Zalapting's arm, pulling the Handler, head and shoulders, into the latrine.

"Don't scream," Indrajit warned the jobber.

The Zalapting kicked and squirmed, but didn't yell. Indrajit dragged the man down into the sewer with them; the spear was too long to fit, until Fix snapped a third off with a sharp blow of his elbow, and then again knocked off another third. He stacked the shattered spear bits in the corner.

Indrajit threw the Zalapting against the wall. "We're going to talk," he whispered. "Keep your voice down and your answers to the point, and you'll go home tonight."

"*You* won't," the Zalapting said.

Fix scooted into the corner of the sewer, keeping an eye out through the latrine seats for approaching lights.

"You think you're so important that we'll get in trouble for...what? Breaking your spear? The Lord Stargazer's going to have us hanged for that?"

The Zalapting laughed. "Nobody cares about *me*. But you killed Ilsa without Peer. And some very powerful people care a lot about her."

"We didn't kill her," Indrajit said.

"That's not what the witnesses will say."

"She's not even dead." Indrajit wanted to test the Zalapting's reaction. He wished he had better light for it.

The Zalapting snorted. "After killing her, you threw her body at my colleague, Pozzi, in an attempt to distract him so you could make your escape."

"That's not Ilsa," Indrajit said.

"That's not what witnesses will say." The Zalapting chuckled. "Don't you get it? You were going to go down for this from the start, Indrajit Twang. No matter how it happened, you were going to end up burned."

Fix interjected himself into the interrogation. "What are you talking about? Why would anyone care about Indrajit?"

"Feeling envious?" Indrajit asked.

"You too, Fix the Trivial." The Zalapting laughed.

Indrajit rocked back on his heels. Did this add up to anything rational? Was the job—were both jobs—nothing but a setup, to have him killed? But that made no sense at all. In the first place, the only person he owed was Holy-Pot Diaphernes, and Holy-Pot had hired him, paid him money. In the second, if the risk-merchant had wanted Indrajit dead, he could have had Yashta Hossarian execute him at the Blind Surgeon.

Still, the Zalapting knew their names.

"Who employed you?" Indrajit asked.

"Mote Gannon."

Indrajit sighed. "You know, powerful people might want to kill us, as you say, but you should think about your answers carefully. There are three of us down in this hole, and you are the smallest, and unarmed. Let's try this again: Who hired Gannon's Handlers?"

The Zalapting hesitated, then answered. "The risk-merchant Frodilo Choot."

"And what was your task?"

The Zalapting hesitated again. "To protect the singer, of course. Ilsa without Peer." Then he chuckled. "From you two."

Indrajit had planned to make another threat at this point, but Fix grabbed the Zalapting by the neck. He cracked the lavender-skinned man's skull against the bricks, softly, and then pressed his cheek against the slime.

"You're a liar," Fix said gently. "Your job was to kill her, and make it look like we did it."

The Zalapting trembled. "My job was to stand guard. Others were going to kill her."

"And blame us?" Fix clarified.

"Yes."

The Zalapting tried to nod, but couldn't, because his face was smushed against the wall. "You weren't supposed to leave the Palace of Shadow and Joy alive."

"You're not very good at your job," Fix said.

"I guess not," the Zalapting admitted.

"Probably Mote Gannon wouldn't miss you," Fix suggested. "I mean, he might kill you himself if you showed up. For abandoning your post."

"Dereliction of duty," Indrajit added. "We should just break your neck. Leave you down here. It'd be the best end for you, really."

Head pinned to the brick, the Zalapting's body trembled.

Fix shook the captive. "Unless, of course, you had more to tell us."

"Like what?" the Zalapting whimpered.

"Like, what does Frodilo Choot have against us?" Indrajit suggested.

The Zalapting shrugged awkwardly. "I don't know. As far as I can tell, it's just business."

"You ever have any business with Frodilo Choot before today, Fix?"

"No," Fix said. "You?"

"Never," Indrajit said. "Never heard the name."

"I don't know anything!" the Zalapting squealed.

"There was a body," Fix said. "It looked like Ilsa, but it wasn't Ilsa. Someone with a dark sense of humor had stashed it in Ilsa's things. I think someone wanted everyone else to believe Ilsa was dead, so they could kidnap her."

"Who would do that?" Indrajit put his question to the Zalapting. "A different opera house?"

"One of the other lords?" Fix suggested.

"I don't know what you're talking about," the Zalapting said. "We were trying to kill you and the singer both."

"Regardless of the extra body," Indrajit said, "Frodilo Choot hired these thugs. Frodilo Choot must have wanted Ilsa dead."

"Is Frodilo Choot an opera fan?" Fix asked. "Does she own a rival opera company? Or is she shorting shares of the Palace of Shadow and Joy at the Paper Sook?"

"Wait," Indrajit said. "What was that last bit of gibberish?"

"Oh, it's just...Paper Sook talk."

"More risk-merchantry?"

"No. Joint-stock companies. Trading ownership, moving capital around, placing bets on the future."

"*Placing bets on the future* sounds like risk-merchantry."

"A different kind of bet."

"Stay focused, Fix."

Fix yelped and let go of the Zalapting. In the gloom, Indrajit saw the metallic flash of a weapon in the little jobber's hand. He grabbed the Zalapting's forearm, trying to immobilize him and stop a second attack.

At the same moment, Fix punched the Zalapting in the throat.

The Zalapting crumpled against the wall and was still.

"Fix," Indrajit said. "Is he dead?"

Fix checked. "Oops. I didn't mean to hit him that hard."

"Frozen hells."

"It wasn't on purpose. Sorry." Fix dropped the Zalapting. "I don't think he knew anything else."

"Maybe not. Are you bleeding?"

Fix shrugged. "A little."

Indrajit sighed and thought for a moment. "I wish I had a better plan, but I guess we just leave the body down here. In a week, some poor sap of a jobber with the sewers contract will find it."

"We should take the tunic and spear, though," Fix suggested. "There are a hundred thousand Zalaptings in Kish, and if one body more or less turns up, no one will pay it any mind. If a body turns up in Mote Gannon's uniform, questions will be asked."

"We will be blamed."

"True," Fix said. "Though in this case, we're actually guilty."

They were quiet for a moment.

"What do we do, then?" Indrajit asked. "Leave Kish?"

"If we do that, your errand fails, doesn't it?"

"My *errand*. You make it sound like I've come to the market to buy crusty bread."

"I don't mean to trivialize it. But surely, you came to Kish to find an apprentice Recital Thane. Someone to follow you, be the four hundred whateverth in the line."

"Four hundred twenty-eighth." Indrajit sighed. "Yes. My people are dwindling in number, and none of the youth has the aptitude or the inclination. But if the Epic dies, then it will be as if my people never existed. In a terrible and real sense, my people *will* never have existed. We will have made no difference, left no mark."

"Grim."

"I came to Kish looking for a way to avoid that. Some cousin people, some lost branch of my kin—the Epic hints at numerous such possibilities—some person interested in becoming adopted into the Blaatshi."

"You could write it down," Fix suggested.

"That would be strictly a last resort."

"We need to find Ilsa," Fix said. "If she's in danger, and we can protect her—and I think both those things are probably the case—then we can still get paid."

"Yes," Indrajit agreed. "And also, we need to go talk to Frodilo Choot, and make her tell us her part in this. Did she want Ilsa killed? And why?"

"I'd like to interrogate Holy-Pot."

"You suggesting necromancy?"

"No."

"I've heard terrible things happen to necromancers," Indrajit said. "Their flesh warps. They get boils, and their skin sloughs off. Something about the living can't abide contact with the dead."

"I'm not suggesting it," Fix insisted. "I'm just wishing out loud."

"Well, maybe we'll be lucky. Ilsa had a double, who was dead."

"Maybe," Fix said. "Though maybe that's something else entirely. Another big reason we need to find Ilsa."

"Maybe Holy-Pot will turn out to have a double, and it will be the double who died."

"Two Holy-Pots," Fix said. "Four faces."

"Frozen hells." Indrajit spat, hoping in vain it would clear the reek of the sewer from his mouth and nostrils. "You don't think Ilsa's double has something to do with the Lord Chamberlain, do you?"

Fix considered this. "You mean, maybe Ilsa was dead from the beginning? And the person we were running around with was Orem Thrush, the Lord Chamberlain?"

"Well, when you say it out loud, it sounds crazy."

"I wouldn't have guessed the Lord Chamberlain could sing like that," Fix said. "But what do *I* know?"

Chapter Sixteen

~~~~~~~~~~~~

INDRAJIT WOKE WHILE IT WAS STILL DARK, THE damp chill of night clinging to his bones and his nostrils so thoroughly plugged with the stench of the latrine that he barely smelled it any longer. What had awakened him?

He heard a groan and saw a flickering light. For a moment, he prepared himself to slip sideways to avoid falling matter from above, but then he realized that the light was at his feet. No, not quite at his feet, but cracking now and then along the floor of the tight, slimy chamber.

A light was shining through the sewer pipe.

It could have been many things, including someone in the basement of an adjoining building, or a jobber working the sewers. But it could also have been some creature, glowing of its own power, creeping up from the lich-dusty Druvash levels to find a meal, so Indrajit jumped into action.

He elbowed Fix, and the short man was instantly

awake. They pushed the dead Zalapting to one side so that the light wouldn't touch him—in case anyone was also *looking* through the pipe—and then climbed out. Indrajit had the gray Handler's tunic balled in one hand.

They crept from the alley. Indrajit's muscles screamed as they slowly uncramped, and the wound in his leg stung him. Once he could see more than a fist's width of stars overhead, Indrajit realized that he'd slept nearly a whole night leaning against the stone. He ached all over, including in his lungs. At the edge of the street, a coughing fit overtook him and Fix joined him in it. For three violent minutes, they hacked phlegm up and cast it onto the bricks of the Crown, and then Indrajit felt he could breathe again.

The air of the Crown wasn't sweet, exactly—in the world's oldest city, the only sweet air was in the gardens of the temples or the wealthy, or on high rooftops—but on top of the sweat of sleepers, the pall of coal fires, and the faint tang of latrines, Indrajit could smell early morning bread, scented toilet waters, and the sea.

"I need a bath," he announced.

"We both do," Fix agreed.

"I have no money left."

"You *are* quick to spend." Fix chuckled, a high-pitched, silvery sound. "No wonder you were in debt."

"Get off your high horse, Fascicular," Indrajit grunted.

Fix nodded. "All I'm saying is that I still have cash. Let's discuss this in a steam bath."

"And at first light, we go talk to Frodilo Choot."

Indrajit kept the gray tunic, just in case. He walked

with his face down and swinging his head from side to side, sweeping the streets around him with his wide-ranging vision. He saw two jobbers in green cloaks with spears—one looked like an ordinary Kishi and the other had cheeks and a jaw that glowed a bright blue, casting light in whichever direction he looked. Jobbers, patrolling the street at night, but they slowly walked away from Indrajit and Fix.

Indrajit didn't see anyone following them.

Thoughts of the Spill reminded Indrajit of the jobbers in orange tunics who had destroyed Diaphernes's office, so they went to a hot bath in the Dregs. The all-sexes common room was cheap, but Fix paid for the best room, a stone grotto six paces long, with a boiling spring at one end whose waters quickly cooled in a series of three small pools before flowing out a crack at the other end. Light came from a heap of blue luminescent stones beside the hot spring.

They piled their weapons in a corner.

Indrajit sat in the middle pool. He felt guilty about taking the warm water, but he needed it for his aches. His guilt disappeared when Fix plunked himself straight into the hottest pool, into heat Indrajit would have found intolerable.

They were alone.

"The first order of business," Indrajit said, "is to raise the possibility that we should split up and leave Kish."

"I'm not leaving Kish," Fix said.

"Because you're in love," Indrajit said.

Fix nodded.

"But that can't be why Holy-Pot wanted you to take the fall. Can it?"

Fix hesitated. "Not exactly."

"Oh ho, now we get to it. You killed someone for love. You're in love with Holy-Pot's sister. You romanced the wife of one of the great family lords."

"I tried to start a business."

"Frozen hells, you are disappointing. I thought we had tunneled to the exciting kernel of your soul, and now you're telling me that for love, you were willing to do...an extremely boring thing."

"I left the Selfless because I was in love. I wanted to become wealthy, so I could convince the woman to marry me. So useless knowledge, you see, would do me no good. And I was learning risk-merchantry from Holy-Pot so that eventually I could start my own shop as a risk-merchant."

"You mean he was training you?"

"No, I mean I was working for him so I could learn to do what he does. You work hard with your eyes open, you can learn any business from any job in the business. In fact, I think there's a big advantage to having worked in the lowest levels of the organization, which in this case is collections—"

"Stop." Indrajit shook his head. "Holy-Pot wanted to kill you because you were going to become his competitor?"

"Well, maybe." Fix dunked his face under the steaming water, and Indrajit flinched, half-expecting the shorter man to die from the heat. "But she was growing impatient."

"Tell me who she is."

Fix fell silent.

"Wait," Indrajit said. "She does exist, right? This is a *real* woman you're talking about?"

"She's gone now," Fix said. "So her identity hardly matters."

Indrajit sensed he wasn't going to learn any more on that subject for the moment. "Okay. She was growing impatient."

"So I went ahead and started my risk-merchantry business," Fix said. "Without being admitted to the Paper Sook first."

Indrajit tried to process this information. "So, contracts not on the Registry."

"Yes."

"Illegal risk-merchantry."

"Unregistered, yes."

"Undercutting Holy-Pot and his friends. Otherwise, how would you get the business?"

"Yes," Fix admitted. "Cheap, illegal risk-merchantry contracts."

"How were you going to pay?" Indrajit asked. "I mean, if you had to pay a...what do you call it?"

"A claim. I took in as many contracts as I could, with as balanced a risk profile as possible."

Indrajit shook his head. "Stop, I don't understand that and I don't want to. Are you saying you ended up in enormous debt to some ship captain or muleskinner chief?"

"No, I did okay in the risk-merchanting business. Made some money, in fact. She left anyway."

"You didn't make *enough*."

Fix nodded.

"But you think Holy-Pot Diaphernes found out you were a risk-merchantry bandit, and wanted you dead for it."

"I guess so."

"So it *was* all about a woman. See, the lessons I learned from the Blaatshi Epic taught me to decipher you, young Fiximon."

"Lucky guess."

"But if you've got a risk-merchantry business going, why were you still taking jobs from Holy-Pot?"

"I can't register my contracts," Fix said. "But the business still takes place in and around the Paper Sook, and I needed a reason to be there."

"You could leave Kish now," Indrajit suggested. "Go take up risk-merchantry somewhere else. Boné or Xiba'alba or the Paper Sultanates."

Fix shook his head. "*She* lives *here*. Besides, this is the biggest market. I don't think those other places have enough room for an operator like me."

Indrajit almost laughed out loud, but caught himself. "Frozen hells, you're a black-books risk-merchant in unrequited love."

"*You* could leave," Fix shot back.

Could he? Indrajit thought about it. "No," he said. "If I leave here, it's to go home and die."

"You couldn't do something else? Just become a fisherman or something?"

Indrajit sighed. "My people are few in number. Three hundred, when I left. Our reproduction is . . . complicated. And our living space is getting squeezed. And none of the youth want to make the mental effort and the life commitment required to master and perform thirty-thousand lines of poetry, with all the epithets and gestures and staging, as well as the tale itself. And none of them want to take on a junior priest in turn, and compose an additional fifty or one hundred lines bringing the Epic down another generation."

"So you came to Kish to find an apprentice."

"It's up to me."

"But why Kish? Your people aren't from here."

"In every generation, there have been leavers. Some of them, or their descendants, must be here. Or if not, perhaps I can find some cousin-folk, some race of man that is our kin, that might be willing to make a home for the Epic. If they're not here themselves, there must be news of them here. All things come to Kish."

They sat briefly in silence.

"If we're not going to leave," Fix said, "then we have a problem."

"If only we had our own jobber company," Indrajit said, "we could fight our way out."

"We *do* have our own jobber company," Fix said. "It's just a bit on the small side."

That thought made Indrajit feel a little better. A little. "Well, if we can't fight our way out, maybe we can . . . I don't know, solve the puzzle?"

"What, you mean figure out who's behind all this and turn them into the authorities?"

"Unless the guilty parties *are* the authorities," Indrajit said. "Which I find depressingly possible. But maybe we could get proof, and hold it over the guilty parties' heads. Make them leave us alone."

"Or maybe, if we got to the bottom of all of this, we'd find there was a single person behind it. And if we just had to kill one person, we could do that."

"I'd be up for killing one person," Indrajit agreed. "If that person was a real bastard."

"Whoever it is, he tried to kill us."

"Or *she*."

"Could be a she."

"Could be Frodilo Choot. She hired the Handlers to kill Ilsa."

"And she's a man."

"What?" Indrajit blinked in puzzled silence. "You're saying that Ilsa's magical power affected Choot, so maybe Choot's not a woman."

Fix shrugged. "Or she's a woman who can be affected by Ilsa's power. So apparently that's a possibility."

"You're right," Indrajit said. "Whoever did this, let's kill him. Or her."

He climbed out of the water and sat in the steam. Sweat beads sprang up on his mahogany-colored skin.

"There is no chance that all this activity is designed *just* to kill us," Fix said. "We're not worth hiring a single jobber company, much less two."

"I make it four companies." Indrajit laughed. "Gannon's Handlers, the boys in the orange tunics—"

"Yes, those are the two I had in mind," Fix agreed. "And I suppose you're counting the jobbers Grit Wopal hired."

"Let's assume they still bear us some animosity, yes. And also Yashta Hossarian."

Fix frowned. "Orange and black? Fellow with no arms, and legs like a bird's?"

Indrajit nodded. "He and his crew are the ones who came for me and forced me to take this job."

"Forced?"

"Okay, strongly encouraged. So one company hired by Holy-Pot, one by Orem Thrush—"

"We *think*."

"We think, one by Thrush's intelligence man, and one by Frodilo Choot. And the goal is not to kill us, but someone has to die or take the blame, and everyone knows in advance it's going to be us. Or at least, Gannon's Handlers know. We're designated to take the fall."

"For killing Ilsa."

"And to keep us from objecting, we're supposed to die. Since Holy-Pot hired both of us, that tends to suggest he knew we'd take the fall. Could he have *chosen* us to take the fall?"

"Why? Because he thought I would be his competition in risk-merchantry?"

Not having a very good answer to the question, Indrajit shrugged. "Why a second body of ... what is Ilsa's race called?"

Fix shrugged.

"Maybe you can look her up in your fascicle," Indrajit suggested. "Let's call the dead one Ilsa Two. Assuming it is dead, and not hibernating or waiting to accept a soul or whatever."

"Why Ilsa Two?"

"Right, good question. Also, doesn't this seem like a lot of trouble to go to just because an opera singer wants to quit her job?"

Fix frowned. "You're saying, there must be some stakes here we're not seeing."

"Yeah. Something that makes this all worth it."

"But it seems clear that the plan is to kill Ilsa. And Holy-Pot is getting in the way, with his pesky jobbers Indrajit and Fix, so he has to die."

"Maybe that's not in the original plan. Maybe that just develops with the turn of events." Indrajit chuckled. "That doesn't bode especially well for the jobbers."

"We have to go talk to Choot."

Indrajit tried to think that through. "Choot knows that Thinkum Tosh took out the original contract, but we know that, too. Maybe Choot can tell us whether she thinks Orem Thrush was the real party behind the agreement."

"Bearing in mind that Choot wants us dead. Also, Gannon's Handlers seem to be in on the mystery here, don't they?"

"They knew they were supposed to kill Ilsa and us. I'm not sure they know *why*. Maybe Gannon himself does."

"Holy-Pot said they were hired by Choot. So I think she knows everything."

"Mote Gannon is my backup plan. But wouldn't you rather try to tease information out of an unarmed risk-merchant, who may or may not secretly be a man, than assault the captain of one of Kish's larger jobber companies?"

"She *did* try to kill us."

"They both did," Indrajit said. "But the stakes have gone up for her, too. Whoever killed Holy-Pot Diaphernes might be after her as well."

"Except that it was most likely Gannon's men, and they most likely killed Holy-Pot at her instruction."

"Right. So we'll go armed."

"As an alternative," Fix said, "what if we found Ilsa without Peer and put some of these questions to her?"

"We *did* put some of them to her." Indrajit stretched his memory back. "She suggested it might be the opera company trying to kill her, or Orem Thrush."

"Thrush still seems likely," Fix said.

"Yeah," Indrajit agreed. "I don't think we can discount either one. Well, if Choot is in on this, it's probably because someone hired her, and the Lord Chamberlain is a good guess. But in any case, I have no idea where to find Ilsa, so for now, that's off the table."

"We could dig into the opera house more."

That was true. Indrajit took up two strigils lying within arm's reach of the water and handed one to Fix. He began scraping sweat and filth from his body, wiping it onto a white linen towel provided for the purpose. "Okay, you're right. And if they're innocent, maybe they know where to find Ilsa."

Fix climbed out of the water and began to strigil sweat from his limbs. "You mean maybe they have her address *written down*?"

"No, you literate bastard, I mean maybe we can shake her address out of one of the clerks. But if Ilsa was right, and they're not innocent, then going to ask them questions might just get us into deeper trouble."

"Of course, we think Frodilo Choot is in on the crime, and we're going to try to get information out of her."

"It's an interesting question," Indrajit said, "what Choot gets out of killing Ilsa. Choot would have to pay if Ilsa died, right?"

"We think so."

"Maybe we should see a copy of that contract."

"You mean *read* it?"

"Don't rub it in. But yes, make sure Choot actually was supposed to pay out if Ilsa died. And if so, then Choot being in on a conspiracy to kill Ilsa means that probably it would make her more money than she would have to pay out."

"So possibly Choot is innocent, and Mote Gannon is the crook."

Indrajit rubbed his temples. "This makes my head hurt."

"Maybe we're not cut out to run a jobber company."

"No," Indrajit said. "Just add it to the list. Talk to Frodilo Choot, interrogate the management of the Palace of Shadow and Joy, put questions to Mote Gannon. Anyone else?"

"Tie Orem Thrush up and grill him. Punch Grit Wopal in the third eye some more. My turn, this time. Get a necromancer and ask Holy-Pot Diaphernes who killed him. And whether his name is really *Holibot*."

"Find Ilsa without Peer."

"Yes," Fix agreed. "Finding Ilsa would be useful."

"What about Ilsa Two?"

"I'm pretty sure she's dead," Fix said. "Are you thinking about a necromancer again?"

"Maybe," Indrajit mused. "But maybe it would help to learn more about Ilsa's race. Ilsa said they were all killed when she was a child, but then we found a second."

"You're making a lot of assumptions there."

"I know. But maybe someone in the Hall of Guesses can help us replace those assumptions with good information. Or if not the Hall of Guesses, is it possible that one of the Selfless of Salish-Bozar the White might help us?"

"You think maybe facts about a nearly extinct race of man might qualify as useless information, and there might be a disciple of the White God who can tell us about Ilsa?"

"Maybe they can tell us whether the race really is extinct. And whether they store extra bodies to transmigrate into, or stuff their dead into trunks. And it doesn't have to be a Selfless, right? Maybe in the process of qualifying a Selfless, the disciples of the White have debated this information. Maybe to prove the information useful, someone has had to master it."

Fix chuckled. "You are thinking like a Selfless, Recital Thane."

"Not I, Godless Outlaw Risk-Merchant. I'm thinking like a jobber."

"Like a jobber *captain*, maybe."

Indrajit grinned.

"Of course," Fix continued, "if some Selfless has mastered all the information about Ilsa's race, and we go get her to tell it to us, she will learn that the knowledge has use. And she will thereupon have to surrender her status as a Selfless. We will have defrocked a priest."

"That thought should please you."

"It does."

Indrajit took a deep breath, letting the steam clean his lungs. "Well, let's go see what we can learn from Frodilo Choot. I'm not putting my old kilt back on after getting this clean, so either we find new clothes, or I go naked."

Chapter Seventeen

"WILL SHE REMEMBER US?" INDRAJIT ASKED. "OR...
he?"

They stood in the walled-in lane in front of Frodilo
Choot's shop. Men with orange tunics still watched from
corners throughout the Paper Sook and surrounding
streets; their arrangement looked casual to the unin-
formed glance, but Indrajit noticed that, wherever they
went in the tangled streets around the sook, there was
an orange-clad jobber watching. The jobbers didn't
interfere with him and Fix, so he guessed they must
be set to watch for Ilsa, or Holy-Pot, or both.

The bathhouse had sold them new kilts and sleeve-
less tunics. Indrajit's weapons and the few objects in
his kilt pocket still smelled faintly of the latrine—the
gray tunic worst of all—but the scent was fading, and
he could ignore it.

"You mean, because when we met her, she was
under Ilsa's influence?"

"You can say *spell*. And yes."

"But you were under Ilsa's spell, and so was I," Fix reminded him. "Did you fail to remember the time while she was dominating you?"

"No, you're right," Indrajit agreed. "Too bad. I think I'd rather she not remember us than that she remember us and think of us as part of the group that enchanted her."

"She seems to want us dead. She'll remember who we are."

"Oh, right." Indrajit tightened his grip on the hilt of his leaf-bladed sword.

"That Pelthite in orange is starting to wonder why you haven't knocked," Fix said. "Do it."

Indrajit knocked.

The door opened immediately, and behind it stood the same doorman: bulky, purple, shimmering, and covered with scales. A bit of his face wriggled, possibly indicating the presence of eyes that were very tiny or nearly shut, and he snorted. Then he backed away, letting the two jobbers in.

They entered cautiously. Indrajit looked into the corners of the room for any indications of a trap or an ambush, and saw none.

Frodilo Choot hunkered behind her work counter. Through the bands of green tooled leather, she stared hostility in their direction. "I should summon the watch," she hissed.

"We haven't done anything," Indrajit objected.

"You and Holy-Pot brought that witch in here. And you brought down Orem Thrush's jobbers, who haven't stopped staring at my door."

"Maybe we should leave by the basement door, then," Fix said. "Just in case."

"Absolutely not." Choot frowned. "Nor will you stay here long, or I *will* turn you in to the watch."

Indrajit was pleasantly surprised that the risk-merchant hadn't already attacked them. "We're on your side." He spread his arms.

"Which side is that?" she asked, ice in her voice.

He watched her eyes closely for any flinching as he spoke. "You bought risk on the life of Ilsa without Peer. You want to keep her alive. So do we."

Frodilo Choot's icy stare didn't falter. "In that case, I have bad news for you. Our side has lost."

"We have...? But..." Indrajit thought of Ilsa Two, and caught himself. "What do you mean?"

"I mean that last night, not too long after you were here, she was found dead at the Palace of Shadow and Joy." The risk-merchant seemed genuinely upset.

"Found dead...*how*?" Indrajit asked.

"Cause of death undetermined." The risk-merchant glowered. "Perhaps from a fall. Witnesses say she was found onstage, or backstage."

Indrajit caught Fix's gaze and they both nodded.

Then Indrajit sighed. "This is going to sound strange, but what if she wasn't dead?"

The doorman hit Indrajit from behind. It was a solid blow and it caught Indrajit by surprise, right at the base of the skull. Indrajit struck the wooden counter with his forehead and bounced backward. Light flashed in his eyes and he sank to his knees.

He had the dim awareness of Fix putting up a better fight, but only slightly. The shorter man's spear and falchion both failed to penetrate the doorman's scales and then the doorman ripped the weapons away and choked Fix until he fell limp.

Indrajit raised a hand to protest, and Frodilo Choot kicked him in the jaw.

Time passed.

Indrajit was dragged somewhere. He hurt. The lights grew dimmer, and that was an improvement.

Was he dying?

Then his hands were tied together, and then his ankles. He was hung on a hook, rough rope suddenly digging into his wrists with all the weight of his body.

Water splashed him in the face, and then again, and then a third time—

"I'm awake!" he spluttered, coughing and spitting out cold water.

"I will not be bullied," Frodilo Choot growled.

"What?"

Fix also made a groggy sound. He was somewhere to Indrajit's left; the room was shadowed and Indrajit's vision was still shaky.

"I will not be blackmailed or threatened." Choot's face swooped in close to Indrajit's own; he saw eyes opened wide, banded in green leather, and he smelled a cloying perfume.

"First of all," Indrajit said, shaking from the chill of the water, "we didn't control your mind. Before. That wasn't us."

"Ilsa," Fix groaned.

"Yeah, that was Ilsa. She has a...power." He didn't say *over men*.

"Where is she?" Choot snapped. "What have you done with her?"

Fix chuckled, a weak, strangled sound. "On your list of people who want us dead, Twang, I guess we can put Frodilo Choot at the top."

The purple doorman lunged from the darkness to punch Fix again. He cried out and fell silent.

"You've got this all wrong," Indrajit said.

The purple doorman hit him in the stomach. He grunted, swung with the force of the blow, and then rocked back and forth slowly, trying to suck in air around the sudden painful knot in his gut.

"Okay," Indrajit said. "Tell us what you want."

"Where is Ilsa?" Choot asked.

Indrajit shook his head. "We don't know. We don't have her."

"Get the knife," Choot said.

"No, really," Indrajit sputtered. "We were hired by Holy-Pot to protect her."

Indrajit's vision had returned enough for him to see that he and Fix hung from a horizontal pole fixed between two walls in an otherwise bare room. Light came in from a high, narrow window. "And you kidnapped her instead," Choot suggested, "and you want me to ransom her from you, because otherwise I have to pay out under the contract."

The doorman handed Choot a knife. It was long and triangular in shape, almost a short sword.

"No," Indrajit tried again, "we got separated from her. Someone is trying to pin the blame on us for her death, and maybe kill us, and we're trying to figure out who. You seemed like an obvious candidate."

"You think I would kill a person whose risk I had bought?" Choot growled. "You think I would commit fraud?"

"It seems like a ridiculous thought now," Indrajit said.

"Tell me where you're keeping Ilsa without Peer." Choot stabbed him in the thigh.

Fix screamed.

That didn't seem right. No, it wasn't Fix screaming, it was Indrajit.

"We don't have her!" he shrieked.

"Who's the beneficiary?" Fix yelled.

The knife poised ready to stab again, Choot hesitated. "What?"

"Who gets paid out under the risk-selling agreement?"

"Frozen hells," Indrajit groaned. "You couldn't say that earlier?" He saw his own blood spatter the floor.

"Who are you?" Choot asked Fix.

Fix was slow to answer. "I'm just a jobber," he finally said. "Holy-Pot explained to me how some of the contracts work."

"Old Two-Face would never do any such thing." Choot pressed the tip of her blade against Fix's sternum.

Despite his pain and giddiness, Indrajit chuckled. *"Old Two-Face.* That's good. Why didn't I think of that?"

"Because it's not one of your epithets," Fix muttered. "You're not a poet. You're not really a wordsmith at all, you've just memorized all the epithets and you lay them together to tell the same story, over and over again."

"I could make a new epithet," Indrajit said.

"You can?" Fix sounded skeptical.

"Yes. In fact, I *will*, just to show you."

"Two-Face would never have taught you anything. He was as stingy with information as he was with money. So I'd better hear a convincing explanation of who you are and what you're doing here in the next twenty seconds, or I'll kill you both."

"I'm a jobber," Fix said immediately. "No company, just solo work. And it doesn't pay much, but I picked up enough about risk-merchantry on the job to under-write a few off-registry contracts, myself."

"Foolish," Choot hissed. "But bold."

"Indrajit and I were hired by Holy-Pot to guard Ilsa, because Holy-Pot had repurchased some of the risk. We think from you. Someone has tried to kill her, but as far as we know, she's still alive. Someone has also tried to set me and Indrajit up to take the blame for her murder—Old Two-Face seems to have had it in for us, but he can't have done all this alone. We're trying to figure out who might be behind all this plot, so we thought you might be able to tell us who the beneficiary is under the risk-selling contract."

"Unless, of course," Indrajit said, "you're the one who wanted Ilsa dead. In which case, I guess Fiximon and I are doomed."

Choot backed away a step, looking at them both.

"You do think someone is trying to commit fraud," she said.

"We were told Thinkum Tosh took out the contract," Indrajit said. His head tingled. The pool of his blood on the ground was disturbingly large. "But we were wondering if maybe the benefactor—"

"*Beneficiary*," Fix said.

"—*beneficiary* might be Orem Thrush."

"You think Orem Thrush set you up," Choot said.

"Someone did." Indrajit felt woozy. "The Lord Chamberlain is definitely *interested* in the situation. We think he's the one who has jobbers watching the Paper Sook."

"Cut them down," Choot said to the doorman. "Bandage his leg."

Indrajit hit the floor hard. Then another period

of time passed during which he faded in and out of consciousness. He was moved to a reclining couch, such as something you might sit on at a fancy dinner party. The purple-scaled man bandaged his leg. When his vision finally recovered, Indrajit was sitting up, a warm and fragrant cup clutched in his hands.

"Is this coffee?" He took a sip. "Or rum?"

"Both." Choot and Fix and Indrajit each sat on a reclining couch, smiling at each other, like characters in some surreal and comical street bawdy. "It'll get you back on your feet."

Indrajit couldn't quite bring himself to say *thank you*, so he just sipped the hot drink. It didn't heal his leg wound or make his head stop spinning, but it felt good going down.

"I think we can work together," Choot said.

It would be nice to get paid again. Indrajit nodded. "Good."

"If you bring me Ilsa alive," the risk-merchant said, "or proof that she's still alive, I'll pay you fifty Imperials."

"Five hundred," Fix said.

The risk-merchant stared at the short jobber, but said nothing.

"Someone has already made a claim," Fix said. "Otherwise, you wouldn't be worried about this. And the policy has to be for thousands of Imperials."

"I could just turn you in to the Paper Sook instead," Choot pointed out.

Fix nodded. "And you could hire other jobbers to look for Ilsa. But those jobbers wouldn't know what we know, and wouldn't have the principals of the scam job—"

"If there is a scam job," Choot muttered.

"—looking for them."

"Three hundred Imperials," Choot said.

"Four hundred," Indrajit said, cutting in, "and you agree to . . . be our risk-merchant when we . . . incorporize . . . our jobber company."

Fix looked at him, nodded slowly, and grinned. "Underwrite our bond."

"Agreed." Frodilo Choot's voice was sour. "Yes, a claim has been made this morning."

"Doesn't the claimant have to prove Ilsa's death to be able to collect?" Fix asked.

"I received an affidavit this morning from a notary's office. Three witness statements, and I saw the body myself."

"Who were the witnesses?" Indrajit asked.

"The director of the Palace of Shadow and Joy and two actors all testified to finding her body."

"Not to seeing her death?" Indrajit pressed.

Choot shrugged. "It doesn't matter whether anyone saw her die. If she's dead, under the contract, I pay."

Indrajit wanted time to discuss alone with Fix. Frodilo Choot, it seemed to him, was a victim. Her money was being taken. But Gannon's Handlers, on the other hand . . .

"What made you hire Mote Gannon?" he asked.

"I needed a jobber company that knew the Palace," she said. "They worked security there last year when that Xiba'albi princess was visiting, and Holy-Pot recommended them."

"Holy-Pot recommended Mote Gannon?" Fix asked.

Choot shrugged and looked away. "Yes. But Gannon's got a track record, he's bonded. He was . . . acceptable."

"Did Holy-Pot also bring you the contract?" Indrajit asked.

She nodded. "Thinkum Tosh came to him, but he didn't have enough available reserves to underwrite the risk, so he brought it to me. I was on the fence myself, given how big the contract was, until he agreed to take on part of the risk as the repurchaser."

"How much are you on the hook for?" Fix asked.

Choot hesitated, but only for a moment. "One hundred thousand Imperials."

Indrajit resisted the temptation to revisit their agreement and ask for more money. This sum, he reminded himself, was an amount she would have to pay, not the profit she was earning. At least, that's what he thought he understood of these risk-merchantry contracts. "So, who is the beneficiary?" he asked. "Orem Thrush?"

She shook her head.

"If someone submitted affidavits in the name of Thinkum Tosh," Fix said, "they're fraudulent. He's dead."

"Is he?" Indrajit asked. "We never actually saw the body."

"The notary submitted the affidavits and the request for payment," Choot said. "On behalf of the estate of Thinkum Tosh, who is dead, and his heirs."

"If he's dead, who do you give the money to?" Indrajit asked.

"What do you think this is, the Caravanserai? Do you imagine that I go find a man in a white turban and give him the money in opals? I pay it into the bank account designated in the contract."

"You just instruct the bank to transfer the credits from your account to the one in the contract," Fix said.

"Of course," Choot said.

"Of course," Indrajit said, pretending to understand.

"Under the contract, I have until the open of business, day after tomorrow. If I don't pay or provide evidence to demonstrate that I have no obligation to make payment by then, the notary will sue."

"We can ask the bank who has the right to access that account," Fix suggested.

"We can ask the notary who he's talking to," Indrajit added.

"Neither one of them will tell you," Choot said. "Obligations of confidentiality."

"I wasn't really thinking of asking nicely," Fix growled.

"Can *you* get them to tell you?" Indrajit asked Choot.

"No," Choot said. "You might get a judge to order it, if you could prove an attempt at fraud. If one of the seven lords, if Orem Thrush, for instance, asked, they might do it."

"We also still need to ask the Handlers what they know," Indrajit said.

"They may not have obligations of confidentiality," Fix said, "but they have weapons. Should we leave that one for last?"

"I have Mote Gannon's home address," Choot said.

Fix nodded. "If you can give us that information, we can find him. I'll know him on sight."

"We can talk to him without his Handlers," Indrajit said.

"It's an apartment in the Crown," Choot said. "He might not be there during the day."

"Perfect," Indrajit said. "We go rattle cages at the bank and at the notary. Then in the evening, we have a private conversation with Mote Gannon. Surely, we'll have this cleaned up before tomorrow."

"Something else is happening tomorrow," Fix said. "Remind me what it is."

Indrajit shook his head. "You're thinking of the Auction. Nothing to do with us."

"Oh, yes."

"This is what comes of reading," Indrajit said. "Confusion."

Fix hesitated. "All of this amounts to an effort to figure out who wants Ilsa dead. Is that really the best thing we can do to try to locate her?"

Indrajit shrugged. "Do you have a better idea?"

Chapter Eighteen

~~~~~~~~~~

INDRAJIT TRIED NOT TO LIMP, WALKING OUT OF Choot's shop. He failed.

"Hey, I have an idea," he said. "Frodilo Choot has already agreed to be our risk-merchant. What was it you called it before?"

"She will post our bond." Fix marched toward the notary's office; he had scratched the address down in his fascicle. "So if our jobber company does anything like, say, drop heavy scenery on top of a crowd of footlings at the opera, or, I don't know, accidentally kill a Zalapting with lots of angry relatives, there's money to pay for the damages."

"The bond, right. So we're halfway there!" Indrajit declared. "And we're on our way to visit a notary, so maybe he'll help us draw up the . . . whatever the notary thing was that you said."

"Organization papers," Fix said. "Our charter. Create our joint-stock company or our partnership. I don't know how jobber companies are organized, actually."

"Right. So this guy can tell us, and then we're in business."

"Keep that in mind as a negotiating ask, then."

"Now all we need is a name."

"And more jobbers. And customers. And marketing."

"Yeah, yeah. In time. I was thinking, what about the *Deep Thinkers*?"

"Sounds like a jobber company that does archival research."

"You don't like it?"

"Or maybe a street bawdy company that only performs parodies of street bawdy, for the benefit of the overeducated elite who pretend to be sneering at street bawdy, when in fact they secretly enjoy it, especially for the naughty parts."

"You hate the name."

Fix shrugged. "Keep thinking of other names."

"But in principle, you're willing to be my partner."

"In principle, I am your partner right now. In fact, I am no expert in charter law, but I believe that since we are no longer employed by Holy-Pot Diaphernes—"

"He being dead," Indrajit interjected.

"—but are jointly undertaking an enterprise with a view to making a profit—"

"Getting four hundred Imperials from Frodilo Choot," Indrajit elaborated.

"—we are partners as of right now."

"Doesn't it feel good?" Indrajit asked.

"Mind you, I could be mistaken," Fix said. "Charter law is definitely regarded as useful knowledge by the Selfless, and therefore disdained."

"We should celebrate!"

"Agreed. Once we have the four hundred Imperials in our pockets, we'll get a drink."

"Another steam bath. With the spiced oils and the massage, this time."

"If we're going to be partners, you're going to have to learn to stick to a budget." Fix stopped. "Here's the notary."

The notary's building was four stories tall, squeezed shoulder to shoulder between two shorter, wider buildings. The flanking buildings were of brick, with canvas awnings extending their premises over the packed earth, but the notary's building stopped sharply at the street and was made of plaster and wood, the plaster painted bright yellow.

"This is without a doubt the ugliest building in the Paper Sook," Indrajit said. "It might be the ugliest building in the entire Spill."

"Banks and risk-merchants want to convince you that they are *enduring*, that they'll be as long as the temples and then some," Fix said. "Lawyers and accountants want to convince you that they're *frugal*."

Indrajit opened the front door, noting that it was anything but cheap. The yetz-wood slab was six inches thick and hard as rock—a direct hit from a ballista bolt might not pierce it.

Behind the door was a waiting room with three divans and a man with skin blue as the sky, standing in front of a steep staircase leading up. He wore gold pantaloons and his bare chest was covered with swirling tattoos reminiscent of waves, and within the waves swam porpoises and orcas. Indrajit wasn't entirely sure, but he dimly thought the man might be of a race native to the Paper Sultanates.

The blue man bowed at the waist. "Is the advocate expecting you?"

"I thought he was a notary," Indrajit said.

"Our master is both," the blue man said. "*Advocate* is the senior title."

"You mean the more *expensive* title," Indrajit quipped.

The blue man smiled.

"The advocate is not expecting us," Fix said. "But he'll see us. We come on behalf of the risk-merchant Frodilo Choot."

"We know the name. One moment." The blue man turned and slipped upstairs.

"Careful," Indrajit whispered to his partner. "He said *we*. The other guy is probably invisible."

"You might not be wrong," Fix whispered back.

The blue man returned, his step brisk. "The advocate will see you."

They climbed the steps, leaving the blue man behind. "That was easy," Indrajit murmured.

"He *has* to see us," Fix said. "We might be bringing money, or some kind of response relating to his request for payment. If he turns us away, he's not zealously representing his client."

"What a strange view of the world you must have."

The stairs were narrow and steep. At the top of the flight they made a one hundred eighty degree turn and climbed back the other way. At the top of the steps stood another yetz-wood door, this one hanging open. Behind the door was an office. Inside, a Wixit stood behind a broad desk and manipulated papers, a clay pipe clamped in its teeth. Shelves climbing around the walls were heavy with scrolls and codices, and a table took up most of the free floorspace, groaning under stacks of paper and pots of ink.

To one side, stairs climbed up again.

The Wixit sucked at its pipe, exhaled a blue cloud, and then smiled, showing all its teeth. "You've come from Choot. About our notice of a claim, et cetera?"

Indrajit blinked. "Your servant referred to himself as *we*, too. Do you both mean you two together? Are you a team?"

The Wixit barked, a sound close to laughter. "When *I* say *we*, I am referring to myself and my client. When little Dromit says *we*, he does so because his people believe they have a collective mind. In their own language, as a result, they *can* only refer to themselves as we."

Indrajit was amused to hear the Wixit, who was the size of a small dog, refer to the blue-skinned man as *little Dromit*, but he managed not to laugh.

"You say they *believe* they have a collective mentality?" Fix pressed.

The Wixit exhaled another cloud. "They believe it, but they're mistaken. His people are idiots. Are you going to contest the claim? Or, for the avoidance of doubt, is Frodilo Choot, in her capacity as risk-purchaser, going to contest my client's rightful claim for reimbursement, et cetera?"

"We're happy to pay," Indrajit said. "We just need to understand who's receiving the money."

"No, you don't." The advocate smiled toothily again.

"The . . . beneficiary . . . was Thinkum Tosh, who is deceased." Indrajit still struggled with the new vocabulary. "We would like to be certain that the correct person is being paid."

"Tosh's legal heir," Fix clarified.

"Fortunately for you and for my friend Frodilo Choot, you need to know no such thing." The Wixit sucked on its pipe and paced back and forth along its desk for a moment, as if collecting its thoughts. "Since you have not apparently read the notice, and are apparently not familiar with the terms of the contract, I will spell it out for you: under the contract, because Ilsa without Peer died—a fact attested by the contractually and legally sufficient number of three witnesses—Frodilo Choot is obligated to pay into the destination account. Ownership of that account is not a relevant term of the contract. Et cetera."

The slippery concepts tumbled about in Indrajit's conception. "You're saying she has to pay, no matter who gets the money."

The Wixit bowed. "Those are the terms of the contract."

"And whom do you represent?" Fix asked.

"My client." The Wixit smiled.

Indrajit fumbled, and found he had nothing more to say. Could they seize the advocate and physically shake the information out of him?

"I detect in this awkward message of yours," the advocate said, "the preliminaries to an attempt by Frodilo Choot to avoid her obligations under the risk-purchasing contract by challenging my client's standing. Please tell her that if she tries to resist us in court, I will not only have the amount of the claim, I will have damages for malfeasance, my client's costs—my fees are steep, I assure you—and a censure from the Paper Sook. I'll have her license to purchase, resell, and repurchase risk taken away. Et cetera."

Indrajit heard a footfall. Turning, he saw a muscled, bronze-skinned man standing on the bottom step of the flight of stairs leading up. He held a heavy crossbow in his hands, aimed at Indrajit. The weapon was cocked, the steel head of the bolt grinning evilly.

If Indrajit were shot, Fix would certainly be able to defeat the crossbowman, and probably shake the information they wanted out of the Wixit advocate.

But Indrajit would be dead.

"Thank you very much." Indrajit smiled politely. "We'll show ourselves out."

They descended the stairs in silence. The man with sky-blue skin and tattoos like the ocean bowed as he ushered them out the front door.

"That was less successful than I had hoped," Indrajit commented, stretching his back and twisting his neck until he felt the bones pop.

A black-and-orange hurricane crashed past him. The sudden apparition hurtled toward Fix, and if it had been aiming at Indrajit, it would have flattened him.

Fix, though, had faster reflexes. Shifting his weight onto his back foot and pivoting on his forward heel, he brought his spear up in front of him. The orange and obsidian meteorite altered its course at the last second, avoiding being impaled and slamming instead into the advocate-notary's door.

Yashta Hossarian. And behind him came a ring of Zalaptings.

"Run!" Fix yelled. He hurled himself at the wall of lavender and broke through. Indrajit followed; the wounds in his legs screamed, and he ignored them. With his longer legs, he was quickly at his partner's shoulder.

The lavender men pursued, but their short, bow-legged gait was no match for the long, loping stride of the Recital Thane or for Fix's tremendous energy.

It took Indrajit and Fix three turns to get into the main square of the Paper Sook, thick with the press of buying and selling. As Indrajit lowered his head to plunge into the crowd of merchants, he heard the scratching of talons on hard earth behind him, and, farther away, the shouting of Zalaptings.

Yashta Hossarian had caught up.

"This way!" Fix plucked at Indrajit's tunic, pulling the poet to the right, under an awning. Tall shelving and stacks of scrolls flashed through Indrajit's peripheral vision on both sides, and Fix kicked at the base of a wall of shelves, pulling it down behind them. Scrolls bounced off Indrajit's shoulders and fell behind him into his wake.

Offended merchants roared.

At the back of the shop—whatever it was—Fix ducked into a split in the canvas. Indrajit followed, and found himself in an alley barely wider than his shoulders. Fix, shorter than Indrajit but also wider, ran with his shoulders twisted diagonally, one shoulder thrust forward as if he aimed to tackle someone.

Indrajit smelled roasting fowl, and suddenly felt hungry.

Fix dodged left, down a different alley, and scrambled up a stack of crates and barrels, piled neatly on the packed earth and roped together for stability. Indrajit followed, reaching a flat, orange-tiled rectangular rooftop. Fix threw himself onto his belly and slunk to the edge of the roof, peering down into one of the alleys below.

Behind them, the shouts of outrage faded, and the dull rumble of buying and selling in the Paper Sook came to drown them out.

"We may have lost them," Fix whispered. "That was Yashta Hossarian and his company. What on earth would they want with us?"

"I told you, they're hired by Holy-Pot."

"Holy-Pot's dead."

"But they don't know that. Or if they do, maybe the fact that he's dead has sent them coming after us." Indrajit shrugged. "Maybe they think we killed him and robbed him, and they want to beat their pay out of us."

Fix's gaze jumped to a spot behind Indrajit, and he sprang to his feet, drawing his falchion.

"Frozen hells." Indrajit turned, arming himself with the leaf-bladed sword.

Two Zalaptings stepped onto the rooftop from the crate- and barrel-made stairs. They held their spears low and glared.

Fix freed the hatchet from his belt with his left hand.

Then two more Zalaptings climbed up, and two more again.

"Three to one," Indrajit observed to his partner. "We have longer reach, but their spears cancel that out. We're probably stronger."

"Still bad odds," Fix murmured. "On the count of three, turn back and run. We'll jump across the alley. They'll never be able to follow."

"I'm not the *best* jumper," Indrajit said.

"One," Fix said. "Two."

Indrajit heard the heavy *whumph* of something hitting the rooftop behind him, and then Yashta

Hossarian's voice. "If you try running again, I shall have to kill you."

Fix didn't count three.

Indrajit turned slowly. Hossarian prowled along the edge of the rooftop, anger flashing in his obsidian-colored face, antennae waving frenetically. Fix kept his back to the bird-legged jobber, facing the Zalaptings, and adjusted his grip on his weapons.

"If you hadn't attacked us," Indrajit said, "we'd never have run. Aren't we friends, Hossarian?"

"Where is Ilsa without Peer?" Hossarian asked.

What did Hossarian want?

What did he know?

"Dead," Indrajit said. "Signed witness statements and all. And so is Holy-Pot. And if you're looking to get paid, we can't help you. Whoever killed that two-faced bastard robbed us of our own payday."

"She isn't dead," Hossarian rumbled, "and you know it."

Indrajit sighed. "I know surprisingly little. But I saw a corpse that looked like Ilsa's. And I saw another that I'm pretty sure was Holy-Pot's."

"Where are you hiding her?" Hossarian raised one birdlike leg, beckoning to Indrajit as if he could coax some answer from him.

"I'm not hiding her. I'm looking for her, because she might be alive. What are you doing?"

"What I do best," Yashta Hossarian purred. "Killing."

"You won't be killing anyone today." The voice was new to the conversation, but Indrajit recognized the accents of the Lord Chamberlain's intelligence agent Grit Wopal.

Chapter Nineteen

"HA HA." INDRAJIT GRINNED AT THE BIRD-LEGGED jobber, trying not to think about Hossarian's general resemblance to a tiger. "Help has arrived!" He had no idea whether Grit Wopal had come to help or hurt him, but he was encouraged at the declaration that seemed to forbid Hossarian from killing Indrajit.

"He's alone," Fix said.

"I see." Indrajit shifted his grip on the hilt of his sword and prepared to die.

"Oh, I'm never alone," Wopal said. Indrajit heard the soft padding of sandals on baked clay and then the Yifft joined him, standing at his side and facing the orange-and-black jobber. Still wearing only a dirty yellow tunic and loincloth, the man looked defenseless.

"If you're seeing some reinforcements in your third eye, Yifft, you might want to go to an apothecary and get your vision checked." Hossarian had a sneer on his face and in his voice, but he spoke with slight hesitation. Doubt?

"Wherever I go, I am cloaked in the authority of the Lord Chamberlain." The Yifft smiled blandly. "Are you prepared to provoke the wrath of Orem Thrush?"

"Thrush doesn't own these men," Hossarian barked.

"You aren't *after* these men. You're after Ilsa without Peer." Wopal spread his hands, a peaceful gesture. "However much you've been promised for her death, you need to stop now."

Yashta Hossarian took one step forward. "I've been promised a lot."

"Then let me make a counteroffer. Your life, spared, if you leave this instant."

Indrajit looked about. Were there archers hidden on one of the adjacent rooftops, and he just hadn't noticed them? But no, Grit Wopal appeared to be alone.

Yashta Hossarian lowered his head. It was an ambiguous gesture that might be a submissive bow, or might be a shoulder lowered in preparation for charging. Wopal stood still, unruffled.

As if finally coming to a decision, Hossarian stepped back to the edge of the rooftop. "I concede nothing." He stepped off the tile and dropped out of view.

Indrajit turned to find the Zalaptings filing away, dropping down onto the stack of crates and barrels and trooping out of sight.

"You made that guy nervous," Indrajit said.

Grit Wopal laughed, a sound that was bell-like, and seemed to ring straight from his gut. "If Orem Thrush threatened to murder you if you *punch* me, Indrajit Twang, what do you think he would do if that jobber actually *killed* me?"

"What's Hossarian doing mixed up in all this?" Fix asked again.

"I'm not entirely sure," Wopal said mildly. "Are you familiar with the concept of a dead man's switch?"

Fix frowned and looked away, as if consulting his memory. "I think it's where a man arranges for something to be triggered by his death."

"Correct. I believe Yashta Hossarian is responding to a dead man's switch, set by Holy-Pot Diaphernes."

Indrajit whistled. "You mean, that guy hated me so much, he paid Hossarian to kill me in the event that he died."

"No, if Hossarian had been paid to kill you, he'd have killed you in the Paper Sook. He wanted to capture you."

"Hossarian isn't after us," Fix said. "He told us so himself. He's after Ilsa."

Indrajit's head hurt. "He would do that, why? Because he didn't want to pay out under the risk-repurchasing contract? Am I thinking of that correctly?"

"Maybe," Fix said.

"But why would he care?" Indrajit asked. "Because he has heirs? So he pays Hossarian and says, if I die, rescue Ilsa without Peer, and then you'll get a bonus payment, for protecting my heirs' money."

Fix pulled at his chin thoughtfully. "I guess so."

"Frodilo Choot is on the hook for a hundred thousand Imperials if Ilsa's dead," Indrajit said. "How much of that risk did Holy-Pot buy? If it was even a tenth, then there's plenty of incentive and plenty of money to pay Hossarian. To set up a dead lever."

"A dead man's switch." Grit Wopal coughed politely. "I, on the other hand, am here to offer *you* money."

Indrajit laughed. "If you'd said that in the first place, Wopal, I never would have punched you."

The Yifft ignored the jibe. "It will likely not surprise you to learn that my master, the Lord Chamberlain, is interested in the return to him of Ilsa without Peer."

Indrajit saw where the conversation was headed and tried to do some fast calculation. He no longer worked for Holy-Pot Diaphernes; he was chasing a bounty offered by Frodilo Choot. He would get the bounty if Ilsa lived.

Maybe, if Orem Thrush didn't want to kill her, he could get paid twice.

Or if Thrush offered a bigger bounty for her dead... Indrajit shook his head. He didn't think he could bring himself to kill her. He certainly didn't want to *be* that kind of jobber.

"I don't know if I can do that," he said.

"What does the Lord Chamberlain want with her?" Fix asked.

Had the shorter man done the same calculation Indrajit had?

The Yifft inclined his head in a nod of respect. "You worry whether the Lord Chamberlain wishes to kill Ilsa. He does not. Of all actors on this stage, he is the one with the strongest interest in keeping Ilsa without Peer alive."

Could that be true?

Indrajit elbowed Fix. "Actors on this stage, see? Like you were saying, Kish is the world is the Palace of Shadow and Joy."

Grit Wopal's brow furrowed, but he stifled whatever questions he had. "The Lord Chamberlain has such a strong interest in keeping Ilsa without Peer alive, that he will give you one thousand Imperials for her return. Since you will also be able to collect from the risk-merchant Choot, that should come to quite a tidy sum."

Indrajit almost asked how Wopal knew they had talked to Choot, but he stopped himself. Of course, the Yifft was following them, or having them followed. Maybe the jobbers in orange kilts answered to him. Maybe the jobbers had followed them into Choot's shop and interrogated her.

If so, he hoped they had been rough on her doorman.

"The promise of a thousand Imperials doesn't exactly guarantee that Thrush wants the singer alive," Fix pointed out. "Maybe he wants her dead so badly, he's willing to pay that much."

"To collect the thousand Imperials," Wopal said, continuing as if he hadn't heard Fix's objection, "you must bring Ilsa to the Lord Chamberlain's palace by dawn tomorrow."

Indrajit shot a look up at the sun. He made it to be early afternoon.

"A thousand Imperials certainly sounds nice," he said.

"We could use some resources," Fix said.

"A thousand Imperials will buy lots of resources," Wopal agreed.

"No," Fix said, "I mean now. The Lord Chamberlain wants his singer back, because he doesn't want to lose the revenue, or he wants to keep supporting the opera house, or whatever. Fine. But you're asking the two least-well-equipped jobbers in Kish to do the job. I mean, we don't have horses. We don't have armor. We haven't even eaten in a day. Or maybe two."

"Pretty sure it's two," Indrajit said. "Feels like a week."

"You may not be well-equipped," Wopal said, "but

you're uniquely well-positioned. And still, you shouldn't assume that you're the only jobbers the Lord Chamberlain has set to the task."

"We've seen the orange tunics," Indrajit said.

"I'm glad the Lord Chamberlain values our position," Fix said. "So maybe you could open those purse strings and give us a little cash."

The Yifft bowed slightly. "I could advance you a little cash."

"No, no advance," Indrajit said. "And no loan. Just cash, no strings attached. Call it a *retainer* if you need to feel official, but give us fifty Imperials now." It was an insane request, and more money than Indrajit had ever held in his hand, but he knew he wouldn't get what he didn't ask for.

"Fifty Imperials." Grit Wopal smiled. "I am willing to give you that, to equip you to serve our master. But you must understand that when you ask for no strings attached, you are talking complete nonsense. When the Lord Chamberlain is involved, there are always strings attached. He might as well write *strings attached* beneath the family crest of House Thrush."

"The horned skull." Fix didn't smile.

"The horned skull." Wopal didn't smile, either. He handed fifty Imperials to Indrajit, then walked to the staircase of crates and barrels and disappeared.

Indrajit gave the Yifft a minute to get entirely out of earshot, then whistled a low note of appreciation. "That was bold."

Fix shrugged. "I took my inspiration from you. If you could ask Choot to put up our bond, bold as brass, I could ask to get paid."

"Too bad we couldn't get the lawyer on our side, too."

"The thing about lawyers is they work for money. If we went back and paid him these fifty Imperials right now, he would draw up and post our charter, no problem."

"Maybe we should," Indrajit said.

"No." Fix tapped his chest. "This thing isn't over, and every time we turn around, we get attacked by someone new. We need to get armor."

"That's pretty time-consuming, isn't it?" Indrajit asked. "The smith has to fit you, and then hammer out a breastplate the right size. We have until tomorrow morning to find Ilsa."

"You're imagining metal, and maybe we could get greaves and vambraces for our arms and legs. But I was thinking linothorax and a studded leather skirt."

"I'm not sure I get the idea of linothorax," Indrajit said.

"Because your people don't wear armor?"

"We are a peaceful folk, living lives of joy and harmony." Indrajit smiled. "But isn't linothorax just made of linen? I mean, does wearing a second tunic really give all that much protection?"

"It's multiple layers of linen, with rabbit glue between them. It's protective and it's light. Which is probably necessary, given all the climbing we've been doing so far. We may need to run and jump and dodge before tomorrow morning."

"I'm not such a good jumper. Let's stick to climbing."

"Also, you can buy the linothorax in a standard shape. Like a tube. You squeeze into it, and then the heat of your body and your sweat make the armor soften up and reshape itself to your body."

"Very nice for you," Indrajit said. "Yours will look

all muscular. Mine will look like the torso of a thin-armed man, with a bit of a belly."

"Just a bit," Fix said.

"I like to think it's dignified. That doesn't mean I want to wrap my belly in form-fitting armor."

"You're a handsome man, especially for someone who looks so much like a fish. But for our purposes, it means we can buy armor off the rack and wear it immediately."

"Can we buy it in the Paper Sook?" Indrajit looked out over the rooftops, realizing that Yashta Hossarian and his Zalaptings could be hiding around any one of a thousand corners. He really didn't want to have to jump across the rooftops.

"We're at the edge of the sook," Fix said, "and there's an armorer a block from here."

They climbed down—just in case, they chose the side of the building opposite the staircase of crates and barrels, dropping first to a sturdy canvas awning and then to the ground. Fix was correct about the location of the armorer, and within twenty minutes both men were wearing undyed linothorax of a tawny yellow-gray color and studded leather skirts over their tunics and kilts. In addition, Fix replaced his spear, and Indrajit got an actual scabbard and sword belt for his leaf-bladed weapon.

Fix got a helmet, steel and plain, with an open face. Indrajit tried on a matching helmet and found it blocked far too much of his field of vision. When he put it back on the shelf and counted out coins for the armorer, a burly man with a third arm sprouting from his side just below his left arm, he found Fix pursing his lips and making a fish face at him.

"I will concede," Indrajit said, "that in this one respect, I am somewhat fish*like*."

Fix shrugged. "It's no big deal. I am very much like a monkey, a fact about which I feel not the slightest sense of outrage."

"Do you have a tail?" Indrajit was curious. "Or are you like a monkey in the sense in which all men are like monkeys, meaning, in general shape, number of limbs, and so on?"

"If you are asking to look up my kilt, Indrajit Twang, the answer is no. We're not partners yet."

"I have sudden second thoughts about this partnership."

They wound back into the sook; Indrajit felt reassured by the weight of the armor on his shoulders and his hips. Fix led them to the second address Frodilo Choot had given them, which was the bank.

The building was made of marble, and did indeed look like a temple from the outside. The blocky, gleaming white building had only two visible doors, both guarded by a pair of spearmen; one door was an entrance and the other was an exit. There was writing in bannerscript, painted onto the marble to either side of the entrance.

"What's that say?" Indrajit whispered to his companion.

"Goldsmiths United Depository," Fix whispered back. "It's the name of the bank."

Indrajit nodded to the burly Kishi spearmen at the entrance, expecting them to demand his weapons. They didn't. Entering, he found himself in a narrow hall that turned immediately right and jogged directly to the exit. The internal walls were made of marble, too, and everywhere he looked he saw trim made of polished brass. On his left were windows, barred with steel bars, and behind them sat clerks. From where he stood, he could see the presence of the clerks, but no details of their faces. Over each clerk, and facing Indrajit and Fix, hung a number. Standing at each window was a Kishi—most dressed in face-concealing scarves or cloaks with hoods or other garments that tended to hide the identity of the wearer—doing business with the clerk.

One of the customers stepped away, and a voice from an unseen speaker called out, "Number three!"

Indrajit strolled uneasily to the third window. "Have you ever used a bank before?" he whispered.

Fix nodded. "I have my savings in a bank."

"That seems . . . elaborate."

"I find if I have my money physically out of reach, I'm less inclined to spend it in every tavern I enter."

"I find that the taverns I enter are more than happy to extend credit when I ask. And I don't even have money in the bank to reassure them."

The bank clerk was a person of indeterminate sex, with gray skin and all the features and personality of a pole. The clerk sat inside a cubicle with charcoal and paper on a desk, and behind it there was a plain door in the wall.

"Account number," the clerk said.

Fix consulted his fascicle and read the account number, which they'd been given by Choot. The clerk took note.

"Password," the clerk said.

Frodilo Choot had given them no password. Likely, she didn't have it, since all she had to do was make a deposit in this account. Fix looked at Indrajit and raised his eyebrows.

Could they guess? Maybe if they knew whose account this was, but since they didn't, the field of possibilities was wide open.

Without a password, the clerk wasn't going to let them in.

If they admitted they didn't have the password, wouldn't it look like an admission that they were trying to steal someone else's account?

"Epic Fish Eyes," Indrajit said.

The clerk made a note.

"What transaction?" the clerk asked.

"Check the balance," Fix said.

The clerk swayed forward, a motion resembling the movement of a palm tree in a spring storm, and left by the door.

"I didn't really think this through," Fix said. "We can't very well pretend to be the account holder and then ask who the account holder is."

"So what are you thinking, then? If we know the account balance, you think we'll better be able to guess whose money it is?"

"It doesn't matter. The clerk is going to check, find we have the wrong password, and alert the guards," Fix said. "We have no chance of getting any information this way."

"I reached the same conclusion the minute she or he asked for a password," Indrajit said. "Let's go." He started walking.

"Number three!" the unseen announcer called out.

Indrajit kept his pace to a casual stroll and pasted a bland smile to his face. He nodded at the guards at the exit, stepped into the Paper Sook beyond, and did his very best to disappear into the crowd.

Once they'd turned a corner and were out of sight, they stopped.

"If you know banks so well, you could have warned me it would be like that," Indrajit said.

Fix shrugged. "You're so quick to talk your way through things, I thought maybe you'd be able to do it with the bank clerk, too."

Indrajit sighed. "Well, I can't fault you for confidence in your partner. What if we ... I don't know, maybe we could follow the bankers home after dark, and force one of them to let us back in. If we just look up the account information, it isn't even really a robbery, is it?"

"I'd assume it's some kind of crime," Fix said. "Misappropriation of knowledge, or something like that. But in any case, the bankers enter and leave by secret tunnels, with bodyguards."

"I guess having a bank account yourself doesn't entitle you to know where the secret passages are?"

Fix shook his head, unnecessarily.

"Probably they go down through the sewers and the old city layers," Indrajit mused. "We could go back to Choot's and ask her to let us down there, poke around."

"Bit of a long shot, isn't it? Especially since we only have until tomorrow morning. Besides, what are we going to do? Knock on every door we find and ask if we've come to the bank?"

Indrajit was grateful for the resistance to his suggestions. He didn't really want to carry out a burglary. "The deadline tomorrow morning is just to get Orem

Thrush's bonus pay," Indrajit said. "Mind you, I *do* want to get that bonus pay. Okay, I think that means our last best lead is to go lean on Mote Gannon, find out why Holy-Pot chose him, how he knows my name, and anything else he can tell us about the plan to kill Ilsa without Peer."

"Or kidnap," Fix added. "Kill or kidnap."

Chapter Twenty

~~~~~~~~

"I DON'T ACTUALLY WANT TO BEAT PEOPLE UP,"
Indrajit said. "I mean, if someone deserves it, fine.
If I need to hurt someone to protect myself, fine. If
someone attacks me, then he has it coming. But I
don't want to hurt people for money."

"We don't have to take jobs like that," Fix said.
"Like collection."

"Could we have the notary write that into our charter? That we just do, I don't know, romantic rescues?"

"I don't think that's a recognized category in the
Auction."

"We could do it privately. For wealthy and deserving
patrons who are star-crossed in love."

"That feels like a small market. Maybe, in addition
to that, we also make ourselves available for Auction
work."

"Maybe we should go listen to an Auction and find
out what the categories are. When is it, tomorrow? Do
they let just anyone in? Or maybe there's a fascicle

somewhere, where you can read the list of contracts that are available."

"They won't let us in," Fix said. "The Auction House is always heavily guarded, but especially during the Auction. I think the heads of the seven families go in person. And I don't know all the contract types, but that's fine—the way to get Auction work is to be known to the seven families. Or their ministers. People like Thinkum Tosh, I suppose."

"And Grit Wopal?"

"Maybe. And we shouldn't have to take any job we don't want to. We can avoid collections. Including tax collection, I guess?"

"Unless the collection is from a bad person, and we're collecting on behalf of someone who is really needy and worthy." Indrajit listened to his own words for a moment. "I guess that's probably silly."

"You did collections for Holy-Pot, didn't you? How did you do it?"

"Badly. The guy didn't have enough money, but I let him off without breaking his legs anyway. And then I felt bad about it, so to console myself I went drinking. And I was hungry, so there was no way I was ever going to be able to resist that roasted fowl. And there were dice being thrown, and of course that seemed like a great idea. I think maybe, in my drunken state, I thought I could win the difference between what the man had given me and what he really owed. Pay his debt myself, out of my gambling winnings. And that's how I spent all the money I *had* collected."

"Which is why Holy-Pot wanted you dead. Or at least was willing to see you killed. No collections," Fix said. "No assassinations or kidnappings."

"Wait, are those even options?"

"Not legal options," Fix said. "But once you start running everything in your city by small companies of armed men, some of those companies are going to get put to nefarious uses. If not by the seven families, then by others. Not all murders in Kish are committed by the House of Knives."

"No assassinations or kidnappings," Indrajit agreed.

"Exceptions only as unanimously agreed between the two partners."

"Right. And no else gets a vote. They can always leave if they want, but you and I decide what jobs we take."

"And I think there's a whole class of other, similar jobs we can rule right out as a matter of course. Arsons, intimidation, burglary. We're going to be strictly on-the-books jobbers."

"I don't know about that," Indrajit said. "But let's be heroes. If we're going to agree to break the law, let's try to do it for a noble purpose."

"That might be a good name for a company," Fix said. "The *Heroes*."

"Hmm. Not totally convinced, but not repulsed, either. I feel like you're close."

"So, what's our noble purpose here?"

"Isn't it obvious?" Indrajit felt genuinely surprised. "Save Ilsa. Stop whatever wicked plan is behind all this mayhem."

Fix was quiet for a moment. They passed from the Spill up into the Crown. "You're thinking about how you'll be written into the Epic, aren't you?"

"Of course, I am. One of my responsibilities is to find and teach a successor. But another is to bring the

Epic down an additional generation. That is to say, to my grandfather's generation. Necessarily, especially in recent centuries, a central figure of each generation's account is the Recital Thane who trained the predecessor of the composing Recital Thane."

"Did it used to be different?"

"Anciently, according to the Epic itself, everyone knew the Epic by heart. It was the curriculum of my people's education, our sacred text, our principal guide in peace and in war. The central figures of those times were noblemen, high priests, and war leaders. But we became fewer, the world became more complex, and the Epic became the preserve of the Recital Thanes."

"So, the person trained by *your* student will eventually write about *you*, and you want to be the noble hero."

"Also, being the noble hero is the right thing to do."

"Yeah." Fix stared off into the deep afternoon shadow piling up on the east side of a gambling hall. "Being the noble hero sounds like a good idea."

"The ladies like it," Indrajit said.

"Do they?" Indrajit thought Fix's expression brightened, but only a tiny bit and only for a moment.

"Speaking of ladies," Indrajit continued, "how exactly do you think our employer—"

"Client," Fix said.

"What?"

"Employees have employers. We are an independent partnership, and we are engaged by clients."

"I don't see the difference," Indrajit admitted, "but I'm happy to learn and adopt the language of the professionals. How do you think our employer has Mote Gannon's home address?"

"I assumed they were once lovers," Fix said. "But

that's probably that, being an aspiring lover myself, I tend to see lovers in everyone around me."

"Maybe that's why the best she could say about him was that he was bonded and acceptable," Indrajit suggested.

Fix nodded.

"If you are wondering," Indrajit said, "I am not anyone's lover."

"No," Fix agreed. "That seemed obvious enough."

"Hey!"

"I didn't say it was *impossible* for you to have a lover." Fix shrugged. "It just seems pretty clear that you don't at this time."

"I haven't met any Blaatshi women here."

Fix nodded. "Many men have not been held back by a similar limitation. But in any case, I suggest that you refrain from asking Mote Gannon whether he was Frodilo Choot's lover."

"I guess you also think I shouldn't ask him whether Frodilo Choot is a man?"

"Correct. As a former Trivial, I believe I can definitively assert that that is useless information."

"Fine." Indrajit shook his head. "So there's no registry of jobber company captains? Maybe Choot just looked his address up in a book?"

"There is a registry, according to the Auction House notices. But the registry can't contain captains' home addresses, for exactly the reason that jobber captains do not want surprise visitors. No one wants surprise visitors, perhaps, but jobber captains, accumulating enemies as they successfully serve clients and as they fail to serve clients, are more likely than others to be accosted by unexpected visitors with hostile intent."

"First of all," Indrajit said, "there are too many registries."

"You were the one who asked the question."

"I know, but still. Why are there so many registries?"

"Before the great families can tax or control anything, they must have it all written down, so they know who to go after and how much to take."

"And writing facilitates this." Indrajit tsked and shook his head. "You see? Not only does writing render the mind feeble, it also enables great wickedness in government."

"Or great efficiency." Fix shrugged. "A state that writes nothing down builds no sewers or great walls and cannot field an army."

"That all sounds fine to me," Indrajit said. "But second, implicit in what you are saying is the likelihood that Mote Gannon, even in his home, will be tough. This is no simple extraction of a sea snail; *poke* and you pull him out. No, Mote is likely to be deeply sunk into a thick, horny shell, with strong, sharp claws to protect him—"

"He will have armed guards," Fix said. "Do you feel at peace with the idea of physically assaulting Mote Gannon?"

Indrajit considered. "Morally, yes. His men knew my name and wanted to kill me. He is clearly in on the plan to set me up, and also to set up my partner, the learned scholar Fiximon Nasoprominentus Fascicular. But as a matter of physical risk, it may be wiser to try another tack."

"Of course." Fix nodded with his head. "This is his building, right here. Keep walking and look casual."

They strolled past.

The building where Mote Gannon lived looked like the palace of some lordly family, four dizzying stories tall, with windows and iron-balustraded balconies starting on the second floor. At the four corners, towers rose an additional two stories; their windows suggested that the towers also contained residential apartments.

A gate wide and tall enough for a carriage opened over a short lane paved with cobblestones. Within the gateway stood two guards. A window in the wall of the gateway arch suggested the presence of a guardhouse, and possibly more security.

Without turning his head, Indrajit's wide vision allowed him to see into the cool, shaded depths of a courtyard beyond, thick with ferns and littered with marble benches and statues. He also caught a glimpse of a walkway at the second story, from which doors entered into individual apartments and onto which windows opened. The whole thing was covered with a coral-pink plaster, bricks peeping out here and there where the plaster had been knocked away.

They passed the end of the building and kept walking.

"All things considered," Indrajit said, "nicer than the places where I've been staying."

"Me too."

"But you have money."

"I have money *because* I haven't been spending it on nice places to sleep. There is wisdom for you in this very point, O Recital Thane, if you are willing to let your mind dwell upon it."

They turned and walked around the block in which the apartment building sat. "Climbing seems tricky," Indrajit said, "notwithstanding our delightfully light armor. Do you think we're too heavily armored to claim to be messengers?"

"It might get awkward."

"Well, we have the one Handler tunic."

Fix looked startled. "What Handler tunic?"

"I took it from the Zalapting. The guy who went poking into the latrine. I have the two orange tunics too."

"*I* might fit into a Zalapting tunic," Fix said thoughtfully. "The height is about right, and if the tunic is baggy enough, I could squeeze in."

"A few torn seams will probably escape casual notice," Indrajit said. "If you're slightly too big."

"Do I say you're a messenger?" Fix asked.

Indrajit thought about it. "Say nothing unless asked. Then glower rather than explain yourself. And if anyone's really interested, say I lost my tunic."

"That's the plan, then."

In the mouth of a dark alley behind a wooden puppet stage, Fix shrugged into the gray Handler tunic, making a face at the lingering smell. Then they hiked back around to the front of the block and walked into the gateway.

The two guards standing in the gate stepped forward to challenge them. They were dressed lightly, with leather jerkins under dusty tunics and kilts. On his tunic, each man had the circular glyph of Gannon's Handlers. Each held a club in his hand, and at their belts they had swords.

One of them stepped forward, pointing at Fix's tunic. Oops.

"They're Handlers," Indrajit murmured. "Forget the plan."

Indrajit admired the instant flexibility of Fix's

reaction. Leaping forward as if fired out of a crossbow, the former Trivial slammed his steel-encased forehead into the bridge of the first Handler's nose. The man crumpled, bounced once on the cobblestones, and lay still. As the second man raised his arm to swing his club, Fix grabbed the raised arm by the elbow, snapping the elbow forward in a direction it was not designed to go. At the same moment, Indrajit wrapped his fingers around the Handler's throat, cutting off the cry of pain and surprise before it could escape.

The Handler thrashed, trying to escape, but together they lifted him off the ground and pushed him against the wall. Indrajit choked harder, pinning the man's legs with his body and his left hand with Indrajit's right, and Fix did the same on the other side.

When he stopped kicking because he had passed out, they threw him to the floor in the guardhouse. Mercifully, there were no other guardsmen there, and they dragged in the second Handler as well. Shoving both men into a corner where they were invisible from the gateway itself, Fix stood guard while Indrajit quickly cut the soft jerkins into strips, tying the men's wrists and ankles and gagging them.

When Indrajit returned to the gateway, two men in riding boots were walking in. He and Fix bowed pleasantly and told the men, when asked, that there were no messages. Once the men had passed, Fix passed the gray Handler tunic back to Indrajit. "Do we run up to his apartment and break in, now?"

Indrajit thought hard. "You know the number, right? We're probably early, but let's go knock on the door. If anyone answers, we attack. We hide the bodies inside and wait for Gannon, if he's not there."

"And if no one answers?"

"We come back down here and wait. Follow him up when he arrives."

They climbed, in a fashion simultaneously as quick and as casually as they could manage, to Mote Gannon's door. It was at the base of one of the towers; it was locked, there was no peephole, and no one answered.

They returned to the guardhouse. The two Handlers were still unconscious. Indrajit and Fix stood in the gateway, smiling at each person entering or leaving.

"What lie do I tell next?" Fix asked.

"Say nothing to anyone, if at all possible."

"But if I *have* to talk?"

"I have no idea," Indrajit said. "It depends on who you're talking to, and there's a pretty good chance we'll get it wrong."

"So ... be ready to fight."

"Be ready to fight, and watch for Mote Gannon. How do you know what he looks like?"

Fix shrugged. "I've seen him in the Paper Sook."

Indrajit nodded. "Also, this might be a good time for you to get religion. Does Spilkar, God of Contracts, have dominion over situations like ours?"

"You mean, because we're trying to fulfill a contract?"

"Yes. Or should we turn to the Unnamed, Queen of the New Moon, patron of thieves and assassins, because, notwithstanding the fact that we are heroes, our actions have the superficial appearance of being the actions of rogues?"

"I don't believe in either." Fix shrugged. "So I say, let's pray to both."

Indrajit nodded. He didn't know the formal prayers,

so he improvised, spitting onto the cobblestones by way of offering.

A matron in green silks asked if she had received any messages, and Indrajit truthfully told her he had nothing for her.

"But your aspiration in life was never to be a jobber captain," Fix said.

"No. Neither was yours. I need to recruit and train a successor; you need to win a lady love."

"Win her *back*," Fix muttered darkly. "But getting a career launched as a jobber company captain might help me. How does the jobber company help *you*?"

"Income," Indrajit said. "And visibility. I'll put it about that I'm looking to recruit a poet. And extra eyes—our jobbers can let me know if they see anyone who looks enough like me to investigate as possible kin."

"They can also look for Blaatshi women."

"I didn't say that."

"We should take long breaks," Fix said, "to give you the time you need for your search."

"Then everyone will make less money," Indrajit said. "You only get paid when you're working."

"Hmm," Fix agreed. "That's a dilemma."

A heavy man with rubbery skin and ears like a donkey's asked them to hail a sedan chair. Indrajit cheerfully flagged down a sedan and took the two bits the man offered as a tip.

"How do we recruit other jobbers?" Indrajit asked. "I've never been a leader. Never hired anyone, or gave anyone directions."

"You'll get over that quickly, once you've got an apprentice. Also, the fame of our deeds will eventually bring in many would-be team members."

"Yes, but until then. Do we post an advertisement somewhere?"

Fix shook his head. "Maybe."

Then the shorter man stiffened and threw an elbow into Indrajit's side. Indrajit realized that they had arranged for no signal to indicate to each other that Mote Gannon had arrived. Also, he realized that if Fix recognized Gannon, Gannon might also know Fix by sight.

The man who entered was serious-looking, with curly brown hair going gray and the fair complexion of someone with northern blood. He wasn't tall enough to be from Ukel or Karth, so that suggested an Ildarian. He was wrapped in leather, including knee-high boots and a long leather jerkin with bronze discs riveted to it; bright red silk sleeves puffed out at the wrist made a stylish contrast to the armor. He had two swords at his waist. Gannon wore spectacles, and as he walked, he read from a sheaf of papers in his hand, pinned together.

Frozen hells, not a sheaf, Indrajit realized.

A *fascicle*.

Another problem occurred to Indrajit, just as Mote Gannon looked up. The jobber captain must know his men should be on guard. No doubt, that was part of his security arrangement. And he would know in an instant that Indrajit and Fix were not his men.

Gannon raised his eyes and frowned.

Indrajit grabbed Mote Gannon, intending to throw him to the wall.

The jobber captain, though, was faster than either of his men had been. He stepped in, turned his body to break Indrajit's hold, and at the same time punched the Recital Thane across the jaw, knocking Indrajit spinning. Then he grabbed the hilts of his swords.

Fix grabbed the hilts too, from behind, wrapping both fists around Gannon's hands.

Off balance, Indrajit seized a chair from the guard-room. The chair was heavy, made of metal-hard yetz-wood and pinned together, mortis and tenon style.

"Fire!" Gannon roared. "Fire in the building!" Then he charged forward, dragging Fix with him. The stocky man barely kept his grip, and when Gannon reached the wall of the gateway, he lowered his head, twisting to throw Fix against the wall—

Indrajit Twang hit him in the temple with the chair. Mote Gannon collapsed.

Fix groaned, trying to stand. "Is he dead?"

Indrajit checked. "He lives. And so do you. Now let's all three of us get up into his apartment and have an intimate conversation."

Chapter Twenty-One

~~~~~~~~~~

GANNON HAD A KEY TO HIS APARTMENT IN HIS pocket, so they let themselves in. Then Indrajit brought up the other two Handlers, one at a time, finally locking the door behind them and then further sealing it with the heavy iron bar hanging from a chain for the purpose.

Then they climbed one more story, on a private staircase with steps made of pristine marble, and into the apartment proper.

Mote Gannon did well for himself. Passing through an entry hall, past a kitchen and a dressing chamber, they found the large, square parlor. As Fix threw the jobber captain onto his back on a table as thick as his hand and stained the color of fresh blood, Indrajit looked about him and whistled. The apartment's tall windows let in the sea breeze and the cry of the sea's birds, but not the tidal stink that engulfed the lower precincts of Kish. Blue silk curtains waved gently in the windows, themselves reminiscent of the ocean below. The marble floor was a pale pink, and covered with thick plush carpet.

Gannon's apartment lacked the omnipresent murals of Orem Thrush's palace and was much smaller, but it rivaled the Lord Chamberlain's home for opulence. Rather than murals, a few sculpted busts in the corners suggested gods Indrajit didn't know, or maybe military men whom the jobber captain admired—Gannon had fought in Ildarion, Indrajit seemed to remember, though the busts looked like Kishi. Tiny model sailing ships stood on waist-high pedestals in each room, complete with tiny model sailors and marines, meticulously painted. Wicker shelves in the corner of the parlor held perhaps fifty scrolls, along with several writing tablets.

"Frozen hells," Indrajit said. "Just when I was beginning to like the man, it turns out he's a reader."

Quick glances into other rooms revealed two sleeping platforms—one adult-sized and one the right size for a small child—austerely covered with a single sheet each, and a bath. Some unseen pump mechanism must bring water up into the tower to fill the bath—tiny waves lapped at the tiled edge of the pool—unless Gannon simply had the money to pay someone to haul water up in buckets.

How deep was the pool?

Indrajit had no time to find out, but resolved that when he was a wealthy jobber captain himself, he'd live in the top of a tower and have a pool in his apartment.

He dragged the two Handlers into the parlor one at a time, throwing each onto a thick-cushioned divan. As the unconscious men sank into the soft pillows,

Indrajit fought against the urge to sit beside them and get a little rest.

Maybe a few minutes of sleep.

Gannon groaned, struggling to sit up. Fix pushed him back down onto the wood and pressed a long knife blade to his chest.

Indrajit didn't like threatening the man's life, but he had tried to kill them first. And Indrajit and Fix were bluffing.

At least, he thought they were.

"Who are you?" The jobber captain asked.

"Ah, see," Indrajit said, "now *that* is a lie."

"What are you talking about?" Gannon lay his head back on the table. Slowly, he brought one hand up to rub his temple. "I just asked a question."

Indrajit rested his hand on the hilt of his leaf-bladed sword. "Yeah, but see, the question implies that you don't know who we are. And we already know that's not true. So you are attempting a subtle lie, lying to us by implication. Maybe you find it easier to lie indirectly—that could reflect well on you, I suppose. It might suggest you're not a habitual liar. Or maybe it just suggests that you have an easier time meeting another person's gaze if the lie you're telling in the moment is an indirect one."

Gannon frowned.

"Do you have anything to eat?" Indrajit added. "I could really go for some cured meat, but bread would do. Fish, if it's all you've got."

"Or maybe he wants to convince us he's been knocked on the head," Fix said. "So he won't be able to remember anything."

"That would present a problem for us," Indrajit

conceded. He abandoned any hope of eating, at least for the moment.

Fix shrugged. "If he doesn't know anything, we just chop him up and throw him down the latrine for the Druvash ghosts to eat."

Gannon struggled to sit up for a moment, but surrendered to Fix's strength. "You broke into my home!"

"Yes, and you might tell someone," Fix agreed. "Some judge or some jobber on a law-enforcement contract. So we should probably kill you, in any case."

"Although," Indrajit added, "if the good captain had something interesting to tell us, maybe we could let him live in exchange for the information."

Gannon said nothing.

An uncomfortable thought began to take shape in Indrajit's mind.

"You were very quick," he said. "With that question and its lie by implication, I mean. You had it ready."

Gannon glared at him.

"And also, your own men were standing guard below. That seems odd, doesn't it? Surely, a high-fee jobber company like the Handlers could make more money working some task for one of the great families, and then just pay a much more low-rent force to work as simple security."

"What are you saying?" Fix asked.

"I'm saying that I bet, usually, the men standing watch down in that gateway aren't wearing Gannon gray."

Fix frowned. "You're saying, you think he knew we were coming."

"I think he thought it was a possibility. So he put his own men on watch at his apartment."

"Listen to me, you criminals—" Gannon started to speak.

"Call me by my name," Indrajit said.

Gannon glowered.

"Go on." Fix tapped his knife on Gannon's chest. "Call him by his name."

"Twang," Gannon said. "Indrajit Twang."

"There it is," Indrajit said.

Gannon shifted his gaze. "And you are Fix."

"I think it must have been the Zalapting," Indrajit said.

"That Zalapting told no one anything at all," Fix said.

"Except that the fact that he never rejoined the company suggested we'd killed or captured him. That put Gannon on notice that we might be onto him. On the other hand, the fact that Gannon here only posted two guards, and that he walked into the apartment without bodyguards, suggested he thought it was only a remote possibility we'd come after him. If he'd thought it was a *likely* event, he'd have had more protection."

"Or he overestimates his personal skill at combat," Fix suggested.

"Or you two got lucky." Gannon sneered.

"Anyway," Indrajit said, waving a dismissive hand, "we're here, and you've admitted that you know us. So I think it's time you just go ahead and tell us everything."

"Hells take you," Gannon said.

"Ah." Indrajit shook his head. "So you're going to show us you're tough, and we're going to have to wound you until you tell us what we want to know. Doesn't that seem tiresome to you?"

Fix shrugged. "Maybe he thinks we'll torture his boys in front of him, and he figures he can take that."

"Well, they would be sad to hear that." Indrajit crossed his arms. "How about it? Should we kill your two employees right off, just to clear the way for you to be honest with us?"

"I think it would focus his mind, too," Fix suggested.

"Let's at least start by telling him what we want to know," Indrajit said. "Maybe he'll find it's something he's happy to tell us. Maybe then we can let him and his men free, and be friends again."

"Were we friends before?" Fix asked.

"Well, we could become friends, then. Maybe we could become Handlers, ourselves. This little caper might turn out to be something like a job interview. You know, the old classic, *Hey, if you can kidnap me and tie me up, I guess I'll have to hire you before you join the competition* move."

"Hells take your mothers," Gannon snarled.

"No need to get personal, Mote." Indrajit sighed. Something about capturing and tying up the famous jobber captain made him feel powerful, or at least capable. "So, here's the question."

"You want to know why I know your names."

"I want to know who told them to you." Indrajit paced back and forth. "Here's how I see it. Someone gets old Thinkum Tosh to sell risk on the life of Ilsa without Peer. Frodilo Choot, down in the Paper Sook, buys that risk, and she hires you."

"Choot told me your names," Gannon growled.

"I don't think so," Indrajit said. "I think Holy-Pot Diaphernes brought the deal to Choot, and you were already part of the deal. Choot just had more money than Holy-Pot, that's why she got involved. She was one of the victims, the one who was supposed to lose her money."

"Indrajit . . ." Fix said.

"Only Choot wasn't just someone with money, was she?" Indrajit probed. "You had personal reasons to want to hurt her."

Gannon shrugged. "I've worked with lovers who had jilted me before."

"I knew it!" Indrajit snapped.

"But she didn't give you our names," Fix said.

"It must have been Holy-Pot who told me your names, then." Gannon's eyes glinted. "I'm sure he can confirm that if you ask him."

"See, now you're taunting us." Indrajit shook his head. "You know he's dead, and you know *we* know it."

"You know so much," Gannon said, "I don't think there's anything I know that you haven't already figured out."

"What I'm looking to find out," Indrajit said, "is whose idea was it? Who was the first mover here? Orem Thrush?"

Gannon started to laugh.

"Was it the opera house?" Indrajit continued.

"And why us?" Fix asked. "If someone had to go down for the murder, why not just grab a couple of beggars from the street and throw them into the mix? What would Orem Thrush or the opera house have against me?"

Gannon's laughing grew louder, and he attempted to speak through the guffaws. "Oh, *fine* . . . I will tell you." Red in the face, he got his laughter under control, but tears of mirth marked his cheeks. Indrajit felt vaguely unsettled. "Killing you was *Holy-Pot's* idea."

"What?" Indrajit felt a cold rock in the pit of his stomach.

"Why?" Fix looked more curious than angry, as if he were solving a puzzle.

"Why?" Gannon laughed again. "I swear, the stupidest people are smart. Because, you hatchet-swinging muttonhead, you were taking risk-contracts off the registry."

"So?" Fix's face was intent. Indrajit eased a step closer, just in case his friend decided to stab Mote Gannon.

"So, you were Holy-Pot's boy. You write contracts off the registry, people assume it's really Holy-Pot doing it. Holy-Pot worried you'd get him into trouble, or if you didn't, you'd do something else to hurt his business or hurt the Paper Sook. So he decided to kill you."

Fix rocked back on his heels, a surprised and thoughtful look on his face.

"*I* wasn't writing risk-contracts off the registry," Indrajit objected.

"No," Gannon agreed. "But you're a screw-up. You owed Holy-Pot money. You spent Holy-Pot's money. You stole from him."

"That's not how I see it," Indrajit murmured.

"As long as you were walking around, you were an advertisement for the idea that ripping off Holy-Pot Diaphernes was no big deal, a deed without consequences. Holy-Pot wanted *you* dead too, Fish Eyes."

"I'm not a fish," Indrajit said.

Gannon's laughter grew louder. He arched his back, as if the laughter might erupt from his belly button.

"You're very amused, for a guy lying on his dining room table at knifepoint," Indrajit said. "What aren't you telling us?"

"Only one thing." Gannon gasped, the laughter choking off in his throat as he sucked air into his lungs.

"The person who wanted Ilsa dead," Indrajit said.

"Orem Thrush," Fix suggested.

"The Palace of Shadow and Joy," Indrajit countered.

Gannon shook his head. "The one thing I know, that I'm not telling you..."

He broke into laughter again.

"Frozen hells, Gannon," Indrajit muttered. He prodded Gannon's shoulder with the tip of his blade. "Tell us now."

"That's the one thing." Their prisoner smiled. "*I* am *not* Mote Gannon."

For a split second, Indrajit smelled water. Not the cool, blue, healing scent of rain in the spring, transforming cracked cakes of dirt back into comfortable mud, not the nourishing green aroma of a spring bubbling up within the secret heart of a thicket or a grove, but the purple reek of a stagnant pond.

Then Fix somersaulted forward across the room.

A flash of yellow at the left margin of his vision warned Indrajit that something—the same thing that had hurled Fix across the parlor?—was lunging for him.

He dropped to the floor. A heavy spear thrust against the wood and bent, bronze head folding neatly with a swift metallic groan. Indrajit rolled beneath the table and under a sudden cloud of curses that exploded in his direction, toward Fix.

The black-market risk-merchant was resilient. He was already shaking himself, trying to stand, leaning against the wall as if climbing a ladder. A knee-tall being with bright green skin and a gray tunic dropped suddenly into Indrajit's view, holding a dagger in one hand that, at the wielder's scale, looked like a sword.

Had the small man been hiding among the scrolls? As he scrambled toward his friend, Indrajit saw who had attacked them from behind. It was the big yellow Grokonk, the female, and at her shoulder stood the Grokonk Third. The Third stabbed with a spear directly at the space where Indrajit had been standing, and would have run the Recital Thane through if he hadn't just moved.

The Grokonk female bellowed.

The Third cursed, then dropped back and turned his attention to untying the two Handlers who had been at the guardroom. The two-to-one odds against Indrajit and Fix were about to become four-to-one.

Indrajit grabbed the imp's wrist. The tiny green man shouted something unintelligible and bit Indrajit's hand. Indrajit ripped away the dagger and wrapped his fingers around the little man, preparing to throw him back at the other Handlers—

But saw that the Handlers had frozen in place.

For a moment, he wondered whether some sorcerer had cast a spell, but then he realized that the Handlers were all staring at the little person in his hand.

Indrajit laughed. "Mote Gannon," he said to the little green man. "Pleased to meet you."

Tiny Gannon spat and tried to bite him again. The doll-like man, Indrajit now saw, had the same features as the taller man they had taken to be Mote Gannon. They could have been twins, only one was a fifth the size of the other and the color of an avocado.

What did *that* mean?

"We could kill him," Fix suggested.

"We need him," Indrajit said. "This was a trap. There were more guards all along."

The Grokonk female bellowed again.

"They knew we'd come," Indrajit continued. "They

realized they'd said my name. They knew we'd come find what was going on, and they waited for us, to finish out their contract by killing us."

The Handlers' expressions were all sour.

Indrajit nodded to the fair-skinned man with spectacles. "Who *are* you, then?"

The fair-skinned jobber stood and straightened his clothing. "I'm Mote Gannon, as far as Kish knows."

"You understand that you were bait. This little guy here was willing to sacrifice you."

Tall Gannon shrugged.

Indrajit flicked the green imp hard in the forehead with one fingernail. It was meant to be just a threat, but the fair-skinned man fell down as if he'd been punched in the face.

"You're connected," Indrajit said.

"If you kill me," the Ildarian said, "I can be replaced."

"And if I kill *him* instead?"

"Please don't."

"We don't want to," Fix said. "For one thing, that would leave a dozen or so angry and suddenly unemployed jobbers."

"Although," Indrajit pointed out, "maybe then you could all join our company."

Tall Gannon frowned. "What company is that?"

"We're still working on a name." Indrajit smiled and backed toward the hall, and then through the hall toward the exit.

The Grokonk female roared.

"Herness would suggest the *Dead Men* as a good name," the Grokonk Third said. The wheedling, greasy look on his face might have been intended to be a sly grin. The Grokonk female bellowed another time. "Or the *Cowards*."

Tall Gannon raised his hands peaceably. "Let them go," he said.

"Very good." Indrajit nodded. "We'll give you boys your dolly back once we get somewhere safe."

"Like maybe Pelth," Fix suggested.

The Grokonk female snorted, a mucus-filled gurgle.

"Herness suggests a grave," the Third said.

"Good to know where we stand." Indrajit smiled. "You stay right here."

Fix picked up his spear, dropped when the Grokonk had thrown him across the room, and the two jobbers hurried down the tower steps.

"The *Dead Men* is not a terrible name," Fix said. "It's a little mystical, and also suggests imperviousness. If we are already dead, who can harm us?"

"We'll think of a better one."

Fix ripped the iron bar from its brackets, letting it bounce against the wall on its chain. Indrajit looked once back up the steps to be certain the Handlers weren't immediately on their trail, and then opened the door.

The slate-blue Luzzazza in a Handler's tunic stood in the doorway, a sword in one hand and a shield hanging on the other visible arm. A scab on his cheek reminded Indrajit that this was the same Luzzazza he had faced twice now in the Palace of Shadow and Joy. Behind him stood Green Skin—the Handler who had attacked Ilsa on stage—and to either side, along the walkway in both directions, stood a file of Zalaptings, three deep.

Chapter Twenty-Two

~~~~~~~~

"CATCH!" INDRAJIT YELLED.

He threw Tiny Gannon.

Indrajit did not have great aim.

Indrajit's people were fisherman, but they fished with bare hands, with nets, and with stabbing spears. He knew of peoples that hunted the great fish of the sea—whales, and porpoises, and sharks, and orcas— with thrown harpoon, and had seen spears thrown on land, by hunters and warriors, and launched from a Xiba'albi throwing stick. But hurling spears, and any other missile weapon, were not for the Blaatshi.

The Blaatshi killed their food and their foes face to face, by hand, with melee weapons.

So Indrajit's aim was not especially good. In the tiny moment of time between when he opened the door and saw the Luzzazza on the other side, and when he threw Tiny Gannon, he worried that if he tried to throw the jobber company captain into the Luzzazza's arms, he'd fall short, and fail to distract the blue-skinned man.

Indrajit's aim was not great, but his limbs were long and well-muscled. Worried he might fall short with his throw, he compensated by hurling Mote Gannon with all the force he could muster with his shoulders, chest, and legs, firing the tiny green man past the Luzzazza and out over the cobbled courtyard, four stories below.

Tiny Gannon shrieked as he flew, a sound like a rat stepped on in the darkness.

The Luzzazza had quick reflexes. A blur of blue, he spun sideways and lurched out over the void. He dropped his sword and grabbed for the flying green man with his long blue arms—

And caught him.

Fix also had quick reflexes. As Green Skin and the Zalaptings turned to watch their employer fly, gasping in surprise at the same moment, Fix lowered his shoulder and charged.

He knocked Green Skin to the floor and kept running.

Indrajit followed. To slow pursuit, he stomped on Green Skin's ankle as he ran over the man.

Pressing his hips against the iron railing, the Luzzazza leaned out over the courtyard, pinning Tiny Gannon with his empty hand into the space inside his shield.

Fix ran one Zalapting through, dropped his spear, then knocked the other two lavender men up into the air as he plowed beneath them. Indrajit threw one against the wall and punched a second in his long, lavender snout.

Fix crashed into the Luzzazza from behind.

The railing snapped, and the Luzzazza fell.

Notwithstanding his bluster minutes earlier, Indrajit didn't want Tiny Mote Gannon to die. Especially right now, with Fix and Indrajit in their sight, Gannon's jobbers might decide to take out their anger at unexpected unemployment by beating Indrajit and Fix to death. At the very least, a criminal prosecution and penalty for murder seemed likely.

Also, he would feel bad.

Fix seemed to care less, or at least, he kept running.

Indrajit skidded to a stop, trying and failing to catch the Luzzazza's long kilt.

The Luzzazza toppled forward, bending at the waist as if he were trying to cradle Tiny Gannon with his body. Maybe Gannon would survive the fall, bouncing off the wreck of the Luzzazza's corpse. Then the Luzzazza somersaulted forward, nearly hitting the back of his head on the railing of the floor below. Death looked imminent, the Luzzazza hurtled on past the third story walkway—

And then suddenly stopped falling.

He screamed and rosettes of blood burst from his ribs on one side, but the Luzzazza hung in midair, as if he had been caught by an invisible net.

Or as if he had arrested his own fall with invisible arms.

Indrajit found himself laughing with relief.

The Zalaptings, scooting around to face him and galloping in his direction, seemed considerably less amused.

Indrajit ran.

Ahead of him, Fix disappeared down the staircase. Indrajit lurched, his legs in agony, both the muscles from exertion and the two not-yet-healed wounds from being reopened again. Thinking he should have caught up with his friend by now, Indrajit flung himself down the stairs. As he plunged toward the railing, grabbing with both hands, he turned his head slightly, and was dismayed to see Zalaptings gaining on them.

Passing the third floor, Indrajit saw a blue hand reaching up from below the level of the walkway and grabbing the rail. Tiny Mote Gannon climbed along that arm and squeezed between the iron bars of the railing.

Their eyes met, briefly, and Gannon turned and ran.

Passing the second, Indrajit saw the Luzzazza, still dangling by his grip on the railing above, and trying to get his sandaled feet onto the second-story railing. The blue man stared at Indrajit with hatred, and Indrajit stepped around the corner from the staircase, momentarily not following Fix down.

"Stop!" the Luzzazza yelled at the following Zalaptings. "He's hiding!"

Indrajit shrieked and leaped from his hidden corner, scattering the small lavender men with sweeping blows of his sword. He knocked the helmet off one, disarmed a second, and slashed into the calf muscles of a third before they evaporated completely before him.

Indrajit took one last look at the Luzzazza before he descended. The blood flowing from his sides clung oddly to something Indrajit couldn't quite see, appearing therefore to outline in red an invisible set of shoulders.

No, just one shoulder. From the other side, much more blood flowed, and there was no shoulder outline.

Indrajit's legs ached and his head hurt. He spat, and continued his descent.

On the ground floor, he would have missed it if he hadn't stepped on it—beneath the Luzzazza, alone and still, lay an invisible arm.

Indrajit stooped to pick it up. As he looked more closely, he saw that the arm wasn't invisible—it shifted color as it moved. Knowing where he was looking and what he was looking for, he could see the arm, but the arm took the color of whatever lay behind it: cobblestones, marble, or even Indrajit's own mahogany skin, with hints of green.

Indrajit squeezed the forearm, and the fingers and thumb of the hand clenched.

"Strange," he murmured.

Shouting above and behind him reminded him that he was pursued. Skirting around the space below the Luzzazza, in case the blue-skinned man fell, he ran toward the gateway.

Fix threw himself against two warriors there—the fair Sword Brother, who now held a long, straight blade with both hands on a long hilt, and a Yuchak woman in furs, who stabbed and swung with two short spears, one in either hand.

The three danced, ebbing and flowing within the narrow space as Fix maneuvered to keep a wall behind him and tried to drive the other fighters away in turn, so that he never really faced more than one at any given moment. He fought with his falchion in one hand and his ax in the other and he was more or less succeeding, but the Sword Brother and the Yuchak were closing in.

Beyond all three stood a Thûlian, face swathed and the match—the long, slow-burning cord that sprang from his headgear and hung in front of his face like a fiery esca—smoldering. The gunman poured Thûlian powder into the mechanism of his weapon. Such powder was of secret composition, known to very few, and said to be the object of numerous bounties offered by princes of the Serpent Sea. The person who obtained the formula of Thûlian powder would be able to retire from public life with great wealth.

Sadly, a mere sample wouldn't do.

The Thûlian raised his long-barreled musket, pointing it toward Fix.

Indrajit threw the arm.

And fell short.

He lost track of the severed limb in the shadow of the gateway, and charged, screaming.

"Heroes!" he hollered.

The Thûlian lowered his head, touching the match to his gun. *Bang!* A plume of smoke erupted from the musket, and Fix fell.

The Sword Brother heard Indrajit's cry and turned to look. Indrajit careened into the Yuchak, dropping a shoulder to throw it into her ribs and send her sprawling into the path of the Sword Brother.

The Thûlian reached into his sash, grabbing the butts of two long pistols. Indrajit fell on the man before he could fire them, jerking the deadly weapons from his hands and knocking him to the ground.

Although as he slammed into the Thûlian, the marksman felt strangely light to him, and soft. Was it possible the Thûlian was a woman? But she smelled as sweaty as any man.

Fix staggered toward Indrajit, bleeding from a wound on the back of one calf. When he had covered half the distance, he slipped and fell.

"Sorry!" Indrajit called. "That's the arm!"

Fix picked up the Luzzazza's severed arm, climbed to his feet, and stared in surprise at the limb as he ran.

The Sword Brother tossed the Yuchak to one side

and advanced again. Indrajit pointed one of the pistols at the fair man. "Fire!" he shouted. "Shoot!"

Nothing happened.

The fair man raised his sword.

Indrajit shook the weapon, and it did nothing.

The Sword Brother swung his sword and Indrajit threw the pistol.

Indrajit missed, but the Sword Brother skewed sideways, and Fix took advantage of his sudden loss of poise, kicking at the man's feet. The Sword Brother crashed to the ground.

Fix dropped to one knee on the man's sternum and punched him repeatedly in the face until he dropped his sword and lay still.

Fix grabbed his weapons and hooked them onto his belt again. Then Indrajit and Fix ran.

"What is this?" Fix shook the color-shifting arm.

"It's not mine!"

"Really? Something got in my way in a fight, and it has nothing to do with you?"

"Okay, I threw it at the Thûlian. But it's not my arm."

Fix grunted, but held on to the arm. "Where did it come from, then? Wait . . . did this come from the Luzzazza?"

"Yeah. I tried to hit the powder priest, but I missed."

"You have terrible aim."

"I am a hand-to-hand fighter."

"It's your fish eyes."

"Really, now is no time to be offensive."

Night was falling, deep twilight drifting down the avenues and boulevards of the Crown like autumn leaves in a thick forest.

"It's not offensive. You just have no depth perception. I guess your whole species has the same problem. No wonder your people have almost died out—your eyes are so far apart, you probably can't hit anything more than ten feet away."

"You are not making this any less insulting," Indrajit said.

They chose smaller and smaller streets, heading, without discussion, for the gate into the Spill. As they turned each corner, they stopped to look behind them.

"Are we going back to Frodilo Choot?" Indrajit felt tired.

"Maybe she can help us get into the bank," Fix said. "We only have until tomorrow. Or maybe she can find us a big jobber company's worth of extra muscle, so we can go back and squeeze Mote Gannon for what he knows."

"They wanted us dead," Indrajit said. "Specifically."

"Not *they*," Fix said. "Holy-Pot wanted us dead."

"But there has to be something more to this, right? This is about the money, the risk-merchantry? I mean, there's no way that Holy-Pot Diaphernes went to all this trouble just to set us up and kill us, right?"

"No, this isn't about us. Killing us was just going to be the gravy on Holy-Pot's duck." Fix stopped. "I'm not saying it's your fault. The vision thing. Look, here's the other effect of your eye placement. Do you see my finger?"

"No, I don't see the fingers on the Luzzazza's hands. I don't know what kind of magic that is, but it's pretty odd. Why would they want to have one invisible pair of arms?"

"I'm not sure about magic," Fix said. "I'm also not sure it's something they want. There are lizards that are hard to see, because their color changes to match whatever surface they're standing on."

"You think the Luzzazza's arms do the same thing? And not on purpose?"

"Yes. Their second pair of arms, their lower set. And I don't know if it's magic, any more than what Ilsa does."

"Ilsa controls minds. That's magical, if anything is."

"Is it? Or is it just a more powerful version of what lots of other women do, too?"

"Lots of other women are attractive." Indrajit sniffed.

"Anyway, I'm not talking about the Luzzazza arm. I mean the fingers of my left hand. Don't you see them?"

Indrajit frowned. "No. Because you're holding them out of sight."

"Where?"

"Down. Low."

"Wrong. They're right in front of you, and almost touching your bony, fishlike nose."

"My nose is not like a fish."

"Turn your head and look."

Indrajit turned his head, and saw that Fix was right. Fix's left hand came into view, fingers extended, fingertips nearly touching Indrajit's nose, which didn't resemble the nose of a fish at all.

"What are you trying to say?"

"That you have no depth perception, and a blind spot right in front of your face. You probably don't like kissing women, do you, because they disappear?"

"Hey!"

Fix shrugged. "You're just fishes. Here, take this."

Indrajit took back the Luzzazza arm, sniffing. "We're not fishes. We're not *descended* from fishes.

We didn't *used* to be fishes. We *eat* fish. Except I don't especially love it myself, which is another, very minor, reason for coming to Kish."

"Fish eat fish." Fix shrugged. "It isn't all that rare that men eat men."

"You are confusing external shape with spiritual reality."

"I don't know," Fix said. "I'm just trying to understand the world from the information it gives me."

"That's a child's way to understand the world." Indrajit wanted to punch the other man, but instead he resumed walking toward the end of the alley. Beyond, he knew, lay the gate. "An adult learns from those who came before."

"You mean, by reading books?"

"I mean, by listening to the Epic."

"Hort's nubbin, you know the same answer to every question."

"Say rather that I have one powerful tool that sets me on the path to finding the right answer to every question."

"Your Epic doesn't say anything about those who came before *me*," Fix said. "I'm not Blaatshi."

"But you have a man's soul. Anyone with a man's soul, any member of any of the thousand races of man, can benefit from hearing and knowing the Epic."

"I'll give you back that much credit, too, despite your fishy ways. You have a man's soul, Indrajit Twang."

They turned the corner onto the crowded avenue, funneling into the gate-bound traffic. Palanquin bearers threw hard elbows trying to block their way, but Indrajit threw elbows back—his peripheral vision let him see pretty clearly who was responsible for each bump and scrape he received, and he tried not to think about the suddenly unnerving possibility that someone might attack, unseen, from directly before him.

The gate was manned by Zalaptings, in armor but not in uniform. Each palanquin or party on foot or rider got a perfunctory examination, passing through. In more fraught moments—during a festival, or when the city was under attack—that scrutiny might be more detailed. Two parties ahead of Indrajit and Fix, a cord-thin Rover leading two mules dragged his feet, drifting into the gate. A Zalapting guard limped over to examine the animals' packs, perhaps searching for contraband: yip, or unstamped metal or yetz-wood or luxury fabrics from Boné.

Something bothered Indrajit, and he wasn't entirely sure what it was.

"I'm starting to not feel good about our chances," Indrajit said.

"Of . . . surviving?"

Indrajit snorted. "No, what are Gannon's goons going to do to us, really? There were a few nervous moments back there, but we're in the city, now. Mother Kish, refuge of every scoundrel, haven of every fugitive. How's he going to find us, if we don't go to him?"

"Yashta Hossarian found us."

"He's unnatural. Got some kind of magic for finding people."

"Hmm."

"Hmm, what?"

"Hmm, I'm not sure I believe in magic. Or maybe, I'm not sure I know what it is."

"*You're* the one who said he was healed by a Druvash artifact."

Fix shrugged. "Speaking of healing, what are you going to do with that arm?"

"Tell them I found it. They can have it if they want it. Fine." Indrajit chuckled. "Disbelieve everything, then, you godless clod. But no, I meant I'm starting to not feel good about our chances of getting paid. By Thrush or by Choot."

Fix rubbed his forehead. "Oh, that's good. I, on the other hand, *am* beginning to worry we might not survive."

Indrajit snorted. "Nonsense. We're immortals, you and I. Eternal beings. But we *do* need to get paid. Even the immortals eat."

"But *what* do they eat?" Fix asked. "Ambrosia? Soma?"

"Fish. Sadly."

The limping Zalapting finished with the party directly before Indrajit and Fix, which consisted of a heavy man in plain white cotton, face veiled, sitting on an open sedan chair. He turned and headed toward the two jobbers, his face a blank slab.

Indrajit felt uneasy.

A second Zalapting joined the first—this one had a dent in his snout, and blood crusted on his upper lip.

They were Handlers.

"Fix," Indrajit murmured. "Run."

They turned, and found themselves facing directly into the broad, open mouth of a Grokonk female.

Chapter Twenty-Three

THE GROKONK SWUNG ONE ENORMOUS YELLOW FIST and knocked Fix sideways. The smaller man tumbled through a procession of dromedaries led by a mule-skinner swathed in linen and armed with two curving tulwars, and then the Grokonk was bounding after him.

The Grokonk Third emerged from a crowd of faces, bearing down on Indrajit with a spear. The Recital Thane leaped back, pulling a pair of drunken young noblemen in silk tunics and kilts between himself and his attacker. The young men, interrupted in a rowdy drinking song that seemed to be about the score of a legendary Rûphat game that decided the holding of the Imperial throne, several hundred years earlier, objected boisterously. When one caught the edge of the Third's spear in his side, his objections became more fierce.

"Who do you think you are?" he demanded in a slurred voice, and then thin dueling swords whisked from their sheaths.

Indrajit chased after Fix. His friend had got out a sword and a long knife, but the Grokonk's longer reach and its spear meant that Fix was on the defensive, backing away through a crowd that had begun to scream and doing his best to parry and dodge each new blow that came thundering his way.

Over the shrieking of the crowd, the Grokonk female roared like an angry elephant.

"I know that tunic!" one of the drunk lordlings harrumphed. "That's one of Gannon's—"

His identification was cut off in a sudden gurgle as the Third ran him through.

The big female cut the outside of Fix's biceps. Swinging with the backward motion of her attack, she clubbed him in the temple with the spear's shaft, knocking him to the ground.

Indrajit had no time to draw his sword. He jumped with hands raised, planning to grab the Grokonk's ankle and at least slow down her advance. But as he charged, the slimy mass heaped up on the big female's shoulders trembled, like an aspic in an earthquake. It might have been his imagination, but Indrajit thought he could see circular black eyes quaking in the gelatinous heap. He felt sick.

The female spun, insanely quickly, and with the back of her hand she struck Indrajit across the face.

The Third tried and failed to yank his spear from the belly of the man he'd killed and advanced on Indrajit.

Indrajit's head spun. Somewhere, he heard Fix shouting. Surely, the Grokonk female would now pound the four hundred twenty-seventh Blaatshi Recital Thane into a paste, and there would be no four hundred twenty-eighth.

Shame filled him, and sorrow.

But somehow, he wasn't pounded. Instead, his vision returned to him, just in time to see two things. First, the Grokonk female wheeled back around and swung the butt of her spear at Fix again. And second, the Grokonk Third ran toward Indrajit, short sword raised to attack.

Indrajit kicked. Raising his legs, he planted both feet in the Third's belly, hoisting the neutered Grokonk up into the air—

The Third screamed in surprise—

And Indrajit planted him, face-first, in the gelatinous mass covering the female's back.

The female shrieked. Indrajit rolled aside, expecting her to turn and trample him. The slime shook and bounced like water on a hot iron skillet; twisting abruptly, the female reached back and gripped her Third by the back of his neck, yanking him from her body and then holding him up before her.

Indrajit stood. He definitely could see black eye-dots within the jelly, shaking. He drew his leaf-bladed broadsword—could the Grokonk be any more warned by her mates? Opposite, standing below the Grokonk herself, and under the dangling feet of the Third, Fix stood. The Grokonk had dropped her spear, and Fix now held it, a look of grim resolution on his face.

But the Grokonk attacked neither of them. She stared at her Third.

In its mouth, the Third had something that looked like a fish with tiny legs, or maybe a very fat, slime-covered yellow lizard, or a tadpole that had developed halfway into a frog. As Indrajit looked, the tadpole—a fertile Grokonk male, if Fix was right, spasmed in the

Third's mouth, and then its viscera erupted over the Third's puckered lips.

The Grokonk roared. Her back quivered even faster, and she punched her fist through the Third's face.

The Third's skull disappeared in a sudden red mist.

Fix leaped up from below, driving the Grokonk's spear into her belly with the strength of both legs. Seeing Fix's attack, Indrajit stabbed with the leaf-bladed sword, pushing it as deep as he could, through the slime, through the body of at least one tiny fertile male, and then, with more resistance, into the muscle and between the ribs of the big female.

She screamed in rage and thrashed, spinning like a child's string toy that scooted across a kitchen floor. As she lost her balance, Indrajit raised one leg to kick her from behind. She fell forward, impaling herself more deeply on the spear, falling and flailing, almost crushing Fix before sliding to an abrupt halt.

Indrajit whooped once, a reflex from his days of hunting river horses in the waters of his home, but then spun around. His hands were empty, but he dropped into a defensive stance, prepared to dodge, or punch, if necessary. He half expected a wave of Zalaptings to flood over him.

Instead, he saw shocked onlookers.

"Constables!" someone shouted. "Get the constables!"

Feet ran off, presumably looking for whatever jobber company had the law enforcement contracts for the Crown.

"Help," Fix grunted.

Indrajit considered several quips that struck him both as clever and also, in the context of having just defeated the Grokonk female, debonair, but decided instead to help. Fix was trapped under the dead weight of the Grokonk, but the heavy spear protruded now from her back, and by hanging from it and throwing all his weight into it as if onto a lever, Indrajit was able to turn the yellow-skinned frog-woman off his friend.

Fix stood. "This is going to sound odd, but I know what to call our jobber company."

"Later." Indrajit pointed. "Here come the constables."

The first order of business was to get out of sight, so that onlookers wouldn't simply point them out to the pursuit. The second was probably to get Grokonk blood and slime from their clothes and their bodies, but Indrajit was scarcely thinking that far ahead. He planted a foot against the big female's side, yanking his sword free—the males were still trembling, and one or two had fallen to the ground—and they ran.

"A latrine?" Indrajit suggested, panting. Pain lanced through the wounds in his legs.

"They'll know we...did that before," Fix pointed out.

"We should...leave false trails. Into latrines!" Indrajit tried to grin nonchalantly, but his footing was tricky in the deepening shadows, and he heard the cries of pursuit.

"If we had...more time!"

They dashed down a relatively narrow lane, gaining a few moments' lead, perhaps, on their pursuers. The lane, still wide enough to allow a Rover clan to pass through, opened into a market square from which exited six streets. In the center of the square, on a low wooden platform, a street bawdy company performed. A rapt crowd, done with the day's shopping and now prepared to stroll and spectate, filled the square. At the edge of the stage, beside bang-harp players and unwatched, sat an open wooden chest, bound in bronze, in which were piled costumes and oversized masks.

"There!" Too tired to point, Indrajit flung himself upon the chest.

Fix followed. They each grabbed a mask first, quickly knotting the leather bands behind their heads. Then they shrugged into loose togas, not the real togas that required folding and holding and marked the city's true upper class, but fake togas, which were easier to slip into and out of and move while wearing, because they were stitched into their hanging pattern permanently.

Indrajit flung a tunic over his shoulders without looking at it, then spun and sat behind the harpists. Finding a timbrel on the earth, he picked it up and shook it gently, large masked head swaying side to side in time with the music. Fix grabbed a black toga and picked up a gourd, patting it with the heel of his hand.

"My sword has slain a Grokonk," Indrajit said. "It has earned a name."

"What?" Fix answered.

"I am thinking of calling it Vacho, after the famous blade of Inder. Vacho, the Voice of Lightning."

Fix tapped his gourd. "That certainly sounds like the weapon of a hero."

"Your timing is off," Indrajit whispered. "If you can't find the beat, use the tips of your fingers and be more gentle."

Fix grumbled wordlessly, but reduced his volume.

Zalaptings and Yuchaks rushed into the square from the direction from which Indrajit and Fix had come. They all wore Gannon's gray tunics and glyph, and they cast bewildered looks about them.

"Who am I dressed as?" Fix asked.

"Plays and stagecraft are not part of your fund of knowledge, I guess?"

"Not even a little."

Indrajit struggled to refrain from laughing. "Your toga's colors suggest one of the Xiba'albi Lords of Death, who are customarily portrayed in black, with thin red lines, such as you see in your garment. Your mask, on the other hand, shows that you are one of the Spring Maidens."

Fix cursed obscurely.

"Keep your voice down," Indrajit counseled. "If anyone notices us, they will expect you to sing in the chorus. Also, if there is a dominant randy character, such as a king or a particularly fierce warrior, he will be expected to chase you around the stage at least three times."

"This is why I hate stagecraft," Fix muttered.

"You've been cast in this part before?" Indrajit chuckled slightly at his own joke. "But what does my costume look like?"

The Sword Brother arrived, along with Green Skin and the Thûlian. Perhaps the Luzzazza was getting healing somewhere. The Zalaptings and Yuchaks took direction from the Sword Brother, and then the Handlers split up, marching with determination down the different lanes. None of them gave Indrajit and Fix a second glance.

"I think you're Orem Thrush," Fix said.

"Skull and horns mask?"

"Yes."

"So I could be the current Orem Thrush, or one of his predecessor Lords Chamberlain. In either case, it's probably incumbent upon me to chase you about the stage. Would you like a head start?"

"Would you like a punch in the throat?"

"No." Indrajit looked down at his own toga. "White. A priest or a scholar, a newborn or someone who is very old. White shows us someone who is mortal, but marked apart from the rest of society somehow. Someone upon whom the ordinary obligations and limitations are not imposed. Someone above it all or outside it all."

"So your costume actually makes sense," Fix said.

"I suppose," Indrajit said. "In a play about the Lord Chamberlain being an infant, or dying, or perhaps getting away with things for which he should be punished."

"Isn't that exactly the play we're in?" Fix asked softly.

Indrajit didn't want to answer that question. He wasn't sure he could, if he wanted to. Instead, he changed the subject. "Okay, then. Tell me the name."

"Of the spear that killed the Grokonk? I left it behind. That was hers."

"Your name for our jobber company. You said the Grokonk had smushed a new idea into your head."

"The *Protagonists*," Fix said.

"The *Protagonists*." Indrajit let the word roll around in his mouth. He liked it, and said it again. "The *Protagonists*."

"It means—"

"I know what it means," Indrajit said. "The heroes of the story."

"Right. But also, someone who acts on someone else's behalf. Someone who fights for someone else's cause. A proponent."

"Also, it means the first actor. And here we are, actors upon the stage of life."

"In the Palace of Shadow and Joy," Fix said.

"It sounds much better than the *Mercenaries*."

"It means much more."

"Good. We were already in business together. Now we have a bond and a name."

"We have a name," Fix said, "and a promise from a risk-merchant to post a bond for us."

Indrajit shrugged. "We make progress. But for now, we must survive."

Fix looked as if he might comment, but he didn't. "So, what do we do? We could get into the basement of one of these buildings and break through a wall, try to get down beneath the city and make our way to the Spill."

"No thanks." Indrajit shuddered. "I don't like doing that when we have a guide. I like doing it much less *without* one. What about climbing the wall?"

"What, building a ladder? Or throwing a lasso? I don't know how to use a lasso."

"I'm game to try," Indrajit said.

Fix laughed.

"We could try bribing guards at the gate," Indrajit suggested.

"Unless they all work for Gannon. Or have taken his money to keep an eye out for us."

"I think this would be much easier if we were wealthy and powerful," Indrajit said.

"Someday, we may be wealthy and powerful."

"But Orem Thrush is wealthy and powerful now. Perhaps he can help us."

"He may want Ilsa dead."

Indrajit considered that. "Yes," he agreed. "He may. But we can cross that bridge when we come to it. In the meantime, he has money to bribe guards, or soldiers to escort us."

"Or lassos, to use to climb the wall."

One of the bang-harp players, a narrow-shouldered Kishi with a sunken chest and long arms, leaned back and whispered loudly over his shoulders. "Shut up." Then he cocked an eye at Indrajit and Fix and frowned. "Say, who *are* you guys?"

"*We*," Indrajit said, "are leaving."

With one quick visual sweep of the square to be certain there were no gray tunics, he undid his mask, shrugged out of his toga, and stood. Fix followed his example, and they walked briskly up toward the Spike and, just beyond it, Orem Thrush's city palace.

"Watch for gray tunics," Indrajit said.

"And orange," Fix added. "And don't forget your friend Hossarian—his boys didn't wear livery at all."

"Fortunately, Yashta Hossarian himself is completely unmistakable. Short of by falling directly out of the sky, he will never be able to sneak up on *anyone*."

They had only walked a block when Indrajit realized they were being followed. Swinging his head from side to side, he noticed the Thûlian trailing them a dozen paces back. With their faces obscured, all Thûlians looked awfully similar, but Indrajit led Fix down two sharp turns, and the Thûlian, though he—or *she*—fell back slightly, continued to follow them.

The Thûlian's match smoldered, visible in the night that grew ever gloomier.

"The Thûlian's behind us," Indrajit murmured. "He must have been hiding in the crowd by the bawdy troupe, waiting for us to reveal ourselves or recross our trail." He left out his suspicion that the powder-warrior might be a woman.

"I'd rather not face the musket," Fix said. "But he can't really shoot at us in this crowd. Let's just pick up the pace. Carrying that long gun, he'll never catch us."

They broke into a jog.

Bang!

Indrajit heard the explosion. Looking back, he saw the Thûlian standing with his musket pointed at the sky. In the greasy yellow light of a winery, the plume of smoke from the gun mingled with the smoke rising from the Thûlian's head and gave him a demonic appearance.

"That's a signal," Fix said. "Run!"

"I do this way too much!" Indrajit grunted, but ran anyway.

His legs hurt. Fix must hurt as much, or maybe more, having been shot and stabbed and beaten, and they were both many hours short on sleep, and hungry.

But they were motivated, and they ran fast.

The Lord Chamberlain's palace hove into view. They were approaching from the side nearest the trades-men's entrance, which was just as well, since it was the only entrance Indrajit knew. Taking a deep breath, he lengthened his stride, ducking past a horse pulling a two-wheeled cart stacked high with small casks—

Something struck him from the side and knocked him down.

The Sword Brother loomed over him, looking unnaturally tall in the darkness, with yellow lamplight running up and down his two long swords like twin lightning bolts poised to strike. He kicked Indrajit in the ribs, which hurt.

But as he was in the act of kicking, a smaller, more compact shadow bowled into him, hitting him between the belly and the knee. In a flash of fair skin, the Ildarian disappeared. Then Fix pulled Indrajit to his feet with hands under both shoulders.

"Knock!" the shorter man yelled, pushing Indrajit.

Indrajit sprinted to the door. Behind him he heard cursing, the clash of steel on steel, and another gunshot. He hammered on the door and the peephole slid open. In the dim light, he could see nothing of the face looking out at him.

"Here to see the Lord Chamberlain! Business about Ilsa without Peer!" Not waiting for an answer, Indrajit whipped back around and drew his leaf-bladed sword.

Vacho, the Voice of Lightning. A sword for a hero.

Fix gave ground step by step, fighting with his ax and his falchion against the Sword Brother's longer weapons. His defense was conservative and brilliant, each step as short as could be, each arm motion as direct as possible. He made bold moves, hooking with the head of his ax, clubbing with the flat of it, darting within the Sword Brother's guard to deliver a sharp elbow to the man's sternum.

Yuchak and Zalapting jobbers tried to dash around the Sword Brother in the narrow alley to join the fight, and each time, Fix rendered the extra combatant harmless in a quick, efficient manner. A deceptively gentle poke with the ax handle to this one's head, a falchion slash across that one's belly, and always the fight whirled around the two men.

Indrajit tightened his grip on Vacho and prepared to charge into the fray. "Protagonists!" he yelled. It wasn't a proper battle cry, but for the moment it would do.

As he yelled, yellow light erupted from behind him. The Sword Brother hunkered and stepped back, shielding his eyes. Fix pressed his advantage for a moment, and then Zalaptings swarmed past him from Orem Thrush's palace, sweeping the Sword Brother and the rest of Gannon's Handlers away.

Indrajit took a deep breath, feeling safe at last, and sheathed his sword. Fix put away his own weapons, and when they turned, they found they were facing Four Eyes again, the Lord Chamberlain's doorkeeper.

"Indrajit," Four Eyes said. "Fix."

Zalaptings returned from chasing the Handlers and surrounded the three men.

"We want to talk to the Lord Chamberlain," Indrajit said.

"Good." Four Eyes smiled. "The Lord Chamberlain wants to talk to *you*."

The Zalaptings raised their spears.

Chapter Twenty-Four

"FROZEN HELLS. I JUST WANT PEOPLE TO STOP pointing weapons at me."

Four Eyes made an expression that wasn't quite a smile, but the spears weren't lowered.

"Fine," Indrajit said. "We want the same thing as the Lord Chamberlain. We want to talk."

"We want to rescue Ilsa," Fix added.

"By tomorrow morning," Indrajit said. "So let's get a move on."

Four Eyes and his Zalaptings prodded and led the two jobbers into the Lord Chamberlain's palace, down two hallways and up a flight of steps, into a room without windows. There was no light in the chamber, but Four Eyes took an oil lamp from a niche in the hallway and raised it over the cell, illuminating bare stone floor.

"The night is warm," Four Eyes said. "You'll be fine waiting here for a little while."

"This is not quite what I had in mind," Indrajit said.

Thrush's men disarmed Indrajit and Fix. Four Eyes and the lavender warriors retreated, spears last and pointing at the two jobbers, and then the door shut, leaving Indrajit and Fix in total darkness.

Indrajit heard the heavy thud of a bar being slotted into place, holding the door shut.

"We'll just wait here, then!" Indrajit called.

No answer.

"Tell the Lord Chamberlain I haven't punched any of his people since we spoke!"

"That you know of," Fix said.

"What?"

"Well, you did punch that Zalapting Handler in the face. What if he's one of Thrush's people?"

"Well, if Gannon's Handlers somehow work for Orem Thrush, rather than for Frodilo Choot . . . or rather, Holy-Pot Diaphernes . . . then we did worse than punch that guy in the face."

"You ripped off the blue guy's arm."

"And stabbed him in the face. And threw Mote Gannon over a cliff. You ran a Zalapting right through with your spear."

"We killed the two Grokonk."

"No. We killed the big female. *She* killed her little neuter buddy. And *he* . . . or *it* . . . killed the little male. Bit him right in half." Indrajit shuddered.

They were silent for a bit. Indrajit eased himself into a sitting position on the cool stone. He heard Fix situating himself similarly.

"Do you hurt as much as I do?" Fix asked.

"I was keeping track for a while," Indrajit said. "Which muscles ached, where I was wounded. Now it's all just melted into a single ball of pain. Including my stomach."

"Me too. Maybe this whole jobber captain thing isn't worth it."

"If we can rescue Ilsa by tomorrow morning, we might come out of these three days of pain with a thousand Imperials. No, fourteen hundred. I can't read, but I'm pretty sure I'm getting that math right."

"Okay," Fix agreed, "that would be worth it."

"Besides," Indrajit said, "it turns out that the reason Holy-Pot tried to have you killed is that you were taking off-registry risk-contracts. So I'm not sure *that* business is better. Be a jobber captain, we'll work for a year, and then you'll have enough cash to impress your lady love. Buy an island up the coast, settle down, raise a little brood of children. Spoil their minds by teaching them to read."

"She married someone else," Fix said.

"Oh." Indrajit thought about this. It was difficult to concentrate, his head hurt too much. "Then why are you stuck here again? I thought you were trying to make money to impress her."

"I was. Then she married. Now maybe I'm trying to make enough money to impress myself. Prove that I'm the kind of man she might have married."

"That's a terrible way to try to keep score, Fix," Indrajit said. "Maybe the worst."

Fix said nothing.

"On the other hand, maybe she'll find you dashing as a jobber captain, and run away with you. Her husband will challenge you to a duel, you can kill him with a clean conscience, and then you can go live on a private island."

"If I run off with his wife, I don't think I can kill him with a clean conscience."

"Not even if you do it for love? I thought anything you did for love was pure," Indrajit said.

"No, that's nonsense," Fix said.

"You're right," Indrajit agreed. "Pure street bawdy."

"But I need to stay in Kish to keep an eye on her."

"In case he dies?"

"Or in case she needs my help."

"Ah, Fix." Indrajit sighed. "Life is complicated."

"Where do you think Ilsa is right now?"

"I hope she went to ground. Hid."

"I was thinking that maybe Orem Thrush found her. And maybe that's what he wants to tell us."

"I hope not," Indrajit said. "I don't think he'll pay us, if that's the case."

"Frodilo might, though," Fix said. "And two hundred Imperials would be nothing to sneeze at, especially if I could take the money and sleep for a few days."

"Two hundred Imperials would buy a house, so you'd have a place to sleep in."

"Not in the Lee, it wouldn't."

"I was thinking about a house in the Dregs."

"I want a house in the Lee. Or an apartment, at least. But that's a couple thousand Imperials, I think."

"Well, if you're going to aspire to wealth," Indrajit said, "why not aspire all the way? Why not get a house in the Crown?"

Fix was silent.

"Oh," Indrajit said. "*She* lives in the Lee."

"Yes."

They were silent for some time.

"You know," Indrajit said, "we've been in here awhile.

For a guy who urgently needed Ilsa without Peer back by tomorrow morning, the Lord Chamberlain seems pretty content to let us stew."

"I think he's recovered her. Maybe she just came back. Maybe some other jobber found her."

"Maybe Grit Wopal found her."

"Then why would Thrush want to speak to us?"

"Maybe he doesn't," Indrajit said. "Maybe he just wants us killed. Maybe he wants to interrogate us first. Or maybe he'll turn us over to the constables."

"I feel like we keep chasing our tails around a track of endless possibilities."

"Yeah, but in the end, one of these explanations is right."

"Does it matter if we ever find out?" Fix asked. "And how will we know?"

"I want to know the truth," Indrajit said. "But it's not as important to me as, first, survival, and second, getting paid." But was that really true? It was, at least in the sense that if Indrajit died, he'd never find a successor Recital Thane.

"And what about that deadline?" Fix asked. "Tomorrow *morning*. The opera's performances are in the evening, so it's not that he wanted to be sure she made the show."

"If Thrush wants her dead, then he wants her dead by tomorrow morning." Indrajit tried to focus. "So maybe he thinks he's about to kill her, but he's keeping us in reserve just in case he fails, to deploy us again?"

"I feel like there's some central point we're missing," Fix said. "Some central idea that, once we see it, it will cause the events of the last two days to make complete sense."

"I don't think Thrush wants her dead," Indrajit said. "So I think either he's rescued her, and has just forgotten to come tell us about it, or he's about to find out where she is, and then he'll come up and send us after her."

"And the deadline, tomorrow morning? What do you make of *that*?"

Something nagged at Indrajit, but he couldn't remember what.

"I don't know," he said. "Is it possible that he knew something bad was going to happen to Ilsa? With all these armed thugs running around, is it possible that Orem Thrush wants to protect Ilsa? That he knows someone will try to attack her tomorrow morning, and he wants to save her? That whoever attacked her before is going to try again tomorrow?"

"I don't think Orem Thrush wants to save Ilsa," Fix said slowly. "Or at least, not for Ilsa's sake. I think Orem wants to *own* her, like he owns so many other things and people."

"Except *us*," Indrajit said. "He doesn't own *us*." The bluster rang hollow.

"And in your scenario," Fix said, "who tried to kill Ilsa the first time? It wouldn't have been the Lord Chamberlain, if he's trying to save her. So ... are we back to the opera house? We never really investigated *them*."

"Maybe Holy-Pot had something personal against her," Indrajit said. "He tried to have *us* killed, after all. Maybe he wanted *her* dead, too."

"So he entered into a risk-repurchasing agreement that would cause him to lose money if she died?"

"That loss would only make him look innocent, if

anyone investigated. In the meantime, it let him set her up, along with us."

"Interesting," Fix said. "How can we find out if that's true?"

"Well, we're not going to find a note, in which Holy-Pot confesses that he tried to kill Ilsa without Peer. Maybe we *will* have to hire a necromancer."

"Your idea might suggest who killed Holy-Pot, though."

"What? Who?" Indrajit yawned. His aching muscles were knotting up, his wounds reaching that state of scabbing where they no longer felt they were about to tear, and instead began to itch, and he was exhausted. All told, he really wanted to sleep. Almost as much as he wanted fourteen hundred Imperials.

"Ilsa," Fix said. "If we left them alone, maybe Holy-Pot saw his chance and tried to kill her. Only she defended herself."

"Or maybe she knew what he was up to, and ambushed him."

"We'll have to talk to Ilsa to find out," Fix said.

"Or a necromancer."

"I don't believe you can talk with the dead. Or rather, I don't believe the dead can talk to *you*."

"I don't know," Indrajit said. "I've seen odd things. Heard an old cunning woman once, who had a familiar spirit. The thing sounded like it spoke out of her belly, and it had this voice . . . it was like a tree saw was talking."

"You sure it wasn't some little man, hiding down there? Someone Mote Gannon's size? Or someone else talking through a tube? Or maybe the old woman had a second face, like Holy-Pot, only *her* second face was set into her belly?"

"All possible," Indrajit admitted. "Still, I tend to believe."

An iron rasp at the door made Indrajit sit up straight. Moments later, the door opened and a light burned his eyes. After blinking away the initial pain, Indrajit saw that the light came from a single oil lamp—he'd simply become adjusted to the darkness.

Standing in the doorway and holding the lamp was Grit Wopal, the Lord Chamberlain's Yifft spy.

"Good evening." The Yifft stepped into the room and shut the door behind him. The immediately following *thud* suggested that the bar was being put back into place.

Indrajit stayed seated. "Fancy meeting *you* here."

The Yifft chuckled. "I'm glad you have a sense of humor. It's so much easier to work at hard jobs with people who are capable of laughing."

"I'm glad you see us working together," Fix said. "This sort of feels more like we're prisoners."

"Yes, sorry about that." Wopal crouched to set the lamp in the center of the floor, then sat cross-legged against a wall. "There's just a lot of activity out there right now. A lot of *heat*, as you jobbers would say."

"What do spies call it?" Fix asked.

Wopal raised a hand. "And I'm not a spy."

"No?" Indrajit asked.

"I'm a *spymaster*."

"Does that make *us* spies?" Fix asked.

"I might use the word *agents* instead," Wopal said. "Or *assets*, if I wanted to be more vague. The Lord Chamberlain usually refers to his *servants*."

"I like *spies*," Indrajit said. "Though *agents* is okay."

"If jobbers say there's *heat* out there," Fix said, "what do *agents* say?"

Wopal chuckled. "Enough, really. The point is, there are people chasing Ilsa without Peer still. I have not yet determined who they all are or who they work for."

"We're still trying to figure that out ourselves," Indrajit said. "The truth is, we hadn't ruled out the Lord Chamberlain as the one trying to kill her."

Wopal nodded. "Because you're not entirely sure you can trust me. I understand."

"So you're keeping us in here, because we contribute to the heat." Indrajit nodded. "That's not unfair."

"On the other hand," Fix said, "if the Lord Chamberlain really needs to find Ilsa by morning, he can't have much time left. A couple of hours, maybe."

"Oh, the time has run out."

"There go the thousand Imperials." Fix shook his head.

"Frozen hells. But there's still Frodilo."

"Also," Wopal added, "Ilsa without Peer is dead."

Indrajit took the news like a hammer to the chest. It snatched his breath away, and he was surprised to feel so much emotion. He tried to make a joke, and couldn't.

Fix came to the rescue. "Looks like the Protagonists are going to start business thinly capitalized."

Indrajit didn't quite understand, but *thinly capitalized* sounded like *poor*, and that was certainly going to be true. He laughed, but it was a sharp bark that ended quickly.

"What happened?" Fix asked.

"She was killed at the Palace of Shadow and Joy," Wopal said. "I don't know who killed her."

"So . . . we failed," Indrajit said. "Whatever it was the Lord Chamberlain wanted her for, it's over. He's not going to pay us, but also . . ."

"Is he going to kill us?" Fix asked. "Break our legs?"

"No, no." Wopal waved away the thought with a gesture. "Another... avenue... materialized for the Lord Chamberlain, so he'll have what he wants, despite Ilsa's death. And she was unhappy, poor thing, so maybe her passing is for the best. I don't know if the Lord Chamberlain plans to pay you for your work. If he does, I think it's likely that it won't be a thousand Imperials."

"He'll just wait until the heat passes and then let us go?" Indrajit suggested hopefully.

"I've asked him to allow me to continue to engage you as assets," Wopal said. "You're enterprising, dogged, systematic, and clever enough. So even if he doesn't recompense you, I'll pay you something out of my funds, and then I'll engage the... is it the *Protagonists*?"

"Could be worse," Fix said.

"Sure could be better, too." Indrajit shook his head, and then he laughed. "Okay, Wopal. If you don't mind working with a guy who once punched you in the face, I'm in."

"Twice," Wopal said. "*Twice* punched me in the face. I don't mind. And the Lord Chamberlain will be here shortly, to make the details of his will known."

"What avenue?" Indrajit asked.

"Excuse me?"

"What avenue materialized that let the Lord Chamberlain have his way, even with Ilsa dead?" Indrajit asked.

"I take it you know... what Ilsa was capable of?" Wopal asked. "I don't mean her singing."

"You mean how she made men fall in love with her. Made them sluggish and compliant."

Wopal nodded. "The Lord Chamberlain found another of her kind."

"A *third*?" Indrajit asked.

"Third?" Wopal looked surprised.

Indrajit heard footsteps in the hall, and the bar being drawn back again.

"Also," he added, "the *Protagonists* is a great name. For jobbers or agents or whatever we end up calling ourselves."

"Sure sounded good in a battle cry," Fix said.

Grit Wopal frowned and blinked.

The door opened and light flooded in.

Chapter Twenty-Five

〰〰〰〰〰

"ILSA!" INDRAJIT CRIED, ONCE HIS VISION HAD cleared. "Thanks be to every god in Kish!"

"Kish has some dark gods," Fix muttered. "Maybe we don't need to thank the cannibal cults and the kidnappers and the murderers."

Indrajit ignored him.

Orem Thrush entered the room. He was resplendent in a toga dyed deep red, which he held in place with a closed fist over his sternum. He wore sandals of soft white leather, with thin soles. His hair was oiled and pulled back away from his forehead, and perfume wafted from him in waves. He carried no weapon, and something else about him seemed odd, but Indrajit couldn't decide quite what. Altogether, Thrush's costume spoke of wealth and luxury, and a man who had no need to fight or flee.

Orem Thrush must have been bound for the Auction, and meeting with the other six heads of the great families. Would such a costume intimidate the other lords? Would his lack of weapons reassure them? Would they all be dressed like this?

And was it that late in the day? What time was it?

Beside Thrush came Ilsa, squat in the body and long of limbs, wrapped in armor that was lacquered the same red. Her head was uncovered, but in her hands she held a helmet. The helmet looked like a horned skull, and was the one piece of her garb that was colored a bone-white. She wore a straight sword and two long knives at her belt. The costume resembled, slightly, the costume she'd worn onstage during the opera, and at the same time it made her appear as the living incarnation of the Lord Chamberlain's heraldic icon.

Cold relief poured through Indrajit's heart.

"This is not Ilsa," the Lord Chamberlain said. "This is Lysta."

The relief turned into icy dread. Indrajit stared.

"She looks like Ilsa," he said stupidly.

Thrush nodded.

The light seemed to fade from Indrajit's vision. His breath came tight in his lungs and his head swam. "Is she like . . . like you?" he asked. "She takes on someone else's form?" Did Thrush intend to send a mock replacement to the Palace of Shadow and Joy, to continue being paid? But surely, no replacement would sing like Ilsa without Peer.

But Orem Thrush might be able to sell the risk of Ilsa losing her voice, and then collect under the agreement when it turned out that, naturally, the impostor couldn't sing like the real thing.

Frozen hells, he was beginning to think in terms of risk-merchantry.

Fix stared, his eyes narrowed.

Thrush glowered, as if Indrajit had said something deeply rude. "Lysta is of Ilsa's race."

Things were not adding up to Indrajit. He wasn't sure whether he had too little information or too much, but the images of the last two days flashed through his mind in changing and repeating sequence, and wouldn't come to rest: Ilsa on stage, Ilsa in the Fountain, Ilsa in Frodilo Choot's office, Ilsa beneath the Paper Sook, Ilsa Two springing from the blue chest. What sense did all of this make?

"Ilsa told us she was the last of her kind," Indrajit said.

"She believed she was." Thrush nodded a slow acknowledgement. "For many years, I believed she was, too."

"Was there some other community of her people, then?" Indrajit asked. "A village of astounding singers? This is going to be big news for the opera world. I can see the recruiters now, riding out to some remote high valley with letters of credit and promises of hiring bonuses and glorious salaries to be made to young singers. There is wealth in a golden voice."

He did not say, though he was imagining it, that those riders would have to wear sprigs of the Courting Flower. Assuming they were males.

"The lure of wealth is indeed great, for singers and promoters alike." Lysta smiled at Indrajit grotesquely as she croaked. "They are only men, after all."

Indrajit nodded. Something unknown nagged at his mind. "Ilsa was a shockingly good singer. If she was in fact, not without peer, if you can sing like she did, then the Lord Chamberlain and the Palace of Shadow and Joy are both very lucky."

Orem Thrush shook his head. "Her people are destroyed now. There is no community of them left in the world."

"Lysta without Peer?" Fix murmured.

The singer smiled, an expression that was both trollish and gentle.

"What were they called, while they lived?" Indrajit asked.

"Idle curiosity?" Thrush asked.

Fix smiled. "My colleague has a responsibility to produce an epic. I believe he wants to include Ilsa and her kind."

"And Lysta," said Orem Thrush.

Fix tipped his head. "And Lysta."

"I never knew their name." Thrush turned to look at the singer.

"Nor I," she said, with a voice like a sack full of pebbles being ground together, a rumbling croak that sounded just like Ilsa's. "I survived the massacre of my youth and have lived as a beggar and a slave ever since. If you could learn the name of my people and tell me, I'd be grateful."

"You'll need epithets, too." Indrajit thought a moment, then translated his syllables into Kishite. "*Golden of voice, women commanding, mercy at all times to men who are favored.*"

He thought Lysta looked touched at his words. Sad, perhaps.

"They rhyme in Blaatshi," he hastened to add.

"So there were only three survivors, I guess," Fix said.

Grit Wopal stood against the wall and surveyed the others with his eyes in a deep squint.

"I don't know the third," Thrush said. "There was Ilsa. Then, recently, I found Lysta."

"What, back in the same village?" Indrajit asked. "Was she living there alone, all these years?"

"For a race that was supposed to be extinct," Fix observed, "there are an awful lot of these people."

Lysta's nictitating membranes fluttered. "Sadly, I do not know any others. When my people were destroyed, I wandered alone for days. When I was finally rescued, it was by a caravan of merchants bound for the Endless Road. I was sold as a slave in Thûl, and have moved from port to port in the service of different masters, or begging for scraps when between masters."

"Were you rebellious?" Indrajit asked. He was imagining himself in her place. "Was that why no one wanted to keep you long?"

Lysta curtseyed. "The contrary. *All* wanted to keep me, and the price to purchase me rose and rose, until it became a prince's ransom, and only very few could even make a reasonable offer. When possible, I bought my freedom, or I fled."

"Runaway slaves get harsh punishments," Fix said softly.

Lysta nodded. "I was far too valuable to punish. I was a beggar, but I could bring wealth to kings. I languished in Pelth, until the Lord Chamberlain heard of me and made an offer the size of which caused my former owner to swoon."

"You exaggerate," Thrush said. "But the lady was happy with the price."

"Do you sing like Ilsa?" Fix asked mildly. "Did all the women of your race have that gift?"

Lysta nodded, a gesture which made her look like

a toadstool retracting its cap into itself several times in quick succession. "We all do, I think. We all *did*."

"Ilsa, I was deeply saddened to learn, died in the Palace of Shadow and Joy." Orem Thrush frowned. His face was subtly changing again, looking more and more like Lysta's. It was a shocking look on the Lord Chamberlain.

"Who killed her?" Indrajit asked.

"I believe it was someone you know." Thrush met Indrajit's gaze; he looked like a duskier, taller Ilsa. Or Lysta, rather. "Yashta Hossarian."

"Hossarian?" Indrajit and Fix spoke at the same moment.

"He's a jobber," Thrush said. "He has no arms, and a bird's legs, and he's black as obsidian."

"His claws are orange," Fix said glumly.

"We know him," Indrajit said. He wasn't sure he could piece the information in with what he knew already—once Holy-Pot died, Hossarian had indeed been looking for Ilsa, but why would the jobber want to kill the singer?

Or why would Holy-Pot want the singer killed? And what sense did it make that he would want the singer killed in the event that he himself died?

"*I saw the killing*," Lysta sang.

Indrajit's confusion faded, replaced by a deep sense of tranquility, and he believed her. He nodded. "It makes sense."

"It makes sense," Fix agreed.

"I hope that you will remain in my employment," Orem Thrush said, "answering to Grit Wopal. Perhaps one of the tasks you might undertake is finding Yashta Hossarian and inflicting the appropriate consequence."

A wave of warm feeling washed over Indrajit. He felt well-being, contentment, happiness, and a desire to be cooperative. But his feeling wasn't directed at Orem Thrush—it was directed at Lysta. He would do what Thrush asked, because Lysta wanted it.

But then Lysta asked it, too.

"*Please stay,*" she sang, her voice full and operatic and gorgeous. "*Enter the Lord Chamberlain's service with me.*"

"Of course," Indrajit said.

"Of course," Fix added.

"Yes," Grit Wopal said, after a moment's hesitation.

Orem Thrush nodded. "I want you to stay in here for the day. Food and water will be brought to you. I'll pay you for your work—say, ten Imperials? Tonight, I will certainly have work for you to do."

Indrajit and Fix nodded. Wopal followed suit.

"Be careful." Indrajit struggled to find the words, his sense of well-being taking away his ability to think out loud. "Be careful of Hossarian."

"Of course," Thrush said.

"He will...he will think Lysta is Ilsa. And try to kill her again." Indrajit's speech was slow, but he thought he avoided slurring his words. "Because they look..."

"Yes," the Lord Chamberlain said, "I understand. Don't worry, we'll travel protected." He raised a yellow blossom at his breast up to his nose and breathed deeply through it.

Blossom. The Courting Flower.

A dim light pierced a dark vault somewhere in the back of Indrajit's consciousness, but the shaft didn't seem to touch on anything. It moved through the darkness, looking for a connection it couldn't find.

Orem Thrush and Lysta without Peer left, the door shutting behind them. Indrajit didn't hear the sound of a lock turning or a bar being placed into brackets, but Grit Wopal remained in the room with them. The Yifft sat, back against the wall, and hummed.

Indrajit felt as if he was swimming in warm milk.

"Flower," he croaked, a few minutes later. The shaft of light in his mind was shining on a small bush in his memory.

"The Courting Flower." Fix had somehow ended up facedown on the floor, and he spoke without raising his head. "It didn't work."

"Jog," Grit Wopal said dreamily.

Indrajit patted himself on the chest and found the sprig, still in place. It hadn't protected him—was Lysta more powerful than Ilsa? Or did she have her magical power set on a higher setting?

"Jog," Wopal said again.

Indrajit shook the flower, but that had no obvious effect.

Fix laughed.

"No," the Yifft said. "Stand up and run."

Indrajit floated in warmth again for a time he couldn't measure, and then found himself pulled to his feet. Fix steadied him upright, and then pushed him.

"Run," Fix muttered.

They staggered around the room. The first two circuits were painful, as they rebounded off the walls repeatedly, missing every turn.

But then, just a little, Indrajit's head started to clear.

"You know," Indrajit panted to the Yifft, who still sat slumped on the floor. "You studied . . . Ilsa."

"Jog," Wopal groaned.

"The Courting Flower . . . stopped protecting us," Fix grunted.

"Maybe Lysta is . . . too powerful," Indrajit suggested.

"Maybe the plant . . . withered," Fix countered, voice still thick and slow.

Indrajit stopped. He needed fresh Courting Flower.

"Jog!" Wopal tried to climb to his own feet and failed, sinking back to the ground.

Fix grabbed Indrajit and tried to drag him, but the Recital Thane pushed his friend away. "No," Indrajit said. "Wait. I have more. Where did I put it?"

Fix leaned over, resting his elbows on his knees and breathing deeply.

"In my pocket." Fix dug into the pocket of his kilt and found what he only vaguely remembered putting there . . . what, a day earlier? Several bunches of the Courting Flower, leaves still bright green, petals still yellow as egg yolks.

It wasn't fresh, but it was fresher than what he was currently wearing. Was it fresh enough? He placed a sprig to his nose and inhaled deeply.

And his thoughts cleared.

"Frozen hells." He clapped a second bunch into Fix's hand and then pressed it to Fix's nose. While his partner was still inhaling, he did the same thing to Grit Wopal.

The Yifft recovered immediately, springing to his feet. "That was Ilsa without Peer!" he snapped.

Indrajit threw away the old sprig and pinned the new one to his tunic as Fix did the same. "I don't know," he said. "They look pretty similar, but we saw another one of their kind. She was dead and in a trunk, but she looked pretty much identical to Ilsa, too."

Fix furrowed his brow in thought.

"You said *three*," Wopal pressed. "Tell me what three women of Ilsa's race you have seen."

"Ilsa," Indrajit said.

"Then a dead one in a box," Fix continued. "Then . . . who did we just see now?"

"Lysta," Indrajit said.

Wopal shook his head. "Ilsa."

Indrajit's head felt hollowed out by fatigue and hunger. "It's possible. But I don't see any reason to think it's actually true."

"They are only men, after all," Wopal said.

Fix nodded. "Ilsa said that. Several times, while we were together."

"I heard her say it, too," Wopal said. "In the Fountain, and here in the Lord Chamberlain's palace."

"So . . ." Fix said, the struggle to think visible on his face.

"Lysta said it, too," Indrajit said. "Tonight. Just a few minutes ago. Or an hour. Or however long that was. Only she wasn't Lysta. She was Ilsa without Peer."

"She faked her own death," Fix said. "That's why she had the corpse in her trunk, it wasn't some kind of strange species power—she needed a body."

"Where did she get it?" Indrajit asked.

"Lysta came to House Thrush a couple of months ago," Grit Wopal said. "Ilsa had been expressing discontent with her . . . work, and the Lord Chamberlain was preparing to replace her with Lysta. But then Lysta disappeared."

"Ilsa killed Lysta," Indrajit said. "And she was going to use her body to fake her own death, so she could run away, to escape Orem Thrush and her work at the opera, which she had grown sick of."

"But Thrush knew there were two of them," Fix said. "Surely, she would have to expect him to come after her."

Lights flashed in Indrajit's mind. "Yes, which is why she needed to fake her death, and make a lot of money from it. She would use the cash to flee and start a new life." It made a terrible sense. "But why blame her death on Yashta Hossarian?"

"Because there *was* a dead man's switch," Grit Wopal said. "Which can only mean that Holy-Pot Diaphernes thought that Ilsa without Peer would likely kill him. So he hired Hossarian to take revenge, in the event of his death."

"That only really makes sense if he also told Ilsa about the dead man's switch," Fix said thoughtfully.

"Which is how she knows that Hossarian is after her," Wopal added.

"It also only really makes sense if Holy-Pot and Ilsa were in league." Indrajit felt as if his head was exploding. "He was going to help her disappear, and get paid in the bargain. Thinkum Tosh was their go-between—we know how easy that would have been for her. They'd collect under the risk-contract with Frodilo Choot, who was picked as the mark because she jilted Mote Gannon. Holy-Pot would pay back some of that money under his risk repurchasing agreement, they'd split it, and Ilsa would flee, believed dead by most but in fact alive and wealthy."

"Only Ilsa got wary of her help. She killed Tosh, and then she killed Holy-Pot. He didn't trust her, if he had a dead man's switch, so why go into the Palace with us? Maybe he thought he needed to, to help her go through with the plan of faking her death. Or to make her do it." Fix shook his head, a gesture of admiration. "And she killed him. Figuring she could pose as Lysta, get Orem Thrush to kill Hossarian, and then keep all the money for herself. Why kill Tosh?"

"To cover her tracks?" Indrajit could only guess. "He knew too much. Or maybe Tosh got greedy. Gannon's Handlers were hired to kill Ilsa and blame us, killing us in the process to make sure we wouldn't object. But if Ilsa was behind the scheme, she didn't want to die, which means that she thought she could outwit the Handlers. Using her magical power, no doubt she stood a good chance."

"But some of the Handlers came wearing the Courting Flower!" Fix snapped. "Which might mean that Tosh betrayed Ilsa from the start, planning to collect on the contract that was, after all, in his name, when Ilsa died. She figured it out and killed him, but not before the Handlers were warned. Or at least, some of them."

"We have to warn Choot," Indrajit said. "And the bank."

"What bank?" Wopal asked.

"Goldsmiths United Depository," Fix said.

"I'll send couriers to both." Grit Wopal jolted into action, flinging the door open. Indrajit and Fix followed him into the larger palace; Indrajit noted the gray light of early dawn peeping in through windows as the three men headed for an exit.

"I'm astounded, though," Indrajit said, thinking out loud. "All this to escape the opera. I mean, I understand committing crimes to get wealth, but it seems that, with her magical gift, there would be an easier way."

"Ilsa isn't trying to escape the opera," Grit Wopal

said. "If all that was at stake here was the opera, no one would have died in the first place, and Ilsa would simply have left when she grew tired of singing."

"I don't understand," Indrajit said. "You told me she was tired of her work."

Wopal stopped and spun to face the other two men. They stood in a room with a single wide table, on which rested Indrajit's and Fix's possessions. "The opera house is where Ilsa *diverts* herself."

"The *Auction*," Fix said. "Her work is at the Auction, ensuring that Orem Thrush gets exactly what he wants, every time. No wonder he wouldn't let her leave."

"Oh, no," Indrajit said. "Without the money, and trapped again, Ilsa has only one move left. She's going to kill him."

Chapter Twenty-Six

"MAYBE GATHER UP A SQUAD OF ZALAPTINGS?"
Indrajit buckled his sword belt over his kilt and
headed for the palace's back door on Wopal's heels.
Fix followed two steps behind, given the larger number
of weapons he had to collect.

Four Eyes the doorman, newly deferential in their
presence, stepped aside into an alcove with a single
cushioned chair. Close to the door as it was, it might
have been his official station, a place to wait for
knocking visitors.

"Zalaptings are weak," Fix grumbled.

"Yeah, but they're so plentiful," Indrajit countered.
"That's why you say, of mosquitos, for instance, *these
things breed like Zalaptings*. It means they spawn in
huge numbers."

"I know what it means."

"And I'd love to have a wall of Zalaptings to take
a few hits for me, you know?"

"No time!" Grit Wopal threw open the bar holding
the door shut.

Yashta Hossarian crashed through the door, opening it with his body and knocking one of the hinges loose. Four Eyes immediately shrieked, not a mindless alarm but a string of high-pitched, compact syllables that Indrajit couldn't decipher.

That ended abruptly as Yashta Hossarian flicked the sharp tip of an orange talon across Four Eyes's throat. Bright red blood spouting from a severed artery and all four eyes opening into blind circles, the doorman sank straight down into a puddle of flesh on the floor.

Fix leaped past Indrajit, falchion in hand, but he didn't attack. As the obsidian-colored birdman jobber recoiled into a defensive position, Fix grabbed the Yifft by the elbow and yanked him back. By the time he was shoulder to shoulder with Indrajit and the spymaster was behind them, Indrajit had out his own blade so that the two men formed a defensive wall protecting Grit Wopal.

"Fear the Voice of Lightning!" Indrajit cried.

Hossarian coiled, legs bent as if prepared to leap forward. "I'm here for Ilsa without Peer." His voice rumbled like the bottom of a river.

"You want to kill her." At the sight of the long, powerful muscles on the big jobber's body, and the smell of blood rising from Four Eyes, Indrajit's grip on his sword felt slippery and unsure. "I understand. You're keeping faith with Diaphernes."

"Faith has nothing to do with it." Hossarian sniffed at the air. He shifted his weight from side to side, changing stances as if testing Indrajit's and Fix's reactions. Indrajit wished his heart weren't beating so loud. "I am keeping my contract."

"For honor's sake?" Indrajit asked.

Hossarian blinked at him without expression.

"Someone out there is holding a final payment of money," Fix said. "When he proves he killed Ilsa, he'll get the cash."

"Gentlemen," Grit Wopal whispered. "There are other doors. Let's back away calmly."

Indrajit and Fix retreated, slowly and together. Hossarian advanced a step for each step back they took.

"But you know there's a dead body," Indrajit said. "Not Ilsa's, but another of her kind. Why not present that one?"

"Maybe the other party knows about the dead body already," Fix suggested.

"Stop trying to talk him out of leaving us alone!" Indrajit hissed.

Hossarian chuckled, a low rattle. "There is also honor."

"She's not here, anyway," Indrajit said.

"No?" Hossarian sniffed the air again. "I smell her. But I think you're right, it's an old scent."

"If you can smell her," Fix muttered, "maybe you should try tracking her." He and Indrajit retreated farther. The hall was barely narrow enough for the two of them to defend it, and they entered a stretch without side tables or statuary. From a mural, some former Lord Chamberlain frowned down at them with gaping eye sockets.

"But *you're* here." Yashta Hossarian smiled as he followed. "And you two fools are hells-bent on saving her life."

"No," Indrajit said quickly. "We were, but now we're . . ." He thought for a moment, jaw working without words. What *were* they doing now? "Now we're trying to save Orem Thrush."

"Interesting," Hossarian purred. "Why?"

"Because..." Indrajit said.

"Because..." Fix added.

"Because they're the Lord Chamberlain's servants," Wopal said.

The floor just in front of Yashta Hossarian disappeared, falling away in the form of a trap door that opened beneath his feet. The gap that suddenly appeared was the width of the hall, and beneath it was a lightless shaft.

But the jobber was already moving.

"Stop him!" Wopal yelled.

Indrajit surged forward, Vacho up to try to keep the orange talons from his throat. Fix did the same, but Hossarian wasn't attacking; he was trying to get a grip on the stone at the lip of the pit, and he teetered, struggling to find purchase.

A brown object half the size of a fist sailed forward past Indrajit's ear; but for his excellent peripheral vision, he probably wouldn't have seen it at all. It struck Hossarian in his antennae-like tentacles and burst, unleashing a glittering black cloud that stung Indrajit's nose.

Pepper.

Shrieking in rage, Yashta Hossarian waved at the cloud in front of his face and then fell into the shaft.

"This way!" Grit Wopal called. As the three men ran through the palace's corridors, guided by the Yifft, Zalaptings with long spears and short swords swarmed past them in the other direction. "Hold him!" the Yifft barked to the Zalaptings.

After sprinting down a short hallway, they encountered two more Zalaptings. These men were unarmored and carried only short swords—they looked as if they were off-duty, or maybe they were house-servants rather than soldiers.

"Follow me!" Wopal barked, and the two Zalaptings obeyed.

Two more long corridors, and suddenly they were at the other door of the palace. Lizard-like men in Thrush's livery bowed and opened the door, ushering them out.

The Auction House was only a few blocks away. They ran.

"Won't the other lords . . . think there's something strange . . . when the Lord Chamberlain . . . shows up . . . looking like Ilsa?" Indrajit asked, huffing.

"Why should they?" Wopal asked.

Fix laughed.

"Because he'll . . . look like Ilsa?" Indrajit felt stupid. "But no . . . they don't know what she looks like . . . she sings in a mask."

"And if she always . . . goes to the Auction," Fix panted, "maybe for years now . . . then maybe they're used . . . to Orem Thrush looking . . . like her. Maybe they think . . . he naturally looks like that."

"Or they think . . . she's his favorite bodyguard . . . and he always looks . . . like her."

Grit Wopal nodded to all their guesses. "They won't see . . . his face at all . . . beneath his mask."

Arriving at a small elbow of street corner just out of sight of the Palace of Shadow and Joy and the Auction House both, they stopped to catch their breath.

"How will she kill him?" Indrajit asked.

"She's armed and he isn't," Wopal said.

The two Zalaptings stared. They looked too frightened

to ask what was going on, and they tightened their grip on their swords.

"It'd be easy enough," Indrajit admitted. "All she'd have to do is get the sprig of Courting Flower away from him, then knock him silly with her magic. He'd probably slit his own throat, if she asked nicely."

"What a power to have," Grit Wopal muttered. Straightening his clothes, the spymaster led them into the plaza in front of the Auction House. The low steps before the shut door were occupied, by men in two different sets of livery. Indrajit ignored them for the moment, focusing on his companions.

"You'd like to have that power, too," he guessed.

"It would make my job very easy," Wopal admitted.

"I've been thinking about it," Fix said. "I think Ilsa's power has to be tied to reproduction."

"Oh, wait," Indrajit said. "I haven't had a good chance to use the word *fascicle* for almost an entire day."

"I didn't read this in a fascicle, I'm just thinking about it."

"Planning to read a paper at the Hall of Guesses?" Indrajit teased his partner. "Give anatomy lectures?"

"I wouldn't mind dissecting Ilsa," Fix admitted. "With some Vin Dalu help. I might be able to test my idea."

"I also wouldn't mind dissecting Ilsa," Wopal muttered.

"I think if reproduction were really hard for your race," Fix said, "and it had something to do with the female—for instance, maybe if the female were only fertile one day a year, or something—then it would be very helpful for the female to be able to order males to step up and...do their job, so to speak... at that precise time."

"You say that as if the females *choose* to have that power," Indrajit said.

"I don't exactly mean it like that. But maybe when they were ... created ... it was chosen for them."

"You mean, the *gods* gave them that power to overcome a limitation in their reproductive arrangements?" Indrajit resisted the urge to sneer.

"Fine," Fix said. "Maybe it was the gods. Or whatever power or process made them. I'm just saying, the parts of any successful creature tend to fit together, and that's how I imagine Ilsa's people might need such a power."

"Do you two ever shut up?" Grit Wopal asked.

Chastened, Indrajit faced forward just in time to step up onto the lowest of the stairs in front of the Auction House, and realized that the two liveries worn by the men there were that of the jobbers in orange tunics, and the gray tunic and circular glyph that identified Mote Gannon's Handlers.

"Ah, frozen hells."

Tall Gannon rattled down the steps, drawing a long sword with each hand as he did so. Fix also drew his weapons, ax and falchion, but Indrajit raised his hands to try to avert a massacre.

"Hey, listen." He looked around for indications of the presence of the little green Tiny Gannon, but didn't see any. Did the minute fellow—apparently, the thinking or controlling part of the Gannon-entity—have to be close? Was he sitting in his swampy pool in his tower, half a mile away, seeing through Tall Gannon's eyes? Was he hiding inside Tall Gannon's body? "Listen, Gannon. We've had some disagreements this week, but I think it's safe to say we can be on the same side now."

At the last moment, as Fix was tensing his muscles to leap to the attack, Tall Gannon hesitated. "How do you figure that?"

Why did Indrajit think there could be peace? After all, Gannon's Handlers had been in on the plan to kill Indrajit and Fix and make them the patsies for a murder.

"You were engaged by Holy-Pot Diaphernes, really," Indrajit said hastily. "We were also engaged by Holy-Pot—"

Gannon took a swing.

Indrajit stepped back quickly, but Fix's move was even quicker. The shorter man leaped in front of Indrajit, caught Gannon's sword with the head of his ax, and shoved him away. The two Zalaptings fell in behind Fix, shaking.

"We are not the marks anymore!" Indrajit screamed. He wanted to yell, *If Orem Thrush dies, I'll make sure you get the blame!*, but that didn't seem wise. "Holy-Pot's gone, and won't pay you! If you kill us, Frodilo Choot won't thank you!"

Gannon regained his balance with a thoughtful look on his face. "I can't say I'm too afraid of the wrath of a single risk-merchant." He raised his weapons into a defensive position. "Especially that one."

Fix countered by dropping into an attack stance. "Why are you doing this?"

Tall Gannon smiled coldly. "It's personal."

A Kishi or a Zalapting or some other man with eyes set in the front of his face would have missed the attack. Indrajit, though, was Blaatshi, and as Tall Gannon said the word *personal*, he saw a flash of slate blue racing toward him at an oblique angle, from nearly directly behind.

He threw himself backward. Grit Wopal yelped, Tall Gannon attacked, Fix attacked back with two weapons, the Zalaptings dove in like lavender dogs, nipping at Gannon's heels, and Indrajit slammed his chest into the attacking Luzzazza's ankles. As they tumbled together, calculating that he had only moments of seized initiative left, Indrajit drew his leaf-bladed sword.

They rolled to their feet at the same moment, rage in the Luzzazza's face and a long spear in both his hands. Indrajit was too close for the spear to hit him, so the Luzzazza stepped back, looking to put the right distance between them.

Indrajit stabbed him as hard as he could, in his remaining invisible arm.

He could tell which side of the body it was on, because the other side had a visible bandage where the Luzzazza had lost a limb. And he could tell that he'd scored a hit, because his blade sank deep into flesh, struck bone, and then showered very visible blood all over the cobblestones.

The Luzzazza roared. Twisting, he jerked leaf-bladed Vacho from Indrajit's hand and then stabbed with the spear—

Indrajit stepped in again, and grabbed the spear with both hands.

The Luzzazza was bigger and stronger, and should have been able to seize control of the disputed weapon. But the Luzzazza was also freshly missing one arm and freshly wounded in another, and it was therefore in pain and distracted.

Indrajit yanked away the spear.

"This way!" Grit Wopal called.

Tall Gannon backed away from the battle. Indrajit picked his sword up from the cobblestones. Fix, in turn, grabbed Indrajit by the arm and dragged him out of sight after Grit Wopal and his Zalaptings. Turning down a side street, they stopped and looked back over a baker's stall and three children playing a game with sheep's knucklebones.

The gray-clad Handlers stared after them, or helped the Luzzazza. The jobbers in orange stood aside and watched, weapons ready.

"Aren't those orange tunics on our side?" Indrajit asked.

"They're hired by the Lord Chamberlain." Wopal panted. "The Auction is always guarded by at least two jobber companies, engaged by two different lords. But they don't know who I am and won't take direction from me."

"So, Gannon?" Indrajit asked.

"In the service of the Lord Stargazer at the moment." Wopal shook his head. "Our bad luck that he appears to hate you."

"What are we doing?" one of the Zalaptings asked.

Wopal fixed him with a firm eye. "Rescuing the Lord Chamberlain. I hope you're both prepared to be heroes."

The Zalaptings gulped.

"I do still have two orange tunics," Indrajit pointed out. "And one gray one."

"That's not going to work." Fix shook his head. "Not if they look at us directly."

"Frontal assault is right out," Indrajit added. "Sewers?"

"We'd need time to explore, and digging equipment."

Fix looked to the Yifft. "Unless you know a secret door in."

Grit Wopal shook his head. "If there are secret doors, I don't know them. I've never been inside the Auction House, much less the Auction Chamber. The heads of the great families go nearly alone, taking a single bodyguard each."

"Some spymaster you are. How about secret powers?" Indrajit asked. "Maybe you can use your eye to put all the jobbers to sleep?"

Wopal didn't even bother to chuckle.

"What we could really use is Ilsa's power," Indrajit reflected.

"Or the power of flight," Fix added. "With time, we might be able to get down into the roof of the Auction House by rope from the top of the Palace of Shadow and Joy."

"But we don't have rope or time, any more than we have the power of flight, or Ilsa on our side," Indrajit said. "Ilsa's inside that Auction House, and she might already have killed Orem Thrush."

"No," Wopal said. "If someone had killed one of the lords, we'd know it by now."

"Unless Ilsa has them all in a trance," Fix pointed out.

Indrajit pulled the gray and orange tunics out of his pocket and looked at them. They might still have value, but only if they weren't scrutinized too closely. "What we need," he suggested, "is a distraction."

"We could light a Zalapting on fire," Fix said.

Both lavender-skinned men scooted away from him.

"What we need," Indrajit continued, "is Yashta Hossarian."

Wopal frowned. "Why would Yashta Hossarian help us?"

"He won't," Indrajit said. "So *we're* going to have to help *him*."

"You want me to free him," Wopal said.

Indrajit nodded. "And tell him where to find Ilsa."

Chapter Twenty-Seven

WOPAL SENT THE TWO ZALAPTINGS. THEY RAN OFF eagerly.

"Will Hossarian tear up the Lord Chamberlain's palace?" Fix asked.

"I doubt it," Wopal said. "He would have to fear a terrible retribution, and besides, we're giving him what he wants."

Indrajit and Fix nodded sagely.

"A more serious possibility is that he might decide to avenge himself by killing the three of us." Wopal smiled. "Fix, I suggest you put on the gray tunic. It's far too small for Indrajit."

Indrajit handed over the tunic and Fix wormed his way into it. Indrajit and Wopal then donned the orange garb. "I guess we're betting that Hossarian will show up and cause a scene, like he did at the Lord Chamberlain's. And then we'll run in."

"Hold on." Grit Wopal smiled at Indrajit and opened his third eye.

Indrajit again saw the yellow flesh, the thick mucus, and the horizontal slit of an iris. He felt relieved when the Yifft crouched at the mouth of the alley and turned that strange eye on the Auction House.

"Are you going to stun them with your eye, after all?" He grinned.

Wopal ignored him. "Fix, you see those two Kishi at the right end of the men in gray?"

Fix looked. "One has long, curly hair and the other has a shaved head."

"When the noise starts, head directly for them."

"Can you see weakness or something?" Fix asked.

"I see their uncertainty. They're young, probably new."

"The Luzzazza is near them," Fix pointed out.

Wopal nodded. "But the Luzzazza is wounded."

Moments later, Yashta Hossarian exploded onto the plaza.

He was alone, and he was running. He charged the Auction House, heading not directly for the front door, but for a corner of the building.

He was as fast as a horse, and he took the jobbers by surprise.

"What's he doing?" Indrajit asked.

"Remember him jumping up to the rooftop?" Fix asked. "Let's go, we won't have much time."

They trotted down an alley and around a corner so that they came out onto the plaza from a different street. As they emerged, the jobbers had organized into something like a defensive wall. Arcing around ninety degrees of the building's circumference, composed of both gray and orange tunics, the wall of men faced Yashta Hossarian with spears lowered and shields forward.

Fix marched briskly toward the two Kishi Wopal had indicated. The Luzzazza had moved into the defensive wall, but two jobbers in orange tunics stood with the Kishi now. One had a fish's head, and the other had skin the color of ebony, and pointed ears.

Indrajit tried to look at his feet, feigning dejection. His wide vision served him well yet again, letting him observe keenly as Yashta Hossarian charged the wall of jobbers—

And then leaped right over it.

Those enormous legs, bent backward like a bird's, sent him flying from the ground while he was still out of reach of the spears and hurled him up over the heads of the mercenaries. Several of them jabbed gamely with their weapons and came up far short. A few hurled spears and missed.

Several shot bows, and two arrows struck Hossarian's body.

Hossarian didn't have wings, but he seemed to fall slowly from his jump, drifting down toward the rooftop of the Auction House. As he fell, the wall of jobbers pivoted to follow him, ignoring Indrajit and his companions.

"Hells take me," one of the Kishi said as Hossarian flew.

"Fire!" Mote Gannon yelled.

Hossarian hit the rooftop. He landed with a staggering, off-balance movement that suggested that his wounds were serious. A third arrow immediately struck him, and then Indrajit was too close to the Auction House to see what was happening on its rooftop.

Fix opened the door and they entered.

Behind the door, a single hallway appeared to

encircle the entire smallish building. Its outer edge
was square, to match the exterior of the building,
but its inner wall curved, suggesting a circular room
occupying the building's center. The hall was two
stories tall and its walls were bare to the point of
resembling a prison cell.

A person standing alone, a quarter-turn away along
the hall, suggested where the door could be found.
Indrajit sized the person up as they approached: short
and narrow, dark red, four teeth like tusks. He'd seen
this race of men before—hadn't there been one at the
opera house?—but he didn't remember their name.
Walrus Tusk stood beside a pair of double doors of
plain yetz-wood.

"No one can enter," Walrus Tusk said. "The Auction
is in progress."

Indrajit listened, imagining he'd hear shouted bids,
but there was silence. "Can you take a message in
for us, then?"

Walrus Tusk shook his head.

Indrajit dug into his kilt pocket, looking for his purse.

Fix punched Walrus Tusk in the face, felling him.
"Too much talking," he said to Indrajit, and then he
opened the doors.

Indrajit stepped over Walrus Tusk and into the
Auction Chamber.

He expected something like an amphitheater, with
rows of seats cascading down into a well of furious
action. In hindsight, given what Wopal had said about
the Auction, that was a ludicrous image. Still, what
he did see was surprising.

"Spilkar's thorny pants," Grit Wopal murmured.

The Auction Room was not two stories tall, but

three. Its walls, like the walls of the encircling hallway, were stone, decorated only sparsely and strangely with the occasional plain gray blanket, and they rose in a cylindrical shape to a ceiling made of glass. Beyond the panes, Indrajit saw a blue, cloud-free sky.

The room's floor was fifteen feet below Indrajit's sandals, reachable by a narrow staircase winding down around the inside of the cylinder. In the center of the floor rested a ring-shaped table, within which stood a podium. At the podium was a very ordinary-looking Kishi woman in a plain black tunic and breeks. She labored at a book that lay open on the podium, making annotations as she spoke to the men sitting at the table.

There were seven men sitting, and behind each stood an armored warrior. Indrajit only recognized Orem Thrush, who wore a red toga and a mask that looked like his livery, a horned skull; armored and helmeted, and wearing a heavier version of the same headgear, Ilsa stood behind him. But the other six seated men must be the other six lords of Kish: the Lord Farrier, the Lord Usher, the Lord Gardener, the Lord Archer, the Lord Stargazer, and the Lord Marshal.

"Frozen hells," he murmured, "it's the seven most powerful people in Kish."

"And Orem Thrush is still alive," Wopal noted.

"Eight," Fix said.

"Eight what?" Indrajit asked.

"The eight most powerful people in Kish," Fix explained. "The woman in black is the Auctioneer. She has the only permanent government post in the city."

Everything else the city did was auctioned off to one of the seven lords.

"I should have brought a bow," Grit Wopal said.

"I'd just shoot Ilsa from here." He started padding down the steps.

"This is the quietest auction I ever heard," Indrajit whispered, and followed.

"And most important," Fix said, bringing up the rear.

As Indrajit descended, he saw more detail of the room. Multiple doors were set into the walls—unless they opened to very small closets, that suggested that the Auction House expanded horizontally underground, beneath the streets. Did it go farther down? What was in such rooms? Living quarters for the Auctioneer? Storage? Food and water? Written documents? The Auctioneer was writing in a book. Could there be rooms of such books stored down here? Written copies of contracts?

He snorted. If a man wasn't going to keep his word, Indrajit didn't see how showing him a written version of the promise would have any effect.

The stretches of wall between each pair of doors was thickened with another undecorated gray blanket. Were the blankets above and below trapping the sound? The men sitting at the table were indeed talking, though in ordinary tones and ordinary volume, but the sound didn't seem to rise or echo, as Indrajit expected it might.

A device to prevent eavesdropping, or to make conversations comprehensible and echo-free? Or both?

As he reached the floor, immediately on the heels of Grit Wopal, he finally heard some of the conversation. Orem Thrush was speaking. "I realize this is a modest amount to bid on the Paper Sook Regulation Contract, but you know I've had difficulty with enforcement in recent years, and I can't really afford to bid any more. I hope you will indulge me with this smallish payment, in this one case."

"*Please*," Ilsa without Peer sang, with a beautiful melismatic flourish. Indrajit was grateful for the sprig of Courting Flower at his neck. He had enough in his pocket for the other six lords, he thought, but maybe not for their bodyguards as well.

Ilsa's brief song must surely be a breach of the Auction House's rules, but no one objected.

"Contract for the Regulation of the Paper Sook," the Auctioneer intoned. Her voice had the listless, drugged quality of a person under Ilsa's influence. "The Lord Chamberlain has bid one hundred Imperials. Are there any other bids?"

The other six lords sat, silent.

Indrajit's head spun. Didn't having the Contract for the Regulation of the Paper Sook mean that the Lord Chamberlain would impose taxes on the risk-merchants and bankers and lawyers of the sook, to recoup what the contract cost him?

Frodilo Choot was on the hook to pay one hundred thousand Imperials. The Paper Sook was *vast*. Surely, the right to tax it would bring in thousands, maybe tens of thousands of Imperials into the coffers of Orem Thrush. That one contract would bring the Lord Chamberlain fabulous wealth . . . and he was buying it for one hundred Imperials?

But the other lords sat in silence, and made no counterbid.

Ilsa. This was her doing. This was her value to the Lord Chamberlain. He wouldn't have to win all the contracts, just a few big ones at steep discounts, and it would keep him fantastically rich.

This was why he couldn't allow her to escape. Not only could she not quit, but Orem Thrush would never take the chance that she might reveal to the heads of the other families that he had been defrauding them.

Of huge amounts of money.

Perhaps for years.

It struck Indrajit as incongruous and maybe even hilarious that Thrush would bid one hundred Imperials. Why not bid *one* Imperial, if he thought he was guaranteed to win, regardless? Maybe some vestige of a conscience, or a belief in propriety, caused the Lord Chamberlain to pay an amount that was slightly less offensively low.

Fix's footfall on the floor behind him brought Indrajit from his meditation.

"Contract assigned." The Auctioneer made some notation in her ledger.

And then Indrajit realized that Ilsa's helmeted head was turned in his direction. She was looking at him.

She drew a sword.

"Ilsa!" Indrajit called. "Don't do it!"

Orem Thrush sprang to his feet. He yanked off his mask, revealing a face contorted and screwed up into a ball—it looked as if someone had taken a statue of Ilsa and slapped Indrajit's eyes on it. In jumping up, Thrush knocked his chair back, and Ilsa leaped out of the way.

The other six lords climbed to their feet, each bodyguard drawing a sword or taking an ax or a spear in hand. "What is this?" a man in a green toga demanded woozily.

"*Kill Orem Thrush!*" Ilsa sang.

She turned and ran.

Fix seized the spear of a bodyguard to his left and wrenched it from the man's hands, sending him away with a kick to the thigh. Then Fix and Grit Wopal rushed two more bodyguards from behind, scattering them.

The other three bodyguards, and their clients with them, charged Orem Thrush.

Indrajit took a start of two running steps and leaped up onto the circular table. To his satisfaction, a sheaf of papers—maybe a whole fascicle's worth—and note cards tumbled to the floor. He landed in motion, and yelled at the Auctioneer: "Move!"

She ducked, cowering beside the podium.

Indrajit raised both hands and leaped again, hurling himself toward the podium.

He landed off-balance, with one foot at the corner of the podium's surface. The lectern lurched sideways and Indrajit jumped again.

A warrior in lacquered blue armor raised an ax over his head, aiming at Orem Thrush—

Indrajit tackled the man, knocking him to the floor. They rolled together on the stone and the ax went flying.

Fix jumped over Indrajit's head to attack a fighter in purple armor, forcing him back from the Lord Chamberlain. Grit Wopal took Orem Thrush—looking like a deeply shocked Indrajit Twang—by the hand and dragged him back toward an open door.

An open door. The same door by which Ilsa had left?

"The flower!" Fix shouted.

The Courting Flower! Indrajit managed to disentangle himself from the fighter in blue and step back three paces. A warrior in yellow charged toward the Lord Chamberlain swinging a long-handled mace, so as Indrajit grabbed the flower, he ducked and stepped under the yellow-armored man, throwing a shoulder up into his midriff and pinning him against the blanket hanging on the wall.

The yellow warrior choked, then inhaled deeply, and his motions suddenly became hesitant.

Seizing his opportunity, Indrajit leaped for the warrior in blue, who was climbing to his feet. Indrajit slapped a big handful of Courting Flower against the grill of the man's helmet.

The warrior in blue inhaled and then staggered back.

Indrajit stepped back and found himself shoulder to shoulder with Fix. "You're under a spell!" he called. "Smell this!" As men in purple and green and orange came forward, but more hesitantly, he threw each man a small bouquet of the countermagical flower. "This is the counterspell! Breathe through it! It will clear your head!"

Maybe Ilsa's spell was fading, and maybe the plant had its effect. As each warrior sniffed the sprig and then passed it his master, their facial expressions changed from lethal rage to confusion to calm curiosity.

"Hey!" The shout came from above. Indrajit looked up, flinching involuntarily, and saw jobbers in orange spilling in through the door.

The one in front was a heavy Xiba'albi with a topknot and an obsidian-spiked club. "Interlopers! Trespassers!" the Xiba'albi bellowed.

For a moment, Indrajit grinned. Then he realized that the jobber was talking about him.

"No, wait," he said.

Fix pulled him backward by the shoulder, and Indrajit drew the leaf-bladed Vacho.

"Gentlemen," Fix said, "we came here to stop a murder."

The warrior in yellow shook his head. "You've trespassed on the Auction. The penalty is death."

"Trespassed . . . what are you . . . it's just an auction!" Indrajit protested.

The yellow warrior raised his mace and advanced.

The other warriors in lacquered armor picked up swords, spears, and axes, and ranged themselves in a semicircle around Indrajit and Fix.

The jobbers in orange poured down the steps. Behind them came men in gray, with Mote Gannon's glyph on their tunics.

"The door," Indrajit whispered to his partner. With the muffled walls sucking sound out of the chamber, he could barely hear his own words.

"There's only one open," Fix said. "All three of them went into it."

The bodyguards stepped closer, spreading themselves to have the optimal amount of space to create a lethal killing field.

"Now Orem Thrush will try to murder Ilsa," Indrajit predicted.

"I'm kind of inclined to let him."

"I'm still running out that door. You ready? On three."

The lacquered warriors raised their weapons.

CRASH!

The window overhead shattered, and something huge and black and orange fell down into the room.

Chapter Twenty-Eight

〜〜〜〜

THE BODYGUARD IN YELLOW LEAPED FORWARD, swinging his mace at Fix; the other fighters in lacquered armor fell back.

For a split second, Indrajit felt offended that the yellow warrior was attacking Fix, rather than him. Did he not look as formidable as his partner? But his indignation ended quickly, as the yellow fighter snapped his arm in Indrajit's direction and a gleaming blade affixed to the end of a long, fine chain hurtled toward the Recital Thane.

He dropped backward to the floor. The chain and blade whizzed directly over his nose, missing his face by inches. At the same time, he saw Fix step in to his attacker, catch the handle of the mace with his ax, and stab with his falchion up into the man's belly.

Indrajit rolled to one side, lurching to his feet with his blade up in front of himself defensively. The black and orange object hit the ground, flexed, and bounced, and then Indrajit put enough pieces together to recognize what it was.

Yashta Hossarian tore into the bodyguards of the great families like a pit lion tears into a pack of fighting dogs. They nipped at his sides, stabbing with spears and slashing with swords, and he seemed not to care as their blades nicked his jet-black flesh. The ichor that dripped from his flanks didn't flow like blood, and Hossarian's talons slashed the hamstrings of one man, dropping him to the floor, and then tore the head off a second.

Indrajit stepped forward, thinking he might intervene in the battle, and then fell back again. The bodyguards shouted threats and curses, and called out directions to each other, trying to coordinate an encircling motion. Hossarian worked silently and efficiently, his face giving away no intentions and his talons as sharp and fast as they were long. The bodyguard in blue armor circled behind the armless jobber, and it looked for a moment as if he might have a clear aisle of attack into Hossarian's back, but then Hossarian spun about, seizing the man's head in one claw.

The blue warrior screamed once, and then Hossarian squeezed. The fighter's skull and helmet crumpled instantly.

Indrajit had the sinking feeling that *he* was going to be held responsible.

"Indrajit!" Fix hissed.

Indrajit's Kishi partner was grappled fist to fist and toe to toe with the warrior in yellow. The mace and ax had fallen to the floor and Fix's blade was still impaled in the other man's belly. The chain-blade lay snaked across the stone, still attached to the bodyguard's wrist, but useless until the man in yellow could free himself from Fix's grip.

Indrajit grabbed the chain just below the blade. The

bodyguard stared vitriol at him and tried to pivot, evading or possibly trying to throw Fix into his path, but the off-registry risk-merchant was too solid to throw so easily.

Indrajit looped the chain around the yellow warrior's neck and yanked it tight. When the bodyguard let Fix go, Fix yanked out his blade and kicked the yellow fighter into the path of Yashta Hossarian.

Indrajit didn't wait to see the result. "Go!" He scooped up Fix's dropped ax and tossed it to him as he raced for the open door.

Fix followed.

They entered a hallway whose walls were lined with shelves. Other hallways intersected this one at right angles every few paces, and those intersecting halls were also lined with shelves. The shelves were stacked high with scrolls, codices, and baked clay tablets.

Indrajit hesitated.

"The door!" Fix threw his shoulder against the door, slamming it shut. "There's no bar."

"Sure there is." Indrajit jumped, grabbed a set of shelves as high up as he could reach them, and pulled them down in front of the door. Scrolls and wood planks collapsed in a tumble in front of the door, nearly raining down on Fix's head, but the Kishi fighter managed to leap out of the way.

From the chamber on the other side of the door, more screaming.

Indrajit grabbed the shelves on the opposite side of the passage and pulled them down, too. The jumbled shelves and writing material amounted to a barrier nearly as high as Indrajit's waist.

"Well, don't look so gleeful about it," Fix grumbled.

"I'm just happy to finally find a decent use for

writing," Indrajit said. "Would you care to throw your fascicle onto the pile?"

"No." Fix's voice was sour. "But I bet the weight of a Recital Thane and all fifty thousand lines of the Blaatshi Epic would really slow down an intruder."

"Thirty thousand," Indrajit said. "Depending on how much you want to embellish particular scenes. Fifty thousand would be a lot of embellishment. It might feel repetitive."

"I find that hard to believe."

"That way." Indrajit pointed at a greasy yellow light coming from the back of the corridors.

They ran.

"What are these papers?" Indrajit huffed.

"You want me to stop and look?"

As if to punctuate Fix's question, they heard a *THUD* at the door behind them.

"I want you to guess!" Indrajit said.

They turned left with the corridor they were in, and reached an abrupt end—except that the shelves covering the end of the hallway had swung away from the wall, revealing a hinged mechanism by which the shelves moved, and also a space behind the shelves. The yellow light came from that open space, which had crumbling red brick walls and reeked of the dank, close, musty smell of mold and rot, with a faint hint of not-too-distant sewage.

"Contracts," Fix said. "Purchase orders. Statements of work. Change orders. After-action reports. Census tallies. Tax rolls. Maybe even literature."

"Forget I asked." Indrajit stepped through the opening, Fix following.

Crash!

"That's the door," Fix murmured.

"Shh." Indrajit pulled his friend into the tunnel with him and pulled the shelves shut. They swung into place with a soft *click*.

"I think Hossarian can smell us," Fix said.

"Then try being less stinky," Indrajit suggested. "Also, quieter."

They followed the tunnel toward the yellow light at its end. At irregular intervals, the floor was scored with iron grills covering descending shafts—air rose from the shafts in breezes that were alternately warm and cold, salty and musty, stiff and gentle.

Indrajit stopped over one shaft and pointed down— faint green light was visible below, and the smell of oil oozed up through the grate. "What's down *there?*"

"If I say *statements of work*," Fix muttered, "will you stop asking me stupid questions?"

Passages opened to either side. The smells of mold and rot nearly overwhelmed Indrajit, but the light ahead led him on. He loped quickly, almost running. A short flight of brick steps leading up ended in a wooden door that was swinging shut.

"No!" Indrajit sprang up the steps, Fix behind him, and the door shut, plunging them into darkness. Indrajit pressed his shoulder to the cold wood, pushing, and then hitting, and the door didn't budge.

"It's locked," Indrajit said.

"I didn't hear a lock."

"You're right, it's barred. Silly me."

"Get out of the way."

"Am I in your way? I can't tell where you're standing."

"It's too bad your strange eyes don't let you see in the dark."

"My eyes aren't strange," Indrajit snapped. "And besides, you're the one who's trying to get past me."

Fix groped his way, shoving Indrajit aside. Indrajit heard the whisper of steel emerging from a sheath in the darkness.

"Don't stab me," he said, half joking.

"Don't tempt me."

"You're not going to be able to cut through the door. You'd need an ax. And fifteen minutes."

Another crash at the far end of the brick tunnel made Indrajit jump. Dim yellow light trickled into the passage from that end now.

"I've got a thin blade." Fix grunted. "I'm trying to lift the bar."

"And?"

"It's heavy. Can you help?"

The loud scratching of talons on brick echoed down the passage, and the light flickered in and out of existence, blocked by something large that rushed down the hall toward them.

Indrajit grabbed Fix by the wrists, turning his friend's hands to angle them upward, to turn the blade of Fix's long knife into a hook. Then he hoisted.

Their joined hands rose, heavy with an unseen weight, and they let the point of the knife drop. The weight abruptly disappeared—

CLANG!

The sound of talons paused.

"Go!" Fix pushed Indrajit toward the door. Suddenly unbarred, the door opened outward, and Indrajit stumbled from one dimly lit space into another. He nearly tripped on what he thought was a body, but then realized was a dummy, sprawled across the floor in a heap of scarves. Fix rushed afterward and they both fell into a rack of clothing. Fumbling on the floor, Indrajit found the iron bar they had dislodged and shoved it into the brackets that let it pin the door shut.

THUD!

Something heavy slammed into the door from the other side.

"Where are we?" Indrajit whispered.

Fix pointed. "Don't you recognize that trunk? We're beneath the stage, in the Palace of Shadow and Joy."

Not only beneath the stage, but in the tiny room that had been exclusively given over to Ilsa's trunk, containing Lysta's body. Light filtered in from an oil lamp that burned in the larger space directly beneath the stage. Confused memories flashed across Indrajit's mind—on the night the Handlers had tried to kill her, Ilsa had wanted to flee under the stage. She had said there was a way out, hadn't she?

So this was her planned escape route: a secret passage that connected the Palace of Shadow and Joy and the Auction House. Surely, she hadn't built it, but it was easy to imagine how she might have learned of its existence.

"No!" A muffled shout came through the ceiling. It was Grit Wopal's voice.

"He's alive, at least." Fix turned and ran for the corner of the space. Indrajit followed, recognizing that Fix was heading for the stairs up. "Hopefully Thrush is, too."

"Is that our job now?" Indrajit asked. "Save Orem Thrush?"

"Let's save everyone," Fix said. "Frodilo Choot can pay us for saving Ilsa, and in gratitude for saving his life, Orem Thrush can pay us as well."

"Frozen hells, Ilsa's got cash, too. They can *all* pay us."
THUD!

Indrajit and Fix emerged onto the stage of the Palace of Shadow and Joy. Light, bright enough to see by, poured down onto the stage from windows set into the walls and the ceiling high above the audience's seating. Ilsa without Peer, helmet off but still wearing lacquered red armor, stood over Grit Wopal with a sword raised over her head. The Yifft sat at her feet, wearing a red toga and a stunned expression on his face.

Only it wasn't Wopal, it was Thrush, his face having metamorphosed into an imitation of his spymaster's. The sprig of Courting Flower had disappeared from the Lord Chamberlain's breast.

The real Yifft lay crumpled at the edge of the stage.

"I didn't do it," the Lord Chamberlain murmured.

"*Tell the truth now,*" Ilsa sang.

"I didn't do it."

"How are you resisting?" Ilsa growled. "Have you been immune all along?"

Indrajit checked to be sure that his own sprig was in place, and then walked toward the singer. "Ilsa! Ilsa! Let's stop this!"

In his peripheral vision, he saw Fix kneeling over the fallen Yifft. Wopal's yellow tunic was dark with blood.

Ilsa without Peer turned to look at the Blaatshi, her nictitating membranes flickering briefly over her large eyes. "Don't make me kill him," she rumbled.

Indrajit took a deep breath, then drew the Voice of Lightning from its sheath and laid it on the floor. "You don't need to kill him. Or anything."

"I'll spare him," she rasped, "if he confesses."

Confesses to rigging the Auction? But no, there was nothing to confess. Ilsa had been Thrush's conspirator, and they both knew good and well that they had gamed the Auction. "Confesses to what?"

But in the instant he asked, he knew the answer.

"Orem Thrush killed my family," Ilsa said.

"I didn't." Thrush's voice was weak.

"Liar." Ilsa raised the sword as if to strike.

Indrajit took two long steps forward, arms raised to get Ilsa's attention.

"Wopal's alive," Fix called. "But he needs help."

THUD!

"Why?" Indrajit shouted.

Ilsa looked at him and blinked.

"Why do you think it was him?" Indrajit asked. He could guess motives—if the Lord Chamberlain had realized Ilsa's powers, he might want to have exclusive control over them, and exclusive control would require ensuring that Ilsa was the only surviving member of her race. Or at least, the only surviving woman.

"Lysta told me," she groaned.

Indrajit eased a few steps closer. He heard the sound of cloth being torn. "What happened to Lysta?"

"I had to do it." The singer's nictitating membranes flickered and a tear ran down each cheek.

She had killed Lysta. "You were trying to escape."

"I had to." She pointed at the Lord Chamberlain with her sword. "He had found another one. He was going to replace me."

"I had to." Orem Thrush's voice was remote. "You were going to leave."

"*You were going to kill me,*" she sang, "*like you killed all my people.*"

"I didn't," he murmured. "I rescued you. I tried to rescue Lysta, too, but she was mad."

"You would have replaced me with a madwoman."

"Only if I had to." The Lord Chamberlain seemed half-asleep. "Was it so bad, helping me win the Auction? I gave you every luxury. You had fame. You loved singing in the opera."

Tears trickled down Ilsa's cheeks. "A bird in a cage is a slave." Ilsa shifted her sword to the other hand, and then back again. "Even if her masters enjoy her song, and even if the cage is made of gold."

Indrajit took two steps closer.

"I kept you too long," Thrush said. "I should have set you free years ago."

"Before I killed Thinkum Tosh?" Ilsa asked. "And Lysta? And Holy-Pot Diaphernes?"

"Stop," the Lord Chamberlain murmured. "Stop confessing. Go now, I won't follow. Go, and live your life in peace."

"You say that now," Ilsa said. "But you would change your mind. You would be afraid that I would join one of the other lords, and you would have me hunted down."

No answer.

"*Tell the truth,*" she sang.

Orem Thrush seemed to struggle, but finally nodded. "I might. The stakes are very high, and the lord of a great house cannot always afford the scruples he would like."

"*The stakes have always been high,*" Ilsa sang, and then her voice fell back into its guttural rasp. "That's why you killed my family!"

She raised the sword over her head—

Indrajit hurled himself forward, covering the Lord Chamberlain with his own body, and Ilsa's sword bit into his shoulder.

He collapsed onto Orem Thrush.

Crash!

"Indrajit!" Fix yelled.

Lying on his back on the floor, Indrajit looked over his head. Upside down, he saw Fix setting the Yifft on the floor. Fix's gray tunic had been torn into strips and wrapped around Grit Wopal's wounds.

Indrajit wished he hadn't relinquished his weapon.

"Ilsa," he groaned. "Fix."

Ilsa raised her sword again.

"Indrajit!" Fix yelled. "Hossarian's coming!"

Ilsa hesitated.

"Ilsa," Indrajit murmured. "My sword. Don't kill Thrush."

Indrajit was losing blood.

Ilsa stabbed Orem Thrush.

The Lord Chamberlain bellowed in pain. Indrajit levered himself up onto his elbows and knees and dragged himself across the wooden stage. He slipped in blood—his? Wopal's? Thrush's?

But then he wrapped his fingers around the hilt of his leaf-bladed broadsword. The act of holding the weapon poured strength into his limbs, and he forced himself to stand.

Like a hero.

He found himself facing Yashta Hossarian. Blood spattered the jobber's talons nearly all the way up his legs and speckled the jet-black flesh of his chest. His antennae were extended straight out to the sides, making his head seem much larger than it really was.

"Get out of the way," Hossarian croaked. "You don't have to die."

"No one has to die," Indrajit answered. "We can all take a deep breath and walk away."

"The singer is a murderer," Hossarian said.

"She killed Holy-Pot." Indrajit nodded. "And others. Holy-Pot at least deserved it. Her victims can't walk away, but we still can. All of us."

"No," Orem Thrush groaned. "Don't let her."

Ilsa ignored him, backing slowly away toward the edge of the stage, bloody sword raised defensively.

"You'd defend a murderer?" Hossarian took a step forward on his long, red-stained, birdlike legs.

"There's been too much killing," Indrajit said. As he said it, he felt tired. Ilsa wasn't the only killer on the stage—he and Fix had killed the two Grokonk—well, along with the tiny males, however many there had been of *them*—and the Zalapting in the latrine. The Grokonk had been attacking them, and the Zalapting's death had been an accident, but they were all dead, nonetheless. "It's not my job to bring her to justice."

Hossarian smiled without humor. "But you see, it *is* my job. It is *exactly* my job."

Without warning, Hossarian launched one of his feet toward Indrajit. Indrajit flinched too late, eyes widening as he saw his jet-black doom hurtling toward his face.

But the two-legged jobber snatched the Courting Flower from Indrajit's tunic, hurling it into his own mouth.

Then, with a single great bound, Yashta Hossarian leaped over Indrajit's head, hurling himself at Ilsa without Peer.

Chapter Twenty-Nine

~~~~~~~~~~

INDRAJIT STABBED AT HOSSARIAN'S LEGS AND MISSED.
He lurched about just in time to see Fix throw his
body against the singer, knocking her spinning across
the stage. Hossarian crashed into Fix, flattening him
to the floor and pinning him under his orange claws.

Indrajit rushed toward Ilsa, to put himself between
her and her attacker, as a shield.

Ilsa raised her sword and pointed it at Hossarian.
"Kill the monster!" she sang.

Indrajit fell on Hossarian with energy, hacking at
his back. This close, and attacking as he was, he could
now see that the jobber's muscles rippled beneath
a scaly, callused hide that resembled the skin of a
chicken's feet. It was also resistant to the sword's
blade, though not impervious—swinging with all his
strength, Indrajit nicked the jobber, drawing a thick
trickle of black liquid to the surface.

Hossarian turned, leaving Fix—was Indrajit's partner still breathing?—and springing at Indrajit. Indrajit

leaped sideways and found himself unexpectedly blinded, wrapped in a heavy red curtain and stumbling through with no view of his own feet. He heard Hossarian crash to the ground in some metallic stagecraft apparatus that rang like a whole forest of timbrels, and then he heard Fix's voice.

"Back off, Hossarian. We don't want to kill you, but we will."

"Kill the monster," Ilsa shouted.

Indrajit heard clicks as Hossarian stalked sideways, extricating himself from the curtains and stepping out onto the stage. He managed to untangle himself and get a look at the stage. Grit Wopal struggled to sit up and Fix and Orem Thrush stood side by side. Thrush held Fix's falchion, extended before him; Fix held a long knife and his ax.

Ilsa stood behind the two men.

Orem Thrush cleared his throat. "Whatever you're being paid right now, I can afford to double it."

Hossarian changed course abruptly, swiveling one hundred eighty degrees and clicking back the other direction with unnerving ease. "Of course, you can. But you can't buy my honor. And you can't buy the reputation I would earn as the jobber who stood up to Orem Thrush."

"You don't need that reputation," Thrush said. "You can work for me, full-time."

Indrajit saw that Fix had split his sprig with the Lord Chamberlain, so Thrush had a bit of green and yellow pinned to the top of his toga again.

"Or the jobber," Hossarian continued, "who *killed* Orem Thrush."

"Is that what this is about?" Thrush asked. "One

of my rivals is angry at my outmaneuvering him at the Auction, and wants me killed as punishment?" He laughed. "Don't you know that any one of the others would have done exactly the same thing in my place? Come, let's be businessmen. At some price, you'll switch sides."

"Stab him in the back!" Ilsa sang.

Indrajit felt overwhelming need.

He charged.

Grit Wopal, at the same moment, lurched to his feet. The Yifft had a long, triangular knife in his hand, and he threw himself at one of Hossarian's flanks while Indrajit attacked the other.

Hossarian sprang sideways. With his bulk, he knocked Wopal to the floor again. Spinning, his face now pointing Indrajit's direction, he opened his mouth wide and spat. Something large, white, and hard, too large to really be emerging from the gullet of a man, hurtled from the jobber's open maw and struck Indrajit in the eye.

Indrajit fell, in pain.

The sense of desire leached from his flesh as he slammed hard to the wooden floor, banging his head and his heels simultaneously. He still felt well-being, associated with a vague memory of Ilsa without Peer, but she seemed far away.

He was holding a small skull, for some reason.

Hossarian scooped him up and threw him against the wall.

If he'd hit differently—head first—the impact would have killed him. Instead, Indrajit saw a second's view of the wall, approaching him quickly, and then the next thing he knew, he was lying on the floor and Grit Wopal was kneeling over him.

"Fix is down," the Yifft said. Indrajit's vision swam, and when he managed to focus, turning his head slightly so his unbruised eye could gaze on Wopal, he saw that the Yifft's third eye was open. "Fix is down."

Indrajit struggled to sit up. "Dead?"

Wopal shook his head.

Indrajit looked and saw Fix lying in a pool of blood in the center of the floor. The Lord Chamberlain, who now looked like Fix but wearing a red toga, backed across the stage with Ilsa behind him, weaving a defensive curtain before himself with Fix's sword. The Lord Chamberlain was a good swordsman, better than Indrajit and maybe better than Fix, but he was being forced back.

Was he defending Ilsa out of gallantry? Out of a sense of his own guilt?

Or was he trying to save her, so he could force her to continue to work for him?

Where were the orange-tunicked jobbers, who had come flooding into the Auction House? Gannon's Handlers? And the bodyguards? Had Hossarian killed them all?

Or had he simply blocked the path behind him, more effectively than Indrajit and Fix had?

"Get Fix out of the way." Indrajit dragged himself to his feet and patted the wooden floor, finding his sword hilt again.

The Yifft blinked once with all three eyes—not quite in sync—and skittered toward Fix. Indrajit looked for a ladder.

He'd attacked from behind, to no effect. He couldn't attack the man face-on and hope to survive.

Maybe he could drop something on him.

He couldn't find a ladder, and didn't know where to find stairs, but he found the pyramid. It was the same one he and Fix had knocked into the footlings; it appeared to be intact, and it stood in the wings, off stage.

"Indrajit Twang!" Orem Thrush shouted.

Indrajit ignored him and climbed the pyramid.

The top of the pyramid wasn't within reach of any dangling ropes, but it was adjacent to a curtain. Indrajit tugged on the thick velvety fabric, and was happy that it didn't fall. He was even happier when he put his weight on it, swinging out over the stage floor, and the curtain held.

Grit Wopal dragged Fix toward Indrajit and the pyramid. Fix was moving, though sluggishly.

Indrajit hauled himself onto the catwalk. He trod quietly, trying not to catch Hossarian's notice, as he positioned himself above the jobber and simultaneously looked for things to drop. A sandbag? A coil of rope? A backdrop?

His sword?

Indrajit leaned over the catwalk railing and looked down. If he dropped it just right, point-first, he might be able to stick his sword, like a dart, into the top of the jobber's head.

He shook himself, chasing out the insane thought.

The catwalk trembled slightly. Indrajit spun to see what was approaching from behind him, and found Fix.

Bleeding, grim-faced, and determined.

"A curtain," Fix growled. "We drop a curtain on the bastard. Then we jump down and attack him through it."

Orem Thrush was bleeding, too. He was fast, but

Hossarian was faster, and the bird-legged jobber didn't seem to mind any of the wounds he took, while the Lord Chamberlain looked more drained by the moment.

"A curtain." Indrajit nodded. "But I have a better idea than swords."

A feint by Yashta Hossarian caught the Lord Chamberlain out of place. As he knelt to unhook a curtain over the combatants, Indrajit expected to see Orem Thrush run through or decapitated.

But the jobber leaped past the swordsman, and stabbed one long talon into the center of Ilsa's chest. The claw sank through the lacquered red armor of her breastplate, the talon disappearing entirely into Ilsa's body.

In her moment of death, Ilsa looked magnificent. She rose to her full height, short though it was, and looked forward. She threw her shoulders back, as if daring an audience to love her. She opened her mouth, and a trickle of blood came out.

Hossarian removed his talon.

Ilsa without Peer sang a long, single, rock-solid, golden note. It bore no words, but the pure sound of it broke Indrajit's heart.

Then the note ended, and blood gushed from Ilsa's mouth and from the wound in her chest.

She fell forward slowly, and with her seemed to fall all Indrajit's memories of childhood, his desire to recite the Epic, his love of home. All collapsed slowly forward into a pale, shapeless sack, which bounced once off the wooden stage floor and then lay still.

Indrajit opened his mouth to scream, but Fix clapped a hand over his face, stifling the sound.

Yashta Hossarian turned. He sniffed at the air, looking briefly puzzled, then turned to face Orem Thrush.

"You just cost me a lot of money," the Lord Chamberlain said quietly.

"I don't know anything about that." Hossarian's voice was terse and his posture a near-crouch, as if he still might spring into combat. Orem Thrush held his sword pointed upward and turned as the jobber walked around him, keeping the blade between them. "I know I fulfilled my contract."

"Murder is murder," Thrush said. "Even if some client, even if one of my rivals, contracted you to kill someone, it's murder."

"Unless the Auctioneer sold the contract," the jobber said.

"Don't imagine that your knowledge of the system makes you my peer." Orem Thrush's voice was gravelly and severe. His face was shifting, darkening from the brown of imitating Grit Wopal to a dark black—he looked more and more like Yashta Hossarian himself, by the second. "That would make every jobber captain the head of a great family."

"Moments ago," Hossarian said slowly, "you were offering to hire me."

Fix leaned in close to Indrajit's ear and whispered. "Hossarian is out of position."

"We could jump on him," Indrajit whispered back.

"Suicide," Fix said. "We get the curtain on him, and then what?"

Indrajit explained his plan with two words and a gesture.

Fix nodded. "So we just need him to get into position."

But Hossarian wasn't in position. He wasn't beneath any curtains at all.

"Moments ago," the Lord Chamberlain said, "it looked as if you might come around to my point of view."

"You don't respect my integrity?" Hossarian continued to circle, and his eyes narrowed. "You don't admire the way I keep my contract?"

"I'm the richest, and can always be the highest bidder." Orem Thrush's voice was cold. "I have no use for a jobber who can't be bought."

"Frozen hells," Indrajit muttered, "he's getting farther away."

Fix was staring at Thrush. "He's going to get himself killed."

"Maybe he's trying to help," Indrajit suggested. "Maybe he thinks he's distracting Hossarian, so we can ambush him."

"If we had, say, javelins, or crossbows, that would be a great idea. Since our plan is to drop a curtain and the target isn't in position, the Lord Chamberlain is going to get himself killed."

"With Ilsa dead, that means no payment from anybody." Indrajit's heart sank.

"Getting out of here alive might be our only victory," Fix suggested. "All things considered, I think would be a pretty good one."

"I will see you tried before an Auction-appointed court." The voice was Grit Wopal's. The Yifft stood almost directly below Indrajit and Fix, feet planted apart, arms crossed over his chest.

"They're both going to die," Fix murmured.

"No." Indrajit pointed. "Look. He knows." He grabbed two hooks holding the heavy theater curtain and lifted them almost out of their brass eyes. "Are you ready?"

Fix grabbed two more hooks and lifted. They were holding the curtain up by main strength, and it was heavy.

Indrajit hoped he was right.

"Will you?" Yashta Hossarian asked. Then he pounced.

He slammed like a tiger into Grit Wopal, who didn't flinch. The ball of orange smashed the intelligence agent to the floor and then rose above him, orange talons flashing in the air and preparing for the kill.

"Now," Indrajit murmured.

They threw the curtain.

Wopal had positioned himself perfectly. The heavy curtain fell—interminably slowly, it seemed to Indrajit, but perfectly, billowing out, spreading—right on top of Yashta Hossarian, covering him entirely.

As the curtain was still falling, Indrajit and Fix scrambled to their feet. Indrajit gripped the catwalk railing with one hand, raised his sword, and checked to see Fix's progress; the shorter man was similarly positioned, ax held high.

"Now," Fix said.

They cut the ropes holding up the catwalk.

As he swung, Indrajit worried that one of them would cut through and the other wouldn't, causing the catwalk to dump them, rather than fall, or that neither would cut through his rope, and they would have attracted Hossarian's attention for nothing.

But both ropes split and the catwalk fell.

Fix lost his grip as the platform swung down, and was cast aside. The curtain writhed and shrugged, and then Hossarian's head and antennae emerged, enraged face glaring upward—

Right into the oncoming catwalk.

The iron of the catwalk smashed into Hossarian's torso with a *CRUNCH*, and its weight drove it down through his body entirely, until it struck the wood. The two orange legs leaped sideways, took three steps as if they had a mind of their own, and then fell sideways off the stage. The jet-black mouth opened, and spewed out a thick stream of mucus that stank of bile and phlegm.

Contact with the stage jarred Indrajit, tossing him sideways. He lost his sword in the tumble, and then found himself sitting dumbly, staring at the jobber.

Hossarian's mouth opened and shut wordlessly. His antennae scratched at the floor as if to pull him forward, but in vain, and then he collapsed.

Indrajit hurt. He stood, and fell, bones and heart aching.

"Wopal!" he called from the floor. "Grit Wopal!"

A murmur and a wiggling of the curtain answered.

Fix lurched across the stage. Indrajit could see now that his partner was spattered in blood from head to toe, his face shining with sweat. "Wopal!"

Indrajit dragged himself across the floor and helped Fix pull away the curtain. Wopal lay still, most of his body trapped beneath the fallen catwalk and Yashta Hossarian's torso.

But he was breathing.

Indrajit found he had tears on his cheeks. Relief that Grit Wopal wasn't dead? Or that, finally, someone had survived? Tears for Ilsa without Peer?

Orem Thrush offered him a hand and he took it, rising to stand unsteadily. Fix pushed against the catwalk with his shoulders, raising it a few inches so that Thrush and Indrajit could drag Wopal out. They pulled the Yifft to the far end of the stage, near where Ilsa lay, cold and still.

Wopal began to come to, woozily.

"I could use men like you in my service," Orem Thrush said. Disconcertingly, he looked just like Yashta Hossarian from the neck up.

"You could have had *him*." Indrajit indicated Hossarian. "He was way better than us."

"He's dead," Thrush pointed out.

"Dumb luck," Fix said.

"Hey," Indrajit objected. "We had a plan. At the very least, it was *smart* luck."

Orem Thrush shrugged. "He's dead, regardless. You killed him. I don't care if you're good because you're lucky or you're good because you're smart or you're good because you have eyes in the sides of your head."

"Hey," Indrajit said again.

"I need good people. And I think you need jobs."

"By *good* people," Indrajit said, "do you mean men who are *ruthless*? I'm not sure we're a good fit for you."

"Despite everything I have ever said to you," Orem Thrush answered, "I do care about justice. And I care about this city."

Indrajit nodded. He thought maybe he should feel exultant, but all he felt was tired.

Wopal sat up gingerly. "Remember that I sent a messenger to the bank."

Indrajit felt dull. "So?"

"So we'll see what happened," Wopal said, "but if you saved Choot's money, she might be persuaded to pay you something."

"She *will* be persuaded," Thrush said.

That thought lightened Indrajit's heart somewhat.

Money meant he could eat again, and live to continue searching for a successor Recital Thane.

"What's that?" Fix wobbled as he pointed across the stage.

Worms crawled away from Yashta Hossarian's body. Not worms, Indrajit realized, but the antennae that had sprouted like a hedge around his neck. They had detached themselves and now wriggled away.

Even as he started across the stage, several of the worms had disappeared, squeezing into cracks between the floorboard, disappearing under curtains, or falling off the front of the stage. Indrajit and Fix smashed every worm they could find beneath their heels.

Many got away.

Indrajit looked at the mess on the stage. "Frozen hells."

Chapter Thirty

BOLO BIT SODANI, THE LORD STARGAZER, WAS SO thin, he looked as if a strong breeze might lift him entirely off the ground. He wore a toga of green silk, and his skin was transparent—Indrajit tried not to stare at the sight of muscle and sinew coiling and uncoiling as the Lord Stargazer moved his arms, and tried even harder not to imagine what it would be like to see the man's torso.

Or worse.

"I don't think you understand," the Lord Stargazer said, and Indrajit yanked his thoughts back to the conversation at hand. "We are not requesting that you make peace. We are instructing you that you will be removed from the Auction House Registry if you attempt any sort of retaliation against these men."

Indrajit smiled, trying to look charming.

The Lord Stargazer smiled too, and the effect was grotesque. His face was heavily made up, covered with powders and paints, and the smile shifted just

367

enough of the concealing artifice to expose bare skin, which then looked as if his face had cracked open, revealing slices of yellow tooth, bright red gums and tongue, and white skull.

Orem Thrush, the Lord Chamberlain, sat beside Bit Sodani in his red silk toga. He might have been smiling, but his expression was hidden by the horned skull mask. Through the eyeholes, Indrajit thought he saw a dark complexion around the Lord Chamberlain's eyes. Mahogany, perhaps, with a hint of green? Did that mean that if he removed his mask, the Lord Chamberlain would look like Indrajit again?

He thought he should probably find that flattering, though he wasn't entirely sure why.

The Lords Chamberlain and Stargazer sat at a table with Indrajit, Fix, and Tall Gannon. Tall Gannon had a sour expression on his face, a bruised cheek and a bandage covering half his scalp. He was unarmed, as the summons had required, but he wore a leather jerkin with bronze rings stitched onto it. Outside the room, which had been rented for this conference, bodyguards waited. Grit Wopal had declined to participate at all—the fewer the people who knew his face, the better.

The purpose of the meeting was to prevent further violence between Gannon's Handlers and the newly bonded and registered jobber company, the Protagonists.

"They broke into my home," Gannon complained. "They killed a large number of my team."

"You can count the Grokonk as two," Orem Thrush said. "Think through the math carefully. Did they kill a large number, or did they kill *three*?"

"Three." Gannon's voice was sour. "Three is a lot

of murders. And they maimed my Luzzazza. And sundry other injuries."

"Sundry—" Indrajit started to object, but Fix kicked him under the table.

"*Murders* is a strong word," the Lord Stargazer said. "The Protagonists were attempting to carry out their contract, and your men attacked them."

"I was carrying out my contract, too!" Gannon banged his fists on the table.

"A contract in which, if I understand correctly, you may have been *conspiring to commit murder*." Orem Thrush's voice was grave. "Speaking of that strong word."

Gannon paled.

"Indeed," the Lord Stargazer said.

"Or risk-contract fraud." Orem Thrush shrugged. "Is this how you want this conversation to go, Gannon? We can request that an Auction Court be convened."

Tall Gannon ground his teeth.

Where was little green Tiny Gannon, and was he grinding his teeth at the same moment?

"You're a good captain, Gannon," the Lord Stargazer said. "We'd hate to see you come off the Registry."

"Or be exiled," Thrush added. "Or executed."

Tall Gannon pounded the table again. "We entered the Auction Hall because we had to! We saw that... creature..."

"Yashta Hossarian," Indrajit said helpfully.

Fix kicked him again.

"Enough protest," Orem Thrush said. "You can agree to peace with the Protagonists, or you can suffer the consequences."

Tall Gannon swallowed, then looked down at the

table. He was quiet for long seconds, and Indrajit began to suspect the man had fallen asleep. Finally, he looked up. "I can't stop my men from carrying out any private vendetta."

The Lord Stargazer nodded. "But we will hold you accountable if they do, regardless."

"Fine." Gannon ground his teeth. "I accept."

Orem Thrush produced a rather large coin purse and threw it across the table in Gannon's direction. The captain of the Handlers caught the money and secreted it within his jerkin.

The Lord Stargazer turned to Indrajit and Fix. "And you."

"No vendettas, no grudges." Indrajit spread his hands in friendly agreement. "We never wanted to hurt anyone in the first place. Happy to agree."

Fix nodded.

"In that case," the Lord Stargazer said, "your bond and your joint-stock certificate appear to be in order. You'll be added to the Auction House Registry by next week."

"Thank you." Indrajit wasn't quite sure how he felt about the news. He looked across the table and met Fix's gaze. Fix's eyes looked puzzled for a moment, but then he grinned. Indrajit grinned back.

The Lord Chamberlain tossed Indrajit a purse, as well.

"Peace comes to the Palace of Shadow and Joy," Orem Thrush said. His voice sounded sad.

◇   ◇   ◇

"The purse is a little heavy," Indrajit said. He and Fix were crossing the Crown and heading down into the Spill, where they had rented an extremely spare room in a nondescript inn on a side street angling off of the Crooked Mile.

"Ah," Fix said, "I have accidentally gone into business with a man who not only spends his money quickly, but also loathes being paid."

"I like being paid," Indrajit shot back. "I'm just afraid I might open this and find a Thûlian grenado inside."

"I am happy to open the purse."

Indrajit handed the money to Fix and stepped into the courtyard of the nameless inn. Two donkeys, an ox, and a small pack of dogs lazed on the hard-packed earth, soaking in the morning sun. Indrajit turned and climbed the baked clay steps up to the second story, where their rented room perched above the stables. The location meant that the room smelled of horse and occasionally Ylakka, but it also brought down the weekly rate.

The choice of room had been Fix's idea. Indrajit had talked down the rent.

"This *is* heavy," Fix said as Indrajit opened the door. "If it's not a grenado, we should deposit it in the bank."

"What for?" Indrajit asked. "Doesn't that make it harder to spend?"

"In your case," Fix said, "controlling spending might be desirable. Though for large sums, a good banking relationship might actually facilitate payments. We'll be able to write drafts, for one thing."

"I don't know what that means," Indrajit admitted.

"It means you can just write down on a piece of paper or parchment or a potsherd an instruction to the bank to pay someone. Then that person takes the potsherd to the bank and the bank pays her."

Indrajit snorted. "Curse you and your writing, Fiximon. And you have made me change my mind about banks. We're going to bury the money in a hole in the ground."

"If the bank holds the money, they will pay us for the privilege."

Indrajit tried to think why that would make sense, and couldn't come up with an explanation. He snorted again. "Now I know you're lying."

"No, the bank pays you because, until you come take the money out again, they use it."

"What, they spend it?"

"They lend it out to other people. And the interest those borrowers pay them lets the bank hold your money without charging you for the service."

"Wait . . . they pay *you* interest?" Indrajit unlocked the door. "And if that guy doesn't pay back the loan?"

"It works sort of like risk-merchantry. The bank makes lots of loans, and so even though some don't get repaid, it still makes enough to make a profit. And the banks have agreements among themselves to help each other out in case of a cash crisis."

"You say it works like risk-merchanting," Indrajit said, "but the one thing I have learned for sure this weekend is that risk-merchantry doesn't work."

"*I* made money buying risk," Fix said.

"And Frodilo Choot almost lost a fortune."

"Well, she was the victim of fraud," Fix pointed out. "If a blacksmith is robbed, you don't say, *See, look, blacksmithing doesn't work.*"

"I might," Indrajit said, "if the way blacksmithing worked made it especially likely that a blacksmith would be robbed."

"Maybe I should handle the banking," Fix suggested.

"No banks." Indrajit shook his head and pushed the door open.

Inside stood two beds, two chairs, a table, and a chamber pot. Grit Wopal sat at the table, third eye closed, smiling at them.

"There must be four hundred Imperials in here," Fix murmured.

"Time to get better rooms," Indrajit said.

"That's it, I'm going from here to the bank. If you don't want to have banking authority, I'll handle all of it."

"Gentlemen," Grit Wopal said. "You got the money."

"Frodilo Choot paid?" Indrajit asked.

"She paid some," Wopal said. "The Lord Chamberlain made up the difference."

"That's generous," Fix said.

"No, it isn't," Indrajit shot back. "He's buying us."

"Don't be dramatic," Wopal said. "He's paying you for past services. For future services, he'll pay you again. This is what it is to be a jobber...or have you changed your mind?"

Indrajit felt deeply conflicted about how his experience with Ilsa without Peer had gone, and three days of rest and recovery hadn't let him sort it out to his satisfaction. Ilsa and Holy-Pot Diaphernes had conspired to fake Ilsa's death, a plan which incidentally foresaw that Indrajit himself would take the blame, and probably be killed.

But Ilsa had been a prisoner. And the man who had been her captor, Orem Thrush, had used her to garner huge wealth. With that wealth, he had bought off Indrajit's enemies and funded Indrajit's new partnership. Indrajit and Fix were experiencing success—but Indrajit wished it had come by some other route, and from some less morally ambiguous person.

He sighed. "I have not changed my mind, Grit Wopal."

"Good." Wopal grinned. "I was a little nervous you were going to punch me again."

"Never say never." Indrajit flopped down on the corner of his cot, leaving the second chair to Fix. "But probably not today."

"By any chance, are you here bringing us work?" Fix asked.

"Say rather that I am giving you advance notice of work that is coming your way."

"I don't know," Indrajit said. "I'm not sure I can eat advance notice."

Wopal smiled. "You can buy a lot of food for four hundred Imperials."

Indrajit shook his head. "Fiximon is going to give the money all to the bank."

"Somehow, I think you will not starve." Wopal continued as if the subject were closed. "I understand that you are aware that the Lord Chamberlain has the contract for regulating the Paper Sook."

Indrajit's heart fell. "What?"

"Yes," Fix said. "We were there."

"The Lord Chamberlain is impressed with your knowledge of the Paper Sook."

"Thank you," Fix said.

"No," Indrajit said. "No. No, no, no."

"He expects you will be involved in regulatory and policing and inspection and investigation work for incidents involving the Paper Sook."

Fix nodded.

"Of which there are many," Wopal said.

"Isn't there something else?" Indrajit asked. "Latrine work? Well digging?"

Grit Wopal shrugged. "The Lord Chamberlain doesn't generally bid on such contracts."

"We may need more resources," Fix suggested, a sly gleam in his eyes.

The Yifft returned the sly look. "We believe that you may be more effective operating as a pair. Lower profile. No uniform."

Fix sucked at his teeth. "Indrajit was really hoping for a uniform."

"No, I wasn't." Indrajit's head spun.

"Formal occasions only, then," Wopal said. "You won't be standing guard openly at the market, you'll be knocking on doors and asking questions."

"Breaking into offices at night," Fix said.

Wopal nodded. "From time to time."

"Tailing suspicious types?" Fix asked.

"Definitely."

The burglary and footpad work sounded more attractive than the idea of asking bankers questions. "Roughing up thieves?" Indrajit asked hopefully. "Recovering stolen funds? Protecting widows from predatory bankers?"

Wopal nodded. "You get the idea."

"The risk-merchanting and joint-stockery and bank-drafting details are all on you," Indrajit said to Fix.

Fix nodded.

"We're in," Indrajit said to the Yifft.

Grit Wopal left and Indrajit moved to the table. For a time, they sat in silence.

"What about your lady friend?" Indrajit asked.

"In time," Fix said. "And your apprentice Thane?"

"I guess I'll be looking for him in the Paper Sook." He didn't mean to, but Indrajit made a facial expression of distaste.

"It might surprise you how many former notaries turn to poetry," Fix said. "Bankers, too."

"It wouldn't surprise me to see a risk-merchant turning to any other trade. Including Smork-herding."

"What's a Smork?"

"I don't know," Indrajit admitted. "But I understand they're disgusting."

Another minute passed.

"Are we going to be able to be heroes?" Fix asked. "I mean, acting like spies and burglars on behalf of Orem Thrush, a man who is clearly ruthless and self-interested...he says he wants justice, and to benefit the city, but can we trust him? *Can* we help innocent victims, and make a difference? Can we be men whose deeds would be recounted in your additions to the Epic?"

Indrajit took a deep breath. Outside, he heard the *clop-clop* of hooves, and the rattling sound of wheels running over hard earth and cobblestones. Somewhere down the street, he heard the shouted jeers and scoring of a Rûphat game, and maybe the rhythmic playing of a bang harp. He smelled roasted meat, baked bread, and the sea.

"I don't know," he admitted. "But we're going to try."